"Could be the most delicious Washington novel in recent memory . . . keenly observed, compelling . . . the novel uses a scalpel where others might deploy a hatchet. . . . *The Cave Dwellers* would be a page-turner no matter when it was released, but in today's climate . . . it practically qualifies as required reading."
—*TOWN & COUNTRY*

"Through blunt caricatures and sharp characterizations, McDowell . . . combines social satire with moral outrage to offer a masterfully crafted, absorbing read that can simply entertain on one level and provoke reasoned discourse on another."
—*BOOKLIST* (starred review)

"McDowell's mordant debut novel sends up the Washington, D.C., establishment . . . the drama is thick . . . the satire cuts deep."
—*PUBLISHERS WEEKLY*

"Author Christina McDowell . . . is back with her unputdownable debut novel, where the aristocratic bloodlines of Washington, D.C.'s high society—the Cave Dwellers—are forced to reconcile with the changing world around them when one of their own is brutally murdered."
—*VERANDA*

"After reading this ruthless satire of their behavior, [the Capital's oldest and wealthiest families] probably can't sue for slander, but they might want to beg for mercy. . . . For its merciless humor and brazen exposure of salon secrets, *The Cave Dwellers* should join that small collection of essential Washington books. . . . After all, this is an author who knows her victims' antique attitudes and traditions as well as Marjorie Merriweather Post knew her china settings."
—*THE WASHINGTON POST*

"A delicious take on the one percent in our nation's capital." —*TOWN & COUNTRY*

$

ALSO BY CHRISTINA McDOWELL

After Perfect

The Cave Dwellers

❖ A NOVEL ❖

CHRISTINA McDOWELL

SCOUT PRESS

New York   London   Toronto   Sydney   New Delhi

Scout Press
An Imprint of Simon & Schuster, Inc.
1230 Avenue of the Americas
New York, NY 10020

First Scout Press trade paperback edition March 2022

SCOUT PRESS and colophon are registered trademarks of Simon & Schuster, Inc.

For information about special discounts for bulk purchases, please contact Simon & Schuster Special Sales at 1-866-506-1949 or business@simonandschuster.com.

The Simon & Schuster Speakers Bureau can bring authors to your live event. For more information or to book an event, contact the Simon & Schuster Speakers Bureau at 1-866-248-3049 or visit our website at www.simonspeakers.com.

Interior design by Jaime Putorti

Manufactured in the United States of America

10 9 8 7 6 5 4 3 2 1

The Library of Congress has cataloged the hardcover edition as follows:

Names: McDowell, Christina, author.
Title: The cave dwellers : a novel / Christina McDowell.
Description: First Scout Press hardcover edition. | New York : Scout Press, 2021. |
Includes bibliographical references.
Identifiers: LCCN 2020027812 (print) | LCCN 2020027813 (ebook) |
ISBN 9781982132781 (hardcover) | ISBN 9781982132798 (paperback) |
ISBN 9781982132804 (ebook)
Classification: LCC PS3613.C39484 C38 2021 (print) | LCC PS3613.C39484 (ebook) |
DDC 813/.6—dc23
LC record available at https://lccn.loc.gov/2020027812
LC ebook record available at https://lccn.loc.gov/2020027813

ISBN 978-1-9821-3278-1
ISBN 978-1-9821-3279-8 (pbk)
ISBN 978-1-9821-3280-4 (ebook)

FOR MARA AND CHLOE

How could they see anything but the shadows if they
were never allowed to move their heads?
—Plato, The Allegory of the Cave

The Cave Dwellers
CHARACTER FAMILY TREE

• THE MAIN FAMILIES •

The Banks Family
(Cave Dweller family)

Genevieve + David Banks
(husband and wife, deceased)

Audrey
(daughter, deceased)

The Bartholomew/Morrison Family
(Cave Dweller family)

Elizabeth Spencer Morrison
(Meredith's mother, deceased)

Meredith + Chuck Bartholomew
(husband and wife)

Elizabeth aka Bunny
(daughter)

Cate
(Bunny's cousin, niece of Meredith and Chuck)

The Wallace Family
(Political family)

Betsy + Senator Doug Wallace
(husband and wife)

Mackenzie
(daughter)

Haley
(daughter)

The Montgomery Family
(Military family)

Carol + General Edward Montgomery
(husband and wife)

William aka Billy
(son)

The Williams Family
(Media family)

Linda + Chris Williams
(husband and wife)

Becca
(daughter)

• THE CLIQUE •

Bunny Bartholomew
(Billy's girlfriend)

Billy Montgomery
(Bunny's boyfriend)

Stan Stopinski
(son of the Russian Ambassador—
aka "Putin")

Marty Robinson
(son of Howard University School of Law professors—
aka "Smarty Marty")

Chase Cowan
(son of the director of the CIA and star football quarterback)

Mackenzie Wallace
(daughter of Senator Doug Wallace—
aka "New Girl")

Part One

*The names in this book have not been changed
so as not to protect them but rather to expose them.*

❖ PROLOGUE ❖

*H*e takes off his jacket and then his mask, lights a match, and dumps kerosene into the limestone fireplace—for *ambience*.

Dusk in this town is a distraction: broken Metro lines at rush hour, passengers covered in righteous martyrdom riding beneath replicated Parisian circles and monuments of men that smell like piss.

Most burglaries happen in the middle of night: the beeping of alarm systems, the searching for bogeymen in closets. Not on this October day. Above the flooded tunnels where no exits are built, where blue jays fly in the autumn and carved pumpkins grin, a colonial mansion rests on the fringes of Rock Creek Park, a vast and dark wood next to a neighborhood that has no name.

The garage door had been left open, Mr. Banks's red Ferrari still ticking from the heat of the engine when the unknown man followed him inside. The mailman, just up the sidewalk, had his back turned, a satchel over his right shoulder, earbuds stifling the National Cathedral bells ringing from a tower named for the Christian hymn "Gloria in Excelsis."

*   *   *

The unknown man places the bottle of kerosene on the mantel next to family photographs with Washington's Very Important People: ambassadors from European countries, the US secretary of defense, Prince Bandar bin Sultan of Saudi Arabia, a senator, and members of the Walton family.

Mrs. Banks, the Bankses' young daughter, Audrey, and the housekeeper have no idea anyone else is in the home. If not for the padded wallpaper the decorator installed weeks earlier to benefit the home theater, they might have heard the *whoosh* of the firelight, beyond the silence.

The unknown man approaches Mr. Banks first, watching from the shadows of the powder room as he removes his branded cuff links, heated marble below his bare feet, and climbs into gym clothes. He confronts Mr. Banks without a beat in his step, wrestling him to the ground, tying his hands with rope behind his back and then shoving a gag in his mouth, explaining what he wants and what he is going to do to get it.

"Dad?" Audrey yells from her bedroom down the corridor. "You ready?"

She has been looking forward to test-driving the new BMW X5 with her father when he got home from work.

When the unknown man walks into Audrey's room, she stands staring at him in her St. Peter's Academy sweatshirt and Kate Spade leggings, confused. They're both startled by the sudden gust of wind, branches slamming against her windows; then the unknown man lunges for her, grabs her by the face, cheeks bulging between his fingers. He ties her to her favorite chair, the one with little fairy-tale scenes sewn into the fabric, and keeps her mouth ungagged. The walls are too thick—the house is too large for any neighbor to hear the echoes of terror soon gifted to her parents.

* * *

Mrs. Banks notices the shriveled petal on her white orchid, French doors open to the loggia behind her as photographs of the family's Christmas card photo shoot at their château in the south of France slide across her computer screen. She is at her desk scrolling down her contact list, the setting sun creating shadows of wild tree branches climbing the walls, when she hears the first round of Audrey's primal screams.

In the laundry room, down the basement steps next to Audrey's play-room, the housekeeper loads bottles of Cakebread Chardonnay into the second refrigerator. She can hear nothing but the tumbling of washer-dryers and the clanking of glass against plastic shelves.

It isn't known whether or not Mrs. Banks made it into her daughter's bedroom to see her, touch her, smell her, love her one last time. The only retraceable steps at that hour are those outside of the mansion. The minutes between darkness and light no one ever seems to notice. *Where did the light go?*

A neighbor swishes through dead leaves walking his French bulldog, inhaling the crisp smell of a distant fire, and thinks: *It's my favorite time of year.* A private security car cruises by, as smoke rises from Audrey's chimney like a misty ghost. The security guard waves to the neighbor, then heads toward the bridge in the deep valley of the park, scanning the woods for female joggers. He stops. Shuts off his headlights. Cracks his window. Waits. Hears the sound of his run-ning engine, the hooting of an owl in a distant tree. Then cruises back up the hill, just missing a young girl riding her bike behind him.

❧⋅CHAPTER ONE⋅❧

EARLIER THAT DAY . . .

*D*oug Wallace pants while struggling to reach for the remote control on the edge of his desk. He fails. He lowers his head and wipes sweat with the back of his forearm, then tries again. His tailored J. Press suit pants, which make him feel superior, are around his ankles as he takes Cate, his new press secretary, from behind. She's sprawled out on his mahogany desk. *Yes.* Blond, a good Christian girl from San Diego, small breasts, but he doesn't care, her face, *oh her face is fucking beautiful.* He flips her over, so young and sunkissed; he doesn't want to break her spirit, but he can't help himself, this compulsion—he feels he *needs* her. He's tired of looking into the dispassionate eyes of his wife, which are now tattooed with eyeliner. He can't believe he's been made senator of the great state of North Carolina, can't believe this is his life now: the pounds of mahogany wood, brass doorknobs, a view of the Capitol. People want to hear what he has to say. The cliché would be unbearable if state officials and politicians had never coerced young interns into having sex with them in what was simply "the conference room" throughout history: drawn curtains, empty walls, a cold wooden table. At least Doug had a leather desktop; *this is progress, not perfection!* A photograph (when Doug still had a full head of hair) with two college buddies at President Ronald Reagan's inauguration stares him down on his bookshelf: *Look how far you've come.*

On the television screen in Doug's office—a millisecond: *WARN-ING: This footage contains explicit content. Viewer discretion is advised.* Static, then a shaky camera before interspersed sound bites of civilians: "Is that *gunshots?* . . . OH MY GOD, *IT'S GUNSHOTS!*" The sound of bullets like thundering raindrops, probably an AR-15. Civilians cast guttural screams that melt into sobs, beer cans and red cups scatter on top of what is becoming a bloodbath of average citizens that, let's be honest, we don't *really* care about. Perhaps the sound of a ticking bomb is nearby. No one knows. Not even the FBI agents. The broadcaster: "*LIVE!* From our nation's cap—!"

Mute.

Doug drops the remote. It hits the side of his desk and falls to the floor with a pathetic thud.

"What's wrong, are you okay?" She speaks. She's worried about *him.*

"Nothing, nothing." Doug's focus reverts to Cate. He puts his hand over her mouth, cupping those plump lips, a loving gesture, because he doesn't want to be reminded by the look of horror that will soon encompass that sweet face, a young Republican who surely must believe in sensible gun control. When she sees the young and slaughtered, she might not understand that his stocks are rising. *AR-15 semiautomatic weapons are selling up to a total of fifteen every hour* scrolls at the bottom of the screen.

"Yes," Cate groans, turning her baby face from left to right, grabbing her breasts, assuming Doug is catching glimpses of her ripe nipples, watching *her.* But Doug isn't looking at her at all. In fact, neither one is looking at the other. Cate, lost in her own fantasy of what she believes this is, reminds herself that she is *worth it,* worth losing his marriage, his children, his reputation, his self-respect—*this is love,* she tells herself. But really, she's confused. She thinks about how she's going to start her public relations firm after they publicly declare their coupling—Doug will be her first client. They will build a political empire together. Spend winter weekends hidden at the new seaside mansion in Nantucket; maybe she'll buy him pants embroidered with baby whales on them for Christmas, he'll love that. . . .

Doug humps like a pubescent boy, sweating profusely now, watching the TV as his gun stocks rise. Cate notices he's not looking at her; she wraps her legs around his waist, pulls him into her with his tie, their noses touching. But Doug can't bring himself to look at her. He closes his eyes, imagines the prostitute he met on a business trip to China, the porn star from the Pornhub video he watched in his home office last night before bed. He knows he's made a mistake. He opens his eyes. He looks up. Closed captions on the screen: *The AR-15 is the country's most popular rifle, now a symbol for all sides of America's gun debate. Gun advocates say the problem isn't the weapon—it's the shooter.*

"Oh God, I'm going to . . ."

⤫

It's one of those damp fall sunsets when red and brown leaves stick to the street as the new season descends upon the nation's capital. The barricade outside the Russell Senate Office Building, which blocks pedestrians from getting anywhere near the parking garage, lowers into the ground, releasing Doug in his black Porsche 911 out onto the streets of Southeast DC. Bureaucrats scatter toward the Metro like little windup toy soldiers—they have no opinions. No identities, no ability to see any kind of truth other than a biweekly paycheck. Several white vans with FEDERAL POLICE: HOMELAND SECURITY written across the side blaze past. Doug doesn't notice. He's too busy searching for the hand sanitizer in his glove compartment while he's calling Tim on speakerphone. *Goddamn it.* Doug slams the glove compartment closed, unable to find it. He sniffs his fingers.

"Hello?" A voice on the other end of the phone.

"Hey, Tim, it's Doug," he says, panicked.

"Hey, Doug, how are you? Haven't heard from you in a while." Tim's serenity is unnerving.

"I thought about our last conversation, maybe I do have a problem. I suppose . . . Cate could be anyone." Doug waits for Tim to respond, but there is only silence. "It's just . . . I understand that she *could* be anyone from an *intellectual* place, but I just don't *feel* that, I don't know. I don't know what I'm saying." Doug lets out a chuckle dabbled in shame.

"Uh-huh." Tim doesn't offer advice. "Well, I'm about to walk into Al's right now. You are always welcome back."

Doug tightens his grip around the steering wheel. "I'm on my way."

Doug speeds down Rock Creek Parkway, the remains of Oak Hill Cemetery climbing the hills above him, passing hundred-year-old tombstones, stone crosses, weeping angels, cenotaphs, and mausoleums. *One day I will be buried there*, he often thinks—with the generals, mayors, bankers, and senators who came before him. Famous men! With the Corcorans and the Grahams! Doug is completely unaware of his delusions of grandeur, just like most people he encounters. He is only certain that he was born a "well-mannered" southern boy, son of the district attorney of Durham, North Carolina. His mother ran the local Sunday school while his father was busy locking up Black and brown people. (Doug doesn't really *get* this, of course.)

As Doug slows down to look for the entrance he's seeking, he remembers his older brother, Ken. Ken was born blind, and Doug blames his mother: despite her religious beliefs, she loved a dirty martini, a Marlboro Red, and Elvis. But Doug's mother blamed the doctors. During a difficult labor, Ken was pulled out with metal tongs, crushing his soft head. This is the story his mother told, but he never tells. Ken died just before his eighteenth birthday after numerous health problems. His organs were weak. The memory of his mother's phone call flutters through Doug's brain—the sound of her rocking on her knees, her sobbing groans letting him know, "He's dead, he's dead"—as it often does while he's alone, driving in his car. The rage he holds for his mother rises in his chest. Ken's death, the neglect Doug suffered as a child, his father's empty bottles of bourbon are the instruments of his so-called *intimacy issues*, Doug's undying need for power, achievement, and attention from women. The problem was first addressed long before he married Betsy. When Doug was seventeen and he discovered that his mother was having an affair, he decided to fuck the family housekeeper. Days later, his father's name and paycheck sent her back across the Atlantic to her family in Ghana. They never spoke of it again. And neither did Doug.

He looks down at the address in his phone, then squints at the gold numbers clinging to the side of a redbrick post anchoring two arches of a towering wrought iron gate. Wait a minute. He knows this property! A Vanderbilt, a Mellon—he can't remember, but it's tucked high above the park where various gruesome and innocuous things have happened: the rotted flesh of a White House intern found, rape, impassioned lovers, tourists, the laughter of schoolchildren running around Peirce Mill, an old flower plantation where Black people were enslaved and later escaped. The horror and the glamour feed off each other in some diseased symbiosis necessary for making the town of Washington all at once riveting and disturbing.

Doug's Porsche follows the beaming headlights to the front of the estate, beckoning him as if it were the solution. Tim stands illuminated in between enormous Doric columns with his arms folded: gold Rolex, boat shoes, argyle sweater. Doug parks, gets out, walks up, and shakes his hand. Tim pats him on the back as he leads him inside.

The walls of this mansion are covered in law books, encyclopedia collections, and photographs of foreign diplomats, kings, queens, and presidents—and Jeff Bezos. An original Chagall hangs above the library's green marble fireplace, near which seven men are seated in Chippendale chairs that form a circle. The men are hard to differentiate from each other, rich white men who are undoubtedly power players. But you'd have to know what kind of car each one drives or the neighborhood in which he lives to truly know who he is: Kalorama, McLean, Chevy Chase, Georgetown. You probably wouldn't find any of them in Silver Spring, Bethesda, Arlington, or Old Town; those neighborhoods are for the average man at the Pentagon, or worse, the Chamber of Commerce. You might find one in Potomac or Great Falls, but only on acres of land on the cliffs above the Potomac River, and he's retired and well into his seventies and refuses to admit he's lost all his money and will soon file for bankruptcy and settle for a condo in Reston, Virginia.

More than half sit in J. Press suits, others in polos and khakis, maybe a red sweater tied around the shoulders. Glasses or mustache or clean-shaven—all have their legs spread, rubbing their hands up and down their knees.

They look up at Doug. "Welcome," a few mutter, some nodding to acknowledge his existence because he's important enough to be there. The hero, the *lawyer!* The man who, before taking office, bailed out the economy (AIG specifically), the man who saved their bonuses! *Hear! Hear!* The man who knows they'll return the favor with political funding.

But Doug can't believe he's back in this room, and the self-hatred consumes him. His cheeks turn the color of his Nantucket-red pants that are folded in his wife's cedar closet. He sits in an open Chippendale chair. There's a book resting on it for him with the engraved initials *SAA.* But the first thing Doug notices is the tufted ottoman in the center of the circle with various pamphlets fanned out on top of it. It's the same ottoman his wife circled for him to review in the Kellogg Collection catalogue earlier that morning. He'd forgotten. It was supposed to be confirmed for the dinner they're hosting tonight. *The dinner.* Doug panics. The meeting begins.

Jeff, late fifties, gray comb-over, puts his round spectacles on and reads from a binder: "Hi. My name is Jeff, and I am a sex addict. I will be the leader for tonight's meeting. The focus of this meeting is the eleventh step, which states: 'Sought through prayer and meditation to improve our conscious contact with God as we understood Him, praying only for knowledge of His will for us and the power to carry that out.'"

Doug glances up from his phone to assure that no one is watching him eviscerate his secretary for not reminding him about the dinner he and his wife are hosting in a few hours. *Send.* He puts his phone in his lap. He waits. He breathes slowly, listening again to Jeff, but not really. He's thinking about what Betsy is going to say to him when he arrives late, sweaty and smelling like a bottle of whatever floral fragrance Cate wears. *Ping.* Doug flips the switch to turn his ringer off, then refreshes his e-mail. His secretary *did* forward him an e-mail reminder an hour and a half ago. *Goddamn it.* He was with Cate.

"We will now take a ten-minute meditation. During this time, we encourage you to reflect on the issues that brought you here and how you want to live your life in recovery. The timer will sound when the meditation time has come to an end."

Men around the room make adjustments in their seats, positioning themselves for meditation: arms resting on knees, legs spread with hands resting between them, chests inhaling then exhaling. *For Christ's sake.*

Washington Life Magazine

Washington Life Magazine: The Insider's Guide to Power, Philanthropy, and Society *has been the leading DC magazine covering all of the most important social events since 1991. It often categorizes events by hierarchical rank depending on the guest list. There are wealth lists, social lists, gala lists, and power lists. Owned by a billionaire who resides in Kalorama and moved to Washington with a sense of social agency, the magazine is the ultimate symbol of Washington status, aimed at shining light on and preserving current power structures. Those who enter Washington with an ambitious appetite will avidly subscribe. Though largely unknown to those outside the nation's capital, the magazine is important because it serves as a window into the financial funnels of the most powerful in politics and media, guided by the influence of where individuals are giving their money away, shaping politicians', philanthropists', and socialites' personal and professional narratives. In an article published in the Daily Beast, it is noted that the forty-fifth president of the United States has "seen" (not read) every single issue.**

---

* Asawin Suebsaeng, "Trump Is Oddly Obsessed with This DC Society Magazine," Daily Beast (website), December 4, 2019, https://www.thedailybeast.com /trump-is-oddly-obsessed-with-washington-life-a-dc-society-magazine.

❧·CHAPTER TWO·❧

*B*etsy Wallace stands in their new Artisan home in McLean, Virginia, pressing her French-manicured hands around her Peruvian housekeeper's cheeks, and plants a wet kiss—*"Gracias, cariño"*—leaving a stain of lip gloss across Teresa's sweet flesh. It's so *nice* that she can speak to the help in their native language. With both children attending different campuses of the same private school, Haley at the lower school and Mackenzie at the upper school of St. Peter's Academy, her life is just exhausting. She needs the silver polished while she goes to pick up the girls from their after-school activities. Their guests will be arriving in two and a half hours: two of Doug's biggest donors, a venture capitalist, a tech entrepreneur, a private banker, a member of the Mars family, an attorney, a political affairs strategist (with a social media intern), and their wives. But, most important, a photographer from *Washington Life Magazine: The Insider's Guide to Power, Philanthropy, and Society*. Doug, Betsy, and the girls will have their photographs taken in front of their limestone fireplace. It's the kind of ostentatious spread Betsy has campaigned hard for in order to get just the right exposure as the new-to-town couple.

It's been years since Betsy lived in the district. She has managed to keep it quiet that she was once married to a powerful lobbyist twenty years her senior in the early 1990s who, shortly thereafter, suddenly died of "cancer." Following two years of infidelity on his part, she finally left him. After the divorce and on his deathbed, he'd confided in Betsy that he had been having sex with men for the duration of their marriage; she'd held his head as he took his last breath. He'd died of AIDS. It was a good thing he never wanted to sleep with her. By then, Betsy had moved back to her hometown of Raleigh and met Doug at a mutual friend's cocktail party. A handsome and powerful attorney with political ambitions, he was perfect. Now in her midforties, Betsy knows this is her second chance at climbing the Washingtonian social ladder. Perhaps, she thinks, it's fate.

Before leaving the house, Betsy places three country club applications with gold paper clips on her Kellogg Collection desk: the Washington Club for the white Protestant, Columbia Country Club for the good (probably Irish) Catholic, and the Kenwood Country Club as a backup since they were the first to allow Jews. It might be a stretch, she thinks, given that they don't have any real history in Washington like most of the other families, but her husband's current position of power should help their chances.

"Ciao, *cariño!*" Betsy takes one last look at herself in the antique gold-leafed mirror and purses her lips. Her blond hair has so much spray in it, if she were to quickly move her head from left to right, it would hold as still as a rock.

⌒✲⌒

Betsy pulls up to the lower-school curb in her blue Jag and waits for Haley, her youngest. Also: the pretty one. Across the street young professionals sip on happy-hour frozen margaritas at Cactus Cantina; teenage girls in tight buns, ballet leotards, and windbreakers gallop with their Starbucks cappuccinos from the Washington School of Ballet nearby. Betsy is focused on the mothers in front of her in their Range Rovers and Mercedes SUVs with vanity plates like TENSTAR (Tennis Star) and BLU DVLI (Blue Devil) and 1 800-GD (1-800-*GOD?*). A few waving to each other and blowing kisses, reminding each other of "Lunch! The benefit dinner! Yoga class!" *Democrat, Democrat, Democrat.* Betsy is desperately trying to find the Republican moms she can power-walk with when she spots Linda Williams walking to her parked car ahead. Linda is the wife of the famous hotshot Fox newscaster Chris Williams, last moderator of the presidential debates before the GOP took the Senate and the House. Betsy jams the steering wheel all the way to the left so she can cut in line and get closer to Linda.

"Li—Lin—Linda!" Betsy waves from where she is parked, but Linda doesn't hear her or notice her frantic waving as she climbs into her Audi station wagon. Betsy looks around, frustrated, as children run to their designated cars, then resorts to tapping on her horn. *Beep. Beep.* Betsy waves again. Finally Linda looks in her direction— but she isn't looking at Betsy. Linda's daughter, Becca, mousy brown hair, a plaid skirt over her riding pants, is passing Betsy's car. "God-damn it," Betsy mutters.

Haley, blond, blue-eyed, not quite old enough at eleven to develop an eating disorder yet, *but soon*, follows behind Becca, pulls open the front passenger-side door.

"Ah, ah, ah, in the back, we're picking up your sister, she's driving us home."

Haley groans and pulls open the back door. She's wearing a red party dress and carrying a Saks Fifth Avenue vinyl garment bag in one hand and dragging her cello case with the other.

"Oh good, you're wearing the dress I bought you."

Betsy crosses Massachusetts Avenue and heads for Cathedral Heights, speeding through stop signs and flashing crosswalks.

"Why don't you have a playdate with Becca Williams, honey? She seems nice."

"Ew, no." Haley sneers. "She's weird and doesn't talk."

"Well, sweetheart, maybe she's shy and needs a friend!"

Haley stares out the window.

"I could take the two of you shopping in Georgetown, wouldn't that be fun?"

"Maybe."

They speed past the abandoned Iranian Embassy and the Naval Observatory. The sun is fading into the bright headlights of cars. Betsy reaches the white picket fence surrounding the upper school to find Mackenzie standing curbside under a streetlamp illuminating the color of bile. She holds her violin case and lugs her Kate Spade monogrammed backpack (copied from the popular girls) in the other. Her hair is brown and abnormally thin. There are faint bald spots toward the back of her head, a few hairs matted across her forehead. Mackenzie began pulling out strands of her hair three months ago when they moved to Washington. A nervous tic Betsy's determined to get "under control."

"Oh, honey, honey, honey, why are you not dressed for our dinner tonight? I repeatedly told you."

"I didn't have time, Mom! I have SO MUCH HOMEWORK."

Betsy tries to keep her cool as she hands Mackenzie the keys to the car, then climbs into the passenger seat, careful not to scrape her Manolos.

"Ew, you smell," Haley says, pinching her nose.

"Shut up, you little bitch," Mackenzie snaps.

"Girls!" Betsy yells. "Enough."

⟡

As Mackenzie eases out onto Chain Bridge Road, Betsy decides to bring up the fact (again) that she is not dressed for dinner.

"The photographer from *Washington Life Magazine* is taking our family photograph this evening. I told you this a thousand times. *How could you forget?*"

Mackenzie taps on the brakes a little too hard, jerking Betsy's head forward.

"You're the *worst* driver," Haley says, slowly and with perfect diction.

"Shut up, you cunt!" Mackenzie cries.

Betsy whips around to point at Haley, tightens her lips. "No more talking until you're home, got it?" She whips back and looks down at her diamond Cartier watch. "I want you dressed and ready for guests by seven fifteen with your violin ready, you hear me?"

"No! I'm tired, I don't wanna play, Mom," Mackenzie whines.

"Mom, *noooo*," Haley cries.

"Girls, we have guests coming! It's very important to your fa—"

Mackenzie hits the brakes. "NO!" The car slams to a stop.

"That's it, pull over, you've lost your driving privileges."

"NO!"

"You pull over right this minute or you're grounded."

"MAKE ME."

There's a red blinking light up ahead at the crossing of Georgetown Pike.

"Pull over." Betsy tries to grab the steering wheel as Mackenzie jerks the car, her front wheels skidding over the double yellow lines, when out of nowhere a black town car appears—

BEEEEEEEEEEEP!

Mackenzie jerks the car back into her lane as the town car blows past them. She screeches to a halt. Betsy throws open the passenger-side door, hysterical. Haley, now silent, remains buckled in the backseat, terrified at the potentially fatal consequences of the moments past and the moments that lie ahead.

Beads of sweat begin forming on Doug's upper lip as he listens to the story of a man who can't stop compulsively masturbating in the bathroom at work. Doug's cell phone lights up: Babe Calling (Betsy). He knows it will take him at least thirty minutes to get over the bridge and into Virginia. Doug hits the Decline button on the side of his phone and places it in the inside pocket of his jacket. "Thank you for sharing," the men say in unison, mirroring compassion despite such a shameful act. Doug gets up and mouths *Betsy* to Tim and points to his phone in his pocket, tripping over the tufted ottoman as he stumbles quickly out the door.

⁓৩৫⁓

Guests are arriving in an hour. Teresa greets Betsy in a panic. Mackenzie and Haley drag their instrument cases up the front steps of the house. Betsy turns around and waits for them at the entrance and glares at Mackenzie. "*Upstairs. Now,*" she says through clenched teeth.

As guests begin trickling in, they stand among tufted ottomans, Chippendale chairs, balloon curtains, and Kellogg Collection credenzas, lamps, and pillows with fringe, plus a brand-new grand piano topped with photographs of the family in Nantucket, the Hamptons, various European castles. Eating crudités and holding flute glasses filled with Kir Royales, they're talking about tax reform and Medicaid.

Doug sneaks in through the garage door, tiptoeing for the back stairs, and makes his way up to the master bathroom where he splashes water on his face. His phone lights up on the edge of the sink: WHERE THE FUCK ARE YOU.

Doug looks at his reflection to psych himself up for his friends (donors) downstairs. He's not a sex addict, *no-ho-ho*, he's just a regular man with needs like his father was and his father's father was and his father's father's father was. He puts on a freshly pressed shirt and blue-and-white-striped tie, then dabs cologne behind his ear and wipes away a tiny trace of lipstick.

As Doug heads down the corridor for the front staircase, Mackenzie appears in the doorway of her bedroom. Finally changed for dinner, she wears a tight black miniskirt, maroon Doc Martens, and a peach spandex tank top from Reformation. Her hair is teased in the back to hide her bald spots. Doug can't help but notice, in this passing moment between them, her enormous breasts spilling over the brim of her top like bobbleheads. It stops him in his tracks.

"Hey, Dad."

"Huh?" Doug, tongue-tied, is suddenly reminded that his daughter is only a few years younger than Cate. As if coming out of a trance, he snaps, "*Christ*, Mackenzie, go put a sweater on. We have guests."

Mackenzie backs up into her bedroom and slams the door.

The doorbell rings. It's one of those cheesy singsong tunes. Tony, the photographer from *Washington Life Magazine*, steps into the foyer. Trendy Warby Parker glasses, bronze skin, he wears skinny jeans and a button-up. Chic. He carries a camera case and appears more Hollywood than Washington. Tony photographs the *Who's Who* of the political and financial power players—mostly the wives—and he's always at the most exclusive social events: book parties, embassy parties, election parties, charity balls, luncheons, and funerals.

Betsy greets him in the hallway with a wide smile and open arms as though she's known him for years despite not knowing him at all. "Tony, darling!" She kisses him on the cheek.

"You look stunning," Tony says, grabbing her forearms. He knows the game. "And where is that brilliant husband of yours?" He shakes his head a little.

Doug comes up behind them and pinches Betsy's ass. She lets out a high-pitched squeal, hops around, and places her French-manicured hand on his cheek.

"There you are!"

Doug leans in to shake Tony's hand. "Doug, pleasure."

They walk toward the living room where Haley has set up her music stand; her cello rests beside her, ready to be played. Guests mingle by the piano overlooking the tennis courts, while others sit on the floral sofas eating Brie and carrot sticks. The wives cluster together in their layers of gold necklaces and diamond pins—a firefly, a horse, a cross—while the men stand, some in red bow ties, others in white polos and sports jackets, silk handkerchiefs peeking through the tops of pockets. Except for the tech entrepreneur, who's in jeans and a black long-sleeved shirt—he doesn't need to impress these people; he just needs Doug to ensure the tech world remains free of regulation and maintains net neutrality, as God and Mark Zuckerberg intended.

Mackenzie appears in a conservative dress holding her violin and bow. She pulls a chair over next to her sister's, making a screeching noise across the wood floor and smiling with her mouth closed.

To the donors and constituents, the night is seemingly smooth. Betsy stands holding her flute glass, smiling at her daughters as they strum their instrument strings with fevered passion. Doug comes around to place his arm around Betsy's waist. Tony snaps candid photographs from each corner of the living room before the final still as guests are in awe—of the parenting, the couple themselves, and the political agenda. They're all so charming in that initial meeting kind of way, in the way that you can only see from afar: in an article, a Facebook profile picture, a family Christmas card—or a photograph in *Washington Life Magazine*.

CHAPTER THREE

*E*lizabeth (Bunny) Bartholomew gazes through a large window. The glass is ancient, the kind that makes the world look wobbly. Her reflection: pale face, freckles, strawberry blond hair, distorted and staring back at her. The sunset behind the glass is colorless; the white Adirondack chairs are scattered at equal distance under an enormous oak tree, its bare limbs poking every which way; the scene: traditional yet uninviting. Almost every single staff member at the Washington Club—server, bartender, valet driver, bathroom attendant—is Black, and every single club member being served in the dining hall is white.

This is fucked up, Bunny thinks.

The Washington Club was one of the first country clubs in the United States, originally known for its fox hunting pursued by cabinet secretaries and generals and various top government officials. Over time it became a haven away from city life for the white Protestant families in the district, and Bartholomews have been members since the founding.

Bunny wears a pleated skirt and baby-blue cashmere sweater because jeans aren't allowed (club rules!) and sits between her parents, Meredith and Chuck Bartholomew. She turns back to the main dining room and sees that every single father wears a white or pastel polo shirt and every single mother wears a silk scarf around her neck with diamond studs because pearl earrings are for the teenagers.

"I'm in a horror film," Bunny says.

"What's that, dear?" Meredith asks, placing a roll of bread for Chuck on his side plate like we've time-traveled to the 1950s. Meredith's hair is short and white around her forehead line. It's angled toward her chin, giving her a regal edge, sharpening her jaw-line.

One might think Bunny, at only seventeen, is emotionally intelligent, but it isn't that at all; she is simply becoming awake to the way things are in her inner circle—her pedigree—her *whiteness*. She isn't special; she is just paying attention. Her mother is a Democrat, for God's sake! And her father, an "old-school" Republican, is, as they say, "fiscally conservative." Meredith still has an Obama bumper sticker on the back of her 1998 Volvo station wagon, which she refuses to give up for sentimental as well as practical reasons. They just couldn't be racist! Though the Bartholomews belong to the most exclusive clubs in town, they most certainly are not considered greedy or flashy by any means, but rather understated, classy—*old money*, if you will, and Bunny is starting to pick up on this.

"I said I'm hungry." Bunny takes a sip of water, not ready to confront her parents for their unintentional racism. Ever since her grandmother died, the matriarch of the family, Elizabeth Spencer Morrison (Bunny's namesake), Meredith has become increasingly fragile and obsessed with contacting her mother's spirit, convinced she hears her banging on her headboard at night. "Do you ever experience that?" she'll ask Bunny, clicking her mouse back and forth on different psychic medium websites while in her study. Bunny doesn't have the heart to tell her that she doesn't believe in past lives or future ones, that when we die, it's just a vast black of nothingness for eternity.

What Meredith is having trouble with is the slow disintegration of power the Morrison and Bartholomew families are experiencing. Both Meredith's and Chuck's lineage traces back to the beginning of Washington—the bishops, the mayors, the colonels, whoever "built" the city, families whose names no one's ever heard of because they don't need any public notoriety, so they say. Meredith's family money comes from supplying half of the gunpowder used by the Union Army in the Civil War and more than five billion pounds of explosives for World War II. Chuck's grandfather helped create the atomic bomb, the family fortune built on nuclear energy and then later on chemicals used to manufacture heat-resistant products, waterproof clothing, etc.—things no one ever thinks about. Theirs was an arranged marriage of fortunes simply built on weaponry and war.

A Black server with the name tag LANCE comes to the table to take their order.

"Lance! Honey, how are you?" Meredith asks. She's *so* nice. She shakes his hand for *so* long, enthusiastically asking about his family: his mother's health, his brother who's studying law at Howard University. Bunny notices this. It irks her. It feels phony: her mother's wide smile, her veneered teeth.

Meredith has always believed that true equality is unattainable; it does not and will not ever exist. She appears to be in acceptance of this—how easy it is for her. Her grandfather, whom she knew as a young girl, always instilled a great pride in the ideologies of capitalism, putting the interests of their family first because of a deep-seated fear of communism. And yet, after the death of her mother, something inside of Meredith is beginning to unravel.

"And what can I get for you this evening, Mrs. Bartholomew?" Lance asks.

"I will have the Cobb salad. *Honey, thank you.*"

Bunny looks at Lance, doesn't smile, her usual self. "I'll get the cheeseburger and fries. Medium, please."

"And for you, sir?"

Chuck folds his menu and whips it in Lance's direction without looking at him. "I'll have the chicken piccata."

As Lance turns away, Meredith remembers Cate.

"Oh! Lance, honey, we forgot Cate's order, she's meeting us, she should be here any minute." She turns to Chuck. "Did she text you her order?"

Chuck looks at his Samsung. "Cobb salad with blue cheese."

"I'll get those right in for you all."

Meredith leans over and reaches for Lance's arm, again. "*Thank you*, honey," and if words were just sounds you might think she was saying, "*I'm sorry*, honey." Meredith had been to a Black Lives Matter rally with an old friend from Yale University, her alma mater, earlier this week.

Cate gallops into the dining room, out of breath, holding her jacket—black pencil skirt, hair in a disheveled bun. With clothes on, she's almost unrecognizable to us, except that the back of her pink thong is hiked above the waist of her skirt, her blouse aggressively tucked into it. Bunny notices this as Cate takes the seat next to Chuck, but doesn't say anything.

"Hi, guys, sorry, the Red Line derailed again. No one got hurt, thank God." Cate throws her hand-me-down-from-Meredith Burberry plaid jacket over the back of the chair.

Chuck shakes his head. "See, what did I tell you about the infrastructure problem."

"Honey, you should really think about getting a car here," Meredith says, concerned. She's only ridden the Metro once—to get to the Women's March a year earlier.

"I don't know, I kind of like not having a carbon footprint."

"Hey, now, I thought you were a Republican," Chuck says.

"Uncle Chuck. I believe in global warming."

"Millennials . . ." Chuck downs the last gulp of wine in his glass.

Cate clears her throat and puts the white cloth napkin in her lap. "I'm assuming you all heard about the horrific shooting at the Midlands music festival."

"What's that?/Where's that?" Meredith and Chuck say simultaneously.

"Missouri," Bunny says, scrolling through her phone; she's in the vortex.

Meredith plays with her gold bangles and sips her wine, feigning interest. "No, honey, I didn't see that."

Chuck nods with pursed lips. "Ah yes, I saw something about that tonight."

"Honey, do you feel safe at school?" Meredith asks Bunny.

"There's secret service at my school, Mom," Bunny reminds her, scrolling through her phone. This sort of thing will never be a by-product of her kind of upbringing.

"Oh, right." Meredith sets down her glass.

"I think I'll be promoted soon." Cate takes a large sip of water.

"That's great, honey," Meredith replies.

Chuck turns to Cate, folds his hands on the table. "I'm confident you will do a great job, but listen to me carefully. As you climb the political ladder, remember to always remain a private person, as much as you can, so you can live as you want—free—rather than create expectations in others that you feel compelled to meet."

Cate thinks on this for a moment. But isn't she supposed to meet the expectations of others in politics?

"Always put your own interests first," Chuck says, pointing his finger at her.

Cate listens to Chuck like a good girl. She knows this, but she also knows that today *fame* is what you need to succeed in politics. A *high* profile, not a low one. Chuck is dead wrong about privacy. Cate smiles with her hands folded in her lap, looking around the room, scoffing in her head at the professors, the partisan journalists, the old political wonks and their dopey-looking wives. Fame is a necessity if you want to win. And Cate wants to *win*.

Lance arrives at the table carrying a massive tray of food; a bus-boy probably about Bunny's age trails behind him and hurries to unfold the stand on which the tray will be placed.

"Thank you." Meredith leans over, piercing the young boy with her well-intentioned eyes, and slips him a twenty-dollar bill, then winks.

Embassy Row

In the early twentieth century, Massachusetts Avenue between the vice president's mansion and Sheridan Circle was known as Millionaires' Row, housing the nation's elite in gilded mansions.* But when the Great Depression hit, it forced many to put their mansions up for sale. Soon after, social institutions (exclusive clubs) and diplomats started moving in. For example, the British Embassy was built in 1930 and the Japanese Embassy by 1931, and by the 1940s the area was dubbed Embassy Row.

Today diplomats and their families who live in Washington are protected by something called diplomatic immunity.** It means the sons and daughters of ambassadors (and the ambassadors themselves) are not susceptible to lawsuits, arrest, or prosecution under American law. For example, rumors circulated around town that there was a fraternity thrown out by American University (reasons unclear). But the fraternity still continued admitting members, becoming the frat for many international students. Around 2014, after a pledge decided to drop, three frat members assaulted him in a garage. One assailant, the son of a diplomat, served no jail time and fled to his home country, while the two others each served 120 days in jail and 100 hours of community service.

---

* Scott Harris, "Ten Facts You May Not Know About DuPont Circle," DCist (website), January 30, 2017, https://dcist.com/story/17/01/30/you-know-it-as-one/.
** United States Department of State, Office of Foreign Missions, https://www.state.gov/wp-content/uploads/2019/07/2018-DipConImm_v5_Web.pdf.

❧ · CHAPTER FOUR · ❧

*F*rom her bedroom window, Bunny watches Chuck pull in the trash cans. She listens to the familiar rhythm of the wheels rolling along their cobblestone driveway. The redbrick mansion across the street, once home to then General Ulysses S. Grant after the Civil War, is twinkling with lights, revived by a tech billionaire from Silicon Valley. Bunny's been spying on the new family of late, no details to report yet, other than that they own a Cavalier King Charles named Steve Jobs that the maid walks every morning.

Bunny turns around to close her bedroom door, a Feel the Bern poster glued to the back of it. She hears Cate giggling on the telephone with a friend from California in the guest bedroom across the hall. She waits for the *beep beep beep beep* of Chuck setting the house alarm for the night—007 with an extra 0 is the code. Her backpack is zipped and filled with Bernie Sanders rolling papers and condoms she took from a trip to Planned Parenthood. Once the alarm is set, Bunny flips the lever of the lock from left to right, then slowly pulls the top half of the window open, chucking her backpack so it lands in the boxwood bushes below before climbing out. Last year when her parents were on a golfing trip to Ireland, Bunny discovered a loophole in the alarm system: pull open the top half of the window and the alarm won't sound.

Bunny rides her bike down the uneven brick sidewalk along R Street, passing Katharine Graham's abandoned estate on her right, Oak Hill Cemetery on her left, its black wrought iron gates chained and locked, protecting the ghosts of Washington royalty from unworthy intruders. Rats scurry behind trash cans and raccoons into the alleyways beneath the old gas streetlamps of Georgetown.

When Bunny stops at the light before Sheridan Circle, the intersection of Kalorama, Dupont, and Georgetown, she peers up at the statue of the Civil War general atop his horse posturing before it bucks, his arm stretched out behind him, an invisible sword ready to defeat the enemy—*a hero before he slaughtered the Indians in the Great Plains!* Bunny waits as the metropolitan police blast sirens at all exits of the circle. The vice president's motorcade comes barreling through, one police car after another, the caravan of black Suburbans, the black limousine, American flags stuck to each side of the vehicle waving in the wind before the bomb squad trails behind them. She's accustomed to this kind of interruption.

Kalorama is the wealthiest neighborhood in the district, the milieu of politicians (Trumps, Obamas, Clintons, Tafts, Roosevelts) who have lived or currently live there, along with Supreme Court justices, media moguls, and international royalty. It is an old neighborhood with clustered colonial mansions sitting almost on top of each other—Embassy Row is just behind it. France is twenty feet to the right. England: twenty feet to the left. Afghanistan: make a right up Wyoming Avenue. When Bunny was little, she and her friends would joke that if one of them were from, say, Albania, and committed a murder, they could run to the embassy for protection and never get arrested as long as they stayed on the foreign property. Kind of dark for eleven-year-olds to think about, but normal in Washington. Kalorama is not the kind of neighborhood where one strolls across the street to ask a neighbor to borrow some milk, not if their people committed genocide against your people just a few decades ago.

The secret service is parked on either side of the street, barricading the entrance where the former president resides. Family members of the current president reside on the block behind it, so close that a baseball could be thrown between the two homes to shatter a window. In fact, most political veterans (both Democrat and Republican) share the same neighborhood. Always have. Always will. *Always* remember that.

Flags with Arabic symbols and colors blow in the icy wind; the smell of burning wood lingers from some mansion nearby. Only the occasional clanking of metal can be heard as Bunny chains her bike to the green fence behind the mosque. The vice president's mansion is a few blocks up the street. Surveillance cameras are hidden in stoplights, in trees, on the corners of nearby embassies pointing in every direction, pointed like guns. Bunny whips her backpack over her shoulder, throws her hoodie over her head, and marches toward her boyfriend's house. Maneuvering through a minefield of government cameras doesn't make sneaking out of the house easy. She and her friends learned their lesson last year when sophomore Teddy Rasmussen tried to throw a party but was quickly shut down by the security officers of Uzbekistan. The kinds of problems facing the offspring of the Washingtonian elite are unprecedented compared to those of children throughout the rest of the world. Only in the days to come will Bunny begin to question the lot in life she's been so freely given.

❖ CHAPTER FIVE ❖

The chairman of the Joint Chiefs of Staff, General Edward Montgomery, stands between the Doric columns of his home, an old colonial schoolhouse along Massachusetts Avenue converted into a live-in mansion. A towering figure, he stands six feet four with wide shoulders, though age has curled them. Known for fighting in the Persian Gulf War, the Iraq War, and the War in Afghanistan, he has more decorations than any other general in America and is now in charge of the most powerful military in the world. Even at home with his youngest son, Billy, he speaks in military jargon: *affirmative, negative, copy that.* He expects beds to be made with crisp hospital corners, rooms to be tidy, shirts to be tucked in, and never a hat worn at the dinner table—or any other place, really, except for a baseball field. In addition, it is always *yes sir, no sir,* when one is spoken to. The general comes from an extraordinarily humble and religious upbringing in coal-mining Virginia where the divide between the haves and the have-nots widens every day. The military provided a way out for the general, which he credits with giving him the abundant life of service he leads today; it's only as of the last several years that the Montgomery family has grown accustomed to power and wealth.

Several government SUVs line the semicircular driveway, block-ing cameras and any passerby from seeing something that might appear suspicious. Bunny watches, hidden across the street behind the hedges of the Haitian Embassy, waiting to sneak around the side to the service entrance where Billy awaits her.

The general shakes the hands of the unknown men in black suits. They climb back in their government SUVs, and General Mont-gomery stands in the cold air watching as they disappear down Mas-sachusetts Avenue, his breath visible as he exhales, his shoulders reaching toward his ears. He looks up to the bright, round moon, then turns around, steps inside the house, and slams the door behind him.

⟨⟩

Carol, the general's wife, sits in the kitchen nook folding laundry. On the television screen in front of her, *BREAKING NEWS* interrupts Fox News's already-breaking coverage of the mass shooting. *White House Chief of Staff is accused of domestic violence. No comments yet from POTUS. . . .* scrolls across the screen.

Carol is composed, easy-breezy as she folds the next towel. She's known for weeks this was coming, but hasn't said a word to anyone except when discussing the matter with her husband. The general can rage, but he's never hit Carol before. He's hit his sons, but never Carol. Carol is still dressed in her tweed blazer, red reading glasses left atop her head of silver hair. She spends most days volunteering at the public library, helping recovering vets use the free computers and Internet. She loves a good Danielle Steel novel, but she'll never tell you that; she keeps them hidden upstairs in the guest bedroom. A devout Catholic from a small town in Connecticut, she spent her after-school hours bagging groceries for her dad, who owned the local grocery store. Carol doesn't fit in with the elites of Washington, nor does she care to. She can't wait for the day her husband retires and they can move back out to Virginia, where they recently purchased a farm—an old corn-mill plantation built before the Civil War.

Hot Fox News reporter Chris Williams's face appears: "The White House accumulates more chaos. Just in, we have a photograph of the White House chief of staff's wife from the police report filed several weeks ago." An image appears of the woman with no makeup on, a swollen blue and brown circle around her right eye, a split lip, and bruises around her neck.

"Jesus," Carol says under her breath, throwing the last towel in the pile next to her. She gets up to turn the television off just as the general walks into the kitchen. He stands in the doorway. Carol turns to face him, terrified of what he is about to tell her.

⟿⟾

"Get in, quick." Billy ushers Bunny into the old service elevator in the basement. "Shhh." He puts his fingers over her mouth. The elevator wobbles when he shoves the gate closed and presses the fourth-floor button.

"If this breaks down, it means we have to get married," he whispers.

Bunny giggles and tries to put her hand up Billy's sweatshirt. "Show it to me," she says. Billy's hair is light brown and tousled up at the front; he has a baseball player's body: tall and lean. He pitches for the high school team and was MVP last year. He'll never show it, but Billy is remarkably sensitive, given who his father is.

"Oh, now you want to see it?" Billy playfully pulls Bunny's arms down, exerting twice the strength she has. He leans in to kiss her. The elevator abruptly stops, bobbles up and down; the door opens.

"Guess we're not getting married," Bunny says.

Billy pulls Bunny into his nautical-themed bedroom, trappings of a high school boy on the verge of manhood, sheltered and yearning for adventure. Bunny trails her fingers along his wooden desk. She notices an extra-large bottle of protein powder, leftover Halloween candy from a year earlier, and Abercrombie & Fitch cologne. His bed is made, crisp and smooth, and there's a giant box of Goldfish under it, conveniently located for weekend hangovers. An Xbox is sprawled on the floor, Vineyard Vines collared shirts hanging perfectly in his closet. A yellow Gadsden flag is strung above the headboard of his bed, the coiled image of a rattlesnake above the words DON'T TREAD ON ME.

Bunny tries to put her hand up Billy's sweatshirt again and he flinches in pain. "Careful." She lifts the shirt all the way up to reveal a white bandage under his heart.

"Oh my God, your dad's gonna kill you."

"He'd kill me if he knew a lot of things." Billy moves his hand up Bunny's pleated skirt.

She pushes it away. "Hold on, I'm not done talking yet."

Billy takes his hand away, both hands up, *not guilty*.

"What is it?" Bunny asks of the tattoo, inching toward the windowsill.

"It's a secret," Billy says.

Bunny shoves open the window and climbs out. "Come on, tell me."

"No!" Billy teases, following her.

Bunny strolls along the balcony, looks at the moon then back to Billy, her elbow propped next to a stone gargoyle. "Has your dad seen that?" She takes a cigarette out of her pocket and lights it.

"Are you insane?"

"I meant your sweatshirt." Bunny exhales, pointing to the logo: NYU.

"Oh, not sure."

"When do you hear back from the academy?"

"Don't know." Billy inches toward her; he wraps his hands around her waist, nuzzling his head into her chest. "Are we done talking now?"

Bunny gently moves him to the side, walks to the other end of the balcony. "Not yet," she says, teasing him.

Billy sighs, leans over the windowsill, grabs his ukulele resting against the wall of his bedroom, and pulls it outside. He strums, completely avoidant of any discussion having to do with his father and the expectations coming for him after graduation.

Bunny notices and changes the subject. "Who was your dad talking to outside this late?"

"I don't know, but my mom was being super weird in the kitchen."

"William . . ." A voice is heard through his bedroom window.

"Shit, it's my dad. Hide!"

Bunny stubs out her cigarette on the railing and crouches down in the corner as close to the side of the house as she can. Billy hops inside, slamming the window shut behind him, leaving Bunny out in the cold.

Billy stands in front of the large glass window, the ukulele dangling at his side.

"It's late, Son, you should be in bed instead of playing that stupid-looking thing."

Billy sets the ukulele down behind him, turns around, and stands up straight. "Yes, sir."

"I need to talk to you about something very important. I'm speaking at the National Press Club tomorrow and I'd like you to come."

"What about school?"

"I've already spoken with the school."

"Okay. Copy that, sir," Billy replies.

The general glances at his sweatshirt then turns to walk out of the bedroom, always brief, yet his presence powerful even with his back turned.

"Good night, Son."

"Good night, Dad."

Billy exhales—then *tap tap tap*; he has forgotten Bunny is still outside hiding. He turns around and bolts for the window.

"What was that about?" Bunny asks, climbing back inside.

"Nothing, he's speaking at the Press Club tomorrow, wants me to go."

Bunny wraps her arms around him, looks him in the eyes. She understands that Billy doesn't want to talk about his father, that the general thinks his love of music is a waste of time, the expectations he has for and of his son—to go to West Point, the U.S. military academy, to follow in his father's and older brother's footsteps. What neither she nor Billy understands is how those expectations will inevitably tear them apart. Love, they will come to learn, will never be enough.

Bunny places Billy's hand up her pleated skirt. He looks into her blue eyes and kisses the fair freckles on her nose as she exhales with innocence and pleasure. Billy smiles, backing her up to the foot of his bed. "Shhh," he teases. "Be very, very quiet."

❧•CHAPTER SIX•❧

Officer Gomez and Officer Nevins are parked outside the Wells Fargo bank in Cleveland Park typing up a police report before they begin their midnight shift. Nevins looks more like a teacher's assistant at Georgetown University than a cop. White, average build, blond hair, and he wears wire glasses that slide down his nose, while Gomez, shorter, stockier, is Latino with a handsome jawline. They spend most shifts "chasing the radio" in the wealthy suburbs, rescuing old people who fall down a lot.

Officer Gomez is swiping through his Tinder app when an old white man—popped collar, silver hair—approaches the vehicle and taps on the window.

"Here we go," Gomez quips, cracking the window just enough so the old white man can see his eyes clearly.

"There's a homeless man sleeping inside the ATM area of the bank right now," says the old white man, noticeably perturbed.

"Has he caused you any harm? Has he attacked anyone?"

"Well, no," says the old white man, "but—"

Gomez cuts him off. "Sir, he's in there because it's cold outside."

The old white man is now leaning toward Gomez's window, gazing beyond him and into the eyes of Officer Nevins in the driver's seat, obviously hoping for a different answer than the one he doesn't like. There is a long and uncomfortable pause before the old white man responds, "So what are you gonna do about it?" He's crossing his arms now.

"Sir, unless we get a call from the bank, we are not permitted to go inside and remove him without cause. He's just sleeping."

The old white man huffs and puffs. "Ridiculous!" he says, shaking his head. But he is the old white man who is a progressive! Who voted to help the homeless! To build shelters, not put them in prison! How can this be? *Disgusting*, he thinks, a homeless man sleeping in the ATM area of *his* bank.

"Have a good night, sir." Gomez would tip his hat if he had one. The old white man storms back to his Audi sedan parked behind them.

"Every fuckin' time," Gomez says, rolling up his window.

"Take a look at this." Nevins pushes the computer screen on the dashboard to face Gomez, who looks up from his phone to review the report when—

The radio crackles to life: "Dispatch for two-one-two-two-one, reports of fire, address is five hundred Wildwood Drive, armed suspect reported, district fire department are on their way."

Nevins throws his backpack in the backseat and adjusts his glasses.

"Go, go, go," Gomez says, watching as a fire truck and ambulance speed past them in the opposite direction. Before Gomez can buckle his seat belt and Nevins can turn on the engine, two more fire trucks follow with a second ambulance, speeding faster.

"Woo!" Gomez yells. "We got a big one. Let's go, let's go!"

Nevins turns on the siren before skidding across all lanes, chasing the ambulance in front of him. They turn on Massachusetts Avenue; as they cut around the ambulance, they see a young white girl riding her bike along the sidewalk, a backpack slung over her shoulder: Bunny Bartholomew.

A glass streetlamp explodes; shards of glass shatter over the windshield as Nevins approaches the flames engulfing a nine-thousand-square-foot colonial mansion. Black smoke billows through weeping willows warping around Wildwood Drive, naked limbs blowing toward Rock Creek Park. A place no longer safe for children to play, no longer safe for tourist horse-and-buggy rides or walking dogs.

The ambulance and fire trucks are blocks behind them. Most nights it's a game for the officers, to race their fellow servicemen and -women, but not tonight.

Nevins gets out of the car, covering his mouth with his forearm. "Jesus! Gomez!" he yells above the approaching sound of screaming sirens, the deep sound of the fire truck horn penetrating his gut. He takes out his gun. Gomez darts toward the back of the house, leaving the car door open, coughing, squinting up at the violent flames bursting through crown molding above expensive windowpanes, charred drywall falling into the dead boxwoods below. The fire is coming from the second level.

"I hear screaming! Someone is screaming! Gomez!!!"

Nevins, coughing and swallowing, grabs the radio attached to his chest as he moves closer to the front door. "Two-one-two-two-one, for dispatch this is Officer Nevins, we need backup, I repeat, we need backup!"

Gomez sprints to meet him. Nevins stands with his ear to the door, trying to pinpoint exactly where the screaming is coming from.

"Do you hear that?" he asks Gomez, a moment of silence between them and the crackling fire when suddenly the front door blows open, knocking Nevins and Gomez to the ground.

Gomez sits on the curb breathing into an oxygen mask while Nevins is taken into an ambulance with severe burns on the side of his face. A body is dragged out of the mansion by a lone fireman as a dozen others attempt to tame the fire; the body is a woman.

"She's breathing! She's breathing!"

Blood smears the sidewalk as a stretcher is rushed to her side. The firefighter snips the woman's top, maneuvering around what look to be stab wounds amidst the burns. In order to preserve the evidence, he carefully places the remnants of her clothing on top of a plastic bag.

Seconds later, another firefighter wobbles empty-handed out of the mansion, red-faced, covered in soot, smelling of acid and unknown chemicals. He falls to his knees and vomits.

The fire chief walks over to him. The fireman is hyperventilating in between gasps: "Sir, I have a daughter, I cannot tell you what I've just seen." He hawks up saliva and spits into the ground. He repeats, over and over, "I have a daughter, I have a daughter, I have a daughter. . . ."

It is written in the papers that David and Genevieve Banks, Audrey, and the housekeeper were brutally tortured before the house was set on fire. The bodies of Mr. and Mrs. Banks were found chained together, charred and limp, gags in their mouths, shadows of their lives dancing across the wall in front of them. Audrey had been beaten with an autographed Ted Williams baseball bat. Mr. Banks's vintage samurai sword from a work trip to Japan was used to slice her up, then what remained was left to burn.

It had been the housekeeper who managed to call 911 after being beaten and burned and left for dead; the lone woman, still breathing, still trying to do her job, and eventually dragged out of the house by one of the firemen. She'd died in the ambulance on the way to the hospital. There were no survivors.

But what was more disturbing than the murders themselves was the fact that not one neighbor stepped outside to see if everyone—*anyone*—was okay. Not one. They didn't notice when the midnight flames tore through the roof. The gut-thumping sirens driving by merely woke them from a bad dream, or caused the switching of sides of a pillow until they fell back into a peculiar slumber. It was only the next morning, when the news crews showed up—and the FBI—that the Washingtonians emerged, standing protected behind their hedges and fences, mouths agape, hugging their spoiled children.

No one in Washington wants to be part of a scandal. The consequences are fatal, socially and economically. Survival in this town requires playing chess, and playing it well. Every move calculated. Never being vulnerable, or someone will inevitably prey upon your weakness and turn it into shame. One wrong move could have you ostracized from all social events, removing any chance for leverage and power moves.

Take the Dobkin family, for example. Mr. Dobkin, a financier, threw a million-dollar wedding for his daughter, and instead of hiring a local wedding planner, chose a celebrity wedding planner. The goal is *Town & Country* or a *New York Times* wedding announcement, not the *Daily Mail*. Turned out said celebrity planner sued for nonpayment, splashing the tabloids with epithets like *greedy*, *cheap*, and *fraudulent*. It was a nasty game of telephone before Mrs. Dobkin was eventually pushed to the outer circle and then picked off for good. Removed from the boards of directors of her charities—she couldn't keep up with her philanthropic commitments. Mr. Dobkin lost all their money after that in a bad deal. Eventually their house foreclosed and they were forced to rent in Annapolis, Maryland.

⟆⟨⟨⟩⟆

David Banks was a quiet man; his weapon of power was silence, and buried beneath it was a family line of money so deep, it was hard for anyone to follow. He preferred a low profile as one of the wealthiest men in Washington. When you googled his name, the only article that came up was an obscure PDF—something about the wiring of funds to some bank in order to pay Ariana Grande for a surprise appearance at one of Audrey's birthday parties—and it was on page four or five of the search. He wore Brioni suits and collected vintage Ferraris. Rumor was that he'd had a garage built on the property of his château in the South of France to hold all sixty of them. Mr. Banks's family money originally came from American oil. His grandfather had got in early with the Bolger Brothers back in Texas in the mid-twentieth century, then expanded into several industries such as plastic ware, textiles, and cement: things no human ever thinks about. So that's why Mr. Banks bought Mrs. Banks a line of linens—the brand that Jackie O and Princess Margaret used for their master bedrooms, children's rooms, and guest rooms—something a little more glamorous than Tupperware. She wanted to do something with her time other than organize benefits and luncheons at the Sulgrave Club and the Cosmos Club for the arts. She wanted it to be glamorous and provide social status beyond Washington.

Genevieve Banks was the epitome of chic. She never left the house without stockings or her signature Yves Saint Laurent hot-pink lipstick with Chanel beige lip gloss slathered on top. She was no dummy. A buyer for Lord & Taylor in her early twenties, she'd met Mr. Banks when he was still a young lawyer. "I just knew he would make a lot of money on his own," she would say to her girlfriends, as if his family money weren't the reason she'd decided to marry him. But there would always be money—and she deserved some sort of prize for it. Mrs. Banks was a girl of good breeding: educated, Ivy League parents (though her parents didn't come from money, they were intellectuals, upper middle class). She was "good enough" to marry up, but she never felt good enough. Not many people knew this, but she was often a jealous person, competitive with her friends; it made most wonder if she even had any real ones. She was the kind of woman who knew how to find a man and, more important, how to keep him. When she and Mr. Banks had sex, she often sounded like she was tasting apple pie for the first time: "Mmm, mmmm, mmmmm!" She embodied a whole new vision of "fake it till you make it."

When Mrs. Banks became more notable in the Washingtonian social circle, hosting book parties and election parties and fundraisers for nonprofits like Teach for America, then moving up to hosting events at the French and British Embassies, she became known not just in Washington but through the social ranks of New York. This made Mr. Banks nervous because he couldn't control her or keep his family contained anymore, which meant he would have a harder time protecting them: *Washington Life*, New York Social Diary, the *Washington Post* Style Section, *The Glam Pad* blog, Facebook, Instagram!

And Audrey, poor thing, was Little Miss Popular, because it was becoming easier and easier to pay for friends, creating a curated virtual path into the life of a rich kid whom everyone could envy and want something from (Instagram stories on private jets: prayer hands, heart emoji!). Which, of course, posed an even greater risk of breaching the privacy Mr. Banks tried so hard to protect—something the old families of Washington coveted. A "quiet" reputation was desired among the elite of the elite. Those whose old money and manner lurk through the cobblestone streets of Georgetown, Kalorama, and Capitol Hill; those whose names can only be found in the exclusive Green Book—a discriminative, secret diary founded by the niece of Edith Roosevelt's social secretary—the names of Very Important People. Everyone inside it is wealthy, everyone inside it is powerful, and everyone has a reputation to protect. The pecking order at the top, the aristocratic bloodlines woven into the fabric of Washington, generation after generation after generation, only socialize within their inner circle, which is impenetrable—turning a blind eye to those who come and go on the political merry-go-round, yet rooted within the very foundation America was built upon.

But what they have failed to understand is that the world is changing. It wasn't until the Banks family was murdered that everything about their legacy was called into question.

They're called the Cave Dwellers.

CHAPTER SEVEN

A running lawn mower vibrates; its bent blade chops through wet grass, drowning the sounds of ice cubes knocking around in Betsy's glass of orange juice. She takes a sip at the hand-painted desk recently shipped from Paris, opens her laptop. At the top of her home screen are trickling red letters: *Breaking News: Wealthy Family Found Dead in DC Mansion.* Surprised and curious, she clicks on the link. Fox 5:

Two adults and one child were found dead in a mansion, which caught fire on the 500 block of Wildwood Drive, home to some of DC's most elite families near the Washington National Cathedral. Additionally, one woman was initially found still breathing but later died in transit to the hospital. Officials say the fire, reported in the early hours of Friday morning, is being investigated as suspicious. Police have not yet identified the victims.

Betsy takes a deep breath of relief. Despite the city's gentrification, which Betsy is *so pleased* about, she still thinks of the inner city as the murder capital of the United States as it was in the nineties. She thinks Georgetown is dangerous. McLean, where they live, is home to the Cheneys, the Saudi princes, and the CIA, a wealthy enclave on the edge of the Potomac River with winding wooded roads and expanding cliffside mansions.

Betsy clicks open a new tab and googles "The Washington Country Club," then clicks on the link and waits for the page to load. A clever slogan appears first in white letters: *We Are the King of Clubs*, before the rest—line by line—(history stands still . . .):

Rules: At all times—No jeans, collarless shirts, swimwear, bare feet, bare midriffs, or hats. Jackets and collared dress shirts and trousers for men and the equivalent for ladies. As for the Tap and Card Rooms: Country Club Casual (CCC) golf and tennis attire permitted. Please note: Public Display of Affection (PDA) is forbidden.

For a moment, Betsy can't remember which religion she should check on the application. Do they want Catholic or Episcopalian? Should she buy a bigger diamond cross, or more Ralph Lauren? Should she confirm with the reverend at the National Cathedral for a meeting if, in fact, Episcopalian is what they want, or the priest at Holy Trinity? Lord knows she must be the right religion. Back in North Carolina, Doug and Betsy attended the local Catholic church, filling their insides with the blood, body, and soul of Christ at each Holy Communion, *cross your heart, hope to die.* . . . Betsy knows only a fool would think that just because private institutions legally can't discriminate on the basis of race or religion, that stops the unconscious attitudes of committee members from making discriminatory decisions.

Most don't know that Betsy was twenty years old the first time she flew in an airplane, that she attended public school and Georgetown University rejected her, forcing her to settle for Gettysburg College. Years of her life have been spent crafting a family identity in order to protect her; and because Doug is now a senator—*especially* because Doug is now a senator—they only have half of the pedigree needed to be accepted into the elite country clubs. All the rest will come by word of mouth and nominations, or else the damning fate of Washington rejection awaits.

Betsy looks up at her Cartier art deco rock-crystal-platinum-with-white-enamel-diamond table clock, then opens her new Instagram account to post the first digital photograph of the family that Tony has sent her via text message. She captions it, "About last night . . . 🖼 , 🏳." She posts the photo, then presses the refresh button several times so that she can see the notification of "likes" pop up in her feed. She had a social media tutorial with an American University student last week after Mackenzie refused to help her. Betsy types "Washington Country Club" under the hashtag search in the application. Once the page pops up, Betsy scrolls through and looks for the most elegant bridal photo she can find in order to locate the church where they were married. And what do you know: a photograph of a groom dipping his beautiful bride outside the flying buttresses of the National Cathedral is the second photo in the second row. *Bingo*. Episcopalian. *Check*. Betsy picks up the phone and schedules an appointment with the reverend. Calculated. Surely in a few weeks time, he'll make a great reference for the family.

Betsy clicks back into Instagram, returning to the photograph of the groom dipping his beautiful bride, then taps, *very carefully*, on the 237 "likes" so that a list of the names of those "likes" pops up. She taps on the round profile picture of a blond woman she finds strikingly beautiful; seeing a photograph of what looks like a castle, she taps the photograph and reads the detailed caption: "We flew into Munich last week. . . . A few days ago . . . we drove miles in the Range Rover and each morning I would see a glimpse of the most enchanting Bavarian countryside, Alps with a little sugar coating of snow, spring flowers and grass, fields upon fields of yellow daisies and charming chalet villages, immaculate—it is simply the best!" Betsy taps into her 1,349 "likes" and sees another beautiful blond woman; she clicks into her page, sees a photograph of a long, regal-looking dining table with three hanging crystal chandeliers, sun striking the credenza against the wall, caption: "The brick floor! To die for! Color scheme obsession! Magic hour! Adore these ochre walls, I need these chandeliers and my winter guest list under them for dinner! ▮▮" Betsy clicks on her 1,899 "likes"; the fifth photograph down is another little circular head shot of a glamorous-looking woman:

red hair blown out perfectly with trendy dangling earrings that look like three giant green balls hanging loosely from her earlobes, familiar. . . . Betsy taps on the image, which takes her to the one and only Linda Williams: "Mother, wife of the wonderful Fox's Chris Williams, Washingtonian, French student."

Betsy's neurological reward circuits light up as if she's had an orgasm. She scrolls through Linda's page the way an FBI agent scrolls through suspects. Parties at embassies: *Italy, France, England!* Photographs of her back garden: hydrangeas in the summertime, a stone swan, intimate candlelit dinner tabletops, décor—Dorothy Draper/ *Architectural Digest*-esque, her summer home in the Hamptons. And last but not least, a recently posted video of Linda learning French at the Alliance Française located around the corner from the embassy in the heart of Kalorama. Betsy stays on the page of the posted video so it repeats itself over . . . and over . . . and over. A broken record: *"Je voudrais un croissant, s'il vous plaît,"* a montage of Linda, over . . . and over . . . and over, *"Je voudrais un croissant, s'il vous plaît," "Je voudrais un croissant, s'il vous plaît."* Linda's wearing a black Chanel sweater set and those dangly green ball earrings as she repeats, over . . . and over . . . and over, *"Je voudrais un croissant, s'il vous plaît."* Betsy notices the location tag at the top of the photograph: Alliance Française, Kalorama, Washington, DC. *Posted one week ago.*

Betsy clicks open a separate tab, googles "Alliance Française," and dials the number.

"Bonjour. Alliance Française, how may I help you today?" The voice pierces Betsy's eardrums as if awakening her from a trance or emotional coma. Betsy clears her throat, covering the telephone speaker for a moment. "Yes, hello, this is Betsy Wallace calling. I'd like to take one of your classes—my husband, Senator Wallace of North Carolina, and I will be traveling to France again this summer, so I wanted to brush up."

"Yes, of course, Mrs. Wallace, we would be delighted to have you join us."

Betsy looks down at Linda's hashtags to make sure she gives the right class, date, and time. "I'd like to join the Tuesday and Thursday evening class, please."

"Not a problem, Mrs. Wallace. I'll just need you to fill out a few forms with your credit card information and scan them back to us. Do you have an e-mail address I could send those to?"

"Oh actually, you know what, I'm going to be in the area this evening to pick up my girls—how about I just stop by and fill everything out there, easy-peasy."

"Well, if it's not an inconvenience for you, that'd be just fine."

"Not at all, see you soon. *Au revoir!*" Betsy leans back against her newly bought Chippendale chair. If she can lock down Linda Williams to nominate her for the Washington Country Club, the family will be a shoo-in.

CHAPTER EIGHT

The Russell Senate Office Building is filled with an unconscious bureaucracy of young staffers constipated on corporate chains and bad fashion: *Chop't! Cava! Potbelly!* Oversize suits and Mother's pearls, white tights and black patent leather shoes (*YIKES*). Most likely hired through a friend of a parent who's a donor or does law work for a super PAC, they're only there for the year before applying and getting into Georgetown or Harvard Law—their life: a factory of privilege. Their parents: churning out little replicas of who they used to be and who they have become.

But not Cate. Cate might be a Bartholomew, but her father is the bastard who left her, her mother, and her baby sister high and dry. A deadbeat alcoholic in prison for aggravated assault and tampering with the odometers of used cars. Cate was fourteen when he left. Her uncle Chuck stepped in to cover tuition costs and helped Cate secure her position on the Hill, a staunch donor to the Republican Party. No one speaks about her father; he's been shut out of the family inheritance, left to rot in a desert state prison in central California.

Cate stomps around an intern, heels clopping along the concrete tunnel connecting all the Senate and House office buildings, where staffers travel like they're in some kind of ant farm, the Capitol at its center. For security, they do not walk between the offices in the light of day, outside, with other people.

"Good morning." Cate smiles, passing a security guard at a clearance checkpoint. She flashes the ID that's dangling around her neck.

"Good morning, Ms. Bartholomew, ready for the day?"

"Putting on my rubber gloves for this one." She winks. Her sass, she believes, is her asset. In a village so jammed with decorum, most don't know who they are anymore.

Cate makes her way up the marble staircase, her Ann Taylor dress restricting her strides, forcing smaller steps. She passes the office intern, twenty, already has his master's, about to sip from the water fountain.

"I wouldn't do that," Cate says. The intern lifts his head, gives her a quizzical look. "There's lead in that water."

Cate enters the senator's office: vintage brown Kensington Chesterfield tufted sofa, the *Washington Post* resting, unopened, on the coffee table. Headlines read:

MASS SHOOTING AT MIDLANDS MUSIC FESTIVAL
WHITE HOUSE CAUGHT IN DOMESTIC
VIOLENCE PROBE
Wealthy Washington family held hostage before slain and burned
in DC Mansion

Cate stands holding a paper plate with a blueberry muffin while she waits for the coffee to finish brewing. As she picks up her muffin and takes a small bite, Walter Stevens, the senator's top aide and lifelong friend, early fifties, fat, wearing a navy suit, swoops around her.

"Did you color your hair?" Walter asks, grabbing the muffin out of Cate's hand.

"Um, no," Cate replies, watching Walter take a bite, crumbs falling down his tie and onto the floor.

"Huh, looks more blond," Walter says with his mouth full, then drops the muffin back on Cate's plate and wipes his hands on the side of his pants. He pulls out his ringing cell phone and answers.

Cate stares at the enormous bite taken out of her muffin. Her face melts into repulsion before she turns and throws it into the trash can.

"Fox News wants a statement about the administration's domestic violence case," Walter says to Cate just as Doug walks through the office door. Cate side-eyes the senator, flipping her blond locks to the side as she listens to Walter give her direction, taking notes with her cell phone, knowing Doug will *absolutely* look at her, see her hand running through those sun-kissed strands as she serves this great nation and *God will it turn him on.*

Doug gives an extra formal "Good morning," nods to his staff, trying not to acknowledge Cate out of utter fear someone will notice the undeniable chemistry between them. He walks into his office and closes the door.

Walter receives another call. "I have to take this, please handle Fox. I have to be in a committee meeting in ten minutes."

"On it," Cate replies delightedly, and heads for the senator's office.

Doug leans back in his swivel chair with his arms folded above his head as Cate stands before him. They each take a deep breath, not having spoken since last night. Doug tries desperately to compartmentalize: *I am not sex addict. I'm just like my father, and my father's father, and my father's father's father. . . .*

"So, Mr. Senator," Cate begins, a little nervous, wavering between personal and professional, "we need a statement from you in light of what's happened with the president's chief of staff. . . ."

A long pause, while Doug gathers his thoughts. . . .

"We need to get this out as soon as possible before a replacement is announced later this afternoon," she persists. "People want to know where you stand on this issue." Doug is completely unfocused, his eyes locked on Cate; despite his lust for her, there's a kind of vacancy to his intense gaze that Cate notices but doesn't acknowledge.

"What issue?"

"Domestic violence . . ."

A moment before he snaps back to it. "Oh, right, right, well, reprehensible, of course."

Cate waits for him to finish, assuming he has more to say. . . . He does not. Cate knows that part of the job is thinking on her feet. Swift. She must prove her worthiness over and over. She won't admit it because the chemistry between them is too blinding for her to see that she is in a vast ocean, alone, treading just to keep her head above water, all while smiling and making sure her hair looks great and the office's public relations strategy is bulletproof.

"How about this: 'I was shocked to hear of the allegations released against White House Chief of Staff Tom Derby. There is no place for domestic violence anywhere. I look forward to a prompt and orderly resignation.'"

Doug thinks hard for a moment. "Were you a journalism major at UCSD?"

Cate smiles and lifts an eyebrow. "Mr. Senator . . ." Doug smiles back at her, exuding the kind of charm that makes all the southern women swoon over him no matter how shiny his bald head might be. "I have to finish this."

"Excellent, publish it," Doug replies, removing his arms from behind his head, repositioning himself at his desk as if he is ready to get to work.

Cate takes a few steps forward. Doug, regretting having just flirted with her, tries to take an action, any action, to stop her from getting too close to him. He grabs the newspaper, shuffles it around, and throws it on the corner of his desk as though he were a childish boy trying to throw something at his kid sister to keep her away from him.

*   *   *

Cate stops *Did I misread him?* She looks down at the strewn news-paper.

WILDWOOD DRIVE MASSACRE:
WEALTHY FAMILY SLAIN.

"That's not far from where I live. When did this happen?"

"Oh, umm"—Doug glances at the headline—"last night, tragic, just tragic, a classmate of one of my daughters."

"Oh God." Cate moves a little closer but notices Doug is not engaging; his personal cell phone lights up.

Tim Cell. Doug looks at his phone, trying not to believe that this is God's way of telling him he has a problem.

"Ah, I'll let you get that." Cate runs her hands through her hair again, disappointed. "Got to get this statement sent out." She waves her cell phone, where she has written notes, then turns toward the door. Doug's eyes revert straight to her butt, staring at it as if staring into an abyss, losing himself completely. Cate glances back, catching him in the act. She smiles, she loves it, bites her lower lip, validated, then spins around to shut the door ever so gently behind her.

Doug's personal cell phone is now violently vibrating on his mahog-any desk.

"Hello? Tim? . . . Yes, yes, all was fine last night, it was my wife, Betsy. I felt terrible, I had to get back, you know, with everything that's happening right now, it's never been a more important time—it really made me realize how much Betsy loves and supports me, it just threw me into gratitude. . . ."

He listens to Tim. Then interrupts: "I really appreciate the con-cern, I really do, and you know, she was just in my office, and it was professional. Last night was the last slip, you know, or . . . I just don't think, Tim, that I'm an addict. It's not like I'm grabbing women by the pussy! Look at my life; I couldn't have made it this far if I was so self-destructive. I appreciate the concern, Tim, but I'm just not one of you."

Doug hangs up and sets his personal cell phone next to his work cell phone. He bobbles back and forth in his chair and locks his arms above his head again. He stares at the framed vintage original print of Ronald Reagan with a gun in his pants and a cowboy hat on his head. The film: *Law and Order.* The tagline: *His Guns Were the Only Law!*

Doug picks up his phone—the brilliance, the control he has! He searches for Cate's personal number; without a thought, he texts: Did I tell you how sexy that dress looks on you 😃? He puts the phone down with a sense of relief, a rush of excitement!

He waits for her response.

Ten minutes pass. He waits. For Christ's sake—more crises than the Hill can handle, and Doug hasn't looked at one goddamn e-mail. He waits.

He picks up his personal phone and goes to his messages. There's no text thread with Cate. But he just texted her, how can this be?

Oh *no.*

In this utterly blasphemous moment, Doug freezes. He quickly gropes for a reason, any reason, to justify why he has texted her from his work phone and not his personal phone. He prays, *Please, please, do not let her respond on my work phone. You can't expense sexting with taxpayer money!*

His work phone lights up. A text message. His heart falls to his feet.

He opens the text. It's the agriculture commissioner from North Carolina confirming dinner next week. *Relief.* As Doug wipes the sweat from his upper lip, his personal cell phone lights up.

Naughty texting from your work phone. Asking for trouble, Mr. Senator? 😃

Doug chuckles at the screen—he loves it! He knew she was smart; it's why he hired her! *Good girl*, he thinks. He throws his head back, laughs louder to himself again. It's overwhelmingly jolly. *Good girl.*

*   *   *

Cate sits at her wooden desk wearing a mischievous, blushing smile, when her work phone lights up. A text message, Senator Wallace's Phone. She opens it: Oh, I'm so embarrassed, that was meant for my wife Betsy, my sincere apologies.

No worries ☺ Cate replies.

Doug swivels a bit more in his seat, taps his fingers compulsively atop the leather on his desk. Picks up his phone. Puts it down, taps, then picks it up again, texting: I forgot something, can you come back in my office for a minute? He drops his phone again.

Cate looks over at her screen. Her heart pounds exceedingly hard when she sees that Doug has asked her to step back into his office.

Cate swoops her hair over to the side and knocks while opening the door, smiles. "You wanted to see me again?"

Doug gets up from his seat, puts his hands in his pockets, and walks around his desk as Cate steps in, closing the door behind her. Doug perches himself on the edge of his desk, crosses his arms and his ankles. "You know I have daughters . . ." he says.

"Yes. Two, right?"

"Fox has invited me to come on-air tonight to discuss the domestic violence issue, but I think you should do it in my place. Be the face of our team."

Cate feigns simultaneous surprise and humility. "Oh, wow, thank you. . . . Yes, I would be happy to—*honored* to."

"From a strategy standpoint as well, I think it looks good to show people that I work closely with women and will not tolerate abusive behavior—not just in the home, but in the office."

"Oh, absolutely. Would you like me to reiterate that you have daughters as well? And God forbid this should ever happen to one of them?"

"Yes," Doug says, then inhales, puffing up his chest. "And in the office . . ."

"Of course," Cate says, smiling, confirming their little secret.

CHAPTER NINE

*A*n army of black Suburbans with government tags is parked beneath the five American flags waving above the National Press Club building. Before Carol and Billy, the general's wife and son, make it to the elevators, they are bombarded by a dozen television screens on the wall in the lobby, each with its volume turned up, a talking head debating another talking head, sometimes a third talking head, occasionally a fourth talking head, even a fifth talking head—a legion of heads, as if an art curator had come from the Met to do a television installation providing the sensation of disorientation complete with a warning label for those prone to seizures, panic attacks, and possible brain aneurysms. CNN, Fox, NBC, ABC, CBS, MSNBC, C-SPAN: "The White House today / by the FBI, the attorney general, and / domestic violence found / the mass shooting yesterday / dozens dead including children/ good news for gun owners as gun stocks rise / more shakeups in the White House administration / Russian intelligence officials have not / the family murdered in a DC mansion . . ."

Inside the elevator, a security guard pulls a key fob out of his pocket and places it against the panel next to the thirteenth floor.

Carol adjusts Billy's navy striped tie, and he pushes her away. "Mom, it's fine."

"We're going to be on-camera, just making sure it's tight." Carol's hands are a little shaky. "Make your father proud." She's wearing a modest charcoal knee-length dress from Anne Klein she found on sale at Macy's. Trailed by three security guards, they step out of the elevator onto a blue and gold carpet. A security desk stands in front of them with two more security guards.

"May I help you?" the receptionist asks.

"The Montgomery family," the head of security replies.

"Come right through." She motions to the clear glass doors, which open electronically. "They're in the Zenger Room today."

As Billy and Carol pass through the halls of this journalism bastion, it is rather evident that this is an old boys' club that has gone sorely out of style. It is nothing but dull to Billy, who isn't entirely sure what he and his mother are doing there. Where are the modern tech rooms with Ping-Pong tables and food trucks waiting outside? Instead, these halls are flooded by old white men, many now retired, yet still they show up each morning in a suit and tie, plant themselves in the exclusive bar area on the tufted oxblood leather couches, amid burgundy velvet pillows and matching curtains, burled wood, brass and silver trinkets on shelves laden with musty donated books, watching multiple television screens as bow-tied Black and Hispanic servers come to take their orders.

Passing several framed historical newspaper headlines—

TERRORISTS HIJACK FOUR AIRLINERS, DESTROY WORLD TRADE CENTER, HIT PENTAGON; HUNDREDS DEAD
UP TO 25 DIE IN COLORADO SCHOOL SHOOTING
JOHN LENNON SHOT!

—Billy and Carol arrive at the Zenger Room where a press coordinator and the president of the club descend upon them. All of the famous faces of prime-time television news are sitting in the front row; a few stand holding a microphone, sound-checking, in full makeup, scrolling their Slack channels. An empty podium before them stands in front of a backdrop declaring THE NATIONAL PRESS CLUB in blue letters. Billy and Carol are led in by a woman wearing an earpiece, the beads of sweat on her forehead and her frantic gestures indicating that she is under extreme pressure to not fuck up one moment of her job. *The nation is waiting.* All eyes fix quickly on mother and son, particularly Billy, who is noticeably being groomed to follow in his father's footsteps.

Billy, seated, turns around to the back of the room to see a row of cameras, so many that they bleed into the aisle next to him. He notices one cameraman—slightly overweight, kind of burly, his beard hasn't been trimmed in weeks—who's got earbuds in and his head buried in a copy of Mark Twain's *The Adventures of Huckleberry Finn.* Billy wonders whether the book is a shield to protect him from the constant news cycle, or a symptom of how numb he has become to it.

A prime-time face stands in front of his cameraman, waiting, begins to read his phone when he gets the alert.

"Just in: General Edward Montgomery has been nominated as secretary of defense. . . . This is unprecedented." LIVE! In the back of the room, several television screens show the president at a rally: ". . . I have decided to nominate General Edward Montgomery as secretary of defense!" The crowd somewhere in the Midwest roars on the television screen. The volume goes dead.

Another prime-time face: "Let's go, you rolling?"

"They'll be here in three minutes, they have entered the building, three minutes!" a PA yells to the back of the room.

Billy turns, searching for a reaction from his mother. Carol just sits with her hands folded in her lap; she turns her head slightly and smiles at him, a closed-mouth smile. Carol isn't comfortable in the spotlight. She swallows. She waits. The room gets quiet, and the president of the National Press Club steps over to the podium.

"Good morning. Just a few minutes ago the president announced that General Edward Montgomery will be nominated as secretary of defense. General Montgomery is certainly no stranger to this administration and to the Senate Armed Services Committee. We've known him as the chairman of the Joint Chiefs of Staff, as a commander in Afghanistan, and in many posts before that. He is a warrior and a leader of the highest quality of our great nation, with twenty-five years of distinguished service, and we are grateful to have him here with us today. General . . ."

Billy watches his father walk through the doors and around the PAs strapped with wires and walkie-talkies, earbuds and clipboards; it feels more like a production set in Hollywood than a political press conference. His father wears his decorated costume: his four stars pinned to the large shoulder pads of his uniform, his jump wings, his colorful badges of honor and courage. Assistants and bodyguards trail behind him.

Billy sits with his ankles crossed, his knees spread, his arms in his lap, stiff posture, his head slightly cocked back, aware that people are watching him. He knows he will never live up to who his father is and who, in this moment, he has just become. His eyes trail his father's as he makes his way to the podium; Billy hopes he will make eye contact, smile in his direction even, just for being there. The general is poised, proud, confident, his head held high. He walks past Billy without any acknowledgment, climbs the towering podium, and looks straight in the direction of the cameras that are surely entering the living rooms and offices of millions upon millions of Americans, and perhaps countries all over the world.

"Good morning, and thank you for the opportunity for me to be here before you today. I am truly honored by the nomination as the United States secretary of defense. Our department—the strongest military department in the world—stands as the guardian of this great country, and I want to thank the president for his confidence in me. I look forward to my confirmation hearing and continuing to serve our nation. Thank you, and God bless America."

Billy doesn't realize that his jaw is clenched and his right hand is curled into a fist. He feels a sense of conscious pride, and yet the kind of guilt that isn't available to feel at such a young age, the kind of guilt that insidiously bleeds into resentment and, later, raw and violent misplaced rage—that his father will always, no matter what, put country before family; that the world only sees a sacrificial warrior, whose family is constantly *thanked* for their support, they're so *supportive*. And yet, were they ever given a choice?

But Billy isn't thinking about this at all; in fact, Billy isn't fazed, the same way a kid in the Midwest isn't fazed by his orthopedic surgeon father's conference at the Courtyard Marriott. He's more conscious of how he is being perceived than anything else. It's only in quiet moments, or obliterated drunken moments, when he feels it.

The general steps off the stage, swarmed by security detail and a White House aide. Billy doesn't yet understand the new level of scrutiny his family is about to endure from the media. He watches. He forces a half-smile for the cameras when his phone buzzes. A text message from Bunny:

Did you hear the news? Audrey Banks is fucking dead.

Washington National Cathedral

The construction of the National Cathedral began under President Theodore Roosevelt in 1907. It was modeled after many of the eighteenth-century Gothic cathedrals with pointed arches, flying buttresses, and stained glass windows (there's also a Darth Vader gargoyle). Located on the highest hill in Washington, it's where many of the political and social elite often pray, marry, and are laid to rest. President Woodrow Wilson, Helen Keller, and Matthew Shepard are among those interred here. In 1953, the United Daughters of the Confederacy lobbied for two stained glass windows commemorating Generals Stonewall Jackson and Robert E. Lee, commanders of the Confederate Army. They prevailed and the windows were installed.* A recent task force report states, "The windows provide a catalyst for honest discussions about race and the legacy of slavery and for addressing the uncomfortable and too often avoided issues of race in America. Moreover, the windows serve as a profound witness to the cathedral's own complex history in relationship to race."** One window depicts Jackson kneeling with a Bible in his hands; the other is of Lee, his back to us, arms spread like an eagle, with the words: "So he passed over and all the trumpets sounded for him." In 2017, the stained glass windows were removed; however, they have yet to be replaced, as a private donor must be found to pay for it. Not one community member has offered to make the donation.

---

*   Colbert I. King, "The Removal of Confederate Windows at National Cathedral Was No Cause for Celebration," *Washington Post*, September 8, 2017, https://www.washingtonpost.com/opinions/the-removal-of-confederate-windows-at-national-cathedral-was-no-cause-for-celebration/2017/09/08/0d75b59e-9406-11e7-8754-d478688d23b4_story.html.

**   Washington National Cathedral website, https://cathedral.org/press-room/cathedral-to-explore-racial-justice-through-public-forums-arts-worship/.

❖ CHAPTER TEN ❖

St. Peter's Academy is a college preparatory school planted like a Gothic dome on the highest hill in Washington. Shadows of the National Cathedral—looming towers, flying buttresses, gargoyles, and stained glass windows of dead Confederates and Jesus, Mary, and Joseph—cloak the brick plantation like a holy veil.

The faint synchronized rhythm of young aristocratic blood flows through the reverend, his eyes closed as he begins the Lord's Prayer:

"Our father, who art in heaven, hallowed be thy name, thy kingdom come, thy will be done, on earth as it is in heaven. Give us this day our daily bread, and forgive us our trespasses, as we forgive those who trespass against us; and lead us not into temptation, but deliver us from evil, for thine is the kingdom, the power, and the glory, forever and ever. Amen."

The reverend's eyes open. He raises his hands. "May the Lord be with you."

"And also with you."

Completely unaware of the way in which they're being groomed, institutionalized, these children—stuffed with American fairy tales, verses of scripture capturing the pathways of their brains; funneled into the superior life of ambassadors, CIA agents, financiers, Kennedys, lobbyists, congressmen, presidents, for the only choice they have is *up, up, up!* The children who will never grow up outside of make-believe, invisible boundaries keeping them separate and apart from the inevitable leaking whispers of failure—deaf to the screams of financial suffocation.

The students of St. Peter's Academy scurry out of the nave in dramatic heaps of tears at the news of the deaths of Audrey Banks and her family. They are *devastated.* So much so that they can't help but talk about how it's affecting them. Particularly the popular girls, they're leaning their heads on their crushes like perpetual twists and turns of such *adversity*, giving the boys total hard-ons.

Before third period begins, Bunny sits on a stone neoclassical swan garden bench in a secluded section of Bishop's Garden, home to student recess where virginity is lost and drugs are sold just beyond the cathedral. Ivy trails up and around like a snake behind her head; green moss covers what looks to be some kind of cenotaph. She lights a cigarette. Over her uniform—green plaid skirt, navy collared shirt with the school's crest and motto, *Fidelitas et Integritas* (Fidelity and Integrity), sewn on the pocket—she's wrapped in a red hooded jacket lined in Burberry check. She hears the clip-clop of dress shoes coming down the stone steps. Stan Stopinksi, the Russian ambassador's son, wild, gregarious, and a ladies' man. Bunny, Billy, and their friends nicknamed him Putin 2.0 for his eerily similar look to a young Vladimir Putin: Aryan blond hair parted to the side, plump lips, round tip of the nose, deep eye sockets slanted upward, and high cheekbones. All of seventeen, he has an Eastern European swagger that none of the other boys have and a sharp wit. A polka-dotted silk handkerchief is tucked in the pocket of his navy blazer.

Stan calls Bunny Elizabeth (*Lizbet*) because he decided freshman year when he arrived in the States that the name Bunny was a joke played on him by his other classmates, "ridiculous" (*"vidiculus"*), he would say, swatting them away like flies. Today, years later, he still calls her Lizbet, though the Russian accent has waned into a more interesting transatlantic one, perhaps with more flare. Stan wanted to know who this strikingly interesting-looking girl was, with her strawberry blond hair, translucent skin, wide eyes, and fair freckles, her skinny legs and bony knees. There was an emotional curiosity at the root of her conversations, sprinkled with a sarcastic sense of humor but not annoyingly so. When Stan saw she belonged to Billy Montgomery, the musician, the academic, the gorgeous jock—the kid who could do anything right and nothing wrong—he backed off. Instead, he befriended them, and the trio inevitably became best friends because Stan was fun and different and mischievous and supplied the vodka at parties. Billy and Bunny inducted him into their circle of exclusivity almost instantaneously.

But Bunny hadn't always been part of an exclusive circle at school. It wasn't until Bunny started dating Billy that the popular girls, like Audrey Banks, noticed her. Though Audrey and Bunny had known each other since nursery school—some of Bunny's happiest memories: playing with Audrey's potbelly pig in the back garden when the Bankses once lived in Georgetown, and their matching Corolle Mon Premier Poupon Bebes when they played house together. Yet once they reached middle school and Audrey began shaving her legs, she formed a little "cashmere mafia," the beginning of her clique of cool girls who bragged about their periods before anyone else, leaving Bunny behind in her prepuberty existence. It was the summer before junior year when Bunny's legs grew long, her breasts filled out, her wit became charming and funny, a new kind of confidence marked the way she walked down the hallway of lockers, and Billy was the first to notice her—to fall in love with her. And all the popular girls followed, including Audrey. But Bunny would always remain skeptical of the friendship—of the way Audrey circled back to her.

Stan sits next to Bunny, who stares into a maze of headless pink roses.

"Wanna know how she died?" Bunny asks, setting the tone for gossip more than grief. "She was chopped up, then they burned—"

"*No, no, no*, Lizbet, I can't . . ." Stan shakes his head to extinguish the gruesome thoughts; he grabs the cigarettes from Bunny's hand, pulls one out for himself. "Who would do something like that?"

"The reverend didn't *say it* in there, he didn't say *how* they died. I googled it during the Lord's Prayer." Bunny stabs her cigarette against the stone bench, wipes it as if it were a paintbrush, then flicks it into a boxwood bush.

"I'm deleting my Finsta," Bunny says. Her "fake" Instagram account, the dark virtual underground world of gossip, of cruelty, of humor, of taunting and teasing and laughing, where the faces behind it accept followers they deem worthy of the privilege of *seeing who they really are*. Where the "real" Instagram is public domain for parents, teachers, and college administrators to dote over: Soccer goals! Prom photos! Family vacations! Not snorting Adderall, blow jobs, and poverty memes. A reckoning is slithering its way into Bunny's consciousness, however slowly, Audrey's murder prompting a turning point, forcing her to question the role she played as friend and the legacy she'll someday leave behind.

Bunny puts the phone down and looks up. Audrey's boyfriend, Justin Finnigan, plaid scarf, striped tie, khakis, cries into the shoulder of Mr. Muller, the AP history teacher, despite just three days ago hitting sloppy seconds with Lily Anderson in the corner of the Children's Chapel. Tessa Dawson, also known as Testicles, posted a candid photo of the couple that penetrated the darkest tunnels of the gram for everyone to see, spinning Audrey into a vengeful rage.

"What a douche." Stan exhales in Justin's direction, crossing one leg over the other as if in the audience at New York Fashion Week. He swoops his blond hair out of his eyes and to the side.

Their friend Marty Robinson slumps toward them, a long string bean, plaid bow tie, round tortoiseshell glasses, he's carrying a copy of Kate Chopin's *The Awakening* for his AP English class all marked up with notes in the margins and yellow highlighter. His parents are professors at Howard Law School and write books on public policy, though he'll end up at Harvard. Known as Smarty Marty, the only Black kid in their class, he's a straight-A student who could take the SATs stoned and still score a 1600 (2400 including the writing section).

"Hey, guys," Marty says, looming gloom, hand in his pocket, book dangling by his side. Bunny stares at him and Stan nods his head. "Where's Billy?" he asks.

Bunny takes a deep breath, consumed by Audrey's death. "He had to go listen to his dad speak at work or something." She says it so casually, so astonishingly nonchalant, *work or something*, the naïveté palpable on the edge of adulthood, the familial power in the hands of children who don't even know it's theirs.

"Oh, does he know what happened?" Marty asks.

"I just texted him," Bunny says. More clip-clopping is coming toward them down the stone steps; all eyes turn to the wall and traveling ivy as Chase Cowan and none other than Mackenzie Wallace, Senator Wallace's daughter, appear before them.

"Yo, Smarty Marty, New Girl is lookin' for you," Chase says. Mackenzie, Betsy and Doug's older daughter, stands with her hands clamped before her, knee socks, stringy hair hiding her bald spots, nose red from the wind chill. She didn't know Audrey Banks, so she stands with wide eyes, lost and clinging to anyone who will talk to her, just wanting to feel like she's going through this traumatic bonding experience with all of them.

Chase is the star football quarterback; his dad also happens to be the head of the CIA. He's got anger issues as a result of his father's PTSD post-9/11. Chase was born just months before the Twin Towers and the Pentagon were hit. His father, an employee under the director at the time, was summoned on a mission to a base in Afghanistan. He wasn't in the military; he was an intelligence analyst trained as an interrogation guy. Up and away in a warplane; it was imperative to their survival that upon landing the engine not be heard by al-Qaeda or Taliban local militants, so they turned it off and let the plane glide toward base, only turning the engine back on at the last moment, preventing a crash landing by seconds. Chase's father was sure they would die. But minutes later, he was led out of the plane to a secret prison. When he returned, he went through a dark period of extreme paranoia, resulting in mostly absence from a lot of Chase's earlier years. The safe room in their house still exists, though his father doesn't go in there much anymore. Instead, Chase and his friends use it to deal drugs and get high.

Marty walks over to Mackenzie and puts an arm around her, she's not sure if it's friendly or romantic but certainly awkward. "Hey, do you guys know Mackenzie Wallace? She's new. We have English together."

"Nice to meet you." Bunny sticks out her hand because that's what girls with manners do.

"Ah yes, you're in Mr. Watson's calculus class," Stan says.

"Yeah, that's right." Mackenzie smiles, thankful she's been noticed.

"You still having people over tonight, Putin?" asks Marty.

"Audrey died, the party didn't." Stan taps the ash of his cigarette away.

"Jesus, Putin." Bunny punches him in the arm.

"Too soon, man, too soon," Marty says, shaking his head.

"Mackenzie, you're invited to my house tonight. I have lots of vodka to chase our troubles *ahvay*," Stan says in a phony accent. His elbow resting on his knee, cigarette in hand like he's fucking Truman Capote.

"His mansion is dope," Chase says.

"Secret service making a beeline, put your cig out," Bunny says, bumping shoulders with Stan. He reaches for the back of the bench, dabbing the ash, and drops the cigarette behind him.

Two men built for the marines, wearing khakis and white polos with clear wires stuck to the backs of their necks, walk toward this group of inheritance survivors. None of them fazed, only annoyed by their encroaching presence.

"There's a black Escalade in the front circle, belong to any of you?"

"Does it have diplomatic tags?" Chase asks, not giving a shit.

The agents look at each other. "It does," one of them says.

The kids laugh at them. These agents are on their turf. It's not the first time government security detail has been stationed on their campus. The vice president's son is an alum, so is the chief of staff's daughter, and now the current president's daughter is here, a young freshman.

"Yeah, that's Ambassador Rothschild's kid, good luck trying to get him to move." Marty gives Chase a fist bump, letting him know he's gotta get to class; he and Mackenzie walk away. The bell rings. Bunny and Stan leap from the bench.

"Sorry, can't help ya there," Bunny says, scurrying back up the stone steps and off to class.

The two secret service men are left standing there, abandoned by a lack of intimidation. The school flag whips through the icy wind behind them; it reads: KNOW WHO YOU ARE.

CHAPTER ELEVEN

The Winners' Room at the National Press Club is a private room with wall-to-wall blue and gold carpet, several mahogany bookshelves, and photographs of journalism royalty: Bob Woodward, William F. Buckley Jr., Walter Cronkite. General Montgomery's celebratory luncheon is full of Pentagon officials and VIP members of the press club.

Billy sits uncomfortably in between a general he's never met before and his father. He picks at his chicken marsala, the brown sauce oozing into his green salad, thinking about Audrey Banks and wishing he were with his friends at school, feeling excluded from the haunting drama, this day that no one will ever forget. But he keeps her death to himself; he knows better than to drag the attention elsewhere. Things seem to be changing at an ever-escalating pace—a windmill of anxiety spins inside him. And he tries not to keep looking at his phone, knowing he'll be scolded for it. He was raised to always show the highest form of respect at whatever cost to military personnel, particularly those who have worked closely with his father—put their lives on the line for him, for their love of country, for their love of God. He feels his phone buzzing in his pocket. It takes all of his resistance not to answer it.

"William—" says the general sitting next to him.

"Oh, you can call me Billy," he replies before the man can finish. Billy feels his father threatening him with a forbidding look; *never interrupt someone of higher rank.*

"Billy," the man says, picking up his knife and fork, cutting into the overcooked chicken, "you must be proud of your old man."

Aware that his father is listening, Billy takes a discreet breath, swallows. "Yes, sir, very proud. . . ." He forces a smile that feels uncomfortable but looks legitimate.

"Next in line?" the general says, nudging his knuckle bearing a custom-made military ring with an emerald into the side of Billy's arm.

"Well, sir, I could never be my father even if I tried, the man's a legend." Billy chuckles nervously, then looks to his father for validation. General Montgomery wipes the corner of his mouth with a cloth napkin, says nothing.

The messages Billy receives in what his father does not say often drive him to the edge of his insecurity, convinced that his father is unceasingly displeased. Billy can't seem to escape any adult conversation without feeling he could somehow have done it better.

"You're not going into the military?" the general asks, taking Billy's attempt at self-deprecation literally.

"Oh, no, sir, I mean—I'm, well . . ." He stumbles, searching for the courage to say the thing he wishes he never had to say: that he will be attending the academy whether he likes it or not—

Just like his father's father's father, his father's father, his father . . .

"I haven't heard back yet from the academy," Billy says, skirting the question.

"Well, let me fill you in on a top secret, son—*you'll get in.*" The general winks and puts his knife stabbed with chicken in his mouth.

Billy chuckles, then furrows his brow and looks down at his untouched plate searching for something to say, to appease his father's silence, to make it go away. He looks up at the eager-to-be-friendly general. "Thank you, sir."

"So what do you like to do in your free time, Billy?" the general asks. Before Billy can answer, he notices a member of the security team walk over and whisper something in his father's ear, drawing his attention away. Billy feels a moment of relief despite wanting nothing more than for this afternoon to just end.

"Uh, my free time? I, uh, well, I . . ."

"Hobbies—do you have any hobbies, Billy? It's important for a man in the military to have hobbies, for dealing with . . . stress."

Billy momentarily mistakes this question as an invitation for shared honesty and possible commonality rather than a test of one's endurance or tenacity—a trick question only in hindsight. "I love to play music, sir."

The general raises an eyebrow, perks up with surprise. "Ah, music?"

"The ukulele. I taught myself how to play it on a YouTube channel."

"A YouTube channel . . ." The general looks confused.

Billy's father finishes talking to the security officer and places his napkin on the table to express that he is *finished*. Billy glances down and over at the napkin as evidence, acutely aware of its position on the plate, the movement of his father's hands, and the impossibility of navigating the end of this conversation.

"Um, yes, sir, there are channels and lessons on YouTube you can find. . . ." He's searching for a way out, trying to make it sound better than the words he hears coming out of his mouth, revealing the duality of who he really is versus who he has to be. "It's . . . they're free. It's really great that we have all of this free access to information now . . . in a way . . . for things, you know, like hobbies, other hobbies we might want to learn in our free time."

The overly friendly general isn't exuding eagerness anymore, and Billy cringes inwardly at his misjudgment of the conversation.

"Enough," his father says, but whether out of cruelty or genuine mortification (which he thinks he probably deserves), Billy can't tell.

The general leans over to General Montgomery, quick to ease the tension, "Gen Z, General—what are we going to do with them?" He turns to Billy, and puts a hand in his pocket to withdraw his wallet, pulls out his business card. "Here—here's my card. When you're ready for a recommendation for the National War College, I'm happy to be a reference—*not that you need it*"—he winks and knocks him with his knuckle again, his ring digging into Billy's bicep, then teases—*"but you'll need it."* A profound feeling of shame creeps through the blood vessels of Billy's cheeks, and he blushes with utter self-loathing and disappointment in himself and this moment that his father must witness on the most pivotal day of his entire military career—in American and family history.

Billy takes the card with both hands, overcompensating for his human error, studies it, eagerness swapped from general to pupil. "Thank you, sir. That's very generous of you, I will take you up on it," Billy says, waiting for his father to interject, express an opinion, tell him what a great idea that might be. Instead, General Montgomery stands, letting him know in the gaps of his silent actions that the reception is over. And if earth were on the brink of World War III or his father was disappointed in Billy's answers, he wouldn't be able to tell the difference.

⁂

General Montgomery slams the front door behind him. Both Carol and Billy flinch as they stand in front of the coat closet.

"Here, Mom," Billy says grabbing his mother's jacket from her shoulders, ignoring the palpable tension. The Montgomery household, always under the illusion of control, a thick veil of order and tradition. Billy tries to fill the silence. "Here, Dad, I'll take your jacket," he says, extending his hand. The general moves toward the closet, forcing Billy and Carol to step out of the way.

"I'm going to put some tea on, honey, do you have homework to catch up on?" she asks to clear the air, walking into the kitchen.

Billy follows. "Nothing due until Monday. I, um—Stan is having some people over tonight, so . . ."

"Oh, a party?" Carol asks, aware that the general is still lurking in the hallway just beyond where they are standing.

"Well, no. I didn't want to say anything earlier because . . . Well, I got a message from Bunny. . . . Did you know or ever interact with the Banks family?"

"Hmm, it doesn't really ring a bell," Carol says, putting the kettle on the stove. Billy starts to pull up an article on his cell phone that Bunny text-messaged him earlier, but the general walks into the kitchen, and Billy pivots, changing the subject, intuitively wanting to correct the tension. "Dad, it was great to talk with—"

"Listen, no more bullshit uka-whatever-the-fuck lessons."

"Ukulel—"

The general slams his hand down on the counter, an explosion: "GODDAMN IT." His eyes light up with anger as he finally makes eye contact with Billy.

"Honey, it's okay." Carol raises her hands in the air in an attempt to mediate, stepping toward the general from the stove. "We had a lovely afternoon—"

"*Carol*, I AM NOT TALKING TO YOU," the general yells, locked on Billy. Carol takes a step back into the kitchen counter, turns to take two teacups out of the cabinet.

"A four-star general asks you about hobbies, wants to be a reference for the National War College, and you talk about *YouTube* videos?"

"I—I was just explaining that, or thought since he asked about hobbies, you know my lov—my interest in music . . ." Billy says, trying to deescalate where he predicts his father is going. Ever since he was a little boy, he's gotten better and better at reading the general's body language. The first time the general slugged Billy, age five, over a toy airplane that had been left in the living room, it had given him a heightened ability to read other people—to read a room, whether his or someone else's, and without any help or intuition from his mother.

"I have been nominated by the president of the United States as the secretary of defense—do you know what this means now for our family, *goddamn it*? *My* son will not be seen looking and sounding like a *goddamn homosexual*—"

"Father, I'm . . . I'm just—"

"DO NOT INTERRUPT ME WHEN I AM TALKING TO YOU."

A sudden and eerie moment of silence captures the three of them before the teapot screams. Carol runs to turn off the burner, her hand shaking as she twists its knob.

"I want that thing out of this house by tomorrow morning."

"Yes, sir," Billy says. He knows it's an order. He puts his hands in his pockets, surrenders.

The general turns around and walks out the door, down the hallway, and into his study; the door slams.

Carol comes over with a cup of tea. "He's going to be under a lot of pressure for a little while until the confirmation, just cut him a little slack, honey."

Billy takes the teacup, puts it to his mouth for a sip, and flinches. "Hot," he says.

❧ • CHAPTER TWELVE • ❧

*T*he arrival of the arborist had interrupted Meredith Bartholomew at her Baker Queen Anne secretary desk in the
study, copies of the *New Yorker* and the *Washington Post* piled in a
straw basket at her feet, the exclusive Green Book resting on top, for
the Bartholomews have always been listed each year. Meredith had
already spoken to Maureen Harrington, Mary Haven, Jane Smith,
and Karen Miller about the Banks family, a game of telephone
prompting accusations, suspicions, and blame—*gentrification, immi-
gration, the gas company, poor house management*—anything to give
a semblance of meaning and control over the shocking and grisly
news.

Relieved at the interruption, the hysteria beaten to a pulp until
further information is released, Meredith stands in the middle of her
front lawn with a camel quilted Ralph Lauren coat draped over her
shoulders, arms crossed, vintage Cartier Tank watch peeking beneath
one of her long sleeves, the cold air blowing the blunt pieces of her
hair toward the back of her neck, which is cranked at a ninety-degree
angle as she stares up at the two-hundred-year-old tulip poplar tree
leaning toward the chimney of their house. The arborist: yellow hard

hat, clear safety glasses, khakis, and old tennis shoes. He's inspecting the health and structure of the tree, using all kinds of state-of-the-art instruments, searching for its cracks, splits, saturated soils, poor architecture, root problems, and symptoms of decay.

Already hiding her vulnerability, Meredith recently discovered some of her family's financial pressures after a paralegal at a Washington law firm left a message on the home voice mail. It was often said that the level of wealth the Bartholomews locked up was nearly impossible to reach even by a lawsuit, blocked by settlements and payoffs. But when 2016 hit, the ability to get closer to someone's personal records in the age of waning privacy was becoming an increasingly apparent threat. Google somebody's name, and websites such as mylife.com, nuwber.com, and whitepages.com will release the date of birth, home address, and the names of relatives of anyone. Meredith was beginning to worry. And with the murder of the Banks family, about what it might suggest: *Will there be another?*

The arborist drills a hole in the trunk of the tree. He stops, takes out another gadget to peer inside of it, when the sound of the ringing landline echoes through the Victorian stained-glass front door that's been blown open by the wind. Meredith breaks her distressed trance and walks inside, immediately engulfed by red toile wallpaper depicting the image of a family outdoors having a picnic in colonial America. A portrait of Bunny, age three, wearing a smock dress and sitting in a Chippendale dining chair, hangs above the china bowl of potpourri. Meredith enters the kitchen and picks up the cordless phone, reads the caller ID: Phyllis Van Buren.

"Hi, Phyllis," Meredith answers as if she's already spoken to Phyllis several times today. Phyllis Van Buren and her husband have been the Bartholomews' friends and neighbors for nearly twenty years. Her husband is president of the Atomic Heritage Foundation, the organization preserving the legacy of the Manhattan Project and the atomic bomb that addresses the scientific, technical, political, and social/ethical issues of the twenty-first century, working with the government and, most important, the Department of Energy. All those years ago when they discovered the coincidence, it brought the families *close*.

"Did you hear the news?" Phyllis asks, her tone less concerned than riveted.

As Phyllis relays everything Meredith has already gone over within her inner circle, she yanks open the junk drawer, pushing papers and receipts and takeout menus out of the way before she finds her emergency pack of Carlton cigarettes. She holds the phone against her shoulder, banging the pack in the palm of her hand before opening the lid. Meredith notices as she pulls out the cigarette and puts it in her mouth that her hand is shaking. She lights it as fast as she can, takes a deep drag, the end lit like a summer firefly, then raises her right hand to the steel fan above the kitchen stove. She presses the On button, leans over, and exhales into the vent, a vacuum of smoke now circulating through the entire house. Phyllis is still talking. Speculating.

"Meredith, are you there? . . . The police just came by, so I wanted to let you know. They're looking for information in the neighborhood, they think they have a suspect but he's not been arrested yet. . . ."

Meredith does not reply.

"Meredith? Honey?"

"*Jesus*, Phyllis." Meredith, back in her trance.

"I'm so sorry, honey, I know. . . . There will be a service at the National Cathedral next week, I'm sure you will get the details."

"Phyllis," Meredith says, "who did you say the suspect was?"

"Well, everything is just speculation at this point. . . ."

"Is he"—Meredith winces—"*African American? Don't tell me*. . . ." She winces again, this time in pseudo pain: the cliché, the stereotype, if true, does not look good for her newfound liberal politics. She waits for Phyllis's answer.

"He is, honey. Well, that's the rumor anyway."

Meredith cringes as if she's just witnessed a missed serve at Wimbledon. She rinses her cigarette under the faucet and shoves it down the garbage disposal. "How could something like this happen?"

"I know, honey, I think—I think they wanted information, they don't know anything yet, but, Jesus Christ, to tie up and torture someone's child. . . . I can only think that they wanted something— money or, I don't know, information. . . ." Phyllis suddenly seems distracted, "Oh, honey, that's the doorbell—the decorator is here to look at the house. We're on the Christmas homes tour. They start early. You should buy tickets, bring Bunny, it will be a nice mother-daughter day and she's old enough to attend this year."

"Oh, congratulations, sounds lovely, we will," Meredith replies, bleak to be switching gears to Christmas celebrations so soon.

"Call if you need me, dear."

"Will do."

A sharp grating sound juxtaposes the afternoon stillness amidst the clustered town homes of Georgetown. The arborist saws a tiny branch from the trunk as dead leaves swirl around him. He pauses when a district police car bobbles along the cobblestone road, stopping behind the arborist's white truck.

Officer Gomez steps out of the vehicle and approaches the arborist. "Are the homeowners around?" he asks.

Before the man can respond, Meredith steps out into the light. "I am she. . . ." she says, a regal figure among these blue-collar men.

"Ma'am, I'm sorry to disturb you this afternoon, but I'm in the neighborhood to ask a few questions regarding an incident that happened last—"

"I think it qualifies as a little more than an incident, don't you?"

Officer Gomez glances at the arborist: the all-too-familiar upper-class white woman they're used to dealing with.

"It was a horrific tragedy that occurred last night, and I can assure you we did everything we could . . . and we're hoping to get more information."

"Well, I'm not sure how much help I'll be." Meredith purses her lips, swallowing her emotion, and crosses her arms.

"Were you home last night?"

"Yes, I was—well, we were after dinner . . . at the club, we were home by about nine thirty p.m."

"Who else lives in the home, if I may ask?"

"My husband, niece, and daughter were all home."

"Did you notice anything unusual, any cars, or persons walking by?"

"No, just the maid of our new neighbors, whom I don't know yet. She was walking their King Charles across the street."

An old blue Volvo station wagon with academic bumper stickers of privileged educations (St. Patrick's Episcopal Day School, St. Peter's Academy, Yale University) pulls into the driveway. Bunny swings open the car door, almost forgetting to turn off the engine, and runs across the front lawn. Rumpled skirt, disheveled hair—a girl who doesn't know yet how this time in her life will come to haunt her, shape her—the days a person remembers only after they are gone.

"Mom!" She wraps her arms around her mother as if regressing into a little girl.

"I know, honey Bunny, it's okay." Meredith rocks her baby girl. She lifts Bunny's face and places her manicure-free hands around her flushed cheeks. "It's going to be okay."

"Why are the police here?" Bunny asks, as if Gomez isn't standing right beside her.

"They're here to ask a few questions, everything is *fine*."

Bunny turns to Officer Gomez. "Were you there last night?" she asks. "Did you see the bodies? I read online they chopped Audrey's—"

"*Jesus*, Bunny, please, go inside, we will talk about this in a minute."

"Well, no one is *saying* that! Why do *you* think someone would do something like that? You're a cop, what do you think?" Bunny's entangled curiosity and entitlement project a virtuous victim of this story she's decided to insert herself inside of without thinking of the repercussions.

"Elizabeth Bartholomew! Inside. *Now*," Meredith says.

Bunny's eyes linger on Officer Gomez a moment longer than would be considered appropriate. "*Fine*. This is so fucked."

Gomez clears his throat, calm in the face of Bunny's outburst. "I'm sorry for your loss."

Meredith closes her eyes, pinches the bridge of her nose with her pointer finger and thumb while Bunny opens the screen door then slams it shut behind her.

"I'm sorry, this is not a good time. . . ." Meredith pleads.

The landline rings. Meredith looks over her shoulder, then back to Gomez. "Except . . . I, uh, do have one question before you go. Do you . . . or have you or the FBI . . . have they found a motive yet?" Meredith looks increasingly tense.

"We cannot say at this time."

"I see . . ."

Bunny yells down from the top of the front staircase, "Mom! Someone's calling from Geller and Cromwell? They're saying they're an attorney?!"

Meredith, suddenly embarrassed, cuts Bunny off: "Uh, no, honey, hang up! It's just a sales call. I'll be right there!"

"But they're saying it's not!" Bunny yells back, increasingly distraught.

"Excuse me, I have to go attend to my daughter now. . . ."

"Thank you for your time, ma'am." Gomez nods his head, places his hand on his belt, and offers a kind smile before he heads back to the car.

"Excuse me, Mrs. Bartholomew." The arborist walks over. "I'm so sorry to interrupt"—he's trying to appear as diplomatic as possible— "I hate to have to tell you this right now, but I found a fracture, which means this poplar is at high risk for developing symptoms of decay, internal rot, and wood-boring pests. . . ."

❧·CHAPTER THIRTEEN·❧

*B*etsy steps out of her Jaguar decorated with gifts from
Doug: her twenty-year upgrade, a twelve-carat emerald-
cut diamond falling against her pinky from its weight, diamond
hoops, and a designer coat that resembles a superhero cape. With
her peripheral vision, Betsy attempts to search for Linda's Audi station wagon without looking too obvious. The only person she sees is
a young secret service agent strolling behind the guardrail across the
street, the arches of the Taft Bridge visible across the park.

The school is inside an old colonial row house adorned with
arched windows and Corinthian columns. ALLIANCE FRANÇAISE DE
WASHINGTON, DC is engraved in gold on a sign planted in front of
lush boxwood bushes, the French flag neglected and wound tight
around its pole, the front windows glowing from the warm yellow
light of a dangling chandelier.

Upon entering the foyer, Betsy catches a whiff of a musty
odor. It's old, and smells like mothballs. She clears her throat,
breathes out of her mouth. *For the love of God, someone light a
Diptyque candle.*

"*Bonjour!* Alliance Française, how may I help you?" asks the young bilingual receptionist from behind thick glasses, her hair pulled back with a pink scrunchie.

"Hello." Betsy places her Versace Sultan purse on the counter; its chain falls, an embarrassing crescendo of gold against drywall. She gathers the chain quickly with both hands, introducing herself: "I'm Betsy Wallace. . . ."

"Yes, welcome, Mrs. Wallace. I put together this package for you." The receptionist, probably a PhD student, flips through the pages as evidence. "You have the option of group courses, private courses, Skype classes, and other adult learning experiences here including a grammar boot camp and field trips, as well as drop-in classes."

"Oh, wonderful, I will take a look," Betsy says.

"Feel free to have a seat. Would you like a cup of tea? Water?"

"Oh no, I'm fine, thank you."

Betsy takes a look around the room, walks toward the photographs on the wall showing parties at the French ambassador's residence, graduating classes, maps of France, special dinners with foreign dignitaries and cultural festivals. Betsy spots a photograph of Linda and her husband with the French ambassador and his wife. A pang of jealousy hits her as the front door opens and a petite redhead in a white Ralph Lauren sweater, skinny jeans, Chanel ballerina flats, diamond studs, and a Louis Vuitton tote breezes in, the wooden floors creaking even though covered by several Persian rugs. Betsy turns around. It's *Linda Williams*.

"Linda!" Betsy says with a wide smile. "Too funny seeing you here."

Linda gives a phony smile, gauging whether she knows who Betsy is, the way a celebrity might fake it if they thought there was a chance this person was important. "Oh, hello!"

"We met briefly at back-to-school night a few weeks ago. I'm Betsy Wallace, Doug Wallace's wife." As Betsy is attempting to prove her worth, Linda does a quick once-over: the Versace bag, the coat (cape) she's wearing . . .

"My daughter is new at your daughter's school."

"Oh yes, hi, good to see you."

"My daughter, Haley, had wanted me to ask you about having a playdate with Becca," she says, snowballing, "she was just too shy to ask, so I said that the next time I saw you in the carpool line I would ask. . . ."

The invitation has unexpectedly touched Linda in a place that often feels guarded. She and her husband have been "famous" for Washington for quite some time, yet her daughter is perpetually bullied at school. Known for being the "horse girl," she's painfully shy.

"I'm late, but here, take my number down. Becca would love to have a playdate."

Betsy eagerly pulls out her cell phone. Linda holds out her palm, gesturing that it will be easier for her to enter the information herself.

"Oh, here." Betsy hands her the phone.

As Linda focuses on typing her information, she asks, "Did you hear the tragic news today about the St. Peter's student? The Banks family?"

"I don't believe so, no," Betsy says, feigning concern.

"Well, they're in the Green Book," Linda whispers, suddenly feeling very open with Betsy, given their exchange about her daughter.

Green Book, Betsy notes in her head; it sounds familiar, but alas, she does not know it, feeling left out once again. "*No*, what happened?" she asks.

"It's horrific, just horrific, the couple and their only daughter, a senior at St. Peter's, were brutally murdered last night in their home. They're not far from us."

"Oh my God, you know, I did read about it this morning, but I had no idea they were a St. Peter's family. . . ." Betsy places her manicured hand to her chest.

"It's devastating."

"I read about that too," the receptionist interrupts, "so scary and awful."

"Is there a suspect yet?" Betsy asks.

"They think they have a suspect." Linda looks around the waiting area, leans into Betsy's ear, and whispers, *"An African American kid."*

"Oh, that's such a shame," Betsy replies.

"I know. The whole thing is just horrendous. The funeral is next week at the cathedral. They were very active in the community and *very wealthy* and it's just such a tragedy. . . ." Linda notices the ticking grandfather clock. "Oh dear, I am so late, I have to run to my class! We'll get the girls together."

As she begins to leave, the receptionist pipes up, "Mrs. Wallace, if you'd like, you're more than welcome to audit the class Mrs. Williams is in, there is actually one more space available."

"Oh?" Betsy glances at Linda, who shrugs her shoulders, indifferent. "Well, I don't have to pick up the girls from their after-school activities for another two hours. . . ."

CHAPTER FOURTEEN

Cate stares at her reflection in the mirror as the makeup artist wipes globs of concealer under her eyes and sticky gloss across her lips; she is a budding *star* beneath the bright lights illuminating the high cheekbones she inherited from her father's side of the family—the Bartholomews—the side she wants to get closer to and farther away from all at the same time. Tissues are tucked into a smock snapped around her neck like a ruffled Victorian collar.

"Eyes up," the makeup artist says, holding a mascara wand as Cate tries to review notes on the White House domestic violence probe, refreshing the breaking news from the *Post*, Politico, Fox, updated photos appearing on her phone of the White House chief of staff's wife with a swollen black eye and bloody lip. Cate lifts her eyes and thinks about her parents. Flashes of her father running toward her mother: she remembers sitting frozen at the kitchen table, preparing for the possible blow to her mother's left eye socket; but instead of her father hitting her mother, he stepped backward, laughing, *Did you think I was going to hit you?* And she remembers how he never believed Cate would make it in Washington; he didn't think she could make it anywhere at all.

"You good?" the makeup artist asks.

"I'm great," she replies, her A game asserting itself, shoving any nerves to the side. Cate isn't conscious of the fact that what drives her to succeed is an intense need for vengeance against the men in her life even as she simultaneously romanticizes them, holding on to each one even after he falls off the pedestal where she had placed him—where she likes them. A complex dichotomy living deep inside of her that she's still too young to understand.

The makeup artist hands her a Kleenex. "Blot," she says. Cate folds the Kleenex and clamps her lips over its crease. She looks at her face in the mirror, beautiful but not beautiful enough, she thinks. The makeup artist unsnaps the smock, whipping it off like she's the magician and Cate is the prize.

"I like the suit," the makeup artist says, "you look powerful." Cate wears a red Veronica Beard blazer and straight-leg slacks she found on The RealReal for half of this month's paycheck.

"Powerful." Cate lets out a nervous laugh. But it is these moments of validation that she lives for, the kind that make her love being in Washington—what she loves *about* Washington: secrets only few are privy to, the intelligence, the security details and political motorcades, men in uniform holding AK-47s, black town cars like the one that picked her up. And the details—the driver clad in his black suit opening the back passenger-side door for her; being encompassed by black leather seats and wood paneling; a *New York Times Magazine* stuffed in the back pocket because people are *smart* in Washington, unopened boxes of tissues and mini water bottles in cup holders—they make her feel *important*, the kind of treatment she has always longed for, a far cry from night shifts at the local Starbucks after school. Today she got a private taste of it, and she only wants more.

Walter comes barreling into the makeup room holding a manila envelope. "Jesus, you look like a movie star, Fox really knows how to clean you up." He goes to touch the top of Cate's head.

"Don't touch my hair," she snaps.

Walter thrusts the envelope at her. Retaliation from Cate warrants a condescending signal that he's in charge.

"What's this?" she asks.

"Notes for you to review," Walter says.

"But I have them on my phone."

A PA steps in with a wire in her ear and a walkie-talkie. "Cate, Chris is ready for you."

"Excuse me." Cate walks around Walter and follows the PA down the hallway lined with photographs of former on-air guests—Reagan, both Bushes, Putin; she doesn't see a single powerful woman in any of the frames. Cate clears her throat and approaches the double sliding glass doors to the set.

Walter follows. "I'm going to watch from the set, not the green room," he says, asserting command. She can smell Walter's bad breath behind her.

Cate stands at the entrance behind camera operators in jeans and hoodies checking their cell phones. The set has an eerie silence, unlike Hollywood. Muted televisions mounted along the back wall for the news show can only be heard by those with earpieces. The PA hooks up Cate's microphone, connecting her to the control room and the audio of the broadcast when it becomes live for her.

Chris Williams, boring suit, caked-on makeup, and a gray combover, repositions himself at his desk, completely ignoring Cate until she is directed to take her seat next to him. The makeup artist and hair stylist run to him in between takes like crazed fans.

Cate takes her seat on the stool, crosses her legs, and assumes position. A voice sounds in her ear: "We need to check your levels, can you count backward from ten for us."

"Ten, nine, eight, seven"—a bright light beams toward her; she frowns—"six, five, four"—before adjusting her eyes and summoning a confident smile—"three, two, one."

"Cate we're getting a muffling sound from you, can you unbutton the top button of your shirt?" a man's voice says from the control room, a poignant reminder that he can see her but she can't see him.

Cate, confused and not sure she heard him correctly, looks down, hesitating. Chris Williams looks up and over at her for the first time. "Your *shirt*," he says, curt and to the point, "*unbutton it.*"

"Oh." Cate unbuttons the top button of her blouse as fast as she can, her hand visibly shaking.

"Atta girl." Chris winks at her.

"And we're back in ten seconds. . . ."

Chris adjusts his tie, then turns to the camera. "Joining us tonight to discuss the crisis and shakeup in the White House administration stemming from the domestic violence probe into White House Chief of Staff Tom Derby is Cate Bartholomew, press secretary for North Carolina Senator Doug Wallace, who has openly condemned the behavior and called for Derby's immediate resignation. Cate, thanks for joining us this evening."

"Good to be here, Chris," she says as if she's been doing this her entire life.

"Fill us in on what's been happening behind the scenes."

"Well, Chris, as you can imagine, Senator Wallace and other colleagues in the Senate are shocked, and they have launched an investigation into what exactly happened during the background check of Chief of Staff Tom Derby, as it is highly unlikely that domestic violence would have been missed by the FBI at a top security clearance level unless someone, perhaps even the president, had him cleared anyway."

"Are you suggesting the president would hire a *wife-beater*, Cate?"

"Well, Chris, I wouldn't use the term *wife-beater*—it's the twenty-first century, and you're dating yourself to the Detroit case of the 1940s where and when that term came to prominence, but I digress—"

"Well, wait a minute . . ." Chris desperately tries to interrupt her, but Cate doesn't allow it.

"I am *suggesting* that the president overlooked it in an effort to have the circle he wanted around him. And he's going to pay a price now."

"What kind of price, Cate?"

"Well, for one thing, he hasn't said a word, hasn't acknowledged the victim, Derby's wife, and his party is beginning to turn on him. And things are looking pretty good for Senator Wallace regarding our plans to introduce an amendment to the domestic violence bill."

Chris Williams suddenly notices what a knockout she is. Cate crosses her legs like they're her weapons of choice, using whatever has been handed to her to fight right back. She lifts an eyebrow, ready for another question.

Chris looks down at his notes. "That's right, Senator Wallace plans to introduce an amendment to the Violence against Women Act regarding psychological control. Can you explain to viewers exactly what psychological control means? Are you saying men have psychological powers over women?" He looks up from his notes. "Because if so, Cate, I'd really like to try that at home, ha-ha-ha, I mean, what kind of argument is this? The feminists aren't gonna like it, I can tell you that!"

Maniacal in her focus, Cate leans over the table. "Well, let me explain it to you, Chris, you can learn something new every day." Chris chuckles to hide his embarrassment. "Coercive control isn't just about low-level or high-level violence occurring in a relationship. It begins as a psychological state meant to control the partner by instilling copious amounts of fear in them. In the case of Tom Derby and his wife, the photos of her black-and-blue eye and bloody lip are all over the Internet—that is very obvious abuse, but it should never have to escalate to that level. We are interested in catching abuse before it escalates as it *begins* with psychological control, which can come in different forms such as threatening a partner physically, financially, or emotionally—anything that instills fear and therefore compliance. Statistically speaking, if a woman ever *thinks* a partner might hit her—even if she reports it was only a fleeting thought— there's a ninety-five percent chance he *will* hit her in the future. So, to save countless lives of American women, Senator Wallace plans to implement this amendment in the coming weeks, and we hope the nation, and gentlemen like yourself, support us in doing so."

Chris leans back in his chair, places his pen atop his notes, and looks into the camera. "Ladies and gentlemen, Cate Bartholomew, press secretary for Senator Doug Wallace. Thanks for joining us— we'll be back in a moment, stay with us."

Cate walks into the green room removing her earpiece and unclipping her microphone, buzzing with adrenaline. Walter follows her. As Cate hands the PA her earpiece, Walter says, "Excuse me, can you give us a minute?" Alarmed by his tone, Cate walks over to the couch to grab her purse and overcoat; the PA spins back around and out the door.

"Your first time on national television with Chris Williams and you're going to talk down to him?"

"What? I was giving him *facts*, Walter." Cate swings her bag over her shoulder, ready to leave. She checks her phone. No text message from Doug.

"What you said about the president was not a fact."

"Check the polls if you don't believe me. The car is waiting for me downstairs," Cate says, holding up her phone. As she heads toward the hallway, she nearly bumps into Linda Williams, a French textbook poking out of her Louis Vuitton tote.

"Oh, excuse me," Cate says, locking eyes with Chris Williams's wife.

"Linda!" Walter exclaims. "Excuse our clumsy press secretary." Cate glares at him. Walter steps in front of her.

"Walter! Good to see you!" They do a double kiss. "Is Chris still on? I'm trying to catch the end of it. . . ." Linda reaches for her phone in her tote.

"Linda Williams?" Cate says, interjecting herself. "I'm Cate Bartholomew." She goes to shake her hand. "Chuck and Meredith Bartholomew's niece—we met briefly at the Washington Club, they're also members," she adds, attempting to prove her place in Washington society even if only peripherally—even if only by a thread—even if Cate just went live on her husband's show.

"Nice to see you again," Linda says, not remembering her at all. And she doesn't particularly like the Bartholomews—they don't typically mingle with members of the press unless it is to their benefit.

Walter notices Cate asserting her social capital. "Great to see you, Linda, lunch at the Press Club next week?"

"Would love it, darling."

"Lovely to see you again," Cate says.

Linda smiles. "Take care, sweetie."

❧·CHAPTER FIFTEEN·❧

The Russian ambassador's residence is a modern glass palace, an old off-white brick building covered in tiny square windows. Sitting high on a hill at the top of Georgetown next to the embassy, the foreign property is protected by layers of black fences, cameras, barbed wire, and cigarette-smoking Russian guards: EMBASSY OF THE RUSSIAN FEDERATION is branded in gold on a concrete plaque at the "Royal" gates. Stan's father is somewhere in Helsinki on one of his many business trips, his mother mysteriously (always) missing.

Stan glides down the freestanding winding staircase as if descending from clouds; he's dressed in a half-unbuttoned collared silk shirt and tight dress pants. In the living room are emblems of American pop culture: Austin Powers prints, a painting of a modern American flag, Marilyn Monroe's iconic white dress photo, big block letters spelling S-E-X-Y above the fireplace, a swinging clear chair and stripper pole his mother uses for exercise in the corner. Modern sculptures of trolls and dancing ballerinas are found in the dining room and library, near photographs of his father at the Kremlin framed in platinum.

Stan walks over to the light switch—a naked photo of Mick Jagger, the on/off switch in place of his erect penis. A security guard, whom Stan has graciously paid off in cash, monitors the cell phones of addicted teenagers being collected and put into a silver bucket upon arrival. Parents, the few who were ever concerned, know that Ambassador Stopinski has been in the news cycle recently and aren't particularly thrilled for their children to be entering the domain of the enemy. Social media will remain closed to the invitees. Stan knows this much. The subject line of his private invite was, *Baby, I got the tapes.* All of them thinking it was funny, none of them knowing why.

Jermaine Dupri's "Money Ain't a Thang" blasts through the open space, floor-to-ceiling windows; the finest vodka, sealed in wooden cases carved with RUSSIAN EMBASSY on top (an endless supply of gifts to foreign dignitaries kept in the basement vault), is lined up on identical coffee tables. Plastic soda bottles and aluminum expired credit cards next to bags of cocaine and prerolled strawberry-flavored blunts fill the side tables. Carefully selected juniors and seniors of St. Peter's Academy and the surrounding private schools flood in, some completely wasted from pregaming, others beelining for the vodka—girls in their tight polo sweaters, miniskirts, long locks pulled up in messy I'm-not-trying-too-hard buns, and pearl studs; dudes in their Nats hats, Capitals shirts, sagging khakis, and trending kicks (plus the occasional pair of boat shoes with no socks).

Billy and Bunny sit on a leather sofa in the corner; Billy's kissing her neck, his hand on her knee. Mackenzie enters with Marty. Chase arrives with a young freshman, bug-eyed and drunk, smiling and nodding at everyone to prevent vomit from spilling up and out of her esophagus.

"Mackenzie, what can I get you?" Marty asks, the perfect gentleman, red plaid bow tie poking out under his argyle sweater, round spectacles, khakis, and brown loafers.

"Shot of vodka, please," Mackenzie says, trying to fix the extension clips at the back of her head. Bunny notices this, and the diamond-studded Tank watch on her wrist.

"*Ohh*, starting off with shots, I *likey* New Girl," Chase says.

"Shots for everyone!" Billy shouts.

"Is that the Cartier Tank?" Bunny asks Mackenzie.

"My watch? Um, yeah, my dad gave it to me for my birthday."

"Nice," Bunny replies. "Audrey had one, but hers was rose gold. . . . Did you know her?"

"No. I mean, we had religion class together, but I didn't really know her," Mackenzie says.

"Do you know how she died?" Bunny asks, spooking her now.

"Um, I heard in . . . uh . . . their house burned down . . . or something," she says, nervous she might say the wrong thing.

Marty returns with the drinks. "Shots! Shots! Shots!" he yells, passing them around the group.

Billy raises his shot glass. "In honor of Audrey."

Bunny scoots closer to Mackenzie. Raises her glass: "To Audrey!" She throws her shot back, slams the glass on the table, leans over and whispers to Mackenzie, who shivers and slams her shot down next, "They beat her with her dad's autographed baseball bat, then chopped her up in little pieces. We could be next. . . ." Someone passes Bunny a joint; she takes a hit and blows O's into the air, leaving Mackenzie alone with the terrifying unknown and her imagination of bloody body parts.

"Whatever kind of piece of shit did this deserves the same punishment as Saudi Arabia or Iraq . . . sick fucks," Billy says, slamming back another shot. "No one fucks with us."

"Actually, dude, the Senate Intel Committee released the report that proved the US's use of torture post-9/11 was entirely ineffective," Marty says. He takes a shot, then sits next to Mackenzie and starts rubbing her back.

"Oh yeah?" Billy turns his entire body to face him. "Let's try it." It is only when Billy is obliterated that the rage rears its ugly head. "Go get Stan's snowboard, you're gonna waterboard me," he tells Marty, "ask me if I fucked Ashley Waterman sophomore year."

"Fuck you!" Bunny replies.

"Come on, you know what I mean, baby," he says to Bunny, "it's just a game."

Bunny pouts.

"Oh, like you didn't lose your virginity to Charlie Nolan. . . ." he says.

"Okay, we gotta get this on film in case he beats the stat," Stan says, handing Bunny his iPhone, since everyone else's has been confiscated and placed in the silver bucket guarded by the Kremlin. She rolls her eyes and presses the red Record button.

"Okay, I'm filming . . ."

"Okay, dude, but you do know that if it's done wrong the person can die." Marty's is a rhetorical question, and he is nonetheless intrigued by the dare.

"I am aware that you can die from waterboarding, yes." Billy looks to Stan. "Yo, Putin, go grab your snowboard."

"And one of your karate bandannas," Chase pipes in.

"What is waterboarding?" Mackenzie asks.

"Uh . . ." Marty looks at her and kisses her cheek. "You'll see." He looks back to Billy. "Okay, so in all realness, I was watching one of the videos online after Mr. Haight's twentieth-century American history class, and all these research experts were trying to see if they could reach fifteen seconds."

"I bet I can beat that," Billy says. If he's being forced into the military, he might as well prove himself right fucking now. To everyone.

Stan comes sauntering back with his snowboard and an unlit joint dangling from his lips, Billy carves another eight ball into lines, snorts a few.

Bunny zooms in on Billy doing lines but says nothing, noticing how many he takes.

Marty takes the snowboard from Stan and leans it against the couple of steps dividing the two levels of the living room.

"Let me do the honors," Stan says, tying his bandanna around Billy's eyes.

Billy lies down on the snowboard, propped up by the split-level steps. Marty pulls up the demonstration video on YouTube from Stan's computer, which is hooked up to the surround sound.

"We need straps, we gotta strap him down." Marty adjusts his glasses up his nose.

"I have dog leashes!" Stan says, excited, then runs to go get them.

"What is going on?" Mackenzie whispers; everyone ignores her.

Stan leaps back into the room carrying two red dog leashes. He's got two black Bouviers that have to be groomed at least once a week. Chase grabs one of the leashes from him, Stan takes the other, Marty directing them.

"We need something for his face," Marty says. He leans down to do a quick bump, then pops back up. "To drown him." He wipes his nose.

Chase walks over and plucks the white handkerchief out of Stan's jacket slung on the back of a couch. "This should do it," he says.

"Wait, we need a jug of water," Marty says.

"Fuck water, give me champagne!" Billy replies, blindfolded, his torso being tied to the snowboard and the leashes then looped around columns on either side of the steps.

"I got the Cristal, baby!" Stan says as he finishes tying, then runs into the kitchen to grab the jeroboam bottle he was saving for the end of the night.

"Holy shit," Mackenzie says as Stan struggles to carry the jeroboam out by himself. He pops the cork, spraying champagne all over the living room.

"Wait, wait, wait, we need to give him something to hold in his hand to drop as a sign of surrender," Marty says.

"Here." Chase leans over and grabs a porcelain horse off of one of the side tables. "His mom won't notice. . . ."

Marty puts the horse in Billy's right hand "Okay, Billy, drop this horse when you can't breathe anymore," he says. Billy's legs are propped upward on the steps. He wiggles into final position.

Marty and Chase take Stan's handkerchief from Bunny and tie it over Billy's nose and mouth, his eyes still covered by the bandanna, while Stan attempts to lift the jeroboam bottle of Cristal, ready to pour as Marty directs.

"Ready," Stan says, hefting the bottle into the air. Billy takes three huge deep breaths, sucking in the handkerchief, before Stan tilts the jeroboam. . . .

"Make sure to start with little drips," Marty directs. Chase giggles with anticipation.

"You fuckers are crazy!" Mackenzie says.

There it goes, *drip, drip, drip*. Billy tries to gasp in between pours, *drip, drip, drip* . . .

Stan counts, ". . . five seconds, six seconds, seven seconds, eight seconds . . ." He continues to pour, *drip, drip, drip*. ". . . eleven seconds . . ."

Stan and Marty start laughing with Chase, cackling, the alcohol seeping into their guts, and Billy's body convulses as the porcelain horse drops to the ground, shattering into tiny pieces across the polished wood floor.

"Stop!" Marty yells. Stan loses control of the pouring and dumps a little more before Marty and Chase can untie the handkerchief. "Stop pouring!" Billy's body convulses again, reaching a level of violence only seen in wounded soldiers.

"Oh my God," Bunny says, the iPhone in her hand tilting as she loses focus and watches in real time.

"Oh God, stop it, you guys!" Mackenzie yells.

Stan drops the bottle on the floor, a stream of champagne spilling out.

"He's drowning!" Marty yells. Snot and champagne spill out of Billy's nose as they pull off the handkerchief and bandanna, his eyes watering.

"Fuck, fuck, fuck!" Chase unties his body, limp now. Billy rolls off of the snowboard and onto the floor; spread out on his stomach, he vomits a combination of yellow snot and champagne.

"Jesus Christ," Bunny says, watching him . . . the phone still recording, but dangling by her side.

Marty gets on his knees with Chase, Stan following suit. "Billy, man, are you okay?" Marty puts his hand on his back.

"Fuck," Stan says. "You okay, buddy? We're right here. . . ." The entire room is still and scared, everyone staring at Billy groaning and gasping for air. The guys pull him up so he's sitting and leaning against the wall, his hair wet with sweat and bubbles, the front of his shirt soaked in yellow bile. He comes to, opening and closing his mouth—squeezing his swelling eyes as they sting with alcohol, his cheeks flushed, his facial muscles so constrained it looks like the veins in his forehead might explode.

"Fuck, man." Billy breathes heavily, a little more normal now. Trying not to look scared. "That was fucking *epic!*" he says.

Everyone looks to each other in a moment of silence—before they bend over laughing, laughing so hard they can hardly breathe, their faces burning bright red.

Chase points to Billy in between guffaws. "If we ever go to war, dude, and they reinstate the draft, I'm going with you, man."

"Me too," Stan says, swiping his hair out of his eyes.

"Shut up, fucker, you're Russian! We'll be dropping MOAB bombs on your ass." Chase takes a swig.

"What we should do is drop a MOAB bomb on North Korea, extinguish them once and for all from planet earth!" Billy grabs the jeroboam sitting within arm's reach, takes a swig, then slams it back on the floor while making an explosion noise with his mouth, the kind that little boys make when they're playing GI Joes.

❖ CHAPTER SIXTEEN ❖

Church bells echo across Northwest Washington. Gothic towers of the National Cathedral reign outside in the fall chill. The grotesque gargoyles are perched, mouths wide, claws hooked below the stained glass windows and a holy cross as black limousines, town cars, and news crews line up outside the semicircular driveway. Three black hearses and several security details wait with the engines running while rubberneckers creep down Wisconsin Avenue.

Inside, a draft kicks crumpled leaves around the grand aisle, swept in by careless footwork. Guests shuffle in rows before three closed caskets covered in white lilies, center stage. The void instead of a fourth casket: the housekeeper, her family unable to afford participation in the National Cathedral service, the church unwilling to provide a big enough discount, and yet no one seems to notice.

Betsy enters the cathedral wearing a lime-green trench coat, tugging on the arms of Mackenzie and Haley, who have no idea why they're at a stranger's funeral, the dead girl from their new school resting below ancient stained glass windows and cold walls. Betsy smiles for a moment before she remembers it's a goddamned funeral, pinching her mouth closed as they approach the Bartholomews.

Chuck turns around to see Senator Doug Wallace and Betsy walking toward him.

"Mr. Senator," Chuck says, patting him on the back, a friendly reminder that Doug's got his balls wrapped in Chuck's donation dollars.

"Chuck, wonderful to see you. I'm so sorry for your loss. I know David was an old friend of yours from those Hasty Pudding days."

"Ah yes, it's a very sad day," Chuck says.

Meredith approaches with Bunny. She wears a black Chanel suit with pearls and diamond studs, a simple eternity band on her ring finger.

"Mer, sweetheart, you remember Senator Wallace."

"Hello." Meredith delivers a polite but phony smile, then pulls Bunny into the pew beside them, avoiding Betsy Wallace at all costs, passing pockets of Bibles and heading for Phyllis Van Buren and her husband, John, their heads buried in the program as an organ sounds.

"Why is that woman wearing lime green to a funeral?" Bunny whispers to her mother, in reference to Betsy's coat.

Without moving her head, Meredith slides her eyes like lasers to the side, then back again. "She's a *commoner.* . . ." She opens her Bible.

"Mom!" Bunny, shocked at her mother's use of the word *commoner*, wonders if this is the first time she's ever heard her say it . . . or perhaps she thinks Bunny is now old enough to hear it.

"I'm sorry, but it's *true*, she grew up in a trailer park in North Carolina. There's only one reason your father likes them. Now, pick up your Bible, don't be rude." Bunny rolls her eyes, pulls the Bible out of the back pocket of the pew, places it on her lap over her navy J.Crew dress.

Mackenzie waves at Bunny from across the aisle as her mother pulls her into the opposite pew. Bunny sends her a Mona Lisa smile, then realizes that the woman she and her mother were gossiping about is Mackenzie's mother. Bunny studies them. She watches

Mackenzie fumble with the extension clip at the back of her head, something she noticed at school too, sensing her deep need to fit in, reminding Bunny of all the times she tried to impress Audrey at the end of middle school after she had pulled away from Bunny—like the iridescent Miu Miu jacket she begged her mom to buy her like all the popular girls. An irrational boil of rage emerges toward Audrey, and now that Audrey is dead, Bunny fears she'll never be allowed to feel it. She feels disgust for that jacket now. Doug takes his seat on the aisle, blocking Bunny's view.

As the reverend begins, Cate comes tiptoeing down the aisle in a tight black Burberry dress, taking a seat directly behind the senator. He turns his head around and back again, so smooth that no one could catch him.

"We are gathered here today to pay tribute and honor the lives of David, Genevieve, and Audrey Banks. To express our love and admiration for this beloved family and to try to bring some comfort to those who are here and have been deeply hurt by such sudden, horrific death."

Bunny looks around the nave, raised chins, stoic faces, she feels a lump climbing up her throat. She isn't sure if she wants to cry or scream; she is reminded of her bike ride home that night . . . the raging fire truck horns as she crossed Massachusetts Avenue wrapped in her favorite hoodie. She was so close to her, she was so close . . . and why was it Audrey and not Bunny who was murdered? Bunny wonders if it was because Audrey could dangle trips to France on her father's private jet for popularity, because she could host parties at their colonial mansion while her parents were racing in the Grand Prix, and drink anyone under the table. She wonders about all the Instagram posts taken in front of their château in the South of France or the summer estate in Nantucket—or pictures with the president. *But other girls do it too*, Bunny rationalizes, *even the parents do it*. And Bunny thinks about that—the visceral lack of identity; Audrey was becoming nothing but a younger version of her mother. Is Bunny destined for it too? *She's a commoner.* . . . Or maybe Audrey's entitlement was a side effect of age or insecurity, or a kind of privileged life so impenetrable that no amount of experience would require personal identification or self-reflection. At least Bunny's parents kept their wealth contained. Maybe it wasn't Audrey's fault that she was a bad person, or *kind of* a bad person, Bunny thinks. She wrestles with the thought that now she'll never get to confront Audrey for abandoning her before high school. She's angry with herself for it. And now it's too late.

"All rise." The reverend makes his way back to the podium. "Lord of Mercy, hear our prayer. May our brother and sisters, whom you called your son and daughters on earth, enter the kingdom of peace and light. We ask this through our Lord Jesus Christ, your son, who lives and reigns with you, one God, forever and ever. Amen."

As hundreds stand, Cate brushes against Senator Wallace's shoulder as she exits her pew and heads for the winding stairwell behind Woodrow Wilson's tomb, lit by flickering candles.

"We will now turn to Psalm Twenty-Three:

> *The Lord's my shepherd, I'll not want;*
> *He makes me down to lie*
> *In pastures green; he leadeth me*
> *The quiet waters by . . ."*

Doug pretends to get an urgent call on his phone, pulling it out of his jacket pocket. He motions to Betsy, then puts the phone to his ear as he ducks out of the pew. He whispers, "Hello," into the phone as he makes his way down the winding stairwell, security detail standing above it, lips forever sealed. Doug's dress shoes echo from the cold limestone walls. Finally reaching Cate, so young in vulnerable flesh, leaning against a brass crypt. *Someday I will be buried here with the generals, the presidents, the saints!*

Doug grabs Cate by the face with both hands and kisses her. She gasps for air when he lets go. "You were so good on-air." She kisses him back, rubbing her lips into his, and he does it again. Breathing harder, she moves his hand up her black dress—old enough to know better: it's bad manners not to wear stockings to a funeral. Doug reaches the top of her thigh and she exhales as he slides his finger into her, *yes*, Cate's head rolls left then right across the crypt behind her. Doug pushes harder, covers her mouth with his other hand, thrusts his erection into her upper thigh as she moves a little to her left—and that's when Doug sees it, in letters and braille: HELEN KELLER AND HER LIFELONG COMPANION ANNE SULLIVAN MACY ARE INTERRED IN THE COLUMBARIUM BEHIND THIS CHAPEL.

Doug starts to lose his erection.

"What's wrong?" Cate says, panicked.

"It's Helen Keller's crypt."

Cate looks over her shoulder, chuckles, and places her hands on his cheeks. "Doug. She was blind and deaf, it's *fine*." She shoves her right hand down his pants. "Look at me," she says, "*just . . . keep . . . looking . . . at . . . me.*"

Doug puts another finger in her, their noses touching.

"Harder," Cate whispers as he thrusts. "*Harder . . .*"

Upstairs, Bunny scans the rows of social climbers and grieving friends standing and leaning on tombs. The reverend raises his hands, like a holy ghost in his big white robe, as two dozen men in black suits and white gloves approach the caskets. Bunny has never seen or heard of these men before. *Who are they? Cousins? Brothers?* And one by one, the bodies of Audrey and Mr. and Mrs. Banks are carried out and down the stone steps where a sea of grim photographers and reporters awaits beneath the carved mural of a God floating in the wind, chipped pieces of the world—a swirling universe.

* * *

The reverend bows his head:

"Goodness and mercy all my life
Shall surely follow me
And in God's house for evermore
My dwelling-place shall be."

Georgetown Slave Trade

Slave trading in Georgetown began in 1760 and continued for close to a century. Because of the nearby plantations in Maryland and Virginia, and its accessibility through the Potomac River, Georgetown would become the largest tobacco shipping port in the nation as well as the location of the most slave trading. By the year 1790, what is now known as the tri-state area was home to nearly four hundred thousand enslaved people, accounting for over 55 percent of the entire population of enslaved people in America.* It was no coincidence that this would become the nation's capital. Thomas Jefferson, James Madison, and Alexander Hamilton knew that they wanted the epicenter of economic power to be the location where the most powerful institutions would be built.

After slavery was banned in the district in 1862, a huge population of formerly enslaved Black people remained in Georgetown. By 1890, an estimated five thousand Black people lived in the neighborhood, giving rise to the era known as Black Georgetown. But as segregation was implemented and then the Great Depression hit, many Black residents lost their jobs to white workers; and with President Franklin Roosevelt's New Deal programs, more and more white federal employees moved into the district, pushing Black families out of Georgetown and into more hardship.**

---

*   Chris Myers Asch and George Derek Musgrove, *Chocolate City: A History of Race and Democracy in the Nation's Capital* (Chapel Hill, NC: University of North Carolina Press, 2017).

**   Kathleen Menzie Lesko, Valerie Babb, and Carroll R. Gibbs, *Black Georgetown Remembered: A History of Its Black Community from the Founding of "The Town of George" in 1751 to the Present Day* (Washington, DC: Georgetown University Press, 2016).

❖ CHAPTER SEVENTEEN ❖

When Anthony Tell, a twenty-three-year-old Black male, was arraigned and remanded without bail, the Banks murders splashed across national news outlets. Anthony's round face was plastered on television screens in restaurants, bars, airports, and living rooms for approximately two days before the news cycle moved on. That same week, the federal court "coincidentally" ruled the contents of the docket would be sealed.

It isn't uncommon for news in Washington to be buried within minutes, particularly if an administration is riddled with scandal. Once the family television is turned off, residents of the Washington power structure configure themselves back into financial appointments, country club happy hours, church, family dinners, and lacrosse games.

Meredith grunts on her hands and knees, pulling weeds and dead roots under the tulip poplar. She knows why she's doing it, tugging weak limbs from the ground in some kind of transcendental meditation, a pile strewn next to the infected tree like picked-off scabs. Her refusal to confront the spiritual crisis hanging over her:

the meaning of her mother's death, the Banks murders, the lawsuits facing the family business, which she's just become privy to. Chuck has left her to meet with lawyers in Appalachia; *do not answer their calls*, he told her in an effort to keep her from worrying. Meredith decided to unplug the landline to hide everything from Bunny: that they're being sued for millions upon millions, that their family company has been illegally dumping chemicals into small towns rife with poverty.

Meredith tugs harder as she thinks about what could happen to her family, the possibility of losing everything that has been passed down to them, to her. Maybe the murder of the Banks family (and she feels a little guilty for thinking it) was divine intervention. After all, they had been a leading competitor to the Bartholomews in their expanded business, and Meredith didn't particularly approve of the way Genevieve Banks was displaying their family wealth, which wasn't self-made. Meredith would never say this out loud to anyone, of course. The idea of not living the only lifestyle Meredith has ever known is unfathomable to her. When she married Chuck, she'd moved a mere three blocks from her mother, had never lived anywhere other than Washington—other than Georgetown, just like her mother and her mother's mother and her mother's mother's mother. She wasn't about to be the dead end of the gene pool. She yanks harder, a rip in the ground, and falls over, her bum smacking the dirt, holding the root in her hand, examining its long tentacles. She looks down and sees a brown worm squirming back and forth trying to rebury itself.

⚬⚬⚬

Bunny wakes to the sound of her mother's grunts. She stretches her arm to the floor, pulling her MacBook Air into bed with her. A copy of *Tiffany's Table Manners for Teenagers*, which she threw off her nightstand before bed, is sprawled out like a tepee. Little paragraphs inside of it read like the sound of her late grandmother's voice: *You have to learn to tell a fish knife from a meat knife and a fish fork from a meat fork. If there is no fish knife and fork, use the smaller knife and fork for the dish. If you make a mistake, just continue eating. Don't put the silver back on the table. Be nonchalant.* It was the second time since the murders the housekeeper had picked up the book and placed it back on Bunny's nightstand. She's beginning to wonder if it's a message of sorts, a constant reminder of who she is supposed to be and who she might become. Bunny reaches down, grabs it, and chucks it under her bed, then pulls her D. Porthault floral bedspread over her head as she opens her laptop. Bunny hates herself for knowing the names of patterned linens and things—*toile, argyle*—as if they mean anything, which, to most in her world, they do.

Washington's Fox 5 News link lights up the fort she's created with her knees. For the last several weeks, Bunny's been compulsively googling "Banks Family Murders" each morning. Nothing new pops up, just the same written Fox 5 News article proclaiming racial and economic vengeance, declaring Anthony Tell, who had been fired from one of Audrey's father's companies, just another disgruntled employee. She can't find any other network covering it. But Bunny's obsession with the case intensified after she saw his photograph everywhere, his young face, only a few years older than her. *Did he do it because they deserved it? Is he innocent? This is what we do to Black and brown people. We lock them up and murder them.* . . . It enraged Bunny that each time she brought it up, her mother dismissed her curiosity: "It's done, Bunny, it's done. Justice will be served." But Bunny didn't see it as done or just at all. She wanted to know the *why*, and each time Meredith brushed it off, Bunny sensed a kind of fragility in her mother—or a denial, an inability to confront any possibility of innocence—a block of ice she couldn't pick through. Meredith didn't care to know anything more about Anthony, his alleged crime superseding his private identity, indicating he was nothing more than a public criminal.

Bunny studies Anthony's photograph again, zooming in on his face so his eyes are life-size and staring into her. She tries to imagine that he did do it—the facial expressions he might have made upon entering the home, upon slicing Audrey up—but she's having trouble. His mug shot, he looks so somber, so human.

Power feels tilted along Idaho Avenue behind the new Giant Food, Bluemercury, and Barcelona wine bar. Bunny sits in her Volvo waiting to turn in at the old Metropolitan Police Station when a public bus pulls up next to her. She glances over and looks up. Rows of Black and brown and very few white faces gaze out the windows beyond the traffic, beyond their shitty-paying minimum-wage jobs and psychopathic bosses and headaches from the cleaning fluid and the screaming white children and the fancy dog-poop bags thrown on top of public trash cans—a cocoon of fantasy thinking and wishing and dreaming and resentment and injustice and judgment. The engine roars as it goes on to pass her; Bunny coughs from the fumes whipping through her vents. She cracks the window and swats the air with her hand, then turns into the parking lot.

Inside, an American flag hangs on a white brick wall with three random head shots of notable police chiefs. Bunny's only ever been to the police station once, when she was thrown into the "drunk tank" sophomore year—a holding cell for privileged teenagers with missing stilettos and calls made to family friends who are lawyers.

An overweight female officer with bleached hair and thick glasses sits at the desk behind bulletproof glass. She types something into her computer, ignoring Bunny's presence. Bunny waits with her hands clasped in front of her, polite, a backpack slung over her shoulder and a pink wool beanie on her head. Bunny looks around to while away the time; a gumball machine to her right is covered in dust and probably hasn't been touched since 1997. Another minute passes, and Bunny feigns interest in the surrounding government posters and most-wanted photographs and laws to abide by. She exhales and stares down at the officer before she realizes neither damsel-in-distress nor entitlement will get her what she wants. She steps toward the glass window and knocks. "Excuse me."

The officer looks up. Affectless, she presses the intercom button. "May I help you?"

"Yes. I'm looking for Officer Gomez."

"Do you have a badge number?"

"Um, no."

"I need a badge number."

"Well, can't you just look it up in your system, or whatever?"

The officer gives Bunny a once-over. "Ma'am, what is this regarding?"

"The Banks murders. . . . The family that was tortured and burned—"

"Yeah, I remember, that case is with the feds now."

"The feds?" Bunny doesn't understand the language.

"The FBI."

Disappointed that it's not going to be so easy to get information, Bunny scrunches her nose. "So how do I get the police report, then?"

"You gotta go through the Freedom of Information Act."

"The Freedom of Information Act?"

"The Freedom of Information Act."

"What's the Freedom of Information Act?"

"It's where you can submit a request to obtain records—provided that it gets approved, then they'll give it to you."

"Okay, but—"

"It's the Freedom of Information Act. You can go online and find it," the officer says once more, then turns around to give a sheet of paper to an officer behind her.

"Okay, wait, one more question. . . ." Bunny says, and the woman begrudgingly turns to her again.

"Yes?"

"How do I go visit someone in jail?"

"Which jail, ma'am?" the officer asks with increasing impatience.

"Um . . ." Bunny thinks, the officer's tone making her feel like she should already know the answers and ashamed that she doesn't, because why would she? Look at the coat she's wearing. Bunny pulls up the link to the story on her phone. "The DC Jail . . . Central Detention Facility."

"You gotta go on the website and fill out a form with your ID," says the officer.

"Oh, like for a background check?"

"Ma'am, check the website, like I said."

Bunny glares at the officer. "Got it." She drops her phone in her pocket and heads for the metal detectors and out the front door.

Suffragist Statue

It wasn't until 1921 that the depiction of a woman surfaced within the United States Capitol Rotunda, a room at the center of the Capitol connecting the House of Representatives and the Senate. The unveiling of the suffragist statue happened six months after the ratification of the Nineteenth Amendment giving women (white women) the right to vote. The marble statue depicts Elizabeth Cady Stanton, author of the women's bill of rights; Susan B. Anthony, abolitionist and president of the National American Woman Suffrage Association; and Lucretia Mott, preacher and organizer of the Seneca Falls Convention in New York; in addition, an uncarved clump of marble towers behind them. There are different rumors about what that clump of marble symbolizes—for example, are we waiting for the first female president of the United States? Could it be for the next prominent leader of the women's rights movement? The Me Too movement?*

Sadly, after the statue's unveiling, it was promptly removed and placed underground in what was supposed to be President Washington's crypt, but instead was used to house cleaning supplies, brooms, and mops. Congress rejected multiple bills seeking to move the statue into the Rotunda. It was not until the seventy-fifth anniversary of the Nineteenth Amendment in 1995 that women's groups, including female members of Congress, rallied in an effort to bring it out of the closet. Finally in 1997 the statue was brought back to public light, though only because private funds around the country were donated to move it. Speaker of the House Newt Gingrich had rejected using any of the $23 million budget for maintenance and acquisitions around the Capitol.**

---

* Denise Goolsby, "No Room for Fourth Bust on Suffragette Statue?" *Desert Sun*, September 19, 2016, https://www.desertsun.com/story/news/nation/2016/09/19/suffrage-movement-susan-b-anthony-portrait-monument-us-capitol-hillary-clinton/88317362/.

** Lorraine Boissoneault, "The Suffragist Statue Trapped in a Broom Closet for 75 Years," *Smithsonian*, May 12, 2017, https://www.smithsonianmag.com/history/suffragist-statue-trapped-broom-closet-75-years-180963274/.

❖ CHAPTER EIGHTEEN ❖

*D*oug sits at his desk googling himself after everyone has left the office. "Senator Wallace," "Doug Wallace," "Senator Doug Wallace"—all of the different ways someone other than himself might be thinking about him. His increased self-obsession is due to an uptick in voter popularity, not just in North Carolina but across the United States. Cate's words on Fox struck a chord across party lines in the handling of the White House's domestic violence scandal. And given its timeliness, Doug thanks God again and again for the day he made amends with college classmate Lisa Greenberg. He squeezes his erection under his suit pants when he thinks about it.

It was a few years after Doug's graduation from the University of North Carolina that he had his epiphany about entering politics. This made it imperative he track down Lisa Greenberg. Doug had been calculating enough to sense that whenever they bumped into each other on campus, her behavior suggested she felt overwhelmed and awkward. He'd intuited that it was because the night they had sex, she'd kept changing her mind about whether or not he could enter her until *he* decided she meant *yes* instead of *no*, when really it was *no* instead of *yes*. He'd humped her until he came, then left and never called her again. Lisa was *so difficult.*

It never quite dawned on Doug that he had raped her, only that she didn't like him, and he felt he needed to smooth things over for his future political career. Doug had tracked Lisa down one day at her favorite bookstore in Raleigh, cornering her in the New Fiction section near the front window. Startled by his aggressive presence, Lisa had blushed from embarrassment at having ignored all of his calls; she had an understandably incessant need to get away from him. Nevertheless, Doug had persisted: *Hey, can I talk to you for a sec?* he asked. *I'm just waiting for someone,* she replied. *Listen, I'm going into politics and I've been reflecting on my past, and I am sorry if I ever made you feel*—Doug paused in order to find the right word—*uncomfortable . . . you know, the night we had sex. I felt like things got weird after that.* Lisa froze with shame and left her body and said, *It's okay,* because that was the polite thing to say in public, and Doug said, *Okay, cool, so we're good,* and she said, *Yes,* and they never spoke again.

Doug leans back in his swivel chair and squeezes his erection harder, eyes glazed over the computer screen thinking about Lisa Greenberg; he has the overwhelming urge to masturbate. He pleads with himself, *Not at the office.* In North Carolina, after he stopped screwing the producer at the local Fox affiliate, he began compulsively masturbating in the bathroom at work, and had made a promise when he moved to Washington that he would stop. But growing up in the Wallace home, promises held no merit. Doug heads for the bathroom door, unzips his pants, leans forward with his hand against the wall, and goes and goes as fast as he can.

Women all over America seem to adore Doug's message of conservative masculine redemption. As his paranoia and his adoration for himself increase, so do his sexual urges—and he no longer accepts Cate as the answer. In fact, as of late he has gone from being addicted to her to being repulsed by her ambition. It was her assertiveness that flipped the switch, the realization that she is after something greater than him and he is the road to attaining it.

Cate reaches the center of the Capitol Rotunda below the Apotheosis, the radiant portrait of George Washington sitting in the heavens surrounded by "goddesses," not dissimilar to a portrait of Hugh Hefner surrounded by a semicircle of Playboy bunnies, when she realizes she "forgot" her laptop. She forgot her laptop knowing Doug will be working late on the new amendment to the domestic violence bill and she's anxious as to why he hasn't called or texted during out-of-office hours.

Cate tiptoes into the office. "Hello?" she says softly, but only hears the sound of quiet screaming. There is a similar memory moving through her body as she approaches Doug's office door; to reach it she must pass the office bathroom, the door slightly ajar, where she discovers the screaming is coming from Doug's cell phone resting on the ledge above the toilet, his back to her, his head turned to the phone as he finishes, with no inkling that Cate is standing in the hallway behind him. Watching.

If she breathes, Cate feels like she might get fired. She tiptoes backward, her mouth agape, still not breathing, heart pulsating, then closes her eyes hard and reopens them and stands at her desk staring at her open laptop. The toilet flushes, creating a ripple effect of thumping pipes through the walls, *this fucking infrastructure*. Cate grabs her computer and turns around to see Doug standing in the doorway.

"What are you doing here?" he asks her, surprised. He wipes sweat with the back of his forearm.

"Oh! You're still here—I forgot my computer." Cate shoves it in her bag, runs her hand through her blond locks.

Doug approaches her like he might kiss her, stops just in front of her desk.

"Do you wanna crack my back?" he asks.

"Right now?" Cate looks around the room almost as if she never even saw him masturbating to porn in the bathroom just sixty seconds ago. *Was he masturbating because he missed me?* she wonders.

"Yeah." Doug sprawls out on his stomach on the floor in front of her.

Cate can't help but crack a smile, seduced but still skeptical. She kicks off her heels and steps onto his wobbly skin. A balancing act, like a young ballerina.

Doug groans: "*Unhhh* . . . God, that feels good. That's it, to the left, *unhhh*, yeaahh."

Cate drops the balancing act and digs her heel into the side of his spine. "Does that hurt?"

Doug ignores her. "Okay, okay, I gotta turn over," he says. And flips over on his back so they're making eye contact. Cate thinks it's game over; she doesn't realize Doug's in a different game.

He pulls his legs to his chest. "Okay, now lean on me as hard as you can," he says. Cate exhales, gets on her knees in front of him, and leans into his shins so his knees get closer to his chest. They're eye to eye, like two acrobats, but he doesn't pull her in for a kiss. Cate waits, until it doesn't happen.

"*Unhhhh*. Okay, okay, I gotta get up now," Doug says. He shifts her back, then scrambles up, his arms above his head as he yawns. "Gotta get home to the girls, see you tomorrow?" He points to her and heads for his office door.

Cate stands, a wave of humiliation hitting her. "See you tomorrow," she says, standing barefoot, stranded in the middle of the office.

⁂

As Cate stomps down Constitution Avenue, she becomes acutely aware of the fact that on Capitol Hill, human resources doesn't *really* exist. Every senator's office operates as its own kingdom, so if Cate filed a complaint it would have to be with Walter. She knows that if she files, she'll be fired.

When someone hurts Cate, whether intentionally or not, she holds on to it and uses it to thrust her forward, placating and listening and studying whomever it is she needs to overthrow. Cate's always had an intense awareness and understanding of people and their feelings, their shame, their vulnerability; she'll get to know them—what they were like in high school, how old they were when they got their heart broken. She listens for the gems and drops them in her pocket like rocks and saves them until she's ready to scoop and throw. She isn't in touch with why—*why* being that her father abandoned her for prison when she was fourteen, that he hurt her mother, and that she was ostracized for it. She still thinks about the time in ninth grade when Danny Farrell accused her of stealing an Adidas gym bag from the lost-and-found and told her, "The apple doesn't fall far from the tree." No one ever acknowledged the fact that he was gone, only in moments of bullying or gossip behind her back. She received no sympathy from teachers or parents or friends, not even from Chuck or Meredith, who used only their money and connections to support her, to get her into college, to get her the job in Doug's office. No one ever asked if she was okay.

As the escalator descends into the Metro station, Cate tries to shake off the initial shock and humiliation that she knows is not hers to carry. A deep knowing that Doug is turning away from her—her ambition—that this isn't *love*. He used her for sex. A moment of dysphoria before she steps through the sliding doors of the train and is overcome by rage, the kind of rage only a woman without any father, money, or status available to protect her can feel.

⌘

The next day Cate and Walter are hovering over Doug, who sits at his mahogany desk. They're watching the end of an ad on YouTube in an attempt to decide whether or not it's appropriate for Doug's SAVE THE BROS baseball hat to be in the background on his bookshelf in his social media video introducing the amendment to the domestic violence crime bill making psychological control a Class E felony.

On the computer screen: The camera pans to a man wearing a gold chain and wife-beater, who looks directly into the camera: "That's what she said," *wink*. The bros dance and shimmy and high-five and fist-bump and the camera pans out. "Tweet your bro anonymously." SAVE THE BROS! appears on the screen.

Doug spins around in his chair, chuckling at the ad, then sighs.

"I think this is inappropriate and we should replace the hat with your Michael Jordan bobblehead," Cate says.

"It's an advertisement for organic protein drinks, for God's sake," says Walter, pit stains noticeable through his white dress shirt. "We need to appeal to our youth, we need hip things in the background."

A young cameraman enters, begins to set up the tripod. Doug pretends he is invisible.

"But this is for our female base, young *and* old," Cate argues. Doug shoots her a disappointed look, which startles her; she thinks maybe she's gotten a little loose with her decorum around the office, especially in Walter's presence. And after her realization last night, that Doug may no longer have any use for her, she can't afford to make any mistakes. She makes a mental adjustment, runs over to the photographer to help set up, leaving Walter and Doug to review their notes on the announcement of the bill.

Doug straightens in his seat, adjusts his red striped tie, which makes him look more like a male candy striper than a senator. Cate stands behind the tripod watching him mouth his lines into the camera as practice, doubting his abilities.

Walter notices the way Cate is looking at Doug, her longing and disappointment, and walks over with a clipboard holding the script. He extends his arm across her chest, grazing the back of it against her nipple, then lifts his arm gently up and down before Cate grabs the clipboard out of his hand. Cate is in a state of shock, as if a cement of shame has been poured over her, propelling her to pretend it never happened. Walter, satisfied in his crumpled khakis, takes two steps behind her, his foul breath on the back of her neck; he crosses his arms and waits for the cameraman to say, "It's a go."

As Doug settles into his usual political cadence, and Cate stands erect following the script, making sure he hits every mark, the phone rings.

"Goddamn it." Doug leans back in his tufted chair, breaking character like he's onstage in a Stanislavski acting class.

A knock at the door; another young intern pops his head in. "Sir, it's a producer for *All the News with Chris Williams!* on Fox, he wants to discuss some talking points before the show tonight."

"Tell them you're in a committee meeting and call back," Walter says to Doug, who nods at the intern in agreement.

"Betsy and Linda are having dinner together at their country club," Doug says, then buries his head back into the script. "Okay, now where were we?"

"Cate?" Walter says.

Cate fumbles with the script. "Start back with 'Coercive control is not just low-level or high-level violence, it is insidious and calculated, causing emotional and psychological harm. Many victims are left with nonphysical scars, but emotional scars can also last a lifetime.'"

On display where Cate walks in the Capitol Rotunda are the carved marble heads of suffrage pioneers: Lucretia Mott, Elizabeth Cady Stanton, and Susan B. Anthony. A slightly unhinged tour guide of middle-schoolers describes the chunk of uncarved marble behind the suffragettes: "This chunk of marble has been abandoned while it awaits a female president. It's been ninety-nine years and even *you* probably won't see a female president in your lifetime."

Cate maintains her focus and walks toward the back-door exit where black Suburbans wait for their designated senators when Walter calls after her.

"Cate! Cate!!!"

She pretends not to hear him, picking up speed heading for Doug's car, ready and waiting to take them to *All the News with Chris Williams!* Cate's cortisol levels rise as she ties her Burberry hand-me-down trench coat, turning around to see Walter stumbling toward her.

"Boy, you got quite a strut there," Walter says, a crown of sweat on his forehead, wheezing from his walk. "Look, you're doing a great job." He puts his hand on Cate's shoulder, his thumb touching her neck, grazing it as if reaching for her throat. "Doug has given me the reins to let you know when he thinks you're ready to take on more as far as additional public interviews, you know, since his schedule is picking up before election season. We need to be sure you are absolutely ready and steady to take that on."

Cate stumbles to pretend she's not irritated, confused, *enraged.* They've been using her language ever since the bill was introduced.

"When did this discussion happen?"

"The senator does not have the time to think about delegating right now, Cate." Walter asserts his condescension without answering the question, then swings his tone. Moving closer to her, he places his other hand on the bicep of her other arm. "As I said, keep up the great work, you'll be running all things press in no time." He steps away from her, pointing his finger at her as Doug walks toward the vehicle.

"You ready?" Doug asks Cate. "Let's go win more hearts of American women!" He gives her that charming smile, the one she fell for when she first met him.

"Cate, you behave yourself now." Walter points at her again, laughs to himself. "I'll see you guys at the studio after I fire an intern."

In the car Cate is next to Doug, whose head is buried in his phone, supposedly reviewing the bill's amendments as well as various news articles responding to the domestic violence crisis. Cate sits with her hands clasped. She remembers when, a few months ago, he asked her to hold his phone during a vote, and GIFs of men receiving blow jobs popped up in his Safari window. Cate had accidentally hit the tab but clicked out of it, pretending it wasn't even there. It was the first time she'd felt a piercing in her fantasy, a poke in her own denial, too painful to believe—so she didn't. How could she be so tough and so naïve?

❧·CHAPTER NINETEEN·❧

*N*om, do we really have to go?" Haley pleads as Betsy pulls up in their Jaguar behind a 1992 Jeep Grand Wagoneer in the valet line at the Washington Club. A woman steps out of the Wagoneer in a white tennis outfit and diamond studs. Her socks have fringed lace spilling over the tops of her ankles. Betsy's stomach turns, and she fiddles with her twelve-carat diamond before the valet attendant, a Black man in a tuxedo, walks over to open her and Haley's doors.

"Madam," he says, and welcomes them both to the "club of clubs."

Betsy tightens the knot in the center of the Gucci scarf that's draped around her shoulders and motions for Haley to grab the fox coat that is resting in the backseat. Betsy steps out of the car and swings it around her shoulders. Haley wears Lilly Pulitzer as if she's a walking roll of floral wrapping paper.

They enter the club. Behind the whiffs of the grand display of dying lilies is a very specific lingering odor whirling from scratchy old sofas that should have been replaced forty years ago. The floral drapes remind Betsy of her dead mother-in-law's living room in Durham. The place is a dump. And yet the legacy lives on in the sons and daughters of its founding members, proudly bipartisan—and by *bipartisan* they mean *wealthy*, the oldest dynasties mingling in an attempt to keep control of their inner hierarchy and outer legacy, for all at the club of clubs are wobbling on the tippy-tops of golden ladders built by their ancestors who climbed to the top for them.

Like living in an ugly heirloom, Betsy thinks. Dangling her alligator Birkin bag at her side, she walks up to a woman who's let her natural gray grow out, sitting at a secretary desk with a sign-in book and fountain pen. There are no computers.

"May I help you?" the old woman asks.

"Yes, hello, I'm Betsy Wallace, I'm here to meet Linda Williams for dinner."

The butler, or secretary, or whatever she is, leads Betsy and Haley past the bowling alley and cardroom, through the cocktail room to the entrance of the dining room. When they arrive at the still-empty table, Betsy pulls out a comb to quickly brush the ends of Haley's hair.

"Mom, stop." Haley winces and sways her body away from her anxious mother.

As Betsy puts the comb back and snaps her bag closed, a knock at the glass window behind them causes her to jump and spin around. It's Linda, standing in a red St. John knit with an Hermes scarf tied around her shoulders. Becca trails behind her clad in a clashing Lily Pulitzer dress.

Hi, Betsy mouths, and waves. Linda motions that she will be right there.

Five minutes later, Linda trails along the dining hall as if she is the hostess in her own home, exuding effervescent power.

"Bonjour!" Linda leans in to give Betsy a double cheek kiss, "Muah, muah!" She nudges her daughter forward. "Becca, say hi to Haley."

Becca is small for her age, mousy brown hair and an unfortunate mustache forming above her upper lip. "Hi," she musters, having trouble making eye contact.

"Hey," Haley replies, resentment in her tone for this so-called playdate.

"How are we doing this evening, Mrs. Williams?" the server asks.

"Juste merveilleux, parlez-vous français?" ("Just marvelous, do you speak French?") Linda winks at the server, then giggles at Betsy.

"Bonjour! Tu es heureux!" (Betsy means to say, "Hello, I'm happy to be here." Instead she says, "Hello, you are happy!")

"I'm sorry, uh . . ." The server laughs awkwardly to ease his uncertainty and asks to take their order.

"The whitefish is divine," Linda says, peeking over her menu, then orders the chicken piccata, and chicken fingers for Becca.

"I'll have the whitefish then, and chicken fingers for this one," Betsy says, smiling, then hands him her menu.

"Oh, there's Meredith Bartholomew," Linda says, waving like the queen of England as she finishes the *"mew,"* giving a wide fake smile as Meredith does the same while walking to her designated table. The two of them performing like players in a Norman Rockwell painting except everyone is lying to each other.

"Becca, sweetie, why don't you go show Haley the bowling alley."

The girls trail off to "explore" the club—"but not too far, club rules!"

"Do you know the Bartholomews?" Linda asks Betsy.

"Chuck has been a wonderful supporter of Doug's. Meredith, however . . ." Betsy leans over and whispers, "not so much. . . ."

"Oh well, you know why *that* is," Linda says, implying that Betsy must know the answer.

"How do you mean?" Betsy knows gossip is the most dangerous neighborhood in Washington, given how *small* this town is, but she can't help but dip her toe in.

Linda leans into Betsy, a game of seesaw. "They're having money problems."

"Oh, *really*. . . . God, I wonder if Doug knows," Betsy says, concerned.

"Well, you didn't hear it from me."

The server arrives with their wine. Linda takes a sip like a southern belle. *Checkmate*. She knows Doug counts on the Bartholomew donation dollars. "They're tied up in over a dozen lawsuits in different counties across the country for their chemical dumping. But the press hasn't caught on yet, not in the *social political* sense, if you know what I mean. . . . And here's a little twist: the Bankses—you know, *the family that was murdered*—they were their biggest competitors. . . . You wouldn't know it because they socialized together and I think Chuck and David were in the same class at Harvard. Anyway, the stocks are tumbling." She shakes out her napkin and drapes it across her lap. "I'm sure Doug knows all about it—*besides*, look at all this wonderful attention Doug is getting!"

⁂

Becca and Haley stand on the upper level of the bowling alley near the dark and empty popcorn stand. Haley plays a game on her cell phone.

"You can't have cell phones in here," Becca says, "it's club rules."

Haley ignores her, enthusiastically tapping the screen on her phone.

"You're not going to get into the club if you keep playing on your cell phone," Becca says.

Haley keeps her eyes steady on the game. "We already belong to the club."

"No, you don't. You're lying," Becca says.

Haley finishes the game, clicking out of the app and into her camera, then lifts her phone to Becca's face and snaps a photo.

"Stop! You're going to get us kicked out!"

"What are you gonna do, tell Mommy about it?" Haley opens up her Finsta account and creates a meme of Becca. It is a split photograph, on the right the unflattering close-up of Becca, on the other side a Google image of her mother. The caption reads: "Mom, am I ugly? Honey, I told you not to call me Mom in public." *Click*. Haley uploads and posts.

Betsy chews her whitefish despite its funky smell. Fishy and over-cooked, it's hard to tell whether it's gone bad.

"We could do it at the St. Regis during teatime. The girls can get dressed up, maybe we can start with—personally one of my favorites—Nancy Drew." Linda is talking about forming a mother-daughter book club.

As she chatters on, Betsy's stomach starts to gurgle. She burps a little bit, "Excuse me," dabbing the cloth napkin over her lips, a wretched fishy taste swirling around in her mouth.

"Where's the powder room? Nature's calling." Betsy's face turns as pale as a golf ball; she doesn't realize she's still holding her napkin to her mouth when she gets up.

"Down there through the dining room to the right."

Betsy knocks over a young girl in her best attempt to run grace-fully for the powder room, her large intestine about to explode. Sweat forms below her perfect hairline; the lingering taste of fish and the image of an oozing slab of mayonnaise cause her to fall to her knees inside the stall of the handicapped toilet to expel the whitefish, and it is violent. After about twenty seconds, she comes up for air. Spit-ting a small chunk back out in the toilet, Betsy hears "Ew!" and the closing of the bathroom door from a young club member who bore witness to the sound and smell of her explosion.

After Betsy flushes the toilet, she falls from her knees to her back against the side of the stall, mucus running down her nose. She gasps as her stomach begins to gurgle, the feeling of a leaf blower in her lower abdomen, a new wave of panic. She attempts to stand, gripping the white tiled wall—"*no, no, no*"—when she loses all control, a warm oozing sensation flooding her underwear, *please, God.* Then, the morti-fying smell . . . "*Oh God, oh my God.*" Betsy shimmies out of her leather YSL pencil skirt and throws it to the side of the stall. She stands in her control-top pantyhose, which are squeezing her bum closer to her bones, making the mess all the more slathered and unbearable.

"Jesus *fucking* Christ!" She peels down her stockings while kind of scooting her buttocks over the toilet. She burps and breathes. Then she hears the door to the bathroom open. It's club housekeeping.

"Everything okay, miss?" the voice asks in a thick Spanish accent, indicating to Betsy that whoever bore witness to her explosion has tattled.

"Fine! Thank you, no need to be in here!" The woman withdraws. Betsy wipes herself again, and again, and again, and flushes. She pulls her skirt back on, then takes the pantyhose covered in feces and debates whether to flush them down the toilet or wrap them up and shove them in the trash can. The clock is ticking, Linda is going to begin to worry. Betsy stands within these milliseconds wanting to cry like a high school girl who's just gotten her period at a boy's house with no pads, tampons, or toilet paper—humiliation in its highest form, except that this moment is worse. Betsy must act fast. *Pull it together for the sake of your husband's—your family's—Washington reputation.*

Betting against the plumbing of the building, Betsy dumps the stool-covered pantyhose in the trash can. After washing her hands and spraying half a bottle of air freshener in the stall, she manages to make a sly exit sans underwear without another soul from the dining hall noticing.

"Everything all right?" Linda asks, shifting her attention away from her conversation with Becca and Haley, who refuse to make eye contact with each other at the table, picking at their chicken fingers.

"Just a little bit of a wait in the powder room." Betsy takes a seat.

"How bizarre, there's never been a wait in all my years coming here," Linda replies.

Betsy smiles and shrugs, and places the new napkin in her lap covering her bare knees, hoping Linda won't notice her stockings are missing.

"Mom, Daddy's show is on," Becca says.

"Oh my goodness, let's get the check." She calls for the server, then says, "Guess who's on Daddy's show tonight?"

"Who?" Becca asks.

"My dad." Haley smirks.

Becca squints at Haley, then asks, "Mom, are Haley and her mom members of the club too? Haley said they were."

"Haley, that's not true, why would you say that?" Betsy says, horrified.

Linda, embarrassed for Betsy and her daughter, tries to save the awkward moment. "Oh, that's okay," she says, then turns to Haley. "Would you like to be a member here, Haley? It's awfully fun; you can go swimming, and ice skating, and have a bowling birthday party! There's even a high-dive at the swimming pool for big kids."

Betsy smiles, *mortified*.

"Just make sure you're on your best behavior so that Mommy and Daddy can become members. You wouldn't want to ruin it for them would you?" Linda finishes.

"No," Haley says, feeling ashamed.

The server places the check in the center of the table.

Betsy grabs it. "Let me—it's the least I can do, you were so sweet to invite us here for dinner."

"Oh no, no, they actually won't let you since you're not a member . . . yet." Linda winks and lifts the bill out of Betsy's hands.

Outside in the valet line, Linda examines Betsy in a more sober light.

The girls stand in the fall chill under the large green awning, a large bouquet of orange chrysanthemums behind them. As Betsy's Jaguar pulls up and Haley hops into the passenger side, Linda pulls her in. "Betsy, hon, before you go . . . listen, the club really appreciates an *understated* look. I would come without the diamonds and alligator next time—you know how *fuddy-duddy* they can be." She tries to make light of the social divide. "See you at French class this week?"

Betsy smiles. "Of course. See you then."

"Oh, and don't mention you were a practicing Catholic either."
Linda makes a slashing gesture with her hand. "You know those
crazy Catholics!!" She throws her head back and laughs.

"Never!" Betsy jokes back. "You're the best."

"Can't wait to go home and watch our hubbies debate, how fun!"

It's ironic how comfortable Linda feels shaming Betsy for her
wealth when the Williamses' net worth is three times the amount of
the Wallaces'. But a real cave dweller never reveals such information.

Part Two

The Mayflower

The Mayflower, *carrying English Protestants fleeing religious persecution by King James of England, anchored at what was to become Plymouth, Massachusetts, on December 18, 1620. It has been documented that the ship was meant to dock in Virginia, which at the time included land up to the Hudson River in what is now New York, but was unable to do so due to severe winter weather.* As well as 30 crewmembers, there were 102 passengers, known today as the Pilgrims, of whom 41 wrote and signed the Mayflower Compact, providing the framework for the creation of a civil government—the first government of and by "the people" (white men) in the history of the New World.*

During their first winter, many of the settlers died from disease and hardships, leaving only fifty-three in the New World. Given how many had died, it was evident they needed help. A Native American by the name of Squanto from the Patuxet tribe taught them how to harvest corn, among other things.** Though peace initially existed, it was temporary. As the settlements expanded more and more, threatening the ten-thousand-year history of the Native American people and their land, bloody battles were soon waged against the Native Americans in a ruthless attempt at attaining power and control. Until the year 1880, it is estimated between 2 million and 5.5 million Native Americans were enslaved in America.***

---

*   Caleb Johnson's Mayflower History (website), http://mayflowerhistory.com/voyage.

**   Rebecca Beatrice Brooks, "Squanto: The Former Slave," *History of Massachusetts* (blog), https://historyofmassachusetts.org/squanto-the-former-slave/.

***   "Colonial Enslavement of Native Americans Included Those Who Surrendered Too," Brown University website, https://www.brown.edu/news/2017-02-15/enslavement.

The Mayflower Compact:

IN THE NAME OF GOD, AMEN. *We, whose names are under-written, the Loyal Subjects of our dread Sovereign Lord King James, by the Grace of God, of Great Britain, France, and Ireland, King, Defender of the Faith, etc. Having undertaken for the Glory of God, and Advancement of the Christian Faith, and the Honour of our King and Country, a Voyage to plant the first Colony in the northern Parts of Virginia; Do by these Presents, solemnly and mutually, in the Presence of God and one another, covenant and combine ourselves together into a civil Body Politick, for our better Ordering and Preservation, and Furtherance of the Ends aforesaid: And by Virtue hereof do enact, constitute, and frame, such just and equal Laws, Ordinances, Acts, Constitutions, and Officers, from time to time, as shall be thought most meet and convenient for the general Good of the Colony; unto which we promise all due Submission and Obedience.**

* History website, https://www.history.com/topics/colonial-america/mayflower-compact.

❖CHAPTER TWENTY❖

*B*unny spent the majority of the Thanksgiving holiday refraining from reminding everyone about the slaughter of the Native Americans when Meredith printed out the family tree from Ancestry.com to prove that their ancestors had arrived on the *Mayflower*. She dispensed custom-made red, white, and blue "Indian headdresses" at the dinner table before dessert. After Bunny read that her great-great-great-great-great-great-grandfather had had three wives (consecutively) and thirty children, she took off the headdress and smoked a joint behind the dying poplar tree. *That's what they did then, honey Bunny—they spread the seed! We had good seed.*

Later that night under her covers with her mother's stolen password, Bunny discovered their family had enslaved Native Americans. But because Bunny had never even heard of Native American slavery, she wasn't about to put up a fight without a loaded gun. Meredith had conveniently left that detail out amidst her joy during Thanksgiving dinner. Overwhelmed with a sense of truth, Bunny felt like she was just beginning to understand the convenience of leaving the details out of history for the purposes of a narrative controlled by those who have something to hide born out of shame. *What else are they hiding?* Audrey's death, the pall hanging over Bunny's every thought, kept pushing her intense need to meet Anthony, the alleged murderer. Finding all of the paperwork for visitation online, Bunny used her fake ID, passed down from her cousin Grace Morrison on her mother's side of the family when Grace turned twenty-one so Bunny could buy cigarettes without having to pay off a stranger every time. A common initiation from older friends or siblings—and Bunny wasn't ever scared to use it. The Bartholomews are family friends with the United States Attoney General. Bunny is immune to arrest, to risk—living in her gilded existence of privilege, the thought wouldn't even cross her mind.

⤙⚬⤚

Bunny drives east of the Capitol toward a brown cement building. She sees the sign: DEPARTMENT OF CORRECTIONS, CENTRAL DETENTION FACILITY.

She turns right toward the parking lot. Rain pounds across her windshield as she makes a wrong turn into the semicircle of what looks like an abandoned neoclassical mansion with boarded and blown-out windows and shattered glass under dead boxwoods, Corinthian columns, arched windows, a massive double limestone staircase, all having survived nearly a century of neglect. *What is this? It looks like Audrey's mansion—strange*, Bunny thinks. ANNE ARCHBOLD HALL is engraved in the limestone above the rotting wood-covered doors.

Bunny parks behind the abandoned mansion and walks toward a dilapidated building next door where she sees more than a dozen women standing in a single-file line, shivering in the cold.

A female officer with SPECIAL POLICE written across her jacket smokes a cigarette while guarding the entrance. Many of the women are covered in blankets and holding brown grocery bags. Bunny approaches the officer, cutting in front of the line.

"Excuse me, Officer?" Bunny says.

The officer turns to Bunny, her hair in a high ponytail, gold rings on each finger. "Hey, honey," she says.

Bunny notices she's missing a front tooth. "Is this the line for the DC Jail visiting center?"

"Oh no, that's in the trailer around the corner." The woman points her cigarette to what's obviously the jail surrounded with barbed wire, a tower in its center resembling an airport control tower. "It's on the other side of that. Just walk around, you'll come to a graveyard, make a left, then a right."

"Thank you. . . . Um, what's this line for?" Bunny can't help but ask.

"*This* the *women's* shelter," the woman says.

Bunny gazes at the line of women waiting for a bed—for some kind of protection and safety, only to turn around for a view of abandonment and captivity.

"Got it, thanks again," Bunny says.

"No problem, honey." The officer inhales her cigarette.

Bunny walks toward the enormous wrought iron gates of a graveyard, chained with a silver lock at the center. "Redford!" a white woman yells as she chases her Labradoodle, off-leash, trampling the planted headstones with a tennis ball in its mouth. Bunny can see the trailer as she turns left, then right, on the other side of the brick wall separating the graves from the jail, a mystifying nexus between being alive and being dead.

Bunny waits in line under dry heat, which is blasting from the vents. She is, for the first time in her life, a minority. Except for the way in which the systemic world sees her—a silver dollar in a jar of pennies—one against a larger sum and somehow still worth more? Bunny is entirely unaware of this reality beyond the words on a page of her history books, of what she is witnessing—there are no words in any of her history books, they don't exist, only in what she has seen in the news lately: marching in the streets, on the steps of the Supreme Court, the Capitol, the White House. In these moments, the story she thinks she knows becomes warped and ripped from the pages; she feels nauseated from the sight of homeless women in the building behind her, the scattered trash, a jail infested with rats and known to be one of the most violent. The heat blows down her back, beads of sweat forming under her jacket beneath her bra. It is alarming for Bunny; the families and individuals waiting in line are mostly Black. Alarming for anyone who's witnessing a different story than the one they've always been told while cocooned in their own. But nothing could prepare her, no Hollywood movie, news segment, or documentary, for seeing it in person.

At last Bunny approaches the correctional officer and hands her the fake ID, *Grace Morrison.* There are no background checks, there's no reason for anyone to suspect this isn't her. Her whiteness: institutionally free of consequence.

"Cell phones are not allowed, everything you say and do is being monitored and recorded." The officer hands Bunny her ID back.

"Yes, ma'am," Bunny says, relieved her ID worked.

"You can have a seat over there." The officer points with her eyes to the right-hand wall, an empty seat in front of a screen with a handset, like some kind of modern telephone booth. This officer has no interest in who she's visiting—just another day, another body, another visitor.

Bunny walks to the empty chair and screen and stares at it. "Um, wait, what is this?"

"This is visitation," says another officer, standing against the wall behind her.

"But this is a monitor. I'm confused."

"This is how it works. You don't like it, the exit's right there."

Bunny pauses. *This isn't what it's like in the movies.* "Okay, but how can you tell us we're 'visiting' someone and not actually visit them? This is like a government FaceTime."

"Are you staying or leaving?" the officer says; he has no time or patience for her questioning.

"I'm sorry, but . . . so there are no *in-person* visits?" Bunny feels completely blindsided.

"Miss, you can have an in-person after sixty days as long as they don't commit any infractions."

"So as long as he doesn't get in trouble?" Bunny has created a physical change in atmosphere, a stir of attention; she can feel the resentful eyes behind her, hear whispering about wasting time—time they want to spend with loved ones.

The officer is becoming increasingly agitated. Bunny feels the thickening of racial and class tension, a lack of patience for her questioning, perpetuating the cycle of oppression that *she is causing*.

"That's what I said," the officer tells her.

"I see."

Bunny turns around to see Anthony Tell's face on the monitor. She pulls the chair back, looking down, more unprepared for this moment than she'd thought—that he responded, that he's there. She looks up at the monitor, lifts her arm to grab the blue telephone receiver, but Anthony's face keeps disappearing into static lightning. In between flashes of him on the screen, Bunny notices other inmates walking, orange jumpsuits passing through this overwhelming moment for her. She sees a man shackled at his feet and wrists; he waddles behind where Anthony sits, a prison guard pushing his back to move him along, and his torso is covered in blood. Finally the signal sticks. "Hello? You there?" Bunny says, the blue phone pressed to her ear.

"Who are you? My lawyer told me not to talk to anyone," Anthony says, folding an arm across his chest, hunched over.

Bunny attempts to defuse the confrontation. "I was told never talk to strangers, so I guess we're even."

Anthony takes a beat, examines her. "We're not even," he replies.

Stirred, Bunny feels her confidence free-fall at the way that must have sounded coming out of her white mouth—unintentionally, but intentions are irrelevant. Heat continues to blast down her back from the vents; she's soaked in nervous sweat.

"You a social worker or what?" Anthony asks.

"Uhhh, no," Bunny replies.

Anthony loses his focus; distracted, he swerves in his seat left then right, looking to see what's going on behind him, all that Bunny can't see and know and smell and touch: the wet mold from the showers, a man furiously masturbating in the corner, another talking to himself, the straitjackets upstairs Anthony saw upon his arrival, the shanks hidden in the soles of shoes, the sporadic violence forcing him to duck and swerve. In the moments when he is still and looking at the screen, Bunny is reminded that he isn't much older than she is.

Anthony regains his focus. "So you're a reporter?"

"Um, I guess you could say that. My name's . . . *Grace*, my name is Grace," Bunny says, before she accidentally reveals the truth. "I think it's important for people to know your side of the story, so I wanted to come and hear it."

"You fucking people. You don't give a shit about my side of the story, and you don't get a prize for coming here. I'm not your fucking zoo animal." Anthony hangs up, gets up, and he's gone.

Bunny freezes, still holding the receiver. Shaken at the interruption of her entitlement; she's never been dismissed before. (*What?*) As she's about to hang up, an inmate jumps in front of the camera, the static image of a young white girl in a pink beanie staring aimlessly, offensively, terrified in front of the screen. He spreads his pointer and middle fingers into a V and slides his yellow tongue through it, then flicks it at her.

Rocked. "Fuck you!" Bunny erupts, then slams the receiver, gathers herself, fake-smiles at the correctional officer, and runs out the door, back toward the gates of the graveyard.

❧·CHAPTER TWENTY-ONE·❧

*M*eredith slams the screen door. She stands in the foyer next to a full-length mirror, its mahogany frame found in a sunken ship off the coast of Martha's Vineyard when she was a little girl. Meredith inhales her mother's federal town house, its ingrained smell of cool wood and charcoal, age and human odor, the whiff of clammy blouses worn too many times. The musky residual pheromones are redolent of status and memory, a kind of territorial marking that Meredith doesn't want to let go of. But the house is an asset and it must be sold.

The living room is rife with exposed brick, double fireplaces, a glass Tiffany lamp, and black-and-white photographs of her grandparents, two with President Franklin D. Roosevelt and Secretary of War Henry L. Stimson. Presidential inaugural ball invitations and old framed Christmas cards, sketches of their farm in Middleburg and Meredith's horse named Shoo. She's missing that dim light, the feeling of being cocooned by her parents; it hits her all at once, that dreadful pull again, the longing for her mother. Meredith's father died from lung cancer over a decade ago, but it was always Elizabeth (Bunny), the matriarch, who kept the family nucleus strong.

Meredith wills her body into the kitchen, sits at the old wooden breakfast booth by the bay window, and lights a cigarette. She opens her mother's laptop in front of her, the one she never used, googles the name of a psychic hotline, then dials from her cell phone.

A raspy voice answers, "Knight psychic hotline, can I have your name, please?"

Meredith hangs up. Throws her head in her hands. Pops up just to take a long drag and stare at the brick wall in front of her. She squints, cocks her head sideways. *What is that?* Some kind of black object is stuck to the brick, *but that can't be.* Meredith cranes her head forward, takes another drag; smoke pours out of her lips, possessed now, when she sees the object move. It's a black butterfly. Its wings slowly descend as though waking from a dream to reveal two red stripes on its body, before it pushes them up again as if its wings are trying to seduce her. Meredith stubs her cigarette out on the crystal ashtray, tiptoes closer to make sure she's seeing it correctly, a butterfly, *how did you get in here?* As if breaking from a spell, Meredith tiptoes back to the computer and googles "black butterfly red stripe spiritual meaning": *A black butterfly is considered a symbol of misfortune and death. It is also associated with power, mystery, fear, and evil.*

Meredith slams the computer shut. *Stop it, Meredith, stop it, stop it.* The butterfly jets off, looking for a way out.

Meredith takes the ashtray over to the sink, remembers there's no garbage disposal. She opens the cabinet below. A mouse lies sideways, still, its gaping mouth staring up at her.

"Oh, Christ!"

Just as she begins to reach for a paper towel, the doorbell rings. Meredith jumps again. "Goddamn it!"

"Yoo-hoo!" It's Phyllis Van Buren arriving to help clean out the house. Phyllis walks toward the kitchen in her Burberry trench with its faint odor of mothballs and Chanel Number Five, carrying two coffees from Booeymonger, the famous Georgetown deli next door.

"You scared the bejesus out of me. There's a dead mouse under the sink. I can't do it, I can't, I can't . . ." Meredith trails off, her lower lip quivering. She lowers herself to the floor of the kitchen, sits with her back against a closed cabinet door. Lifeless.

"Oh, for God's sake," Phyllis sets the coffee cups down next to the computer, violently rips a paper towel from its roll, then kneels, grabs the mouse, and dumps it into the trash bin. "There. It's done."

"It's still in the trash bin."

"For Christ's sake, Meredith, your mother lived a very long and wonderful life! You need to celebrate her, not wallow in this."

WASPs are not ones to *wallow*.

"Her legacy lives on in *you*, and in *Bunny*, she is her namesake!" Phyllis says, trying to cheer her up.

"What does a legacy even mean, Phyllis?"

Phyllis extends her hand. "Get up off that dirty floor, will you?" Meredith takes her hand and stands.

"I'm serious. What does it mean? This country is *eroding*, Phyllis, as we know it, our children don't care about *capitalism* and they're preaching in our streets, *Black Lives Matter! Down with the one percent and big corporations! Gun control!* And I *agree* with some of what they say, but they don't even know what the *fuck* they are talking about. Remember how fearful our parents were—our grandparents were—of communism?"

"Is this about the Banks murders, honey?" Phyllis is trying to follow, be a supportive friend.

Meredith snatches her coffee, walks into the living room, and sits on the rose-colored sofa, matted and soft from the derrieres of presidents and royalty striking deals and declaring war. "I am *saying* that if a legacy does not remain upheld with dignity and respect, it will become nameless."

"Well, isn't that obvious, dear? And what a legacy you carry." Phyllis smiles, puts her hand on Meredith's shoulder. "It'll be all right, dear."

"We're losing money, Phyllis," Meredith tells her, hesitant at first, but she can't keep it in anymore; her secret is imploding, which she knows is a liability. So she must tell only one person whom she can trust. And it is only because Phyllis has spent the last thirty years of her life protecting and preserving the legacy of the Manhattan Project, considered to be an American victory in spite of killing about eighty thousand people, that Meredith feels confident Phyllis will understand.

"What do you mean?" Phyllis asks as if this is simply not possible.

"We're being sued."

"By whom?" She's still not convinced.

"Hundreds of . . . people in rural states." Meredith lights another cigarette.

"But this sort of thing happens all the time, darling. Look, this is *capitalism* and people just want a piece of the pie."

"No, Phyllis, it will blow up if we do not keep paying."

"Mer—"

"A child has died of cancer, a *child*—from the chemical dumping. Headquarters knew. They *knew* it would contaminate the water, they *knew* the fumes would kill livestock. It doesn't degrade into the environment, and only now are we seeing the repercussions. They *knew*. And did *nothing*. And those lawyers have got doctors and specialists on their side. The magnitude . . . with this much demand for transparency today, at the rate things are changing."

"How many towns?" Phyllis asks, getting to the point.

"I think . . . forty-three states."

Phyllis exhales.

"They will bankrupt us if any refuse settlements and make it to trial. Chuck's name, the family name . . ."

"Well, Bartholomew Industries can't be the *only* ones involved," Phyllis replies, looking for an out.

"No, but we are the only ones left now that the Bankses . . . and, well, their stock is catastrophically plummeting," Meredith says with some satisfaction. "There have also been a few threats on their end, lawsuits that Chuck knows about. . . . We settled just one case, *one*, for six hundred seventy-one million under the condition no one would go to the press."

"Well, how on earth are you responsible for this anyway? Or Chuck?" protests Phyllis. "Yes, it's his family's name, but seeing as neither of you run day-to-day operations—and I would assume there's a trust and management on the ground. I mean, should the auto industry be responsible each time someone dies in a car accident? For heaven's sake! For a century now, Americans have been benefiting in our free capital society from the products and services Bartholomew Industries has provided! *This is capitalism!* And I know your father—bless him—if he were still here, he would agree with me. The services and the good outweigh the bad—nothing that reaches as far and as wide as Bartholomew Industries, or the Morrison family, could possibly sustain a conglomerate without error, it's just not possible, dear. Shit happens. We're still human."

Phyllis reaches for a drag of Meredith's cigarette.

"You cannot say a word. I mean it, Phyllis. I'm trusting you."

"How many years have we known each other now?"

"Don't age us."

"That's right." Phyllis passes the cigarette back. "Where's Chuck? How is he handling this?"

"He's in Ohio at a mediation meeting. Then he goes to Kentucky, and then back to West Virginia."

"And Bunny? I'm assuming she's in the dark and you're keeping it that way?" Phyllis knows best.

"Yes, absolutely. She's been struggling with—well, first it was my mother, and now it's Audrey, and it's all just so horrific, Phyllis. She absolutely cannot find out about this."

"And Cate? She's still living with you?"

"Yes, and she does not need to know. She's hardly ever home anyway."

"Good. . . ." Phyllis thinks for a moment. "Have you and Chuck discussed buying the Bankses' assets? Whoever is in the will, *buy them out.* If the stocks are plummeting, this might be the move. Dear Lord, forgive me for taking it as a business opportunity." Phyllis makes the sign of the cross on her chest and looks up to the ceiling.

"That's what he's thinking. If we can afford it."

"Yes, I see . . ." Phyllis sighs. "The future ain't what it used to be—" Just then the black butterfly descends onto Phyllis Van Buren's left cheek. "Oh! Oh!" She swats at her face until the little black butterfly falls to the sole of her Chanel ballet flat and dies.

"All right, should we begin?"

❖·CHAPTER TWENTY-TWO·❖

*B*unny and her classmates gather around the museum guide, a Black man wearing a uniform with a gold pin, a tiny American flag at its center, and a security earpiece. "I call this the time machine," he says as they wait for the doors of the elevator to open. He is missing his two front teeth. Bunny remembers the officer in front of the women's shelter who was missing a tooth; she wonders if there is a connection or if it is a coincidence. As they wait, Bunny peers around the corner at the welcome center. A huge sign on the wall at the entrance of the National Museum of African American History and Culture identifies its donors: WALMART.

"You will begin at the transatlantic slave trade, then travel through slavery, segregation, and the civil rights movement up until today," says the museum guide. Giant glass doors of the elevator part, and Bunny and her classmates pile in. They descend to the bottom level, passing dates on the wall: 1948, 1776, 1619, 1565, 1400.

The students of St. Peter's Academy join the clusters of little white boys wearing American government propaganda, red hats and T-shirts, strolling through a maze of history. The irony feels breathtaking for anyone who's noticed. The exhibit is dark and there are no windows. Bunny watches in disbelief as her classmates whiz by each story and window display and photograph and map, for they are without supervision—this is a prime environment for academic escapism, flirting, and discreet raucousness. *Museums are boring! History is boring!*

Billy throws his arm around Bunny and reads a quote on the wall below an African queen: "'I admit I am sickened at the purchase of slaves . . . but I must be mumm, for how could we do without sugar and rum?'! . . . Wanna come over tonight? My parents are going to some ambassador event and won't be home till late."

Bunny ignores him, reading a panel about African royalty before the slave trade.

"Hey," Billy says, closer to her ear.

"I can't," Bunny replies, trying to focus on sugar plantations and growing capitalism.

"Why not?" Billy feels irked by her rejection.

"I'm . . . helping my mother clean out my grandmother's closet."

Stan walks up between them to read a description below a photograph of American slave owners: *Plantation owners often enlisted their slaves to take their place in war.*

"Vhat the fuck. Vhat a bunch of inferior pussies," Stan says.

"Accurate," Bunny replies, relieved by the interruption.

"In Rvhussia, vhe just enslave everybody!"

"Come on, you're not going to be at your grandmother's that late," Billy pleads. "What's going on with you?"

Bunny breaks her historical trance and turns to Billy, his back against a display of framed Civil War–era dollar bills. She lowers her voice. "All right, I have to tell you something, but you have to swear that you will not tell *anyone.*"

"Not even Stan?"

Stan skips ahead of them.

"Stop, I'm not joking."

"Okay, okay. . . ."

"You can't judge me, I mean it."

"Okay!" Billy says defensively.

Bunny gives him a mistrustful look; her eyes dart left, then right before she steps close to his face. "I met the man who's been accused of killing Audrey and her family."

Billy furrows his brow; a long pause. *"What?"*

"I went to the DC Jail. I met him. Well, it was more like FaceTi—"

"Wait, *what?*"

"Shhh! I told you not to judge me."

Billy looks around the exhibit to ensure no one is listening, Stan has gone up to the Point of Pines cabin. Billy pulls Bunny's arm, corners her. "What are you talking about?"

Bunny jerks her arm away. *"I—went—to—meet—the—man—accused—"*

"I fucking heard you—but *why?* Why would you do that?" He runs his hand through his tousled hair.

"Because I wanted to. Because we don't have enough information. Why the fuck would someone murder an entire family? *Two reasons:* he's innocent, or they deserved it and we're next. . . ."

"What the fuck, Bunny, what is *wrong* with you?"

"What is wrong with *me?* What the fuck is wrong with all of *you?* No one is talking about this!"

"Maybe because it's *over* and this shit is *dark*, and people don't want to talk about it for a good reason. That psychopath has been put *away*. Drop it!"

"But what if he *didn't* do it? Look at where we're fucking standing! And you know what, I *don't* think he did it," Bunny says, provoking him, even if she's still unsure.

Billy rolls his head back in disbelief. *"Ohhh* my God. *Whoa."* He turns his back to Bunny, releasing her from the corner. He walks away.

"Stop, I'm *serious!*" Bunny says, chasing after him before a stranger shushes her.

Billy pivots back to her. "You're ridiculous *and* fucking crazy."

Bunny stands abandoned by her secret, betrayed by Billy's response. Something has erupted in her and she's not sure what it is; her legs and arms are buzzing. Looking around, she catches Marty and Mackenzie talking on a bench below a glowing portrait of Harriet Tubman. Marty's been to the museum more times than he can count. His parents are board members. He's trying to undo Mackenzie's bra without getting caught.

"Marty!" Mackenzie whacks him on the arm. "Put it back!" Marty has succeeded in unhooking her bra without taking her shirt off.

"I'm sorry, I'm sorry." Marty laughs, trying to rehook it through her shirt. He pushes his glasses up his nose.

Bunny approaches. She needs an ally. She knows Mackenzie feels insecure about her social status. "Mack, what are you doing tonight?"

Mackenzie spins around, delighted to get Bunny's attention and swooned by her new nickname. "Hi, uh, not sure, just homework, I guess. . . . You?" she asks, trying to redeem herself.

"Wanna come see my grandmother's house? It's like a private museum—with a little more *joie de vivre*," Bunny says.

"Sure! I'll text my mom."

"Great." Bunny will tell her tonight.

⤜⧉⤝

Bunny leads Mackenzie into her late grandmother's town house. Mackenzie catches a whiff of Phyllis's Chanel Number Five residue and sneezes. She drops her violin case to the hardwood floor with a pathetic thud.

"I should've warned you about the dust and mothballs," Bunny says, plopping down on Meredith's recently indented cushion on the sofa. She lights a cigarette, cracks open the Coke she picked up at the new Wawa around the corner.

"It's okay," Mackenzie says, wiping snot with the end of her navy sweater. She looks around at all memorabilia left on the bookless bookshelves. "Is your mom here?"

"No," Bunny replies, relaxed.

"Oh, 'cause my mom said I could be here as long as your mom would be here too." Truly, it was under the condition that Mackenzie would report back everything she could gather from spending time with Mrs. Bartholomew.

Bunny blows smoke in Mackenzie's direction. "Do you always listen to what your mother tells you to do?"

"No," Mackenzie says. Trying to relieve the tension between them, she reaches down and grabs the cigarette out of Bunny's hand, takes a drag. Bunny studies her lips, aroused by her new and sudden defiance. Mackenzie pretends to inhale, the smoke swirling around in her hot mouth. She holds out the cigarette to Bunny.

"Keep it," Bunny says, knowing she faked it. "So what's going on with you and Marty?"

Mackenzie inhales again. "Uh—" She tries not to cough, her chest rising, her nostrils flaring before she catches new air. "I dunno. . . ."

"I think he likes you," Bunny taunts. "No. Actually, I think he *loves* you."

"You do?"

"Oh yeah. I've known Marty since nursery school, he definitely wants you to be his girlfriend."

"Really?"

"Uh, duh."

Mackenzie puts out the cigarette on Meredith's ashtray, next to remnants of a lipstick-stained stub, black and red and scrunched. "Okay, can you keep a secret?"

"Pinkie swear." Bunny extends her pinkie. Mackenzie follows, locking eyes and fingers.

"We made out after study group on Tuesday. He drove me home."

Bunny smiles, lights another cigarette, then lights the Dyptique scented candle on the table while she's at it—for *ambience*. "Did you go down on him?"

"Not yet, but I gave him a hand job in the car."

"Nice." Bunny taps the ash off the end of her cigarette.

"Well, except I didn't make him come. My dad kept blowing up my phone because I was out past curfew."

"Oh no, you blue-baller!" Bunny laughs.

"I didn't mean to!"

"Okay, okay, my turn." Bunny twists her body to face Mackenzie. "Can *you* keep a secret?"

"Pinkie swear." Mackenzie extends her pinkie.

"I went to the DC Jail and met the man who murdered Audrey Banks and her parents."

Mackenzie's jaw drops. "Whoa."

"I know," says Bunny. "Let me pour us some shots." She gets up and walks over to the wet bar, still filled with Waterford crystal decanters. She pulls out two crystal glasses and pours a few inches of bourbon in each.

"What was it like?" asks Mackenzie, on the edge of her seat.

Bunny hands her the glass. "Bottoms up." She swigs, then slams the glass on the table. "Well, it was kinda weird because it was over video and there was a lot of static in the beginning. I think he's like just a few years older than us, which is crazy." Bunny doesn't tell Mackenzie that Anthony accused her of treating him like he was her zoo animal to observe, and how the experience shook her, the violence she saw on the screen after propelling herself into a universe that wanted nothing to do with her.

"That's crazy." Mackenzie isn't sure what to say or ask. "So, were you scared at all? Was he scary?"

"No. I'm going to go back and see him again," Bunny says, matter-of-fact, testing Mackenzie's newfound loyalty. She goes to pour another round of shots, hands Mackenzie another glass. "Here, on the count of three—one, two, three—" She throws it back, slams the glass down on the table.

Mackenzie leaves half of the shot in the glass.

"So do your parents know about Marty?" Bunny asks.

"No, definitely not," Mackenzie replies.

"Why do you say it like that? Like it would be the end of the world if they knew?" Bunny asks, fishing for racism.

"Uh, I mean . . . I think they'd be fine with it. I mean, Marty's applying to all Ivy Leagues, so—"

"What's that supposed to mean? Like he wouldn't be worthy if he wasn't applying to Ivy Leagues? Because he's Black?"

"No! No, I didn't mean it like that. . . ."

"Then what did you mean?"

"It's just . . . Okay, you really can't tell anyone this, you *seriously* can't, because I mean, I love my parents. . . ."

"I swear I won't say anything." Bunny squirms closer to her on the couch.

"There was this one time when my grandmama was really sick with lung cancer and she was in one of those homes, you know, where you basically go to die, and anyway, when my parents and I were there with her an . . . African American nurse came into the room and my father was, like, super aggressive with her. He was like, 'Who are you, why are you in here,' and the nurse was like, 'I'm here to help Mrs. Wallace with her medication, sir,' she was the nicest woman, and my dad was a total *dick*, he was like, 'I need you to leave immediately and get someone else in here.' And the whole thing just felt so fucking—"

"Racist." Bunny cuts her off.

Mackenzie is visibly ashamed. "Yeah."

"I get it, it's *super* fucked up."

"It's *so* fucked up," Mackenzie echoes, picking at the back of her head unconsciously, triggered, pulling out a strand of her hair.

"This is one of the reasons I went to the jail." Bunny blows smoke to the side, considering. "There was this one time I was with Audrey, I had taken my dad's Audi to pick up a dime before one of Stan's parties, and we got lost off of I-395 and ended up in some neighborhood in Southeast, it was still light out, maybe around four in the afternoon and we came to a stop sign, had our windows down, Audrey vaping, me smoking, and there was a few Black kids standing on the corner with their backpacks on and one of them shouted, 'Nice car!' And Audrey yelled back, 'Work hard and you can have one too!' and just before she rolled up her window, one of the boys yelled back, 'Yeah, right, your daddy bought you that car!' And Audrey gave him the finger. And then I stepped on the gas, afraid they would jump us. And you know, that kid was fucking right. He was probably, I dunno, twelve years old. I mean, it *was* my dad's car. He was right. And I felt disgusting. It was just a few weeks after that that Audrey died."

Mackenzie gazes at Bunny, but Bunny can't tell if she's listening or if she's dissociated—or if she's staying silent because she isn't sure how to respond and doesn't want to say the wrong thing. . . . A few seconds later, Mackenzie asks, "So do you think one of those boys murdered her?"

"Noooo," Bunny replies, frustrated that her point isn't resonating, a stark reminder of what it is she is beginning to see and can't understand why others might not see it too. "It's just an example of our white privilege, and because Audrey didn't see it, she got angry about it."

"But if you *do* work hard you *can* have a nice car—I mean, isn't that true? That's what my dad always says."

"Your dad the racist?" Bunny says.

It stings Mackenzie, hearing it come from someone other than herself.

Bunny pulls back, remembering she came here to get an ally not a frenemy. This complicated need to be heard—she's unsure if she's willing to accept the cost of it, and what would it mean to challenge her? "I just mean, we were born into everything and those kids saw it, like they knew it just from looking at us, and it makes me think about why this guy would want to murder Audrey's family. Why would he torture them first? I've seen too many movies, and you need a motive. And . . . maybe the Bankses *were* racist. Maybe they *were* terrible people."

Mackenzie thinks for a moment, a look of uncertainty across her face. "Yeah, but that doesn't mean you murder someone for it! And if he didn't do it, then who did?"

"That's what I don't know. . . ." Bunny says.

They stare ahead, a black-and-white portrait of Bunny's great-grandmother looking down at them from across the room, her hair swooped up into a bun atop her head.

"Do you love Marty?" Bunny asks, switching the subject back.

"I—you can't tell him."

"You totally love him, I can tell. . . . Don't worry, I won't say anything."

"What's your Insta handle?" Mackenzie asks, hoping Bunny will follow her back.

"It's bb_queen."

"I'm Mackattack1."

Bunny takes out her phone and opens the app, pauses on Mackenzie's profile for a moment, unsure if she wants to follow her, before impulsively hitting the Follow button.

"Oh my God, look at what Haley just posted, my little sister." Mackenzie hands Bunny her phone.

Bunny looks at the photograph. "Oh, shit, that's Linda Williams."

"You know her?" Mackenzie asks, intrigued.

"My mom knows her, they belong to our club. My mom does *not* like that woman. She says she's a gossip, doesn't trust her. . . . Your sister *slays*."

"I think my mom wants to belong to your club because she keeps showing me pictures."

"Interesting," Bunny says with enthusiastic skepticism.

⚜

Later that evening, when Betsy picks up Mackenzie from her so-called playdate with Bunny, she asks, "So, how did you like Mrs. Bartholomew?" To which Mackenzie replies, "She was lovely. But she thinks Mrs. Williams is a gossip and not to be trusted."

❧•CHAPTER TWENTY-THREE•❧

Spring Valley, the "suburb" of the district, home to newscasters and lobbyists, lawyers and partners at Deloitte, was built on top of WWI bombs and a chemical weapons testing site. Before the gray stone mansions, swimming pools, and swing sets, it was an open valley scattered with buried canisters—chemical mortar rounds and 75-millimeter shells of mustard gas, a lethal substance that causes internal and external bleeding, blisters, and blindness. It was a year before the murders that Mr. Cowan, Chase's dad, was mowing his lawn one Saturday morning when Lincoln, their black Lab, began yelping and whining at the orange plastic fence of the construction site next door for the soon-to-be nine-thousand-square-foot mansion for some diplomat. Mr. Cowan looked at Lincoln to find liquid coming out of his eyes and mouth. Most families agreed to move out after that, to have the ground around their houses inspected for more bombs. Not the Cowans, afraid the value of their house would go down. Men in orange hazmat suits would wave from across the fence each morning while Mr. Cowan sipped his coffee and read the *Washington Post*. He still has his safe room equipped with the lie detector where he will occasionally ask Chase if he's addicted to drugs or stolen any of his money.

Marty, Stan, and Billy are hunched over Chase's laptop. The safe room is covered in blankets and pillows and there's an old television set up for video games; four controllers take up most of the floor space, and it smells like sweaty gym bags. Add in the metal door with gadgets and bolted locks, and it's a cross between a teenage boy's man cave and solitary confinement.

"Watch this, it's going to change your life," says Chase. Stan pulls a bottle of Everclear from his backpack, takes a swig, then passes it to Billy. Chase logs into a private Vimeo account. Marty slides his glasses up his nose and inches closer to the screen as a young brunette makes her way over to a four-posted canopy bed.

"We're going to Paris, baby." Chase laughs. The girl, in her school uniform, green plaid skirt, white collared shirt, Adidas, unclasps her bra from under her shirt and throws it on the floor, her nipples poking through cotton. She places herself on the bed and lifts up her right leg so you can see her pink underwear. This is not a girl from St. Peter's Academy. This is a girl from the all-girls Holden Farms, which the boys from the all-boys school call Ho-town Farms as though they themselves were exempt from any *fuck-boy* titles. Her father is a weapons dealer and spends most of the year in the Middle East; she most often serves along the lines of an expense report rather than a daughter.

She settles into the pillow as a jock steps into the frame wearing a number seventeen jersey.

"Dude, is that Kevin Dallinger?" asks Billy.

"Sure is," replies Marty, "it's your boy!" He pats Billy on the back. Kevin is on the rival baseball team.

"That little fucking slut," Billy whispers at the computer, referring to Kevin, "let's see those ginger pubes."

Stan starts laughing uncontrollably as they watch Kevin on-screen pull down his pants, then climb onto the bed. "I can't, I can't!" Stan doubles over.

"Wait for it, wait for it . . ." Chase's enthusiasm catches fire; he pinches the tip of his crotch, scooting closer to his laptop. "We're goin' to the Eiffel Tower, baby!"

The recording shakes on-screen. The person filming sets the camera down on the fireplace mantel, creating a full frontal shot of the queen-size bed.

As the jock reveals himself on camera, Billy, Stan, and Marty—in unison—cup their hands over their mouths and yell, *"Ohhhh!!!"*

"No fuckin' way is that Danny Davis, I fuckin' knew he was gay." Billy fist-bumps Marty as if they had a bet going. Stan takes another swig of Everclear, then pulls a Juul out of his pocket and takes a hit.

The girl removes her pink underwear, flinging it across the room, and gets on all fours as Kevin positions himself on his knees in front of her. Danny climbs onto the bed, naked, and positions himself behind her, creating the appearance of a girl/boy Eiffel Tower, the girl at its center, the bridge, as she blows Kevin and allows Danny to take her from behind.

Chase falls over laughing. "It's so good!"

"Yo, Billy, I wanna do Eiffel Tower with you and Bunny." Stan does a little dance.

"Fuck you, dude. . . . My Eiffel Tower days are over," Billy says, feigning old-man wisdom.

"Oh, your Eiffel Tower days? As if you had any?" Marty calls bullshit and laughs. "You wish, man."

"Oh yeah, you've never even been to *Paris* yet, you pussy," Billy says, insinuating *virgin*.

"Yeah, Smarty, you gonna tap New Girl?" Chase asks.

"Shut up, man," Marty replies, embarrassed he hasn't lost his virginity yet. "I've been focusing on school and applications and shit, I haven't had time."

"Uh-huh," Billy replies as if that's the lamest excuse he's ever heard.

"Some of us actually have to *work* to get into school instead of having our dad's last name." Marty hits where it hurts.

Billy stays eerily calm as if hunting for prey before he gets up and takes a step toward Marty. He backs him up against the wall, cocked head, eyes locked. "What the fuck did you just say to me?" Billy's mouth is so close to Marty's face he could lick him.

"I said some of us have to *actually work* to get into school instead of having daddy's last name."

Billy grabs Marty by the arms and slams his back against the wall. "Fuck you." Then spits on the floor, walks over, and unbolts the safe room door. Before he walks out, he turns around. "Fucking virgin." Then slams the door on them.

Stan, Chase, and Marty look at each other for a moment in silence.

"Why is he being so fucking sensitive?" Marty asks, trying to defuse the situation.

"Dude, that was so unnecessary—you scored a twenty-four hundred on your SATs and your parents are on the board of like every fucking charity in town."

"Vhait, Billy's dad isn't famous. I don't get it," Stan says.

"He's about to become the new secretary of defense, asshole," says Chase.

"Oh right, well, hope he doesn't blow us up."

Billy walks down the long driveway out to his Ford pickup across the street. The cold wind strikes him as if he's been pushed into an icy pool, knocking off his baseball cap; he catches it midair when he notices a black Suburban in front of the Mexican Embassy just a few doors down, a single man watching from the driver's seat. Paranoid, Billy pulls the baseball cap low over his eyes, jumps in his truck, and peels off.

The first snow flurries swirl above thorn bushes surrounding the frame of the Montgomerys' house.

"Fuck." Billy pulls into the driveway. He can see his mother rinsing a wineglass through the window above the kitchen sink but can't see his father. Even if he tried to sneak in through the basement and take the elevator up to his room, they might hear its creaking, climbing through the walls.

Billy, instead, decides to greet her in the kitchen, praying his father isn't home.

"Where have you been?" Carol asks, the skin on her fingertips white and shriveled, hearing Billy's footsteps behind her. "I texted you multiple times." She doesn't make eye contact with him.

"I was at Chase's studying for midterms. I thought you had an event."

"We didn't go to the event. There was a military emergency." The pressure of Carol's hand on the sponge inside the wineglass causes it to pop and shatter. It slices her hand. She stumbles back.

"Mom." Billy goes to her.

"I'm fine, it's just a little glass." She wraps her finger in a white dishtowel, her back against the corner cabinet. Billy sees her teeth are purple.

"Let me look," he says, seeing blood streaming into the garbage disposal.

"I said, *I'm fine.*" Carol takes a strenuous breath.

"Did Dad say what kind of emergency it was?" Billy studies his mother's body language.

"It doesn't matter. Your father isn't happy, but he doesn't have time to not be happy, or to make sure that we're happy. . . ." She is beginning to ramble.

"Mom, are you okay?" He is attuned to his mother's vulnerability for the first time—the absence of his father, the soon-to-be absence of her last son, plunging her into invisibility—and it unnerves him. Carol's days at the library are quiet, yet the solitude seems to be dissolving into an unexpected kind of cold loneliness.

"You need to confirm you are going to West Point, the press is making inquiries. That's all your father wanted me to say to you."

"Mom, I haven't received an e-mail yet," Billy replies, as if there's still a chance he'll be rejected.

Carol holds herself up with both hands resting on the counter behind her, pink blood seeping through the dishtowel. She locks eyes with him. "Tomorrow," she says, "do not push your father to the edge."

Billy throws her look away deep down with everything else he refuses to release inside of him, and leaves the kitchen. He leaps three steps at a time up the stairwell, a portrait of his grandfather, a D-Day WWII hero and survivor of a plane crash, watching as Billy runs for his room.

Settling on top of his comforter, he taps on his e-mail app.

Dear William Montgomery,

It is with great pleasure that I write to offer you admission to New York University . . .

⊰•CHAPTER TWENTY-FOUR•⊱

Cate sits at her desk, two rooms over from Doug. Another mass shooting has happened since the music festival and now—and in this moment, Cate asks the young intern to change the somehow monotonous breaking news to C-SPAN's White House press conference. She needs to observe, learn, watch, wait, judge. Despite this cozy historical (*hysterical?*) office's privacy, it is public terrain, although average pedestrians often forget that anyone can come knocking. The channel switches.

A knock at the outer office door. The new, overqualified, and wealthy inheritance-survivor intern turns the brass doorknob. A young female reporter stands in Hunter rain boots. She looks overwhelmingly groomed. She probably graduated from Brown.

"Hi, I'm Anne Price with the *Washington Post*, I'm looking for Cate Bartholomew. Is she available?"

The intern doesn't speak, having signed a nondisclosure agreement upon getting hired. He simply turns around and walks to Cate's desk. "Someone is here to see you from the *Post*."

"What?" Cate says.

"She's in the doorway."

"Okay, well, ask her what she wants." Cate's heart starts to pound, belying her smooth outer appearance. *Did they find out about the affair?*

"She wouldn't tell me," the intern says.

Cate glares, beyond irritated but aware she can't appear overly irritated or it might raise a red flag. She removes herself from her written document on behalf of Walter on behalf of Doug on behalf of the committee-of-white-men hearing on the Violence against Women Act on behalf of women, stands, and steps over to the reporter, who is not much older than she is.

"Can I help you?" Cate asks.

"Hi, Cate, I'm Anne from the *Washington Post*, do you have a minute?"

Cate feels as if the police have arrived at her front door with some horrific news. "What is this regarding?" She looks over her right shoulder, Doug's legislative director peering from his wooden cubicle to see who this pedestrian is who has appeared at their office door unannounced.

"Would you like to step outside for a minute?" Anne asks, but it's more of a suggestion.

"Let me grab my coat." Cate saunters to the back of her chair and whips her trench coat over her shoulders like a woman who knows what she's doing.

The strong smell of coffee grounds blazes through the crowded Starbucks on North Capitol. Cate nurses a pumpkin spiced latte.

"You like to do things the old-school way—we don't get reporters showing up at our office unless the Senate is voting."

"In-person is always better than an e-mail or phone call, plus I don't trust anyone in this town."

Cate's radar goes off. *Green reporter and new to Washington.*

Completely evident by the most basic statement Cate's been hearing from Washington newcomers since she was a little girl sitting in Aunt Meredith and Uncle Chuck's living room talking about the political merry-go-round and those who will never make it more than a few years in the swamp. *I don't trust anyone in this town.* The girl has a point, but if you're in it for the long haul, the point is *irrelevant.* Cate does what she's learned to do best in situations where she has the upper hand.

She placates.

"Completely," Cate replies.

"Do you know this man with Senator Wallace?" Anne pulls up a photograph on her iPhone. The photo shows a man with a sad face, round spectacles, gold Rolex, boat shoes, argyle sweater. He is standing between illuminated white columns of an old mansion; his arm is around Doug's shoulders, but Doug's head is turning away from the camera and toward the front door.

Cate studies the photograph. "I've never seen that man before in my life. . . . What is this about? I only have a few minutes."

"We've launched an investigation into several high-powered men, a wide range of cases from verbal sexual harassment, to assault, to rape. A few of these men appear to have met at the home of Albert Rasmussen, former top lobbyist at Hill and Knowl—"

"I've heard of him."

"Well, this is Tim Miller, and several women have come forward with strong corroborating evidence of harassment and assault."

"Okay," Cate replies, waiting for more information.

"Have you dealt with or are you dealing with any inappropriate behaviors by Senator Wallace or any other staffer within your office at the Capitol?"

Cate can't believe this is happening. It's too soon. She's had no preparation. She thought she was in *love.* And she can't throw Walter under the bus—not yet, not until she has a plan. She knows she has to think this through very carefully. Another thing she learned from Aunt Meredith: Washington is a small town. It's not like Los Angeles or New York where you can reinvent yourself; when you're out—You're Out.

"No, no, Doug—Senator Wallace has the utmost integrity. Everyone is very professional and thrilled, truly, to be of service—and to see Senator Wallace get all of this wonderful new exposure."

She is proud of herself for that *thrilled*, a word she picked up from Meredith and her social sector of women who seem to enjoy adjectives like *divine* and *dashing*; it makes her feel mature.

"Cate, you're one of the few new press secretaries who are women, and a very young woman to be in such a position, so I wanted to extend an olive branch—to let you know I am here if anything comes up or if anything has already come up and you're just not comfortable enough yet sharing it. I know there isn't a truly safe place for you to go, so consider me that."

Cate tries not to laugh at Anne's absurd statement. "I truly appreciate it, and the women who are coming forward are so brave and paving the way for our future—here in Washington, and across the globe," she replies without missing a beat.

Anne takes a minute to study Cate's body language, as though connected to a lie detector. "Of course, Senator Wallace *was* with Mr. Rasmussen that night. The night this photograph was taken." Anne pulls up another photograph of Doug, alone, exiting the home through the same moonlit entrance, later the same night.

"And . . . ?" Cate replies, teetering on hardball.

"And you know what they say time and time again: 'Birds of a feather flock together.'"

Cate stands up, feeling on the cusp of disrespected. . . . Has she misread the reporter? Was the statement about trust an affront, a clue, so as to cue Cate to armor up, or is Anne on her side? Does she genuinely want the best for her? Or is Anne just in it for her own personal recognition? If she breaks a big story and knocks out multiple members of Congress and businessmen, what's in it for Cate other than the loss of a job and being victimized? This isn't *Hollywood*.

"I will reach out to you if I experience any misconduct, Anne. Thank you for all that you are doing—for your service to these women."

Anne doesn't budge. "Think about it. My door is always open."

Cate struts down North Capitol whispering to herself: *"Fuck fuck fuck fuck fuck fuck fuck fuck fuck . . ."*

CHAPTER TWENTY-FIVE

The pressure from the flat white sky strains Bunny's eyes into squints as she approaches the wrought iron gates of the graveyard in a black oversize snow coat and backpack, marking her turn to the visiting center when her cell phone rings. Bunny stops in front of the brick fence and picks up. "Hey." She drops her backpack next to her.

It's Billy. "I got in," he tells her.

"To NYU?" she asks, beaming with anticipation.

"Yeah," Billy says, smiling on the other end of the phone.

Bunny can feel Billy's joy in how he says it. She hops up on the brick wall—it's a moment worthy of pausing—lets her legs dangle over a headstone beside the stone statue of a praying angel.

"Holy shit, Billy."

"I know," he says in a more solemn tone.

"What are you gonna do?"

"Send them my regrets and rejection, I guess," he says, wishing Bunny could save him from this truth while knowing she'll never be able to.

"What? Billy, come on, you have to go. This is your *dream*. Fuck your parents."

"You don't get it—"

"Of course I get it, and I say *FUCK—YOUR—PARENTS.*"

"But my dad—"

"You're not your dad, Billy. I know you think you need to be, but you don't. You just don't." Bunny hits where it hurts. And she knows it. She tries to backpedal. "Just accept who you are—it's . . ." She kicks the heel of her boot into the brick sheepishly. ". . . why I love you."

"What's up with you? Why are you acting like you suddenly think you know everything?" Billy says defensively.

"What? What's your problem? I'm trying to encourage you to be free of your dad's fucking rein."

"Who's going to pay for it, Bunny? Who's going to pay for NYU? My father will fucking disown me if I don't go to the academy."

Feeling a headache coming on, Bunny hops off the brick wall, the clock ticking before she needs to walk around the corner to make it in time to see Anthony. She checks her phone. Five minutes.

Billy feels her distance. *"Hello?"*

"Did you call to tell me or to fight with me?"

"Would *you* cut yourself off from *your* parents?" Billy asks. It's a legitimate question.

Bunny starts walking briskly down the sidewalk; a branch grazes her cheek, dripping over from the graveyard, and she whisks it away, rubbing her fingers into broken skin. "I gotta go," she says, stonewalling, unable to fathom an answer to the question, too distracted by her need to get to Anthony.

"You wouldn't, would you," Billy taunts. "You're such a hypocrite."

"I didn't ask for this," Bunny erupts, "and neither did you! Just talk to your dad, bet you haven't even tried! Stop being so afraid of him." She passes a man sleeping in a car, waiting for someone, to visit, or be released.

"Whatever, Bunny, I gotta go," Billy says.

"Yeah, I said that first." Bunny goes to press End, but the button's already disappeared, Billy has hung up. *"Ugh,"* she grunts, and drops her phone in her pocket.

*   *   *

Bunny sits in one of the blue plastic chairs amid mothers and wives, girlfriends, sons and daughters, pulls out a Moleskine journal and pen. The heat is broken today. A fan conspicuously spins above her head, making the experience all the more troublesome and freezing. She waits and glances at the woman in the cubby beside her, yelling something into the receiver, before Anthony appears on-screen wearing an orange jumpsuit, hunched over, his left hand resting in between his knees. Bunny turns her attention to the screen, focused. She wants to tell him the truth about herself, that her name isn't Grace, that she isn't a reporter, that she was friends with Audrey Banks, knew her parents, knew the housekeeper, knows how they died, knew that Audrey was entitled and could be mean, *but so could Bunny*. . . . She's afraid to tell. She can't. Not now, and maybe not ever, as long as they're being watched and listened to.

"Why'd you come back?" Anthony asks.

"Because I *do* care and I . . . question a lot of what's been written about, or what *hasn't* been written about, and I want to understand," Bunny says, her palms sweating over her journal.

Anthony welcomes her moxie for such a white, privileged little thing. "You ever visited a jail before you met me, Grace?"

". . . Yes," Bunny says, trying not to blush from her shame *(liar)*, staring down at her blank notebook. She swallows. Looks up. "How about you? Had you ever been arrested before this?"

"Would it matter?" he says.

Anthony's response catching her off guard, Bunny wonders if it's because her question affirms racist assumptions or is irrelevant given what she's learned from the Black Lives Matter movement, which in hindsight makes her regret asking. She tries to think quickly, shamefully unsticking the question from herself: "To some it might."

Anthony swivels, distracted by commotion in the background again, yelling, pushing, a body slammed against the wall before two correctional officers restrain the inmates. He ducks back toward the screen when it's clear and safe to do so. Bunny watches in distress, relieved when he spins back to her. "Is it like that all the time in there?" she asks.

"Oh, you wanna find out?" Anthony asks like it's a dare.

"Why'd you show up for the visit again if you aren't sure about me?" Bunny asks, challenging him, her fragile ego unable to help from making it about herself.

"Why do you think?" he asks.

Bunny tilts her head, puts down her pen. "Because I imagine given the accusations you probably don't have any visitors."

Anthony chuckles at all that Bunny doesn't know, undeserving of his vulnerability. "Nah, that's not why. . . ."

"Then why?" she asks, more interested and surprised by having not hit him where she assumed it would hurt.

"You look like you have money." He tilts his chin up.

Bunny laughs, uncomfortable. "Excuse me?"

"Your shiny long hair. Fancy jacket. I see you: you're moneyed up. Like a catalogue behind that pen and paper."

In a panic, anything to prevent her from already feeling fraudulent, there's nothing to do but take his side, *take his side and get him to trust you.* Bunny nods, accepting the reality of how she looks against the backdrop of the jail's visiting center. "Yep, that's right," she admits, admitting the thing she's starting to wish she didn't have, realizing in these moments with him that it's better to shut up and listen.

Anthony leans back in his chair, more relaxed, surprised Bunny didn't try to defend herself. Doesn't say anything.

"Okay, so you're right, except it's my *parents' money,* not mine," she says, her immaturity and lack of adulthood rearing its ugly head. Her eyes dart around the room, a spike of paranoia hitting her.

"Same thing," Anthony says.

She's irked, Billy's question lingering in her head: *Would you cut your parents off? Hypocrite.* "What about *your* parents?" Bunny asks. Suddenly realizing *he has parents, must've had parents, or still has parents?* Which is weird to think, because whenever Bunny's seen murderers in the news, it's as if they were created (*poof!*) out of thin air, somehow landing on earth without ever having a family, a mother, a father, a daughter or son, without having ever been human.

"What about my parents?" he asks.

"Are you in touch with them?"

"Course," Anthony says, but Bunny's bias is skeptical.

"Where are they?" she asks, prodding his boundaries as if he doesn't have the right to any.

"Mom's home. . . ." he says, but doesn't continue.

"What about your dad?" She sees Anthony fidget. "Where's he?"

Anthony rubs his forehead and looks down, still holding the receiver to his ear. She hit a heartstring.

Feeling uncomfortable, Bunny fills the silence. "My dad's not around that much either. He works a lot, he's working so much right now I haven't really seen him in weeks, and I turn—my birthday is coming up and he's probably going to miss it. But he'll certainly buy me a nice *shiny present* to make up for it!"

Anthony looks up into the screen. "My pops would never miss my birthday," he tells her with conviction. Bunny's racial bias shatters across her feet, her hope of finding something—anything (*the dad card, surely?*)—in common with Anthony.

"Oh," she replies, embarrassed. "Well, that's lucky."

"My dad's dead, if you think that's lucky too, and if he were alive, he'd *never* miss a birthday."

Shame flips on inside Bunny's head. "I—I didn't realize, I'm sorry. . . ."

"You probably don't realize a lot of things," he says.

Bunny grips the phone tight, clenching her jaw, trying not to show how suddenly fragile she feels. "How did he die, if . . . you don't mind me asking?" Unsure of how a journalist might ask, she opts for *good manners*.

The screen goes static. "Anthony?" Bunny grunts and waits a few seconds before smacking the side of the screen. "*Ughhhhhh.*" She grits her teeth, looks behind her to see the officer glaring *do not hit the monitor, ma'am.*

"Anthony, you there?"

His face appears and then disappears into long squiggles across the screen. "Yeah, I can hear you," he says.

Bunny leans over toward the screen, holds the receiver against her chin, and says in a very low voice, "This system fucking sucks . . . it's garbage."

"Easy, they don't like anyone starting shit over there."

Bunny likes the irony of Anthony telling her to behave, seesawing from believing in his guilt to believing in his innocence. She redirects the conversation back to his father. "I'll behave—and I'm sorry," she admits. "For saying that, or thinking that, about, you know, your dad. And, I shouldn't have."

She looks down at her lap; when validation does not come to her, she looks back up at Anthony, who is silent in his gaze. Bunny wonders about his unwillingness to contain and hold her revelation, as if he somehow owed this to her? Is his silence a semblance of his guilt, or a semblance of his responsibility to protect himself? She stirs, uncomfortable in the nuance; she doesn't understand, cramped inside her own white skin.

"Oh, are you waiting for some kind of *forgiveness?*" he says.

Bunny, tripping over her thoughts: "I . . . no. I'm sorry." She is careful in her tone; a beat between them. "I'm sorry, I'm . . . but can I ask how he died?" Still afraid he'll hang up again, but willing to take the risk.

Anthony examines her, noticing the lump in her throat building. "Lung cancer," he says.

"Was he a smoker?"

"Never smoked a day in his life."

"How do you think he got it?"

Anthony breathes in. "From the chemical plants."

"Chemical plants? Did he work for one?"

"Yep."

"Which one?" Bunny opens her journal again, pins the receiver between her ear and her shoulder.

"Same one I worked for," he says, looking straight into the monitor.

Bunny takes the receiver back in her hand and looks up at him. "But, the company—the Banks family company?" Bunny's heart starts to pound. *So is he guilty?* Confused and refraining from assumption, it hits her in the gut.

Commotion again in the background, inmates fighting, a television blaring, the sound of metal clanking metal, doors opening and locking, static lines again.

"Anthony . . ." Bunny says, hitting the side of the monitor. "*this fucking thing.*"

He appears again. "I'm not supposed to be talking to you," he says.

"If you don't talk to me, how am I supposed to help you?"

"You wanna help me? That why you're here? Really?"

"I—I want to know the truth so I can help . . . but I need to know what happened," Bunny says, trying to keep it vague, trying not to lose her sense of self, the reason she came here to begin with, *selfish and self-seeking.*

"You're not my fucking lawyer," he says, growing frustrated, mistrustful, angry.

"I know I'm not. . . . *Who is,* by the way? And why isn't anyone *talking* about this? About your dad? I don't understand—"

"Who's my fuckin' lawyer? A broke-ass public defender is my fuckin' lawyer, you think I got money to get a fuckin' lawyer for myself? That's for people like you. . . . It wasn't in the news because they don't want people like you knowing the company did anything wrong, that they're all fuckin' killers, that's why."

"But . . . it would give you a motive, it would look clear why you did it, because of your dad."

"I didn't fucking do anything!" he yells into the phone.

Startled, Bunny jumps back into her chair, then composes herself so as not to look vulnerable in front of the guard. "Okay, wait, I didn't mean it like that. . . ." she says, breathing faster.

"I stormed into the owner's office one afternoon, David Banks," Anthony says in angst, "and I cussed the motherfucker out, screaming at him. He killed my pops. He didn't even apologize, he just stood there with blood on his hands and pressed some button on his phone, then security came and took me away. So they blamed me for the deaths."

"I—I'm so sorry, Anthony."

"My father was a good man. He didn't deserve that. I didn't deserve that." He shakes his head in trauma and disbelief.

A moment of silence passes between them, neither one looking into the monitor.

"They said you were disgruntled because you got fired," Bunny says, trying to bury the terror of the possibility that he did do it, confirming the worst of her suspicions.

"Yeah, they fired me after that."

"But they never said why you were fired in the news."

"Nope. . . ."

Bunny hesitates; the ball is moving too fast and she feels a little uneasy, a little unsure if she's up for this, if her gut is right or if she's been misguided.

"So would you help me find a better lawyer then?"

"I—I need to talk to a few people first," she says, looking back into the screen.

"If you can't help me, then get the fuck out," Anthony says. He's about to slam the phone down.

Bunny pleads, "No, *wait*, I'm—I'm going to figure this out—"

The sound of an alarm, time's up.

Anthony calms himself, swivels in his seat.

"I'll come back next weekend."

Visitors begin standing, phones clicking. Anthony hangs up.

*   *   *

Bunny heads for the gates of the graveyard but feels someone watching her. She spins around and looks up. A white man in an orange jumpsuit stands in the window, holding something in his hand, a broom or a mop. The sound of an alarm again. Bunny keeps walking, passing the tower of the jail covered in barbed wire. To her left sits a little blue guardhouse with mirrored windows; she tries to look inside but only sees herself.

CHAPTER TWENTY-SIX

Before Betsy picks up the girls from school, she decides she will drop off the application at the Washington Club in person, for a few more minutes of face time. She has also (upon many nights filled with ambitious dread) decided that prior to setting up the interview lunch with the director, she will take a look at *The Social List of Washington, DC* (aka the Green Book) to prepare herself for the meeting. Because that meeting will determine whether her personality, her social position in Washington, her personal history (she'll deal with her dead ex-husband's reputation later), her immediate family reputation, her husband's job, and how much they give to charity are enough for her to be inducted into *the club of clubs*.

Embarrassed by not having heard of the Green Book in her earlier days in Washington, which makes Betsy feel even more inadequate, and unwilling to ask Linda for a glimpse of her personal copy, she has made an appointment at the Georgetown Library's archives to leaf through it.

Upon entering the Georgetown public library, Betsy is horrified. It smells like an alleyway: garbage and piss with whiffs of old newspaper. As she passes two long tables with computer stations occupied mostly by homeless men using them to look for jobs and check e-mail, she is particularly disturbed by one white man—bald pate, rat ponytail in back—playing a computer game in which a guy in a tank is running over and shooting up civilians with his AK-47; the balding man is whispering to himself, "It means I can kill ten thousand digital bodies."

Betsy places her new Hermès neck scarf over her nose and walks up to the information desk.

A young man wearing a silver bracelet looks up from his magazine. "Hi, Queen," he says.

"Oh. Hello!" Betsy can't help but giggle. "Do you greet the entire general public this way?"

"Oh no, honey." He smiles. "I love your scarf."

"Thank you! I—I'm looking for the Peabody Room."

"Of course you are." He grabs his set of keys on the desk. "Follow me. It's on the third floor."

Betsy watches the young man turn the key next to the elevator's third-floor button, thankful she's on her way to a private room, which she hopes smells better.

"You here for genealogy?" he asks.

"More like . . . *society.*" Betsy winks, trying to make light of it. "A bit of research for a project I'm working on."

"*Ooh-la-la*, nothin' like a little afternoon with the haves and the have-nots!" he jokes. The elevator door opens. He holds it for Betsy but does not exit with her. "No need for a key to get back down. George in the back can answer any questions you have. Ta-ta!"

"Thank you!" Betsy waves. The doors close.

Betsy is relieved to see bygone books in glass cases and DO NOT TOUCH signs on historical documents; there's a not-great but better, more vague library smell. An old man who seems rather disconnected from reality shouts from the doorway to the back storage area, "Can I help you?"

"Oh, just looking for right now, thank you," Betsy replies, clutching her new Gucci purse close to her side. When the man goes back to his desk to resume reading, Betsy takes a gander, trailing along bookshelves. She sees titles like *Black Georgetown Remembered*, which indicates she's going the wrong way. She walks across the room to the other corner and reads titles like *The Georgetown Set* and *The Georgetown Ladies' Social Club* and she knows she's getting warmer. Finally she spots the little green book in between something boring and something else boring, a book the size of a hardcover elementary school telephone directory.

The Social List of Washington, DC is scrolled in gold letters on its cover. Betsy pulls out the two boring books next to it so as not to appear . . . lame, but more like a student doing her diligent research on Washington society. Betsy takes a seat at the mahogany table in the far corner below a portrait of George Peabody, the old "father of philanthropy" and financier who rose from humble beginnings to become a pioneer in American credit and banking.

The Green Book begins with a table of contents of Washington hierarchy: The White House, The Supreme Court, The Congress, The Diplomatic Corps, and Businessmen and Women (financiers, lawyers, lobbyists, etc.), which informs those worthy enough to obtain a copy of home addresses, in addition to the summer, winter, and retirement home addresses, and the occasional fourth home (usually somewhere in Europe). Betsy takes photographs with her iPhone of the addresses she finds in McLean, Virginia, so she can scope out her neighbors. Some of the WASP-y names also tickle her, reminding her of North Carolina: Tutty Fairbanks, Tibby Meriwether, Holly Dutton. Then she flips to the index to find the last names of classmates of her daughters, the Bartholomews of course, the Montgomerys and the Davidsons and the Cowans, which light a fire under her. She flips to the protocol section for entertaining, a fascinating reminder for cocktail and dinner parties in an ever-waning disintegration of etiquette and manners in this modern world, Betsy thinks. For example: *We recommend that name tags not be used . . . they have no place whatever at social events.* Or how one must formally address an envelope to a sultan or sultana—His Highness, Her Highness— or in speaking to them, "Your Highness," always. This also includes princes and princesses. For a king and queen: His Majesty, Her Majesty, "Your Majesty," and so on. . . .

⤙⋘⋙⤚

Bunny sits in the center of the sofa surrounded by presents wrapped in pastel birthday balloon print. A portrait of her great-grandmother hangs in gold above the fireplace mantel. As she waits for her mother to bring out her eighteenth-birthday cake—flourless chocolate, her favorite—she notices the cobweb in the upper corner of the mahogany-framed windowpane above the seventieth anniversary poster for the Atomic Heritage Foundation leaning against it, and remembers what bratty Lily Anderson once told her in the seventh grade: "Did you know that cobwebs are formed from human skin?" Of course this was a lie, but for some reason in this moment, she remembers. She stares at the poster, wondering about all those innocent people bombed, and she has the fleeting thought: *War crimes, fucking war crimes,* and yet her genealogy passed down and down and down and onto her shoulders with pride, and she wonders if it'll ever end, and if she was too hard on Billy. He was hurt that he wasn't invited to her family gathering before her big party; she'd said it was because her mother had something private to discuss. *It's not so easy, is it, Bunny,* he'd pushed back, calling out her hypocrisy again. . . . *We'll be out of the house soon, Billy.* . . . *Sure,* he said, *sure.*

"Happy birthday to you, happy birthday to you, happy birthday, dear Bunny, happy birthday to you!"

Meredith sets the cake down in the middle of the coffee table, nearly setting the presents on fire. Bunny closes her eyes to make a wish, but she panics and her thoughts feel like jumbled blurs; she waits for one more moment but nothing comes to her. She fakes it and blows out the candles. "Yay!" Cate, Meredith, Phyllis, and Phyllis's ninety-year-old husband clap their hands in lame unison.

"I wanted to give this to you before your party tonight, sweetheart." Meredith hands her an envelope. "And I wanted it to be the first thing you opened."

While Bunny rips open the envelope, Meredith walks behind the sofa and drapes an Hermès scarf over her shoulders, making Bunny the spitting image of her mother, Phyllis, and her mother's mother.

"Mom, what are you dong?" Bunny asks, irritated.

"Just draping you in Mother's vintage Hermès while you open."

Bunny unfolds the document inside the envelope: it is her welcome initiation into the DAR (Daughters of the American Revolution) with printed photographs of women in white dresses adorned with white sashes and white gloves as if trapped in a 1950s beauty pageant. Bunny tries to hide her repulsion.

"Are you excited, honey? Now you can join me and Phyllis at functions."

"They will just love you, dear," Phyllis says.

"You've got lineage on both sides," Meredith says. "Daddy is very proud."

"So cool," Cate says, genuinely interested.

"You know, Cate, hon, if you wanted to apply you could, you'll just have to get the paperwork to prove the bloodline on yours and Chuck's side of the family."

"Maybe when I have more time . . ." Cate replies, her resentment almost noticeable but not quite.

"So . . . are you excited?" Meredith turns back to Bunny.

Bunny sits and stares at the envelope. "Thanks, Mom, can't wait," she says, flatlining. The significance irrelevant to all that she is learning, like spinning backward into a historical web she might not ever be able to escape from—her ancestors hanging on with their white claws.

"And before you open the rest, you know how disappointed Daddy is for not being able to come home for your birthday, so he wanted you to have this."

Bunny opens a second "surprise" envelope.

Inside of it: a check for *$100,000.*

"Oh my God, Mom." Bunny looks up.

"It's time to learn how to spend responsibly. This was always going to be gifted to you from Daddy on your eighteenth birthday.

It's just a slice of your larger trust that will slowly start to be passed on to you. This also doesn't leave this room, okay?"

"Money can be fickle, dear, and it's no one else's business," Phyllis adds. She and Meredith shoot each other a look of both knowing and hiding what they know.

"Don't ever forget that it's distasteful to discuss money, okay?" Meredith says.

Cate feels a pang of jealousy in her stomach, of knowing that no matter how they may be connected by blood, she was born to the wrong brother. Though they have generously gifted her checks in the past, she did not receive an inheritance on her eighteenth birthday, nor will she on her twenty-fifth.

At the sight of the check, Bunny feels conflicted; she thinks about Anthony, she wants to know if this is normal, *is this normal?* She doesn't feel gratitude, or excitement, or fulfillment. She wonders if Billy was right, *hypocrite*. She feels irritated with herself, her confusion, her mother and Billy, but she doesn't want to show it, she doesn't want to seem ungrateful on her birthday. Bunny tightens the scarf around her neck, a glorious performance for her mother, and says, "I'll be right back—I'm going to go put it upstairs so nothing happens to it before I can take it to the bank tomorrow!" She leaps from her seat and runs up the stairs, hitting every creak in the floorboards. Bunny walks into her room, flings herself onto her bed, buries her face into her blue toile pillows, and screams. Her check floats like a feather to the floor.

♦

Bunny sits at her vanity, leaning into the mirror as she dabs glitter around her eyes, the $100,000 check still on the floor next to her.

"Hello?" Cate cracks open her door.

"Hey, you can come in," Bunny says. Making sure her glitter placement is symmetrical, she turns her head left then right.

"You excited for tonight?" Cate asks, trying to be friendly, trying to convince herself she can still be the older sister Bunny never had without resentment, until she notices her birthday check on the floor.

"Yeah, should be fun." Bunny sets down the glitter stick and picks up her lip gloss, unscrewing the top.

Cate, refraining from lighting into her, walks over to pick up the check. "Bunny, your check," she says, holding it out. "Be careful with this, you can't just leave something like this out, let alone on the floor!"

Bunny turns and snatches the check out of her hands. "It's fine," she says, placing it across a few bottles of perfume in front of her.

Cate's tone shifts. "It's actually not fine, you can't just nonchalantly leave a check on the floor for a hundred thousand dollars."

"It just blew over onto the floor, relax," Bunny lies, swiping gloss across her lips, not wanting to think about it.

"Why are you being so cavalier about this? Most people don't get a hundred thousand dollars on their eighteenth birthday. Actually, most people won't ever see a check for a hundred thousand dollars in their lifetime—"

"Okay, I'm sorry!" Bunny says, "It's right here."

"I know it's your birthday, but it's not an excuse to act like you're entitled. You're entitled to none of it."

"No, you don't understand—"

Cate cuts her off. "You're lucky your father isn't the one in prison. I would encourage you to start showing some gratitude."

Cate walks out of her room and closes the door behind her. As the door shuts, the light breeze sweeps the check up into the air again. Bunny watches as it lands swiftly at her feet.

A moment of shame and confusion before she reaches for her cell phone and impulsively texts Stan via their Signal app, an encrypted messaging service her parents don't know exists. Baby cave dwellers know that at any time their parents can get access to their text messaging via a request if they want to, but this is the loophole, the way to communicate drug deals, secret recordings, after-party locations, and endless sexting.

I need 200 pills of molly.

Lizbet going down rabbit hole tonight? Stan replies.

Yes, and I'm taking everyone down with me 😂. My treat for everyone. I'll Venmo you.

An unconscious part of her wants to get rid of all her money and
rid of it fast, the balance in her bank account—thinking maybe it can
release her from her family's past.

Done. Vodka?

Obvi. Daddy gave me money for my birthday so I'm emptying my
account 😜 for my birthday. I'm an adult I can do what I want.

Stan replies with two pill emojis x 100.

You with Billy? Bunny texts. Three dots appear and then disappear
and then appear again.

Yes.

Is he coming? The three dots appear and disappear and appear
again.

Yes.

Bunny waits a whole minute to reply: Good ☺. Trying to play it
cool, still feeling guilty but ready to get obliterated.

The Society of the Cincinnati and the Anderson House

The Society of the Cincinnati was the first private patriotic society, founded in 1783 on the patriarchal legacy of the white men who fought to establish American independence during the Revolutionary War. With a chapter in each of the thirteen states (former colonies), its original purpose was to maintain the embodiment of and bond over civic virtue. Membership was limited to direct male descendants of officers of the Continental Army and Navy (including French military service members).* George Washington was the first president general of the society.

The society maintains its headquarters at the Anderson House, a gilded mansion on Embassy Row, formerly the home of diplomat Larz Anderson and his wife, Isabel, an author. The Andersons were known for being entertainers, often opening their home to presidents—Taft and Coolidge—as well as major generals, and members of the Vanderbilt and Dupont families. After Larz's death in 1937, with no children to inherit the home, it was donated to the Society of the Cincinnati, of which Larz had been a proud member.**

---

*   Society of the Cincinnati website, https://www.societyofthecincinnati.org/
** https://www.societyofthecincinnati.org/anderson_house/history

Called the "Florentine villa in the midst of American independence," a gilded mansion resides on Embassy Row dedicated to the memory of white heroes who secured America's independence. Once home to a diplomat who'd served in Europe and Japan, it is filled with carved wooden walls, gilded papier-mâché ceilings, marble floors, iron staircases, and eleven bedrooms reserved for those who belong to the exclusive Society of the Cincinnati, the oldest private patriotic organization of the United States. And the Bartholomews have paid a hefty rental price for Bunny's eighteenth birthday party.

Each drawing room of the mansion has been roped off. Portraits of Civil War heroes trapped in gold hang on every wall. The DJ sets himself up in front of the original nineteenth-century grand piano while Bunny stands shivering at the front entrance between ancient Corinthian columns two stories high. She's wearing a palepink pleated suede miniskirt and white cashmere turtleneck, and her vegan Doc Martens. Her hair is wavy and long down her back; a matching white cashmere turban headband pulls it away from her face.

Billy walks up the cobblestone driveway clad in a blue collared shirt and unzipped black parka, clenching his jaw and carrying a dozen pink roses. Stan skips up to Bunny first in a red peacoat and fedora. He pretends to flash her but reveals two hundred pills of molly in a bag instead of his penis, then shoves the bag down his pants.

"Happy Birthday, Lizbet." He taps her on the ass and steps inside the mansion with his head held high. She spins back around to face Billy. They lock eyes in silence as he hands her the bouquet of roses.

"These don't include the gift I got you," he says.

"They're beautiful, thank you." Bunny places them on the marble and gold-plated table in the foyer. "Go get a drink, I'll see you in a minute," she says, the tension between them palpable.

An Ariana Grande song blasts through the grand ballroom once danced upon in buckled shoes. Adults drink brandy in the roped-off red library filled with velvet chairs and leather-bound books about legacy and war, while about two hundred students from the sur-rounding private schools smuggle in bottles of liquor and dance in dresses and shoes bought on Net-a-Porter.

Bunny immediately turns her attention to Mackenzie, kissing her on the cheek as she enters. Bunny says, "Someone is over by the staircase waiting for you," sliding her eyes over to Marty, looking dapper in a red bow tie and suspenders. When Mackenzie walks over to him, Bunny sees that her hair is parted to the other side of her head, her hair extension clips much more visible to hide the back of her head.

"I got my early acceptance letter from Harvard," Marty says, pushing his new round spectacles up his nose.

"Stop it!" Mackenzie swings her arms around his neck and kisses him, then quickly retreats into her shy self.

Chase catches them in the act of sweet embrace; he stumbles over taking swigs from his clear water bottle filled with the finest Russian vodka. "What's this I hear?"

Marty sees that Chase's khakis are falling below his waist. "No belt? Headed for public school next year, eh?"

"I'm no commoner like you, compadre, I'm headed to the place where the tits and ass are part of the state, where the sun shines"—he opens his arms as if he's won a state championship and dry-humps the air—"and everyone gets a taste of Chase!"

"Oh, you're headed to UDC, that's right," Marty teases.

"Come on! Rollins College, baby! No shame in the game." Chase takes another swig of vodka.

Bunny approaches this cluster of imbalanced entitlement. "Did you all get your little treat from Stan yet?"

"You mean dessert?" Marty smiles and takes two pills from his pocket. He hands one to Mackenzie. "One for you, my darling."

"Where are Billy and Stan, by the way?" Bunny looks over her shoulder and sees Stan sliding down the gold banister like a twelve-year-old. Billy, standing at the bottom, catches him, and they double over with laughter. Others are grinding on the dance floor. Insecure teenagers pop their pills and open the double French doors out into the garden inspired by the Italian Renaissance. They dance around statues of family war heroes and roll around in the snowy grass in their faux fur coats and parkas, watching their breath swirl into the cold air.

"Looks like we're behind," Bunny says. "What? Did everyone pregame without me?"

"Stan had a few people over before and bused some of us here," Chase says.

"Fucking dicks," Bunny says.

"Well, I wasn't invited either," Mackenzie says. "I would have told you, you know that."

"It's fine." Bunny turns to Chase, feeling irritated. "Give me one. I know you took more than your fair share, you greedy bastard, gimme. It's my birthday."

Chase rolls his eyes, guilty; he hands Bunny a pill with a smiley face.

"Come on, Mack, I'm taking you to Alice in Wonderland." Bunny pulls Mackenzie away from Marty.

Mackenzie mouths *sorry* and waves. Marty smiles, acknowledging that he'll see her in a bit. She turns to Bunny. "He just told me he got into Harvard!"

"Great, I'm probably going to get into Yale, now swallow this," Bunny demands, unfazed by Marty's acceptance letter. Unexcited for any kind of future she knows and feels has already been carved out for her.

Mackenzie holds the pill in her hand. "Well, I didn't apply early anywhere, I only applied to UNC Chapel Hill, since that's where my parents want me to go and where my dad went."

"How much money did they give them?" Bunny takes a swig of vodka, swallowing her pill.

"Money? I dunno."

"Well, they probably gave them money, so you'll get in, don't worry."

"Oh, I'm not worried, I'm just saying I didn't apply early." Mackenzie takes a swig and finally swallows the pill in an attempt to defuse her defensiveness, a by-product of a specific kind of academic virus that spreads this time of year.

⋯⋯

Bunny takes in the room and sees Lily Anderson flirting with Billy under the grand archway in the loggia just off the dance floor. Stan blows O's of smoke in the cold air of the doorway to the garden. Bunny tucks her phone in the side of her skirt and takes another swig, feels the molly start to soften her bloodstream, tickle her nerves, loosen her motor skills, tighten her jaw. She positions herself closer to Stan, but so Billy can see her.

"Let me bum one."

Stan hands Bunny a Capri, one of those skinny cigarettes you mostly see in Europe. "Feelin' good, Lizbet?" he asks.

Bunny inhales, the end of her cigarette lit like a burning star. "So good." She exhales in Billy's direction, laser-eyes Lily Anderson's back.

Strobe lights swirl the dance floor as everyone makes their way over. Bunny and Stan sway back and forth together, giggling, then laughing, then laughing harder before they catch Billy's attention. Lily Anderson goes off to get more vodka, and Billy walks over, sliding his arm around Bunny's neck, nuzzling his head into her. "Mmm . . . you smell good. I don't wanna fight anymore."

Bunny inhales the scent of his skin underneath the aftershave and cigarettes and grabs his face. "I don't either," she says and kisses him, and it's slow and teasing, their lips tingling, and charged eye contact when they let go; she pushes him away from her.

"You wanna get rough?" Billy asks playfully.

"You wanna go upstairs?" Bunny asks, the molly making her fingertips tickle his forearm.

"I do," Billy says.

"Copy. Upstairs we shall go," Bunny says in her most playful soldier voice, "to the general's bedroom, where it is proper." She salutes Billy so as to mock his experience since childhood.

"Wait for me!" Stan says.

"Russia!" Bunny shouts in Stan's direction, losing her eye contact from the alcohol and drugs. "I'm sorry, but you're not invited to our peace corps."

Billy laughs.

"Vhut! Aw, man."

"Go make me a snow angel, we'll be back," Bunny says. Stan swirls around in his red peacoat and stumbles into the snowy garden.

Bunny and Billy shuffle into the dim master bedroom, a canopy bed fit for a king on one side of the room and double limestone fireplaces on the other, the floor covered in silk rugs and the ends of drapes. Drake's "Started from the Bottom" thumps on the loudspeakers under their feet.

Bunny wraps herself in the red silk drapes, twirling round and round. "These feel so good," she says, spinning as the curtain rod pulls and wiggles above her head before completely yanking the curtain off of the window. Trapped and wrapped like a mummy, Bunny waddles over to Billy as the second curtain flies through the air like a cape catching wind, and she tumbles into him and onto the floor.

Bunny rolls only partially out of her silk cocoon. "Oops!" she yells next to him, both belly-laughing together. "The general will be so mad at us."

"So mad!" Billy says.

"Mr. Ambassador too," Bunny says again in her soldier voice.

Billy rubs his arms across the raw silk, as if he's making a snow angel on the floor. "You're right, this feels so good."

"I don't think Mr. Creepy up there would be disappointed in me if I took off this bra, do you?" Bunny teases, looking up at the portrait of a significant hero in America's War for Independence.

"Absolutely not, he declares a No Bra Abiding Society!" Billy looks up. "His eyes are moving, black circles spinning . . . whoa," Billy says, tripping.

"Billy, why are you so afraid of the dark?" Bunny slurs, taunting him, unable to withdraw from the more sinister place inside of her, from the place that feels unseen in her quest for the truth about the Bankses' murders.

"I'm not afraid of the dark." Billy sits up, his gaze still on the supposed war hero above him. He takes several large swigs of vodka from a glass Voss bottle.

"Unravel me," Bunny demands. "I'm stuck."

Billy crawls to her and begins to pull on the silk as Bunny rolls out of it and onto the limestone finish of the fireplace, inhaling the smell of cool wood and dust.

She leans over to Billy. "Answer me, soldier! Why are you afraid of the dark!" Bunny is close to his face like a drill sergeant. She arches her back like a cat, leans down and rubs her cheek against his, rubbing them together like Silly Putty.

Spooked, Billy shoves Bunny flying back on her bum. She giggles, not taking it seriously. She stands and finds her balance; extending her arm toward the light switch next to her in the dark, she pulls on it, flickering the bedroom lights on and off as fast as possible. Billy squints.

"Do you hear that?" Bunny asks as if she hears ghosts in the walls. "It's Audrey, it's Audrey! She's begging us for help! She wants to know who killed her?! Was it you?" She makes a serious detective face and looks up at the portrait of the Revolutionary War hero. "Was it you?" She looks to Billy. "Was it I?" She looks down at the floor, hand to chest dramatically, then slams into Billy, who has managed to get up, while holding on to the fireplace mantel as if it feels like velvet. "Tell me," she says.

Billy walks toward her and grabs Bunny by her bottom with both hands, pulling her against him as hard and tight as possible. Bunny tilts her head back, her eyes rolling with it; Billy gently lifts her head back up. He stares down at her lips, still and apart, then caresses her chin. "Kiss me," he says. Bunny does as she is told.

"Do you love me?" she slurs.

"I do," he says.

"Grab my neck," she says.

Billy feels rage and then sudden sadness; holding everything inside of him, his chest rising, his head spinning. He places his hand below her collarbone.

"This is so erotic," Bunny says, feeling his hand gentle on her collarbone. She waits for him to grab her neck. Billy can't bring himself to do it.

"I said . . . grab my *neck*. . . . Or are you afraid to do that too?" Bunny says, staring at him, her eyes glassy and passionate.

Billy outlines her fragile collarbone with his fingers, and Bunny's head rolls back, a combination of laughter and then choking as Billy begins to squeeze it.

Wind throws hail across the glass windows, the sound of ice against copper drains as Billy pushes Bunny down onto the silk rug.

"You like being powerful, don't you," Bunny whispers. "You like where we come from, who we are, don't you." She exhales as Billy removes her underwear, caresses the inside of her.

"Who are we?" he whispers. "Tell me."

"Tell me you love it." Bunny stretches her arms into the deep red creases of the silk curtain.

"We're lucky, Bunny," Billy whispers, then bites and sucks on her neck.

"No we're not." Bunny slaps him and laughs. "Did that hurt?" Billy's head drops then bobbles back up in a blackout. She starts unbuckling his belt.

"Don't be such a *brat,* kiss me," Billy says.

Bunny kisses Billy hard and begins to unbutton his shirt when his grandfather's dog tags fall out, dangling across her lips. She grabs them in her hand.

Billy watches and pulls Bunny up so she's straddling him, her skirt high above her waist; he attempts to pull off her cashmere sweater as he thrusts deeper—then his face goes white as a ghost and small chunks of vomit erupt out of his mouth like the beginning of a volcano. He goes limp.

"Billy, ew," Bunny says.

Billy falls to the side, his eyes rolling deep into the back of his head.

"Oh my God, Billy . . . Billy!" Bunny shrieks, adjusting herself so she's not putting pressure on him. She grabs his shirt, trying to bring him back to consciousness. "What's happening!" she screams.

Bunny, disheveled and still rolling, runs out into the corridor. "Fuck, fuck, fuck. . . . someone help!" The heavy beat of some Jay-Z song blasts through the gilded walls and no one can hear her screaming.

Marty runs out of a second bedroom down the hallway with his shirt unbuttoned. "What is it? What's happening?"

"Call nine-one-one!!!" Bunny yells as she trips and falls, the carpet burning the skin off her knee.

Red flashing lights swirl atop the ambulance that waits between the wrought iron gates of the cobblestone driveway. Hail has turned into freezing rain and Billy is whisked out the front doors on a stretcher, clinging to his every breath with an oxygen mask and two paramedics taking his blood levels. Bunny runs after him, but when she hits the freezing rain, she loses him in her focus, the red lights blurring her vision, her head pounding, her mouth dry. "What's happening?" she asks no one in particular. On the other side of the driveway, Mackenzie and Marty stand with Meredith and Phyllis, who's doing damage control with a police officer. Marty walks over to Bunny and wraps his jacket around her wet shoulders. "Here, Bun, put this on, it's okay, it's gonna be okay."

❧ CHAPTER TWENTY-EIGHT ❧

he electronic sound of a camera flash awakens Mackenzie, whose limbs are intertwined with Marty's. They're lying naked across the green felt pool table in her basement, covered in one of Betsy's nouveau riche blankets (*unclear* what it is made of).

Mackenzie lifts her head, disoriented, when she sees Haley standing at the edge of the pool table with her cell phone pointed in their direction: *snap, snap, snap.*

"What the fuck?" Mackenzie leans over as if she's a hostage inside her own hangover, swats at Haley and misses.

Haley swings her body to the left with a wide smirk across her face. "Blackmail, bitch."

Mackenzie rocks Marty's shoulders. "Marty, get up, *get up!* My alarm didn't go off!"

Marty rolls over, rubs his eyes. "Huh?"

"Get up. *Hurry!* You have to go or my dad will *literally* kill you. Get up!"

Marty sits up, blinks, then reaches for his glasses on the edge of the table. He puts them on, pushes them up his nose, and sees Haley standing at the foot of the pool table smiling at him. "Oh, shit," he

says, Haley's presence propelling him off of the pool table and onto
the floor, panicked as he reaches for his scattered clothing.

For no reason other than to punish and humiliate her sister,
Haley begins to scream: *"AHHHHHHHHHH!!!!!!!!!"* It is guttural,
animalistic—she's a budding actress!

"Haley, *stop!*" Mackenzie whispers, straining the muscles in her
neck.

After Billy's overdose, everyone had been sent home. But Mackenzie was still rolling. She had been staring at her mother's collection
of vintage Waterford crystal service bells in the living room, picking
at her scalp, when Marty called to see if she was still awake. He'd
taken an Uber to the Wallaces' house, sneaked in through the garage
door. Billy's overdose wasn't going to get in the way of losing his
virginity to the new senator's daughter.

As Marty runs to the basement door and out toward the tennis courts, Mackenzie hears the sound of her father running down
the back staircase. She knows the sound of panicked foot-stomps.
Doug appears in his boxer shorts holding a loaded nine-millimeter
handgun.

Marty runs for his life across the courts, his glasses falling off
his nose, shattering to pieces. *Fuck it*, he runs for the exit as Doug
follows him waving his gun in the air like a drunken cowboy who's
escaped rehab.

"DAD, stop!!! STOP!!!" Mackenzie screams.

Marty runs down Chain Bridge Road with no shoes on and an
open shirt in the freezing cold, passing old Hickory Hill, the Kennedy
estate, and various groomed lawns full of government propaganda—
pro-gun, anti-abortion, Blue Lives Matter!

Mackenzie runs topless across the tennis court in a pink thong
screaming at the top of her lungs—a volcano of teenage love erupt-
ing from her postpubescent self: *"DAD, STOP!!!"*

Haley stands shaken by the escalating seriousness of the situation, eyes wide open, her iPhone dangling by her side as she watches
her sister save her boyfriend's life.

"Christ, Mackenzie, what in God's name is going on?! Cover yourself!" Doug's balls hang down the side of his hiked-up boxer shorts as he walks toward her, holding his gun down.

Mackenzie walks swiftly back toward the basement door. "You were going to kill my boyfriend!" She enters the game room and charges her sister: "And it's all your fault!" She lunges for Haley's throat. "I'm gonna fucking *KILL YOU!*"

Haley runs around the pool table like a puppy not wanting to go in its crate.

"She's trying to blackmail me!" Mackenzie yells. "Give me your phone, you little bitch!" Mackenzie picks up her own phone on the edge of the table and throws it at Haley's face. Doug stares in horror at his pre- and postpubescent daughters.

"You're just jealous of me!" Haley screams before Mackenzie's cell phone hits her lower lip, blood bursting down her chin.

Doug runs to Haley, pointing his finger at Mackenzie. "Go to your room before I blow a hole in this goddamn ceiling!"

"She's trying to blackmail me! She's trying to post a naked photo of me on Instagram!" Mackenzie cries.

"I am not!" Haley yells.

"Go to your room!" Doug storms toward Mackenzie, prepared to rip her away from the pool table by the arm.

"Fine! Not my fault if nudes of me show up on the Internet during your next campaign! *FUCK YOU!*" Mackenzie screams a final time at Haley, then snatches up her phone and runs up the stairs.

Doug sets his gun on the counter of the wet bar, grabs a towel from next to the pinball machine. He lifts Haley up onto the counter and dabs her lip.

"Ow, ow, ow." She winces.

"It's not bad, cupcake, but she got you pretty good." Once Doug has the bleeding under control, he takes her cell phone out of her hands, "Hand them over," he says.

"Ugh," Haley grunts.

"You girls better get yourselves under control and not embarrass this family, stop acting so *stupid*," he says. "Show them to me."

"Dad!" Haley begs.

"My father would have taken a belt to me had he heard me speaking the way you and your sister just spoke to each other. Pull up the photos."

Haley opens up her photo app while Doug holds the phone.

"Jesus Christ," Doug says as he swipes through several photos of Mackenzie spooning naked with Marty, then a close-up of her face, midblink, boobs out, arms reaching for the camera, and another one of Marty midroll off the Ping-Pong table, his butt in the air, his flaccid penis dangling as he tries to pull up his pants.

"Who is this boy?" Doug asks Haley with concern in his voice.

"I don't know. She says he's her boyfriend."

"Well, I'll talk to her upstairs." Doug performs an artificial smile as he plops Haley down off of the counter. "Hold that towel there until the bleeding has stopped, there's Neosporin under the sink in my bathroom."

"Where's Mom?" Haley asks.

"She's still sleeping." Betsy *would* have tried to assert some power and control over the fight between her daughters if she hadn't been fast asleep from the Chardonnay and Ambien, decorated with earplugs, an eye mask, and a night guard, wrapped in a heated blanket like a modern mummy.

❧

Doug stands in front of Mackenzie's bedroom door wearing a monogrammed navy bathrobe. He knocks. "Mackenzie, cupcake, I'm coming in." Frightened of her womanhood, Doug wants to be sure she's clothed.

Mackenzie is snuggled in her St. Peter's Academy sweatshirt and leggings under her coral-colored covers. She wears her Apple AirPods, listening to music, and has her iPad in her lap. She refuses to look up when the door opens.

Doug sits on the edge of her bed like he's aiming for father of the year.

"Can you take your AirPods out please?" he asks. Mackenzie rolls her eyes but does as she is asked. Then she quickly, and very carefully, slides her cell phone under her comforter and presses the Record button in her voice-notes app.

"Listen, cupcake, I saw the photos your sister took—"

Mackenzie cuts him off. "I love him," she says in protest.

Doug nods as if to refrain from disgust and outright disapproval. "Mackenzie," he says, trying to remain calm and not overtly racist, "you had a young man over here without mine or your mother's permission. You acted out of faith with your religion, out of faith with what your parents think is best for you, and you disrespected our rules . . . right *after* General Montgomery's son was sent to the hospital for a drug overdose. You understand how this looks for our family? To have some *idiot* running down the street this morning for every neighbor to see?"

"He's not an idiot, he's going to Harvard," Mackenzie says.

"Sweetheart—" Doug scoots closer. "You had a young African American boy in our home who gave you drugs. Is that right?" he asks.

"What? What are you getting at?"

"Answer the question—yes or no."

"NO! He did not give me drugs!"

"I'm not mad, cupcake. I'm not mad. . . ." Doug's calculating brain knows getting upset will escalate the situation, which won't help; he's got to think strategy, *psychology*, the best politicians he knows are psychologically (pathologically) savvy—each trying to outdo the other, a disease that needs its host.

"I'm not mad at all, your dad had some fun as a teenager too, you know. . . ."

Mackenzie softens at her father's touch, his hand moving upon her knee.

"Love . . . is complicated, cupcake. We know he's not the one, right? The one you would want to introduce to Nanny and Grampy?

Love doesn't feel complicated. And . . . with *this* one . . . it feels complicated, Mackenzie. You wouldn't want to put yourself in any challenging position, would you?"

"Well, no, but—"

"Real love feels like—like *home*, sweetheart. Does this African American boy feel like home to you? Or does he feel *different* from home?"

"Different, he feels different, but *good* different. Dad, he's—"

"If he doesn't *feel like home*, then he's not the one, sweet pea. And he never will be."

"But I love him, Dad—"

"*NAH—no, you don't.* No, you don't." Doug shakes his head. "I'm sorry to tell you this—he's just not good enough for you, princess. Do you know what I mean?"

"I mean, not really, but—"

"Can you keep a secret?" Doug asks, interrupting her yet again.

"Yeah, okay."

"Dad's thinking about running for president." Doug's eyes light up as if he's just given his baby girl everything on her Christmas wish list.

"Whoa, really?"

"You want a man who's as good as Daddy, don't you?"

"Yes, but—"

"Do you love Mommy and me?" Doug asks.

"Of course I do! I would do anything for you, you know that."

"Good, cupcake. I would do anything for you too. . . ." Doug leans in and tickles her. ". . . *like shoot one of your boyfriends!*" He pushes her into her pillow.

Mackenzie giggles, not because she wants to but because she's supposed to.

Doug leans back and sighs. Proud of his sensibility! "We good? I deleted the photos out of your sister's phone, so no one has to know what happened. It can stay between us."

"Okay. Thanks."

"You're my little American princess! We'll find you your prince, don't you worry." Doug kisses Mackenzie's forehead, gets up, and closes the door behind him.

Mackenzie sits up in bed, pulls back the covers, hits the Stop button on her phone app, and sends the recording off to Bunny. She texts, This just happened. For the record, I'm NOT breaking up with him!

CHAPTER TWENTY-NINE

*B*etsy and Doug have decided to stay in Washington for Christmas. The positive national attention he's received for the amendments to the Violence against Women Act have kept them circling the Beltway in an effort to maintain the momentum, but it was the invitation to the private White House Christmas party that solidified the decision. Doug's anxiety about Mackenzie's behavior has kept him up into the night scrolling through Pornhub, in desperate need of some relief, someone other than Betsy to make him feel something other than dread, other than the rage still embedded from his mother and father.

The cold marble halls of the Russell Senate Office Building are empty and quiet on a Sunday morning except for the usual security detail. Doug walks holding his Compass Coffee cup, his head held high, hiding his spiral of internal shame. He unlocks his office door to find Cate waiting for him, sitting on his tufted leather sofa in a zip-back tweed skirt, her legs bare and locked together with goose bumps climbing her prickly thighs, her eternal sun-kissed highlights wavy down her chest, cheeks still rosy from the wind. She sniffles and straightens.

Doug closes the door behind him. A wooden sign on his shelf reads:

There are two things that are important in politics. The first is money and I can't remember what the second one is.
—1896, Mark Hanna, Chief Fundraiser
for President McKinley

"Thanks for meeting me at the crack of dawn," Doug says.

"What's going on?" Cate asks, fearing she's about to get fired. Thinking of all the people Uncle Chuck knows to help her lawyer up.

"It's my daughter, Mackenzie . . . she's becoming a liability. And the press is hounding Montgomery, we don't need any external stress."

"Okay," Cate says, relieved. "Well, I'll check in with Bunny. Was . . . was this why you had me come down here so early?" She looks up at him, hoping he can take a hint.

Doug rubs his eyes, exhausted. "Look, I think—I think we should just pause," he says.

"Yeah, that's obvious," Cate says.

"I just . . . I want to make sure you're—we're not getting over our skis."

"Over our skis?"

"Ahead of ourselves."

"*I know what getting over our skis means, Doug.* . . . You want to stop seeing me." She stands and steps away from him.

"No, no." Doug takes a step toward her, afraid to ruffle her feathers. *What have I done?* "I just mean, people are looking closely at me now because of how well I'm doing."

"*We're* doing, Doug."

Doug gives her a blank look. Cate isn't sure if it's disagreement or a black void in giving others credit for his rising success.

"Did you speak to the *Washington Post*?" Cate asks—oh, she's going there, like pulling out a gun from the back of her skirt.

"What?" Doug shakes his head. "No. Why would I speak to the *Washington Post*? *You* released those statements."

"I know," she says casually.

"Why would you ask if I spoke with the *Post*?" Doug asks, paranoid.

"I—"

"Did they reach back out to you?" Doug steps backward into his desk, unzips his leather bomber jacket. He feels hot. The heat is on full-blast.

"I meant to tell you . . ."

"Meant to tell me?"

"An investigative reporter came by the office."

"AN INVESTIGATIVE REPORTER?!"

"She was asking about a man named Albert Rasmussen."

Doug's face goes ghost-white when he hears the name come out of Cate's mouth, a sense of betrayal he hasn't felt since the death of his brother.

"There's a reporter who's investigating accusations of sexual harassment, assault, and abuse on the Hill. She also showed me a picture of a man named Tim, but I can't remember his last name. It doesn't matter—"

"*OH,* Jesus Christ, Cate." Doug swings his arm back as if to hold on to his desk and misses, nearly falling over. He stumbles and clears his throat, tries to stand up straight, wipes his forehead with the back of his hand.

"She said there were a few incidents with some political figures in your circle. So she came to me . . ."

"And? *And? WHAT DID YOU TELL HER?*"

"I had nothing to say to her, Doug. Everything has been *one hundred percent* consensual between us."

"You told her that, you told her that we were—that you and I were—are—?" He's starting to stutter.

"No," Cate says calmly. "She has zero evidence or reason to suspect that we were ever together. Do you think I'm an *idiot*? But even if she did . . . it is consensual." Cate eyes him, looking for validation, some expression of relief at knowing that she cares about him, because maybe he'll say he cares about her too; she still wants him to want her, care for her—

But Doug—Doug isn't thinking about her all. "Did you get her off your back? How did you get her off your back? How do you know she's off your back?"

Increasingly annoyed by his selfishness, Cate says, "Because what evidence does she have?" Still trying to reassure him.

Doug wasn't supposed to be like the men in that room, he thinks, he was supposed to be better than that—*like the Corcorans and the Grahams!*

"Nothing is going to happen. Who is she going to go to—*human resources?*" Cate laughs, not sure if she said that out loud for Doug or for herself.

"Does Walter know about this?" Doug asks.

"No."

"Goddamn it, Cate."

"Fine, I didn't realize you wanted everyone at the office knowing," she says.

"All right, all right. *FUCK!* Fuck, fuck, fuck." Doug paces around his desk, rubs his palm over his bald head. "You have to tell him—he's the fucking director of communications, for God's sake."

Cate stands in her power as best she can, which means she decides to sit, snuggle up on the couch, an air of indifference and detachment, an old-time power move she learned from Aunt Meredith. *Act aloof and no one can touch you.*

"When did this happen—how long have you been withholding this information?"

"I don't know, Doug, a few weeks maybe."

"*A few WEEKS? Oh my God!*"

Cate looks up at him with Bambi eyes, watches as he paces back and forth in front of his Michael Jordan bobblehead.

He begins laughing as if he's drunk. "Well, we have a lot more to be concerned about than my daughter's tits ending up on Wikipedia," he says. "What about Betsy?"

"What about your wife?" Cate says.

"Will they go to her?" he asks, dropping to a new level of seriousness.

"Mmm, probably not."

"*Probably* not?"

"Doug, no one knows anything because there *isn't* anything . . .
right?" Cate bats her eyes, looks down to see if she has any split ends.
"There is literally no reason at all for this *green* reporter to go to your
wife."

"She's green?" Doug says, a moment of relief.

"Yes. She's practically a college student."

"So it's under control?"

"It is under control." Cate stands and moves close to him.

"And you're going to talk to Walter. . . ."

"I will talk to him this afternoon."

"And he still doesn't know about . . . us?"

"No one knows, Doug."

Doug takes a big breath. "Okay, good, very good." He pulls her
into him as he places his thumb over her lower lip, tracing its chapped
crease, her breath warm on his hand.

Before he kisses her, "Wait. Wait," Doug says. "Sit down. Where
you were . . ."

Cate sits back down on the couch and crosses her legs.

"Now uncross your legs," Doug says.

Cate keeps her legs crossed for a long ten seconds while looking up at Doug, taunting him, enjoying the power she feels in this
moment, and not afraid to use it. Then she uncrosses her legs.

"Yes, like that. Now open them a little more." Cate opens her legs
slowly, "*Oh God,* like that." Doug moves closer to her, unbuckles his
belt, his broad shoulders a towering presence over her. Cate moves
her hand to touch herself.

"*No!* No. Don't move, just hold still." Regaining the only sense of
control he feels he has, Doug takes his hard self out, and closes his eyes
until his shame spills all over her. Only this time, Cate doesn't feel it.

Loud crows echo between broken tree limbs and blown-over garbage cans on East-West Highway as Cate steps out of an Uber XL. She approaches the front steps of a quaint Craftsman, rings the bell, and pumps herself up, bouncing on the balls of her suede boots—

A round woman approaches the glass door, opens it. "Cate, what are you doing here?"

"Hi, Janet, I'm sorry to show up like this, but it's sensitive, and you know how technology can be these days," Cate says.

"Oh yes, yes, of course, come in."

"Actually, I'm fine to wait out here. If you don't mind grabbing Walter for me."

"Oh. All right. One moment."

Cate's heart pumps faster as Walter approaches the door. He throws up his arms as if to accuse her of being dramatic.

"Hi, Walter."

"What's all this about?"

"I'm going to make this as brief as possible."

"All right." Walter crosses his arms. He wears a UNC sweatshirt, a coffee stain down the front.

"The *Washington Post* has just launched an investigation into several power players, one of whom is Albert Rasmussen, the others—I can't remember, and honestly, I don't really care, but accusations have been made on record: rape, attempted rape, sexual assault, masturbating in front of staff, the gamut. Possibly even sex trafficking, *looks like the Saudis aren't the only ones!* All of whom are within our circle's reach. Doug's circle. A young female reporter spoke to me several weeks ago and asked about the sexual misconduct happening inside our office. And since I'm the press secretary and human resources doesn't *really* exist—and because I am *very* loyal to Doug—I want what's best for *us*. I want to win. But here's the deal: you gotta go, and you gotta be the one to initiate the going."

Walter stands there, his facial expression morphing into that of a little boy who just got caught stealing. Stealing her dignity, her integrity, the right to do her job.

"I have no idea what you're talking about." He glances behind him to make sure the front door is closed all the way so his wife can't hear anything, somewhere in the kitchen baking snowman cookies for the upcoming cookie exchange women's holiday event.

Cate holds her position and tries not to blush. She has spent countless nights watching and observing every single online interview of Hillary Clinton, taking notes on how it looks when you've got an inner core made of steel, when every single inflection sounds exactly the same, an unbreakable robot.

"Well, let's see how *all of you* will look during our little Me Too movement."

"You can't do this, Cate, you have no evidence."

"I just did, Walter, you can't unhear it. I mean, the truth is, it's either you or Doug that's going down, and it would be such a shame for it to be both, after all of Doug's hard work, and his daughters'—and his wife! *Ooof.* But a lose-lose for you, really. . . . Should we call Anne at the *Post*? I have her number right here." She holds up her contact so Walter can see it. "How should I begin the conversation? Should I tell her how you like to graze my nipples at work? Or—" Cate taps at her phone.

"W-w-well, hold on a minute! Did Doug send you here?" he asks, panicking.

"He did, Walter—but he didn't send me here to fuck you. I did that all on my own." She smiles.

"When is this article coming out?" he asks, his paranoia escalating. He looks over Cate's shoulder, *anyone parked down the street?*

"Mmm, not sure, but you can call Anne if you like and ask—or maybe you can call Albert, or a guy named Tim, or any of those sex-addicted men whose careers are surely over."

"What do you want, you want money?" he asks.

"No, but that's so predictable and thoughtful," Cate says, cocking her head, then settles into the role of negotiator. "I want you to resign effective immediately. Tell Doug you're done, and that I'm the only person for the job. You're handing it to me."

"That's it, you want my job?"

"That's right."

"And you won't go to the press."

"Nope."

"How do I know you won't go to the press anyway?"

"Doug is hitting a high point—you think I'm going to jeopardize his inevitable run for the presidency because some old washed-up aide grazed my nipples?" She laughs, seeing that Walter's more offended by being called old and washed-up than by being pegged as a sexual predator.

The front door opens, and Walter jumps; it's his wife. "Are you two chilly out here?"

"Jesus!"

"Oh, sorry, sweetheart." She laughs. "I didn't mean to startle you, just wanted to offer you some tea?"

"Oh, I'm fine, thank you." Cate smiles.

"No, no, I'll be in in a minute," Walter says, shooing her away. "Please close the door." When she's gone, he says, "No press."

"No press," Cate says, affirming the deal.

"Nothing in writing."

"Nothing in writing, just a verbal agreement and your resignation letter by tomorrow. . . . I can draft a public statement about your decision to retire and focus on family matters, the usual."

The reality of this sinks into Walter and he starts to get emotional as he says, "We have a deal."

"Great, cc me on the e-mail." Cate pulls out her phone and orders her Uber.

"Doug's not going to be happy about this."

"Oh yes he will, Walter, he doesn't need you ruining his legacy."

Walter takes a moment to think about his twenty-year friendship with Doug. Was any of it worth it? At least he can go quietly. But the shame will never leave him.

An Uber XL pulls up to the curb. Cate steps off the porch. She turns around before she gets in the vehicle. "Oh, and Walter, don't try to pull a fast one on me. Lest you forget, my uncle's donation dollars are wrapped around Doug's balls. This is in my blood."

❖• CHAPTER THIRTY •❖

*R*unning as fast as she can in her black snow coat and back-pack, Bunny pulls out her wallet to grab her fake ID, but she can't seem to find it. She stops in front of the blue guardhouse with mirrored windows, plops her bag down, and digs, pulling out a Bernie water bottle and crumpled receipts, when a door swings open. "Can I help you?"

"Found it!" Bunny holds up her fake ID. "Just thought I lost my ID for a minute," she says, breathing hard.

The guard stands with his hands on his hips, his back to the mir-rored door. Bunny collects her things, throws everything back in her bag, and leaps for the trailer.

Bunny sits holding the receiver to her ear, waiting for Anthony, when a man she doesn't recognize appears on the monitor in his place.

"Well, aren't you fine," he says.

Bunny looks at him, her jaw drops; confused, she spins around thinking she should call for security, but thinks better of it, then hears on the other end of the phone, "Get the fuck outta here!" It's Anthony who's threatening the man who picked up his visiting call; the inmate gets up, starts laughing like he's medicated, and strolls off. Anthony takes a seat. "Motherfuckers trying to take our calls."

"I can see that," Bunny says, trying to act unaffected, to ignore how much skinnier Anthony looks than the last time she saw him, and that his right eyelid is swollen. "Are you okay?" she asks.

"I'm probably gonna end up in solitary 'cause someone tried to put a shank through my arm but I stopped it, threatened the motherfucker. He backed off, but he'll come back. Jail's trying to make me a *real* murderer." He shakes his head. "How you doing, Grace?"

Bunny has moments where she forgets that she's hidden her real identity from him, and she feels guilty, sick to her stomach, even if she had to do it to get in to see him. She wants to tell him that she knew Audrey would flash her money and privilege around for everyone to see, that Bunny even enjoyed it sometimes—being accepted into Audrey's circle of popular girls even if she never really felt comfortable there—that being discriminatory about people and places isn't who she really is or wants to be, the shame and guilt she feels for never having stood up to Audrey, or up for anything she believes in, never confronting herself about any of it, until now. And she wants to ask Anthony if he thinks that's why the Banks family was murdered—because of greed? Because of race? Both?

But "they" are listening and she can't.

"I can't stop thinking about what you told me about your dad. . . . Has anyone else been to see you?"

"My mom," he says, "but she's not doin' too well, her mental state is declining. Too much stress . . ."

Bunny thinks about her mother pulling dead roots from under the dying poplar. "Do you have siblings?" she asks.

"I got a sister—hey, how is this relevant to my case?"

Bunny quickly pulls out her journal so as to get into character, having forgotten once again who she's pretending to be. "It's important, you know, for context, to know who you really are so people can understand you."

"Who do you work for?" Anthony asks, catching Bunny off guard. "I realized I didn't ask you before."

Stumped, Bunny thinks fast; seizing on half-truths, she says, "Myself—I'm independent, which is why it's better to talk to me." A good and fast recovery, she thinks.

Anthony studies her through the monitor. "Uh-huh," he mutters, still skeptical. "You're young," he says.

"So are you," Bunny replies.

Anthony swivels around in his seat.

"If it's true, Anthony, I—I really want to talk more about your dad."

"Of course it's fucking true," he says. Bunny can feel his anger seething through the screen.

"When did he start working for the Banks—for the chemical plant?"

Anthony clenches his jaw, but doesn't turn away.

"Please," she says.

He takes a breath and racks his brain. "I was probably about nine or ten, because that's when Mom wanted a divorce."

"Why did she want a divorce?"

"She's always been moody, but Dad going away, commuting way out to Virginia for the job, was hard—but *she* says it was because he fell out of love with her. But I know it was about money, always is."

"I know it's rude to talk about money, but—"

Anthony bursts out laughing. "You fuckin' people," he says, shaking his head.

"*What?* What do you mean?" Bunny doesn't understand why that would trigger him.

"Nah, that's just an excuse for you not to reveal how much money you people actually make compared to the rest of us."

Bunny takes a moment to think about this: *a revelation.* "Huh. That's a good point," she says. Anthony appreciates the admission, leaning back in his seat.

She considers what her mother said at her birthday, Anthony's challenge against the things that are being passed down to her uninvited, *it's rude to talk about money.* "How much did they pay your dad at the chemical plant?" Bunny asks, knowing she'll have little to compare the answer to. The limits of her identity reduced to a birthday check of $100,000.

"Well, I guess it seemed good in the beginning, you know, like a salary he was getting, maybe around thirty thousand, but the commute got hard so he ended up just moving to the town nearby. Once the divorce was finalized, we just saw him on weekends, you know, if we could afford a bus ticket or whatever."

"What did he do for them?" Bunny asks.

"He was a security guard, letting employees in and out of the gates. He didn't have the kind of engineer training and education you needed to work inside the plant."

"I see," Bunny says. "I don't know much about the Bankses' business, you know, I just know they . . . had a lot of money." She fishes for more from him, about money, his thoughts on money, his thoughts about the Banks family.

"*Man*, they got enough money to feed an entire town *they be killing*! People out there are dying, and they're flying around in their private jets and shit."

Bunny wonders if he's referring to Audrey. *Did he see her Instagram page? Did he find her? Will he find me?*

"How do you know they had a private jet, did you see it?" she asks, on the edge of her seat.

"Nah, man, you just know, you just look at these people and you *know*. The way they carry themselves." Bunny adjusts her body language, trying to settle into her seat more, not so erect and alert, like a *real good girl, so polite, so manicured, so refined, so* . . .

She clears her throat. "Where did you work for them? Did you work with your dad?" Bunny looks around to see if any of the officers are paying attention to her.

"Nah, I worked at a warehouse out near Fredericksburg, another one of their companies, and sometimes as a delivery guy."

"Okay, I did read that. . . . So when did you find out about your dad's cancer?"

Anthony scratches his head, the screen goes out.

"Anthony? *Shit.*" Bunny slams the side of it.

"Ma'am! Ma'am, you're gonna be asked to leave the next time you touch that monitor," a security guard says, walking over to her.

"I'm sorry, I'm sorry. . . . Anthony?"

"Yeah, I hear you." He comes back into focus. "About eight months before he died."

"Only eight months?" Bunny says, heartbroken for him.

Anthony coughs into his fist. "Yep." He can hardly look at Bunny, withholding his emotion.

"Were you able to get any help or medicine to try and treat it?" she asks. Bunny doesn't know to ask about health insurance because she's never had to think about it.

"I'm still paying for it," Anthony says.

"What do you mean? You had to pay for it?"

"You think they gave him benefits?" Anthony laughs maniacally. "He wasn't working inside the plant."

"Did you have any savings?"

Anthony leans back. Exhausted from her questions, exhausted from her place in the world, the color of her skin, the assumptions she makes.

"I—I'm sorry, I know I'm asking a lot of questions, but—"

"Savings," he says *at* her. "Savings . . ." nodding his head at how out of touch she is. Bunny is beginning to pick up on this—that savings are a privilege, not a right.

"I'm sorry, I . . . think I see."

"You wanna see how much debt I'm in for tryin' to save my dad? *Huh?* You wanna know what that feels like, having the creditors calling you, threatening to sue your ass while your pops is throwing up blood in the bathroom, nearly passing out from not keeping any food down, which we can't afford?" Anthony reins in his emotion and throws the phone receiver against the screen, leans back, folds his arms. Abandoning Bunny for a few moments, the phone still clutched in her hand, her furrowed brow—she can't feel that she needs to breathe; the only thing she knows is that she's in too deep to back out now, to not do *something*. Still holding the receiver tight against her ear, looking at Anthony to let him know that in this moment she is with him, she's not leaving.

Anthony slowly leans over, grabs the phone back, and puts it to his ear. He looks down at the ground. "I don't have connections, I don't have power, I don't have help, and my lawyer fucking doesn't give a shit about me. What I got is information. . . . The company's rich, and the people who make the company are poor. It's not right, it's *not right*, and you fucking *know* it. I can see it in your eyes. I don't deserve to be here, someone else does. I need a good lawyer, I need a real fuckin' lawyer, Grace! Please, can you help me get a good lawyer?"

"Okay, okay, I—I'll see what I can do. But if you didn't kill them, Anthony, then who do you think did?"

"That's not my fuckin' problem, is it."

❖ CHAPTER THIRTY-ONE ❖

*B*unny ducks under the electronic gate of Georgetown University Hospital's entrance, climbing the steep driveway in her red peacoat. A NO WALKWAY sign is inked in white paint along the gutter, and she remembers the story her mother loves to tell about the morning she was born: "When your dad pulled up to the parking attendant at the gate so we could leave, he couldn't find his stamped ticket. You were bundled in the backseat with me, Dad frantically searching his pockets, the glove compartment. 'Come on, my wife just had a baby!' he pleaded, thinking it would work, but the man would not budge! So he revved the engine and drove straight through the gate, snapping it in half. That's the Volvo you drive, honey Bunny. Let's just say being a new dad was unnerving for him. That's why they don't have an attendant anymore, it's just a machine." Upstairs, Bunny peers into the window of Billy's hospital room, tiptoes in. He's asleep in a white bed, his veins pumping with fluids, hair tousled, stained polo from the night of the party slung over the rail. The room is dark with gray light. The windowsills are empty, and the television blares on the wall, headlines scrolling past on the news ticker at the bottom of the screen: *Iceberg Twice the Size of Washington*

Melts in Antarctica in a Sign of Warming (Warning!) / *Budget Plan Reveals Tremendous Fraud / Virus Death Toll Passes World Record.*

Bunny feels guilty for not bringing him anything. The flowers he gave her for her birthday, resting on the front hall table, are now dry and dead.

"Are there still photographers waiting outside?" Billy asks, peering out of one eye.

"I came in through the parking garage, I don't know. I didn't see any."

Billy lifts his other eyelid. "Nice of you to come visit. Sorry I ruined your party."

"You didn't ruin my party. . . . I shouldn't have bought all that molly."

"I partied hard with Stan before we got there."

"That's obvious."

Billy smiles, but it comes off as forced.

Bunny sits on the edge of his bed. She looks around at the empty room. "Where are your parents?"

"Mom's downstairs getting coffee in the cafeteria. Not sure where my dad is, probably in meetings. . . . But I'll be out by the end of the day hopefully," he says, trying to compensate for his father's absence, allay the impending fear that comes with his silence even though they know what's coming.

"That's good," Bunny says, avoiding the topic of his father.

Billy can sense Bunny's withholding. "So how was the birthday anyway? You're a legal adult now, *woo-hoo.*"

"I mean, minus your overdose it was pretty solid. The 'rents gave me a hundred thousand dollars as a present. Guess it's part of my inheritance."

"Damn." Billy lets the $100,000 sink in.

"I'm not supposed to tell anyone, but I don't know. And I just feel fucked up about it now. I think I should give it away. I don't need it. I'll never need it. My dad has literally always told me, 'Bun-Bun you'll always be taken care of, you'll never have to worry.' So might as well do something good with it, right? *Save the world.* Maybe that's what we should do."

Billy knows that he too will always be taken care of, under the condition he goes to the academy, because there will always be conditions. But Bunny is naïve to think they'll have a choice of what to do with it.

"Or you could give it back to them? Tell them you don't want it," Billy says, prodding Bunny's hypocrisy.

"Reject Meredith and Chuck's gift? Hah! There has to be another way other than cutting off your nose to spite your face, if you know what I mean."

"Right," Billy says, knowing he was right about her, but careful not to rub it in. He feels they're much alike in a common understanding of familial circumstance and entrapment, but she's unwilling to admit it fully.

Bunny hops off the bed, paces around the room. "I'm thinking of giving it to Anthony's family—the man who's going on trial for Audrey's murder. He told me his side of the story, and I've been doing all this research about wrongful convictions, and I am seriously telling you that it is so fucked up—his dad got cancer from the chemical dumping of the Banks family's business! And they didn't pay for it, and he threatened the dad. . . ." Realizing this isn't sounding so good, she turns to Billy sitting up in the bed, neither amused nor surprised. "But I swear, I don't think he did it. It was just easy for them because they wanted to hide all of the people that are getting sick and *dying* from the fumes and chemicals, and he doesn't have a fighting chance because he doesn't come from a family like ours, and if he has the money to fight an equal fight, we can find out who murdered them, and if—"

"Bunny. Seriously, *STOP.*" Billy puts his forearm over his eyes, as if the sheer mention of Anthony is blinding.

"You know, for someone who's supposed to go to West Point, you're acting pretty weak in the violence department."

Billy laughs, feigning shame. "Fuck you, Bunny."

"Aren't you interested in any kind of truth, Billy, or—I don't know—*justice*?"

"Justice for who? Your fake friend or the man accused of killing her?"

"She was not a *fake friend*," Bunny says, covering up that she feels scared and conflicted, all of her resentments she never got to express to Audrey, that she wasn't brave enough to confront her that time in the car, that Bunny has been complicit.

"Oh, bullshit, you guys didn't hang until we started dating."

"That's not true, we hung out when we were little—we were *best friends!*"

"'Cause this is *ALLLL* about you, Bunny. I forgot."

"This is *not* all about me—I am trying to find out what really happened! And I think it's more complicated than people want to assume, because everyone is so fucking scared of the *truth*." Bunny stomps her heel on the floor.

"What the fuck do you know about truth and justice? You think giving a hundred thousand dollars to an alleged murderer will help you find the truth? Will bring Audrey and her parents back? Will somehow make you feel safer in this—this *fucked-up* world?"

"In case you didn't know, nothing is *just* where we come from, Billy." Bunny adjusts her jacket, oozing self-righteous indignation.

"You know what I think? I think you're acting like a spoiled brat who gives zero fucks what her family has given her and instead wants to play a game of *woe is me, I know I don't deserve this, so here, I'll swoop in and save you, I'll give it to an 'innocent' man so that I feel I've contributed to the world*. Stop acting like a fucking martyr when you only care about yourself. It's sick."

Bunny flings her arm up in the air, knocking over a paper cup on a metal hospital tray. "Oh, I'm sorry, are you talking to me or to *yourself*? And I'm not sick, *you're* the one who's lying in a *fucking hospital bed!*" Bunny tries to hold in tears. . . . "I can't do this anymore, I don't want to do this anymore."

"Fine," Billy says, his chin quivering, holding back tears.

Carol opens Billy's door and enters holding a Styrofoam cup of coffee. There are dark semicircles under her eyes. "What's going on in here?"

"Nothing. Bunny was just leaving," Billy says, looking at Bunny.

Bunny wipes away a tear. "Hi, Mrs. Montgomery. I—I'm sorry, I have to go. . . . Lovely to see you." Bunny brushes past her and out the door.

Carol walks toward the empty chair. "What just happened? I could hear yelling from down the hallway, William."

"Nothing, Mom, it's fine."

"Everything is *not* fine. You have embarrassed this family and your girlfriend has gone storming out of the hospital. You better get your act together—for your father's sake, for my sake. For this family. We are going through enough. How could you be so selfish, letting this happen?"

"It won't happen again."

"Well, if West Point finds out about this, we're in big trouble. *Big trouble.*" Carol checks her watch. "I'm going to go see when we can get out of here, this is ridiculous. What are they giving you?" She walks over to the nightstand. "What is this, water? I'm going to go get the nurse." Carol turns away and stands in the doorframe. She stops a nurse in the hallway: "Excuse me, we're ready to leave now, please unhook my son. I have to be on the road in an hour."

"Where you going?" Billy asks.

"To the farm."

"Why? Is Dad going with you?"

"No. He's requested to speak with you alone tonight. And I need fresh air—*Excuse me!*" She tries to flag down another nurse. "Oh, and I saw your tattoo. Say your prayers tonight that I haven't told your father."

Billy throws his head deeper into the pillow and closes his eyes, wishing that for once, his mother would protect him. Would find the courage to use her voice instead of hiding behind her husband's.

❖•CHAPTER THIRTY-TWO•❖

Exhausted, Billy steps into the old rickety elevator. No one ever uses it except Bunny when she sneaks over in the night, but Billy feels compelled to get inside, in a masochistic sort of way, as if he might find her waiting there for him saying, *Sorry, I didn't mean it.* He wonders if this time the elevator will get stuck, God's way of punishing him, or maybe the cables will finally snap and he will plunge to his death. Instead, the elevator wobbles to a halt, releasing him into his childhood bedroom. Billy flips over a photograph sitting on his bedside table, of Bunny with her arm around his neck, kissing his cheek on the bleachers of the baseball field. Half of an Adderall pill crushed like children's chalk is inside the bedside drawer; he presses his pointer finger on top of it so the chalky material sticks to it, then licks it, swallows the remainder without any water. This is what he thinks he needs to prepare him for the beating he's about to take from his father.

The beeping sound of the intercom startles him: "William?"

"Uh, hi, Dad."

"Come down to my office."

"Yes, sir."

*   *   *

General Montgomery's office is covered in historical memorabilia, a wide range of social sectors: his great-grandfather wearing a newsboy cap, proudly holding a shovel in front of a coal mine as though becoming a crown prince. Wooden frames full of cursive and presidential stamps and coats of arms. Three-pronged candlesticks along the brick fireplace mantel, a ticking grandfather clock, and a photograph of the general holding Billy as a young baby in front of a new warplane, a grin on his face. A cross hangs above his desk where he spends the majority of his time when he's not traveling. A random portrait of Queen Maria of England from 1634 hangs over the fireplace, which may or may not have been left by the home's previous owner, an African diplomat. A wooden vintage airplane propeller given to the general as a gift upon his nomination from a friend at the Pentagon rests in the corner.

The general carries his glass of scotch from his desk to the Chesterfield sofa and takes a seat. A chair sits empty across from him.

A knock at the open door. "Dad?" Billy tiptoes in like he's regressed to boyhood, afraid of his father's rage.

"Sit down." The general does not look up but gestures his glass in the direction of the leather chair opposite him, just far enough away to inhibit real intimacy but close enough to be within range of his intensity. The green Tiffany lamp on his desk provides the dim light, the wooden shutters on the bottom half of the windows closed for privacy.

"Yes, sir." Billy takes a seat.

"Your grandfather loved this country," the general says, somewhat nostalgic, which in the moment feels confusing for Billy as he so rarely sees it. "He survived a plane crash in the line of duty, and do you know what he got in return?"

"Uh . . ." Billy flounders for an answer because he knows he won't win; he thinks it's better to be silent than to be wrong.

"He got nothing. Do you know why?"

"Um—"

"Because the country, let alone the world, didn't *owe him shit*. And not once—*NOT ONCE*—did he ever complain. That is the definition of a man of honor. A man who at *any cost* and without *any promise* puts his country first—that's what I learned from him. That's what I've always tried to do . . . *at any cost*." The general takes another sip of his scotch, squinting at the encyclopedia collection on the shelves in front of him.

Billy pulls his chin up. "I've always looked up to—"

"I want you to watch something." The general pulls a burner phone out of his pocket and presses play on a video as he places the phone on the coffee table between himself and Billy.

The sound of muffling and then a shaky camera, ethnic slurs against Middle Eastern culture being shouted into the frame. It's Billy at Stan's party in the Russian ambassador's house, getting ready to be waterboarded. He snorts a line of coke, wipes his nose. Stan strapping him down—it's the video Bunny shot of them that night to see if he could beat the record without dying. His father puts his head down as Billy is forced to watch it, Chase laughing, champagne being dumped on his head and spilling over the handkerchief, himself convulsing on-camera—privilege exploding like balloons hot with confetti. The video ends. Silence. The general cannot bring himself to look Billy in the eye. He gets up and walks over to his bookshelf, stands looking at his framed medals.

"Sir . . . I'm sorr—"

"I built this life for us from the ground up, *oh hell*, from *under* the ground up, and this is how you want to treat our name?" He turns around, rage brewing in his tone, points his finger at Billy. "Let me tell you something. This family might be a lot of things, but we are *not* entitled to behave any way we like. *God* did not put us on this earth for the limited amount of time we do have to be a foil, but to be a *leader*. You have *EMBARRASSED* THIS FAMILY—"

Billy retreats, feeling his father's rage escalating with each sip of alcohol he takes. "I know, it will never hap—"

"DO NOT INTERRUPT ME WHEN I AM SPEAKING TO YOU. You have *embarrassed* this family. There are accusations that will be released by the press tomorrow."

Billy runs his hand through his hair, heart pounding, mouth dry.

"Accusations about not only your *entitled* and *disgusting* behavior . . . but an investigation has started about my role in the military, and your acting out only compounds this very serious situation. It's goddamn Christmas morning for the press, William." He stares him down. "ARE YOU LISTENING TO ME?"

"Yes, sir," Billy says, nodding, a fragile child.

"An antiwar journalist trapped in his ivory tower who can't accept a baby's arm getting blown off in the name of democracy is accusing our military of war crimes, and I just can't tell you the scope of what the media might do to blow this out of proportion. But goddamn it, William, do you understand how you have compromised us? How you have embarrassed ME?"

Billy stands, shocked and confused, assuming it is a rhetorical question, but trying to calm his father.

"SIT DOWN." The general slams his fist on the coffee table, forcing Billy's body back into the chair. "ANSWER ME WHEN I'M SPEAKING TO YOU."

Billy can't help but stutter in fear: "Yes—yes, sir, I understand how it makes us look."

"We will have a family meeting at the farm in Virginia, where we can have some privacy during this time. Security will take you to meet your mother next week. Until then you are forbidden from speaking about this with anyone—the Bartholomews, Stanley, *no one*. Do you understand?" The general points his finger at Billy.

"Yes, Father."

"YES, WHO?"

"Yes, sir. Yes, sir, I understand, sir."

The general takes one last gulp of his scotch and goes to his desk, quiet anger seething. Billy waits for some kind of closure to the conversation as his father fumbles with his papers. "Stand up," the general says.

Billy stands, slowly. The general walks over to Billy, facing him like a drill sergeant.

Billy's nostrils flare, his chin high, his eyes dilating from the Adderall, ready for a blow. Ready to take it like a real man. He winces.

"You are not my son. Close the door on your way out."

The general walks casually back to his desk. Billy opens his eyes, trembling as he exits his father's office, gently closing the door behind him.

❖·CHAPTER THIRTY-THREE·❖

*B*etsy power-walks through the entrance of the Washington Club wrapped in a camel-colored winter coat, swinging her brown Birkin bag. This is her version of dowdy. Her new Ann Hand pin is stabbed above her heart as she makes her way across the musty carpet.

"May I help you?" asks a clean-shaven man in a dreadful suit.

"Yes, I'm meeting Mr. Theodore Yoder for tea."

"Right this way, to the Book Room. As Thomas Jefferson once said, 'I cannot live without books.' And we agree!"

Betsy smiles, hiding the fact she's never once read a book about Thomas Jefferson.

Her guide leads her into a mahogany-lined library with green velvet chairs, gold satin pillows, a roaring fire in the fireplace, and a portrait of the founding president of the "club of clubs" clad in a red-checked bow tie and standing beside a white horse, staring quizzically at his audience. "Mr. Yoder, I have—oh, pardon me, I did not catch your name. My deepest apologies."

"Betsy Wallace," she says, her eyes frozen from recent Botox injections.

"Mrs. Wallace is here to see you."

Mr. Yoder stands and extends his hand. "Nice to meet you."

Betsy is unimpressed. Theodore Yoder looks as though he has risen from the dead, a long-lost descendant of the *Mayflower* buried deep in the archives of the National Portrait Gallery, this upper-crust white man with his white mustache curtaining his upper lip, raw-silk bow tie, and round tortoiseshell glasses, as if Theodore Yoder has hobbled all the way from Constitution Avenue to get here. He certainly did not take an Uber.

"Please, please have a seat," he says. There is a tower of cucumber and egg finger sandwiches before them, pink and purple macaroons for dessert at its base. A private butler scurries around with an enormous tea box. Betsy selects Earl Grey, because that is what she notices Mr. Yoder is drinking.

"So, how did you and Linda meet?" he asks, beginning the formal interview. He pulls a manila envelope from an inner pocket and places it beside his cookie plate.

"Through our daughters at St. Peter's Academy," Betsy says.

"Lovely."

"Well, and then we got to know each other at the Alliance Française." The butler sets her teapot on the table.

"Ah! *Parlez-vous français?*" he asks, which both irritates Betsy and makes her nervous.

"I'm getting there." She laughs, placing a cloth napkin in her lap.

"And how are you finding it here in Washington? Congratulations on your husband's win, by the way."

"Oh, thank you, we are delighted to be here." Betsy stirs her tea.

Mr. Yoder opens the manila envelope and pulls out what looks like a résumé. "So I see Doug's parents were born in Durham. His father was district attorney, is that right?"

"Yes, that's right."

"And you all belonged to the Durham Country Day Golf Club?"

"Yes, we did."

"And you lived in Washington once prior, is that correct?"

"I did. That was when my previous husband died of cancer," Betsy says, the sympathy card she's willing to throw down.

"I'm so sorry, I didn't mean to bring up old wounds," he says.

"It's quite all right. You can either be a victim or a survivor, and I consider myself a survivor," she says, pleased with herself.

"Would you like an egg sandwich?" he asks in a lame attempt to ease the discomfort.

Betsy has a flashback of her time in the bathroom at dinner with Linda, repulsed by the look of oozing mayonnaise. "I'm fine, thank you."

Theodore Yoder clears his throat. "We are very proud of our membership list and, as you know, the wonderful variety of real estate our members have. . . ."

"Oh yes. We bought our property in McLean. Did I mention that in the application? Across from Hickory Hill, not dissimilar to our old stomping grounds and country charm in North Carolina." Betsy sips her tea, pinkie in the air.

"And where do you and Senator Wallace like to summer and winter?"

"We spend our winters in Palm Beach, and our summers in Nantucket, Kenneth Point, named after his late brother."

"Marvelous. Now, I do have to ask . . ." Mr. Yoder looks around the private library just to be sure no one else of value is around. "There was some trepidation from a particular member—one of our longest and most loyal—due to an incident that happened last summer at a rental house on Liberty Street in Nantucket?"

"Yes, we stayed there while they were doing extensive wood restoration on the house—to preserve its history. That was just after Doug had won his seat."

"Yes, yes, of course, we have to update ours on the Cape as well. But what I do have to unfortunately ask about is an incident that happened on Liberty Street. It was brought to our attention that an arrest was made of a juvenile?"

"I beg your pardon, I'm not sure I know exactly what you're talking about."

"Well, just to refresh your memory, it said . . ." Mr. Yoder creates a silent moment of dread for Betsy as she watches him remove his round spectacles and lay them on the table, then pull his reading glasses from his jacket pocket and use both hands to place them on his nose. He begins reading a sheet of paper that he pulls from the manila envelope: "Sibling Squabble over Talent Gets One Sister Arrested."

"*Ohhh*, goodness!" Betsy laughs so hard she snorts. "Mr. Yoder, they never took her to juvenile hall. Once Doug and I called our attorney, they immediately returned her home *and* even *apologized* for traumatizing her."

"I see. . . ."

"The girls can get competitive. Mackenzie just slugged her sister is all, who may have even deserved it, you know what I mean?" Mr. Yoder just blinks. "I mean, who hasn't slugged a sibling? Do you have siblings?" Betsy sips her tea again, pinkie raised.

"I am an only child."

She sets her teacup down. "Well, in any case, they threw out the case and the Nantucket police apologized for inconveniencing us on our Saturday morning."

"In the article it says, 'The young Ms. Wallace was taken away screaming, "*You*"'—excuse my language—'"*fucking cunt*" at her ten-year-old sister.' I do hope, Mrs. Wallace, that this is not language that is tolerated in your household, as it is not language that is tolerated by any of our members."

"Oh goodness, *no*. Linda—I mean, Linda of all people would know that that is not language I would tolerate, and given her position in the world of journalism, she would have known about this incident and whether it was even worthy of mentioning, having referred me—you do know this, don't you?"

"Well, this brings me to my next difficult subject. I must do our due diligence, so please forgive me, as it does tend to get personal. . . .

Are you aware of any suspicious activity within the Williams household?" he asks.

"You mean Linda's home?"

"Precisely."

"No—why, Linda was the person who nominated me, so I'm not
sure what I might know that you don't know." Betsy is acutely aware
that this interview is not only about whether or not the Wallaces are
worthy of being club members, but also about how her family might
reflect back on Linda and her family.

"There have been whispers," Mr. Yoder says, "about an exposé
regarding her husband, Chris Williams, and some violent and sexual
behavior."

"Oh, my word. . . ." Betsy places her hand over her heart.

"You did not hear that from me. And again, my apologies for
having to ask such uncomfortable questions—it's one of the things
that makes my job particularly difficult." Mr. Yoder adjusts his glasses
with his right hand.

"Yes, well, *anything* I can do to be of help, but I really have nothing but wonderful things to say about Linda. After all, I wouldn't be
sitting here with you if it weren't for her."

"I appreciate it," he says, then takes a sip of his lukewarm tea.

"Mr. Yoder . . . I beg your pardon, but why did you have me come
all the way here to meet with you, if you don't trust Linda's judgment,
given her family's private troubles?" Betsy asks sincerely.

"Mrs. Wallace . . ." He removes his glasses. "In politics, you don't
need a weatherman to know which way the wind blows."

"Well"—Betsy smiles—"things *are* heating up for Doug."

"That's right, and I am very impressed with his new amendment
and agenda, and how he has handled the administration's escalating
problems—with dignity and grace."

"He is a mighty winner. I knew from the moment I met him he
would be a wonderful husband, father, and leader."

Mr. Yoder closes his file. "Very good. My secretary will be in
touch."

"Wonderful, it was lovely meeting with you." Betsy stands.

"And I do love that Ann Hand pin you're wearing—she is a dear old friend of mine."

"Oh, why thank you, it was a gift from . . . Doug's mother." (It was a new gift she gave herself).

"Just stunning."

Cafe Milano

"Washington's ultimate place to see and be seen," says the Washington Post *about the famous Georgetown staple where black government town cars and motorcades remain parked along the curb in front of the valet line on Prospect Street. Cafe Milano was founded in 1992 by Franco Nuschese, who came from the Amalfi Coast and has been a resident of Washington for over twenty years.* * *Designed for hosting presidents, prime ministers, diplomats, lobbyists, and journalists, it has four different private dining areas, some with glass doors, others without. Whether someone wants to be seen (but not touched) or to secretly move about (but never be seen), the maître d', Laurent, makes it happen. An elegant man from Nice, France, he's worked for the café for nearly thirty years (a mini American flag always pinned to his dress coat), making both Franco and Laurent bigger insiders than a freshman politician. Ladies' luncheons are typically held in the front private room, where they can be seen (not touched). The Cafe Milano's only other location worldwide is at the Four Seasons in Abu Dhabi along the Al Maryah Island waterfront.*

---

* https://www.cafemilano.com/about/

❧·CHAPTER THIRTY-FOUR·❧

*H*ostess extraordinaire Nourah Al Hashem, the Kuwaiti ambassador's wife, raises money each year for homeless children through one of her favorite local organizations, the Lollipop Kids Foundation. Honoring fifty of Washington's most powerful women, including the wives of cabinet members, in an effort to feed the children, it is *the* nonpartisan ladies' luncheon of the year, and no location whets the appetites of wealthy Washington insiders like Cafe Milano.

By the time Jaguars, Mercedeses, and Range Rovers begin pulling into the valet line, the Frasier Fir candles reek of Christmas, the emerald-green satin linens cover tabletops, and mini Christmas-tree boxwoods in cranberry-colored boxes stand as centerpieces. *Darling!* Double kiss: hands on the shoulders. Laurent knows many of the women on the invite list, the wives of the Very Important Customers. But he also knows who is ranked the wealthiest, based on the strategic seating arrangements. Those who sit closest to the host near the podium in the front of the room are those with the most money. Presumably closest so that when it is time to give, *they give.*

After greeting each arrival, Laurent hands her a table number and paddle for the "ask" at the end of the lunch. Though this Christmas feels more solemn than in the past—Genevieve Banks was always seated at Table One, making a splash with a $20,000 donation at the end of the luncheon—this year Betsy Wallace will take her place. Joining Betsy at Table One are Meredith Bartholomew, Phyllis Van Buren, Linda Williams, Carol Montgomery, Sissy Cowan (Chase's mother, wife of the head of the CIA), and Galina Stopinksi (Stan's mother, wife of the Russian ambassador).

Betsy walks into this group of veteran Washington philanthropists with her head held a little higher knowing that she's most likely going to get into the Washington Club after her interview with Mr. Yoder, and that she has sobering gossip about Linda Williams, which she knows not to reveal until absolutely necessary. There are rules to Washington gossip, and one must know how to use them. Anything related to diseases such as alcoholism, or domestic violence, or severe mental health disorders, should be used against someone only in self-defense, or discreetly, and only within the inner circle.

Wearing a red one-piece jumpsuit and earrings that look like red dining-room chandeliers, Betsy takes a seat in between Linda, who wears a red blazer with a gold leaf pin and diamond studs, and Meredith, in a Ralph Lauren blue-and-green-plaid suit and gold Cartier watch. Poor Phyllis Van Buren, in winter white, has tried lip fillers for the first time; a rookie, she didn't have them done far enough in advance, and her upper lip, albeit slathered in the natural-looking gloss she favors, is swollen, her smile a little lopsided.

"Linda!" Betsy says, leaning over to give her a double kiss on both cheeks before she takes a seat.

"How's my lip?" Phyllis whispers to Meredith through gritted teeth, ignoring Betsy's entrance. A waiter in a bow tie is pouring champagne around the table.

"Fine," Meredith lies with a smile.

Linda sits with her lips pursed. "Hi, sweetheart," she says to Betsy, letting her know who's in charge of the friendship; after all, it was Linda who had placed Betsy on Nourah's fund-raising radar.

"A little more wine, please," says Carol to the waiter when he refrains from pouring champagne into her glass. She looks around the table, completely disinterested in these women, in her gray shift from Lord & Taylor, gold cross dangling around her neck, and a military pin placed just above her heart. Hiding the shame she feels about her son's recent overdose, which all of these women are privy to.

"Anyway, you were saying about the Christmas homes tour this year," Meredith says to Phyllis, still ignoring Betsy. "I didn't know this, but Genevieve Banks was supposed to be on the tour as well, so they had an open placement and gave it to a new family who just moved into one of the former churches. Should be pretty exotic."

Phyllis raises her eyebrows, which tweaks her upper lip to the right, takes a sip of champagne.

An uneasy look crosses Meredith's face. "Well, don't mention it to Bunny during the tour, she's—we're all still shaken from it."

"Of course, my dear," says Phyllis. "We'll have a wonderful afternoon of just us girls looking at splendid Washington architecture, the traditional *and* the avant-garde!"

"Pardon me, I don't want to interrupt—just wanted to say hello to you fabulous ladies," Betsy says, her hand on Meredith's shoulder.

Meredith turns her head, gazes at Betsy's French-manicured fingers across her plaid shoulder pad, hardly a smile. "Nice to see you. Do you know Phyllis Van Buren, one of my oldest and dearest friends?" Meredith says.

"How do you do," Betsy says. She can't help but notice the bruises on Phyllis's lip, *oh poor thing*. Perhaps she should discreetly give her the name of her aesthetician.

Carol downs her wine as she sees Galina Stopinski and Sissy Cowan having a great laugh (heads thrown back, veneered teeth in the air, Birkins dangling from their wrists) on their way back from the powder room.

"Carol," Meredith says, "Bunny mentioned you've been spending a lot of time in Middleburg—you must let me know the next time you're going, and come over to my parents' farm for tea."

"That would be lovely," Carol says to be polite. Meredith smiles; she knows better than to mention Billy's overdose on such an occasion, a social faux pas to ask how someone's child is when you know they're not doing well. It somehow feels like cheating, but manners above care.

"Will Billy be attending the academy?" Linda interrupts. She takes a bite of Caesar salad that's just been passed around. The table is suddenly silent.

"He will, just like his father," Carol declares, sitting up straight.

"What a wonderful legacy to carry," Linda says.

Carol smiles. "Thank you."

"Meredith, where is Bunny looking to attend college?" Betsy asks.

"Yale," Meredith says smoothly without any hesitation; she doesn't even look Betsy in the eye—in fact, her outfit makes Meredith cringe. Why do they still refuse to just seat friends with friends each year? She's contemplating whether or not she'll decline next year's invitation; it's just not what it used to be. The spray-painted gold baby's breath is just *too much*.

Trying not to feel intimidated—it must be nice to be a legacy admission—Betsy realizes she'd rather not go down the old college road, for surely these women all went to Ivies while she was struggling at Gettysburg. Meanwhile, she's praying Mackenzie gets into Chapel Hill.

"Good for her," Betsy says, sipping her champagne. She quickly changes the subject. "Phyllis, do you have children?"

"Oh yes. My boys are all grown up," Phyllis says, covering her mouth with her napkin as she tries to take a bite of her salad. She swallows, clears her throat, and adds, "Princeton," as if that was going to be Betsy's question.

"Her boys are just the most wonderful. Stuart is on the tenure track at Penn, and Alex is working on sustainable energy in East Africa," Meredith says, bragging for her old friend to let Betsy know the rank she's trying to penetrate but will never be allowed into, no matter who her husband is on Capitol Hill.

"Besty, darling, vhere did you get those earrings!" Galina Stopinski says. "Stan gave me vhones with less shape for my birthday but doesn't look good vhith the shape of my face." She cups her chin with her hands, revealing her nine-carat yellow diamond, just a little bit smaller than Betsy's.

"Buccellati—you must see the new collection." Betsy smiles, fingering the bottom tassels below her right earlobe.

"For God's sake," Carol says under her breath across the round table; only Phyllis hears, and chuckles lightly.

Linda hands her salad plate to the server walking around pouring Pellegrino. "I'm finished, thank you," she says, looking at her empty salad plate, implying that he was late to pick it up. She turns back to the table. "Doug was just on Chris's show a few weeks ago," she says, trying to move the conversation away from materialism and into politics. Only in the last few decades have broadcast journalists been inducted into the fold of the Washington power structure, becoming more and more accepted.

"I'm really proud of him, and Meredith's niece has been such a wonderful support!" Betsy says, cupping her champagne glass with her fingers, letting the table know she and Meredith are connected not only professionally, but also through family.

"Chuck got her the job, of course." Meredith smiles at the table. "I'm still a registered Democrat!" She readjusts the napkin in her lap. "Betsy, didn't you live here in Washington before?" she asks, tilting her head, putting her on the spot.

"Oh gosh, that was such a long time ago, I was practically a child."

"Oh, you did?" says Phyllis, leaning over Meredith toward Betsy. "And what were you doing here in Washington, dear?"

"Oh, I was just young and newly wedded and, well, looking for something to do, I suppose!" she says, trying to charm her way out of the conversation.

"So you and Doug left the city for a long time?" Phyllis asks, genuinely curious, seeing as he is getting so much attention in the press.

"My first husband," Betsy tries to say discreetly, hoping the other women around the table will turn away and start their own conversations.

"Well, many of us have been there, I'm sure," Phyllis says.

Betsy smiles, wondering if word has gotten around about her sordid past. She feels it around these women, clinging to Doug's potential for a new family legacy.

"How are all of your children holding up since the Banks family . . ." Linda asks. No one, not even Linda, the wife of a newscaster, can bring herself to say *murders* in front of these women, several of whom were friends, even if only superficially, with Genevieve Banks.

"Well"—Betsy puts her hand to her heart—"Mackenzie didn't know her well enough, but she tells me it's been a little frightening as an observer. Is Bunny doing okay?" she asks, putting the spotlight back on Meredith.

Meredith lets out a big sigh. Normally not one who needs to impress any of these women, she's felt an increasing paranoia about her family, having been a leading competitor in the same field as the Banks family business. "Well I think she's doing the best anyone can to try and handle such a horrific, horrific thing at her age."

"Vhell, Stan was just torn up about it, but he seems to be even closer to his friends now," Galina says.

"Oh, goodness," Carol says. "Billy was trying to—he had mentioned it to me, but I don't think I ever met them."

"Meredith, you knew Genevieve quite well, didn't you?" Linda pries. Leave it to the wife of a newsman to want to dig deeper.

Meredith raises her eyebrows, but looks down at her uneaten anchovies. "Well, you know, we led very different lifestyles and grew apart as the years went on. Bunny and Audrey had many playdates when they were younger, and our families knew each other, though were not particularly fond of one another, just given that we were competitors. But we . . . respected each other. And I know David was getting more politically involved and, well . . . who knows if that had anything to do with it," she says, insinuating: *Republican*—then remembers her audience. "Anyway, our families weren't even that different, but business could get in the way." She sips her champagne.

Meredith looks down at her Cartier watch and up at the podium where the hostess, Nourah Al Hashem, has appeared in a gold suit. She takes the microphone out of the stand. "Ladies, I am so blessed and beyond grateful you could join me this afternoon at our annual Christmas luncheon with fifty of the most extraordinary and powerful women in Washington. I am honored to stand before you, and have the privilege to talk about one of the organizations nearest and dearest to my heart. There are over four thousand children in our beloved Washington today who are homeless and hungry, and over three thousand parents who are joined with them. We know that with the ever-shifting economy, hard times can fall on families, which is why I partner with the Lollipop Kids Foundation and this life-changing work that they do. As most of you know, at this point in the afternoon we like to do our 'ask.' Everyone should have received a paddle when you checked in with Laurent—and let me just say how much we love Cafe Milano and our maître d' extraordinaire, let's give them a round of applause." Ladies clap in their seats, heads turned to the front. Meredith begins to unwrap the lollipop on her dessert plate, while Phyllis frantically reapplies lip gloss.

"So, ladies, let me see your paddles!" The women hold up their paddles as if raising shot glasses. "Okay, very good! Are we ready? We are going to start with a whopping ask of twenty thousand dollars, twenty thousand dollars, would anyone so generously like to give the Lollipop Foundation twenty thousand dollars . . . ?"

Women's heads and torsos and hair-sprayed updos twist and turn in their seats, waiting for someone to raise a paddle. Hearts start to pound; no one wants to feel the shame of not having a single person step up to the plate—when suddenly Betsy Wallace, as if departing from the gates of hell, lifts her paddle and says, "I will donate ten thousand dollars if my friend here, Meredith Bartholomew, meets me at ten thousand even, so you can get your twenty."

Eyes in the audience grow wide; no one has ever propositioned someone on the spot—not here in Washington, maybe in places like Vegas or Los Angeles. Betsy would justify it, were anyone to ask, as taking Linda's advice about not being so "flashy" with her wealth, not as the wife of a new politician who wants to get into the Washington Club. But truly? It is vengeance; Betsy has not forgotten Linda's tidbit of gossip on that dreadful evening of their dinner when she mentioned that the Bartholomew family had quietly been losing money.

Phyllis's jaw nearly drops. Meredith wants to lean over the table and swat Betsy across the face with her paddle, watch her go flying through the glass windows and out into the cobblestone streets of Georgetown, her chandelier earrings flying apart at the clasps. Instead, she musters up a smile whose subtext is: *Isn't this woman atrocious?* "I'll match with fifteen thousand dollars," Meredith counters, unwilling to lose her dignity because of Betsy Wallace.

"Wow!" Nourah claps her hands and struts across the floor in her brown Manolos. "Twenty-five thousand dollars on the first ask! A record . . . I just love my friends, old and new! Okay, our second ask . . ."

"Oh dear." Phyllis downs the rest of her champagne while Galina Stopinksi and Carol Montgomery make the next bids.

As the afternoon progresses, neither Meredith nor Betsy makes eye contact with the other, nor do they engage in conversation. It is only when all of the willing donors line up where they originally checked in to give their credit card information to Laurent that Betsy leaves her final mark as the new-to-town powerhouse of Washington. She hands Laurent her black American Express card and kisses him on both cheeks.

"Don't forget that fabulous coat of yours," Laurent says, gesturing to the coat-check room across from him.

"Ciao, darling," Betsy says.

Meredith approaches Laurent. "A successful luncheon this year," she says.

"Every year, Mrs. Bartholomew," he replies.

Meredith hands him her black American Express card as Nourah comes to say good-bye: "Oh, we are so grateful, my dear friend. I'll have my assistant set up tea at the Jefferson as a thank-you." They kiss each other on both cheeks.

"Um, Mrs. Bartholomew, I am so very sorry—I have tried running the card several times through the machine but it keeps declining," Laurent says in a low voice, glancing to either side, so as not to embarrass her.

"What's going on, sweetheart?" Phyllis says in her ear.

Meredith turns to her and whispers through a smile, "My card was declined."

Phyllis begins to dig through her purse to pull out her wallet.

"Oh, for God's sake, put that away," Meredith says, loud enough for Betsy to spin around from the coat check to see the two women panicking.

The woman in coat check hands Betsy her jacket; she swings it around her back, cape-like, wrapping it around her neck. "Thank you," Betsy says, handing the woman a twenty. She walks over to Laurent at the checkout table, bypassing Meredith and Phyllis. "Here, put it on mine, there's no limit," she says. He swipes: approved. Betsy turns around, smiles, and struts out of the double glass doors, Meredith and Phyllis inhaling whiffs of her ninety-eight-dollar bottle of Versace Bright Crystal.

❧·CHAPTER THIRTY-FIVE·❧

*B*unny waits for Anthony to appear, her right leg compulsively bouncing up and down; she's anxious to tell him about the money. When he appears on-screen with a gash under his left eye, her leg stops.

"Hey, oh my God," she says, looking at the flesh wound under his eye.

"That motherfucker came at me again." The screen goes fuzzy; Anthony's voice cuts in and out.

"Why do they do this? Why do they call this visiting? This is fraudulent! Hello?"

Anthony sits back and listens to Bunny's unfolding enlightenment with annoyance. "Still here," he replies, his face edging back into visibility on the monitor.

"I don't understand why you're still in there if you haven't been convicted yet," Bunny says, getting frustrated. "Isn't it supposed to be innocent until proven guilty?"

"I don't got a lotta time left on my minutes this month," Anthony says, reminding her that nothing she is saying is a surprise for anyone in her immediate vicinity other than herself.

She nods and wipes her cold nose with the sleeve of her jacket. "So I'm not sure I'm the person who can find you a lawyer—but I can give you the money for it. A hundred thousand dollars."

Anthony looks at her, impatient, skeptical. He swivels around in his seat again, paranoid. "Where'd someone young like you—an independent reporter—get *a hundred thousand* dollars? You dealing drugs?" he asks.

"You said it yourself, I'm moneyed up, or whatever." Bunny looks down, trying to not make it a big deal, but it's a big deal.

"All right, where's the money from?"

"My parents, I told you."

"Your parents gave you a hundred K? . . . *Why?*"

Bunny pauses. "That's a question I've never been asked before."

"Right, 'cause you only hang around people like yourself."

Bunny hears this and knows it couldn't be truer. She doesn't have any friends who are unlike her. Marty is the only Black friend she has. From the time she can remember she's been taught to not acknowledge it, or think about it, or ask why.

"So who are your parents?" Anthony asks.

"They're nobody—they just came from somebody."

"Who'd they come from?"

The tables turning, Bunny tries to keep it vague. "I guess you could say . . . war."

"War . . ." Anthony echoes.

"Yeah. War."

"What the fuck do you mean, *war?*"

"Like weapons-ish . . ."

"Your family makes weapons?"

"Not anymore, like *a lonngggg* time ago, like last century," Bunny says quickly. "But my parents are so proud of what our ancestors accomplished, you know? There's so much pride, and I just, I've been thinking about your dad, a man who made his money in an honorable way, in a way that didn't hurt anyone, and didn't think that it would kill him in the end . . . that it's killing the whole fucking planet," she says. "Not him, I mean, you know what I mean, the company."

"Compan*ies*," he corrects her, frustrated that he has to sit here and listen to Bunny recap what he's always known. "The Banks got *companies*. But listen, we don't got a lot of time, my minutes . . ." Anthony says urgently, his stomach churning, anxious for the money.

"Anthony," Bunny says, taking her *time*, "do you think the Banks family deserved to die? Do you think they had it coming?"

Anthony bites his cheek, exhales. "When I'm questioned about it, I'm having to pretend to show remorse, 'cause if I don't it makes me look guilty. But when someone's fuckin' killed your *father*, you don't give a shit what happens to them—in fact, you want the worst for them. . . . How do you think it's going to make me look?"

"I—I don't know, I don't know what it's like to lose a father, I guess. I can't say."

"Mm-hmm." Anthony doubts her honesty.

"I think . . . I think I'm . . . afraid," Bunny continues.

"Afraid of what, we don't got all day here!" Anthony's impatience is escalating as his phone minutes dwindle.

"Afraid that I'm a bad person."

"You want to give me a hundred thousand dollars, and you think you're a bad person? What the fuck's wrong with you?!"

"'Cause the money I inherited is dark and conditional and bleeding all over America!" She wants him to tell her it's okay, she wants him to tell her she's innocent, she wants him to tell her she shouldn't feel guilty, she wants to put the burden on anyone but herself. She wants him to tell her she isn't complicit.

Anthony takes a good long look at her. "You're not bad, Grace, you're not bad."

"Right, yeah, of course," Bunny lies, reburying the shame she feels. "So will you take the money? I want to give it to you, to go after what is fair and what is right—you should have a chance to be heard and the right to a decent fucking lawyer. But I—if you take the money, I won't be able to write about your case. I probably shouldn't," she says, wiggling her way out of "Grace, independent reporter."

"Yeah, yes, thank you. I'll take the money," Anthony says into the telephone. "So what is this anyway, your white guilt? A donation to make you feel better about Black lives?"

Bunny panics, she knows she's gotten too emotional, she's revealed too much, *why did I do that, why did I come here?* "I don't want to end up like my parents," she blurts out. It is the most honest thing she has shared.

Anthony takes it in. "Yeah," he says, "me neither."

For a brief moment they share a look of understanding.

"So who should I give the money to?" Bunny asks.

Anacostia

In 1608 explorer John Smith discovered a village along the Anacostia River that belonged to the Nacotchtank tribe* (Anacostia is the Anglicized version of their name). It turned out to be an abundant trading center frequented by the Iroquois of New York among others. By 1668, the Native Americans were being forced out and uprooted by war. It wasn't until 1854 that Anacostia became an early suburb of the District of Columbia. Known in those days as Uniontown, it was built to provide affordable housing for the white working class until desegregation spread and public housing units were built in the 1950s and '60s. During this time, Anacostia saw a dramatic change, its population quickly becoming predominantly Black amidst cultural, political, and racial tensions.

During the crack cocaine crisis of the 1980s and '90s, Anacostia took a violent turn as an epicenter for drug dealing in Washington, making the city the murder capital of the United States. Its name became synonymous with gun violence for the white elites, perpetuating even deeper racial tensions, gentrification, and segregation.** Once home to abolitionist Fredrick Douglass, Anacostia today is being eyed by aggressive developers eager to build properties as the massive infrastructure project of the Eleventh Street Bridge Park, connecting the Navy Yard district to Anacostia, is scheduled to open in the near future.

---

*   https://www.nps.gov/nr/travel/wash/dc90.htm
**   Asch and Musgrove, *Chocolate City*.

CHAPTER THIRTY-SIX

*B*unny stares down at the brown river as her Uber crosses the Eleventh Street Bridge. She couldn't risk getting lost or parking her car on the street, given what her mother's always told her: *Don't get lost and end up in Anacostia, you might get shot.*

On Bunny's sixth-grade field trip hiking through Great Falls, the only Hispanic kid in her class slipped on a wet rock by the river, splitting his forehead open. When Bunny saw the blood spilling down his cheek, she felt it was the inevitable result of socioeconomic and racial consequences: *This is what happens to Hispanic children.* The thought came to her as though she'd been warned of it her entire eleven years on earth. And for the rest of the school year, Bunny was afraid to sit near him, as if she might catch a fall through osmosis—it was a *white* psychosis. *Slipping: it can happen to anyone.*

For Bunny's entire life, everyone in her inner circle always said not to cross the bridge into Anacostia. But as she enters Ward Eight, passing Fredrick Douglass's large house, its porch buzzing with tourists, the crossing of the wards feels anticlimactic. *Where are all the loose gunmen? Children bleeding and starving in the street?*

They drive down Good Hope Road passing signs for CASH KING and HOPE DOLLAR STORE, abandoned laundromats in art deco buildings hugging corners, liquor stores. Bunny sees an "eye in the sky" tower for the first time. After her visit at the jail, she knows what it's for: government and police surveillance. *Intimidation.*

"Is this the right location, miss?" asks the Uber driver, a Middle Eastern man.

"Yep. Here is good."

He pulls the car over to the curb.

Bunny gets out and checks the address, then looks up to the yellow row house, protected by a chain-link fence. She walks up the porch steps, proud of herself, and reaches for the doorbell, but before she can press it, the door swings open.

"May I help you?" A striking Black woman stands behind a screen door, her long braids swept up into an elegant bun.

Bunny jumps back. "Ohmigod, I'm so sorry, you scared me," she says, catching her breath. Bunny notices the woman's distinctive style, a baby-blue turtleneck sweater complementing her dark complexion.

Bunny waits for her to respond, but the woman remains unmoved.

"Hi, I'm . . . Grace. Did Anthony mention I was coming by? Are you his sister?" Bunny asks, suddenly hating the acute sound of her voice.

"No, Anthony did not tell us you were coming by. . . . Are you a social worker?"

"Oh," Bunny says, trying to hide her confusion. "No, but I am here to—to drop something off for his case."

"What do you mean? I'm not following," the woman says, somewhere between paranoid and skeptical.

"I'm here to provide some financial help. For his case," Bunny says, mustering confidence and pride.

The woman looks up and over Bunny's head, scanning her surroundings. "What? Who sent you here? Did the attorney send you?"

"No one sent me. Well, Anthony told me where you lived. I thought he would be able to tell you I'd be coming by and why—"

"I haven't talked to Anthony in months," she says.

"I'm sure this seems *super* weird, me just showing up on your doorstep on a Saturday morning. . . ." Bunny says, trying to convince her she's not a threat.

"Do you have any identification on you? Or a business card?" she asks.

Bunny's hands begin to shake a little from nerves as she reaches for her tote bag. No one has ever asked her for a business card before. Bunny is unsettled by this lack of trust.

"I have a driver's license. I don't have a business card." She takes out her cousin's driver's license she's been using to get into the jail, several receipts spilling out of her bag in the process. "Sorry," Bunny says, handing her the ID, then kneeling to gather the scattered trash, heart racing.

"Do you work for a clinic?" the woman asks. "You look young."

This isn't how Bunny planned, prepared for, *imagined* it. Instead, this woman is poised, beautiful and intelligent, rightfully suspicious, questioning—everything Bunny's always been told didn't exist over on the other side of the river. In this moment—her learned stereotype obliterated by reality—humiliation courses through her.

"How do you know my brother?" the woman asks.

"I . . ." Bunny thinks twice now about telling her she's a journalist. "I saw what happened in the news and took it upon myself to visit him. I remember when it happened, it . . . was close to where I live, and I began to question whether or not he did it. And no one is talking about it. The information is sealed. But Anthony told me about the chemical dumping. Everyone seems fine with the fact that they think he's guilty. So I want to be able to do something good with the money that I have, and I know Anthony doesn't have a good lawyer, that's what he said. . . . So that's why I'm here, to talk to you—about giving you money for a good lawyer. And—and he told me about your father, I'm so sor—"

"You came by here to give us money?" Anthony's sister laughs.

"What else did my brother tell you? He sweet-talk you into giving him money? How much money?"

Bunny is taken aback by this. "Well, uh . . . like I said, he told me about your father and—"

"How *much?*" she interrupts.

"A hundred thousand dollars—but, really, he didn't sweet-talk me."

"*Ohhh*, this is too much. You got some nerve." She hands back Bunny's ID.

"Okay." Bunny isn't quite sure what to say. "So where should I send the money to? The bank said I should get your routing number."

"*Oh*, sweetie, listen. You don't know my brother, he's no saint. . . . You don't know the situation. *Keep your money.*" She steps backward to close the door.

"No, wait," Bunny says. "I don't understand. I'm serious. I don't want or need this money. I want to give it to you."

"*Look*, I don't have time to *unpack you* right now, and the *last* thing I need is for the feds to be breathing down my neck as a respectable business owner because I got some handout from a stranger obsessed with my brother that I don't need and that doesn't coincide with the agreement with the chemical company."

"I'm really sorry," Bunny says. "I'm not sure I'm following—what agreement are you talking about?"

"Honey, you're not following because you're not on this road. You think it's okay to insert yourself into another family's business because you got money?"

"What? No, I—I think I'm confused. I just want to help. Did the Banks family make an agreement? Like . . . a financial agreement? Like they paid you?"

"*You don't have a right to be here.* I have to get back to my day. I'm not interested in anything else you have to say. Get off my property or I'm calling the police." The door slams.

Bunny stands alone on the porch; her lower lip and legs start

shaking. As she takes herself down to the sidewalk, a German shep-
herd lunges from behind the neighbor's chain-link fence with a
snarl, his jaw snapping. Startled, Bunny throws her hand against her
pounding chest, then quickly calls for an Uber. She waits, vulnerable
in her skin, and tilts her head to the sky to see a government security
camera filming her from atop its long white pole. She stares at it as
if staring directly into the sun.

❖·CHAPTER THIRTY-SEVEN·❖

ou from around here?" Bunny's Uber driver asks. A crucifix dangles from his rearview mirror.

"Uh, yeah," Bunny replies, still shaken.

"A native! *Wow.* Don't pick up too many of those. I was just dropping off a couple at the old Frederick Douglass Museum."

"Yeah, well, the city's changed a lot, or that's what people tell me."

"*Oh*, let me tell you . . ." he begins. "I don't mind all the nice houses and buildings goin' up. I'm a lot older than you, *ha.* I coach a baseball team, and I got people, kids I used to know, who are all comin' back to town after maybe ten, fifteen years, you know, 'cause they got families now, and they're complaining about how it's changed! So this is what I say, I say the city that *you* left, once *you* could afford to, has not become the museum that you wanted it to be, the euphoric *bullshit* recall that you have of it now that you're back. And on top of that, you're complaining about the race of those who came in to buy the homes of the elders that you *did not* stay with. So let me make sure I get this straight—because if it wasn't that, you would have stayed here, been here in a house that was already paid for—"

Bunny's cell phone begins to ring. "Oh, I'm so sorry, I'm—"

"It's all right, go ahead," he tells her.

Bunny answers. An older woman's voice says, "Hello? Is this Ms. Elizabeth Bartholomew?"

"This is she."

"This is Ellen Rivkin with Bank of America calling about your recent deposit."

"Yes, yes, I remember."

"Well, I'm so sorry to have to inform you of this, but it appears that this check has bounced."

"*What?* I'm sorry, I think you're breaking up."

"It appears that the check has *bounced*. It did *not go through*."

"What? What do you mean, not go through?"

"Well, whichever bank the money is coming from, it appears to have insufficient funds. So what I recommend is that you contact the business or individual who issued you the check. I am here if you have any further questions."

"I—I don't understand, there should be money in that account." Bunny's universe is plunging into an unknown dimension. *How is that possible?*

"I'm so sorry," the woman says.

"Thanks for letting me know." Bunny hangs up. She turns back to the driver. "Sorry about that."

"All good, all good," the driver says, cruising over Key Bridge.

"Sorry, you were saying?" Bunny says.

"Well now, so you know, I said, *let me tell you something*, it's not about *color*, it's about *culture*. You know, I said, that's what, you know that's what it's about, and I said, for some reason, we told these folks who didn't have the opportunities or the skills that we had that they were supposed to *stay like they were* when that's *exactly* what got these guys into the pickle that they were in. I said, *you* have to change, *you*, you have to change. And I said, if you notice, the people that are complainin' about this are y'all. It ain't all these elders who actually had to live through the riots and who got five hundred thousand dollars for a house they paid thirty thousand dollars for back in the 1950s. These people are makin' *bank*! And good for them. I don't mind. God bless the free market. That's what I say, *God bless* the free market!"

Bunny's hands are shaking. She asks him if it's possible to turn up the heat.

"No problem. . . . You know, I have elder cousins who lived in the U Street Corridor and they bought their house for fifty-one thousand back in 1949 and it hadn't been updated since the sixties or whatever. And some developers came through because the house was twenty-six feet wide, so they said, we want to split this up into—it was a four-story house, three stories and a basement—they said, look we want to sell three condos, and the basement we're going to rent out and that's going to pay the condo fees for the condo association. *Brilliant!* Just brilliant. So they paid her four hundred thousand *cash* for the place, and they paid her six hundred dollars a month to live there, this was back in 2013. So you know what she did? She went and built her own new house in southeast Virginia where her part of the family is from, and she *still* had money left over. So, so my whole thing is, *how, how, how* is this *wrong*?"

Bunny nods her head, pretending to listen. Thinking about Anthony, the falling dominoes of her preconceived ideas about him, how her fundamental assumptions about his life keep revealing themselves; they feel almost uncontrollable, impulsive, even if she can't see them yet as being derived from something disease-like, so pervasive she feels completely powerless. How her foundation of belief rests on the underpinnings of all the responses she seems to think are right only to come to learn they're wrong.

Her head aches at the thought of having to meet her mother and Phyllis at the Christmas Homes Tour of Georgetown in a few minutes.

"My wife and I live out in the country. I'm done with city life. I have my little piece of earth—sixteen acres of open space behind us. So I got my smoker on my deck. I cooked a brisket this past weekend. The kids can run outside—well, now they're teenagers, but they'd go out and fly their kites. And that's one of the reasons why I love America. I grew up in the projects, my father was an alcoholic. My mother, she was overwhelmed. I was a drug addict when I was a teenager myself, and now I got twenty years sober—look what can happen when we do the work. *Miracles.*" He shakes his head in disbelief.

Light snowfall trickles across the windshield as the Uber driver pulls up to Thirty-Third Street. "Alrighty, I think this is it." He turns his head over his shoulder. "You stay warm now."

Bunny looks up, disoriented, in a different world than the one she's pulled up to. "Thank you."

Bunny shuts the car door, her strawberry blond hair glowing in the yellow streetlight. Lamps adorned with round Christmas wreaths and red bows. A Christmas fairy tale as Georgetown's cobblestone streets bustle with stay-at-home moms in their furs and camels and wools, wine hidden in coffee mugs, ready for the Christmas Homes Tour.

"Sweetheart!" Meredith runs up the sidewalk, the spitting image of Bunny's grandmother in a vintage fur and a hat reminiscent of some kind of twentieth-century bonnet. "Hurry, hurry, put these on before we go inside." Meredith hands Bunny a pair of cloth bootees for her shoes to prevent mud and snow from damaging the expensive rugs they're about to trample. The bootees look like hospital caps, blue netting with white elastic around the ankle.

"I don't want to miss this house. It's supposed to be one of the more exotic homes of Georgetown. New to the list this year. Phyllis is on her way. They just had the last group at her home, she's going to stop at the gorgeous Federal on N Street, one of the Kennedys'. *Divine*—they really ramped up the patriotic feel to it. Anyway, she'll meet us in a bit."

Meredith's excitement feels nauseating to Bunny. "Mom, I need to tell you something—"

"Aren't you *excited*? It's our first year doing this together!" Meredith is not listening, her own anxiety about the family business escalating her enthusiasm into an artificial and forced elation. "Remember when you were a little girl and you would sit on the floor in my study and flip through my *Architectural Digest* pointing at which designs you loved—you loved *kitchens*. You were only seven! But you had a good eye."

Bunny shivers on the brick sidewalk, greeted by the home tour sponsors and hosts: THE KENNEDY CENTER, WASHINGTON FINE PROPERTIES, THE EPISCOPAL CHURCH.

"Mom . . ." Bunny tries again to get her attention. "I got a call from the bank, my money didn't go through. . . ."

Meredith ignores her, adjusting her bootee around her black boot in front of a steel plaque reading: NATIONAL COLONIAL DAMES OF AMERICA (one of Thomas Jefferson's favorite places to get drunk).

"Mom . . ." Bunny's blood feels hot, a tantrum forming inside of her as Meredith walks ahead, stepping into the foyer. Behind her, Bunny hops on one foot, placing the bootees over each Doc Marten.

Hot tea simmers in fine silver displayed on an antique console as Bunny follows her mother inside. The house smells of cinnamon and vanilla potpourri, poinsettias clumped by the foot of the grand staircase.

"Welcome to number Fifteen Fifty-Two on Thirty-Third Street. This is one of the more unique homes of Washington's Georgetown, as it is not a Federal but is built of wooden planks. Rumor was they were from an old ship back when Georgetown was the largest tobacco shipping port in the country," says the real estate agent, who looks like the Monopoly man.

Bunny can't help but notice the wooden beams, the racks of white dishware for decoration. *Who's so boring they put plates on the wall?* She knows it will never be her.

They continue into the double-height living room, nearly twenty-foot ceilings, the walls full of Salvador Dalí prints of elongated animal heads. "How modern," one woman says.

Bunny raises her hand in angst. "When was the home built?" she prods.

"Wonderful question," the real estate agent replies. "It was built in the eighteen-fifties and used to be a neighborhood chapel for African Americans."

"*Oh*. So you mean slaves," Bunny corrects him.

"*Well*, perhaps—but remember, slave trading was banned in Washington City by 1850 . . . so, many were free men and women," he says.

"Well, *actually*," Bunny rebukes him, "slaves weren't emancipated until 1863, and just because it was banned doesn't mean it wasn't still happening. So this was a church for people who were most likely once enslaved."

Meredith, embarrassed, nudges Bunny: *Be quiet.*

"Well, yes, it was a neighborhood church primarily for the African American community. I do believe some were free and others perhaps had not been, but it was where they congregated."

Women's heads tilt up at the high ceilings. "Fascinating," says one, ignoring Bunny, viewing her as nothing more than a rude teenager. They move toward the kitchen.

"*Fascinating,*" Bunny mocks under her breath, following them.

"As you can see"—the agent thrusts his arms forward—"they blew out what was once the back of the church and extended the walls in order to create this stunning white kitchen."

"Oh, feel this marble counter, Marianne," a gray-haired woman says, placing the palm of her hand on the kitchen island, "to *die* for."

"Ah, yes, I believe the owners had that shipped from Rome," their guide says.

Bunny squints her eyes, rage building as the real estate agent shepherds everyone back into the living room. He stops in front of the enormous arched window overlooking the back garden, which holds an ivy-covered brick wall. Enclosed by the wall are four headstones. *HEADSTONES.*

"As you can see, there are still grave markers from the former burial grounds, adding some wonderful historical texture to the home," he says. A blow-up white Santa Claus sits on top of where the bodies were buried.

"Extra *texture*??" Bunny says, nearly exploding in continued shock.

"*Elizabeth,*" Meredith says. Other white women in their bootees and sprayed hair under bonnets turn their heads, look at the art, the new French molding, the limestone fireplace, ignore what's happening. *Pretend* it's not happening.

"Oh, it's quite all right," the real estate agent says, composed.

"What did they do with the Black bodies?" Bunny asks. She has always heard rumors that thousands of bodies are still buried beneath Volta Park across the street, where she learned to climb the monkey bars and ride her bike.

"Elizabeth Bartholomew." Meredith grabs her by the arm. Bunny whips her arm away.

"We get asked certain questions occasionally," the agent says, as more women squirm in their bootees with nowhere else to look. "Once the chapel was bought, I think around 1925, the new property owners were able—through the church—to contact the families and have the bodies returned to them after they turned it into a private residence."

"*They returned the bodies?*" Bunny says, beside herself.

Meredith clutches her arm again, digging her nails into Bunny's jacket. *"Enough."*

Bunny yanks her arm away and walks around the real estate agent.

"Yes, but they kept the tombstones as part of the historical legacy," he says with righteous indignation.

Bunny laughs at him, enraged. "*Historical legacy?* Why don't I repeat the *HISTORICAL LEGACY* for you: we enslaved you, beat you, killed you, *raped* you, now we're going to take your place of *WORSHIP* and *buy you AGAIN* so we can turn it into a mansion and hang these *STUPID* fucking plates!" Bunny storms the wall of decorative plates. She plucks one from the hook and slams it to the ground, shattering it. *"Ugly"*—she takes another plate, slams it on the floor—*"fucking"*—she grabs another, chucks it as hard as she can against the wall—*"PLATES"*—backing up now, breathing hard—"with little fucking—what the fuck are these?—*cockatoos* on them! And pat ourselves on the back for how *rich* and *white* we are. Lock ourselves inside of our ivory castles like nothing else fucking exists!" She stands, a boxer in the middle of a ring. Possessed.

"Oh my God," Meredith says, covering her mouth, shell-shocked. She runs over to the *plates* and gets on her hands and knees, collecting jagged pieces of porcelain. "I'm so sorry," she keeps repeating over and over.

Bunny's entire body trembles with rage and personal legacy when Meredith approaches her. *"Get away from me."* She charges through the foyer; slipping in her bootees, she tips over a china bowl, then runs out the front door.

❖ CHAPTER THIRTY-EIGHT ❖

*M*eredith sprints down Thirty-Third Street in her blue bootees calling after Bunny, "ELIZABETH BARTHOLOMEW!" following her toward Halcyon House on the corner of Prospect where Richard Ewell once lived, a Confederate general under Stonewall Jackson and Robert E. Lee, a colonial redbrick mansion with proud Doric columns and a view of the Lincoln Memorial, now used as a hub for young entrepreneurs who want to change the world.

Bunny stops to remove the bootees from her Docs, chucking them into the trash can on the corner. She sees Meredith sprinting after her. A pang of guilt and shame strikes her gut, the kind that hits when you think maybe you've taken things too far—enough to keep her from running away.

"Stop right there . . . please," Meredith gasps, uncomfortable, sweating in the cold. "I'm not going to yell at you, please just stop running."

Bunny faces her, her eyes blue and translucent; the veins in her temples travel down the sides of her head like lightning strikes.

"The check bounced," Bunny says, "the bank called me. It *bounced*."

"That's not a reason to have a meltdown, goddamn it, you will get the money!" Meredith shouts, as if Bunny should be punished for asking about it—the shame behind the family name tumbling from mother to daughter.

"I don't want to do this anymore," Bunny yells.

"Do what?" Meredith asks, softening a little.

"I don't want to *be here* anymore." Bunny bites her lip to keep from crying.

"Sweetheart," Meredith says, catching Bunny in this perfect moment of vulnerability. "It's been a . . . *crummy* end of the year, I know that." She pulls Bunny in for a hug and rocks her. "But what do you mean, you don't want to be here? You mean home? In George-town?"

Bunny unwraps herself from Meredith's arms. "I mean this, this *lot* that Great-Grandma had and Grandma had and you had and—I'm *tired*—I'm *not* going to wear a fucking white sash and white gloves like it's the fucking nineteen-fifties! Don't you see how fucked *up* this is? Those people removed enslaved bodies from their graves so they could build a mansion for themselves, and Audrey is *dead*, and hundreds of people from the chemical dumping are dead, and it's all our fault!" Bunny breaks down in hysterical tears.

Meredith's heart skips a beat. "What did you just say?"

Bunny sniffles, wipes her tears, inhales. "Chemical *dumping*, the Bankses' family business killing innocent poor people . . . that's why they were murdered, isn't it?"

Relieved that Bunny is talking about the Banks family and not her own, unsure of how she's obtained this information, troubled about where this conversation is leading, Meredith pulls Bunny into her, but Bunny pushes her away, a dance in the snow flurries. "It is *not* your fault, Bunny."

"But why isn't anyone talking about it?"

"Who did you hear that from?" Meredith asks, paranoid, unsure how she's going to get out of this, a crack of truth revealing itself under the foundation of her entire life.

Bunny searches for something to say, afraid to tell her mother about Anthony because she knows she'll be punished for it. "I . . . read it online somewhere."

"Those are rumors—stop reading garbage online written by websites with zero credibility," Meredith scoffs. "Conspiracy theories— *Jesus*, Bunny, you know better than that, and *we know* the truth. That man who murdered the Banks family is a sick, *sick* man who is *severely* mentally ill! And unfortunately, this is a reality we are living in today, and, and . . ." Meredith flounders, desperate to prevent her world from being cracked wide open. "I'm just so sorry that you're privy to so many shootings and so much horror at such a young age," she says, shoving the truth toward mainstream tragedies and away from her complicity. "But there is nothing we can do to change it. Let's go home now, okay? It's starting to snow."

"That's not true!" Bunny says, shivering and blinking and furrowing her brow, the flat light making her eyes hurt, a migraine coming.

"Bunny, you can keep pushing against the grain, but it won't bring Audrey back. It won't fix this. Accept it. *Accept it*, Bunny. Come on. Let's go home."

"I'm not talking about bringing Audrey back!" Bunny yells, wiping her eyes. "I'm talking about entering the twenty-first century. *HELLO*. Look around you, everything is available, any information we want about anyone: their history, their possessions, their properties, their family members, names and addresses and cell phone numbers. . . . Did you know Audrey used to brag about her clothes and jewelry and post photos of herself on her family's private jet? People—*strangers* can see it, *poor people* can see it, people who *WE WHITE RICH PEOPLE* have been oppressing for centuries! And people are starting to talk about it, because people are dying—even the people running for president are talking about it! WAKE UP."

Bunny has knocked the wind out of Meredith, thrusting her own deepest fears into light; connected by blood though alien in ideology, the two women share a history, and Bunny is rapidly pushing Meredith to confront it, unraveling their legacy before her very eyes without truly knowing the depths of it, the horror of it, their own family's part in it.

". . . And maybe that's why some people think they deserved it," Bunny finishes.

There's a look of terror in Meredith's eyes, her nose red from the cold, her cheeks rosy. "I don't even know who you are right now. How *dare* you insinuate something like that? No one on this earth deserves to die."

"That's right, Mom. No one. Including those they killed."

"This conversation is over, I'm going home." Meredith begins to cross the street.

"What do you know about the Bankses' business? Did they pay families off? *Billionaires just buying everyone off!*" Bunny shouts.

Meredith turns around, stunned; she actually wonders if her daughter has bugged the house, is she listening to her conversations with Phyllis? "What are you talking about?"

"It's a question I'm wondering whether you know the answer to? Did they pay off families that they killed from their chemical dumping?" Bunny crosses her arms.

Meredith, frozen from fear, bewilderment, literally laughs. "Bunny, sweetheart, I don't know what you're talking about. I think you need to go home and get some sleep, it's been a very tough few months," she says, gaslighting, condescendingly brushing off Bunny's accusations.

"Are we going to be next?" Bunny asks. "Because I'm not interested in being on the wrong side of history."

"You stop it, stop it right now." Meredith points her finger at her. "Your father and I have given you a *spectacular* life, don't you *dare* insult the hard work of your ancestors, your great-grandfather, a World War II hero."

"If killing thousands upon thousands of innocent children and mothers and fathers means he's a war hero, *sure!*" Bunny yells, refraining from more tears. Everything is unwinding within her, her sense of history, her pride, her family values, her moral compass swaying with each assumption that's been proven wrong. She doesn't know who to turn to when she doesn't want her future and she doesn't want her past.

"Are you insane?" Meredith says. "No more news for you. No more Internet, I'm going to take that phone away from you if you keep this up. Is this how you want to remember a lifelong friend? Is this how you want to honor her legacy? By trampling all over it with resentments from strangers and false, *ridiculous* conspiracy theories? Is this how you'd want us to be remembered? Your father is going to be so disappointed when he finds out about this." Meredith reaches for the weapon she's always had: "Start insulting your grandfather and he'll start deducting your inheritance."

"If there even is one," Bunny shouts.

Meredith turns her back on Bunny, crosses the street. She feels an overwhelming sensation—*jamais vu*—descending through her consciousness, a sudden eeriness where nothing looks familiar: the gargoyles on stone towers, the rats scurrying behind trash cans, the plaques memorializing faded American history. Meredith has walked these streets every day of her entire life, but she doesn't recognize a thing.

⋙⋘

The next morning, Meredith stands at the kitchen stove fingering her cigarette, exhaling into the electric fan. Cate sips coffee out of a white Santa mug in the red-toile-lined kitchen nook.

"How is she?" Cate asks, referring to Bunny. When Bunny finally got home after the fight on Thirty-Third Street, she and her mother hadn't spoken a word to each other, except when Bunny asked for a sleeping aid.

"I sedated her," Meredith says. She takes another drag, her eyes squinting in the smoke. Ice thaws outside the kitchen window into the crunchy boxwood bushes. They hear footsteps coming down the back staircase, creaking.

"Mom?" Bunny appears with disheveled hair and swollen eyes, her voice raspy, wearing an extra-large *Everytown for Gun Safety*

T-shirt. One eye is open. "Can I borrow your sleeping mask? The sunlight is too bright in my room. My eyes hurt."

"There's an extra one in the bottom drawer of my vanity," Meredith says.

An electric saw rages through dead limbs of the poplar tree in the front yard. "Jesus . . . what is that noise?" Bunny asks, pressing her palms against her ears as tree limbs fall to the cold grass.

"The arborist is here, he's trying to save our tree." Meredith ashes her cigarette, looking out the window. "Go back to bed, he'll be done soon."

"*Ugh,*" Bunny groans. She walks back upstairs, slamming her door, shaking the frame of the kitchen.

"Well, I think the benzos are working, but anything beyond that is . . ." Meredith blows smoke into the vent above the stove. "Cate, I'm worried about her. Ever since we lost the Bankses—Audrey, and my mother—and Billy—all of it. She hasn't been herself. . . . Do you think she should see a shrink?" Meredith ashes her cigarette on a porcelain spatula plate with some presidential inauguration date on it.

"I'm so sorry, you all have been through so much. You know, I wasn't sure if I should mention this or not, but the senator said his daughter Mackenzie has been spending some time with Bunny and her friends and seemed a little worried about her too. Sounds like they're just going through a lot, and the pressure with school . . ."

"Oh well, that's taken care of, we don't need to worry about college." Meredith shoos away the thought like a fly. "Maybe . . . if you don't mind checking on her for me in a little while, maybe give her a little pep talk? She's always wanted a sister. Maybe you can show her how . . ." Meredith searches for the right word. ". . . *grateful* you are, you know, for where you are now after what you and your sister and mother went through with your father. I don't think she knows how *lucky* she is. And she's never been through any kind of *adversity*—I mean, not that . . . maybe *adversity* isn't the right word, but *tragedy*. And to be taking it out on her community?" Meredith is *flabber-*

gasted! "For her to be insinuating that this—the Bankses' murders—has *anything* to do with race, or you know, *money*, or—their entire family was killed, for Christ's sake! Nothing justifies that."

Meredith has always had an uncanny way of making Cate feel both validated and small at the same time. "You know, I have tried to mention it, well, once before, on her birthday. I'm not sure she was feeling so receptive." Cate pauses; Meredith inhales her cigarette, doesn't say anything. "Maybe keep her away from the news for a while, you know? I know you like CNN, Aunt Meredith."

"Oh, stop it. Besides, I've already told her that."

"I'm teasing. Don't worry, I'll . . . try again. I'll have a chat with her when she's feeling better."

"Thank you. Let's change the subject—how are *you*? Senator Wallace seems to be turning the tide, are you the one behind this?" Meredith asks, pouring herself another cup of coffee, cigarette still in hand.

"I'm behind *all of it*," Cate replies, unabashedly confident.

"Oh, *really*—I'm so proud of you." Meredith places a hand on her cheek and takes a seat across from her in the breakfast nook.

"What do you know about his wife?" Cate asks.

Meredith squints out the window. "I can't stand that woman. I do have a little pity for her though."

"Why is that?"

"Why is what? Why don't I like her, or why do I take pity on her?"

"Both?"

"She's the most wretched social climber I've ever encountered in my life, and she's married to a politician, what could be worse? It's like being married to a used-car salesman, if you've never heard *that one* before." Meredith stops herself, realizing she might offend her poor little niece. "You know I'm very proud of you, but you must never trust a politician, especially when he sticks his dick around town, excuse my French." Meredith lights another cigarette. "Don't go falling in love with one, that's my only advice. You can take over the world if you like, run for president for all I care, just don't fall in love."

Cate, trying not to blush, takes a large sip of her coffee before she musters up the courage to ask, "Aunt Meredith, is . . . who . . . how do you know the senator is"—she can't bring herself to say "dick" in front of Aunt Meredith—"sleeping around town?"

"I don't," Meredith says, matter-of-fact. Cate feels like she can breathe again. "I just know the weaselly type. Sorry, dear, I know he's your boss, but I have psychic intuition about this one."

Cate, always feeling slighted, tries—politely, of course—to stand up for him, but really for herself. "Well, I'm being promoted to communications director, the announcement hasn't been released yet—but you know, Aunt Meredith, he's inevitably going to announce a bid for the presidency."

"Oh, sure, sure, they all do," Meredith says, unimpressed, whisking away the smoke between them. "But congratulations, my dear, that is so exciting." She tries to form a smile, sound enthusiastic, but the congratulations feels moot. The shifts of power among the family feel too threatening for Meredith, her whole identity wrapped up in what was given to her rather than what she created for herself. She crosses her arms, holding her cigarette up in the air.

Cate quietly sips her coffee. She feels hatred toward Doug, toward this city, toward her aunt. Once hopeful of a better future for herself, she's starting to fear an endless power game of Whac-A-Mole.

Suddenly the smell of burning. "Aunt Meredith!" Cate says, panicked. "Your cigarette!"

The end of Meredith's cigarette is touching the red toile wallpaper behind her, burning a hole in the head of a colonial family member.

"Oh, shit," Meredith says.

❦

Later that afternoon Cate knocks on Bunny's door. "Come in," Bunny says, propped up by another frayed decorative pillow, a silk eye mask the color of a ruby shielding her eyes from the sunlight. Cate tiptoes toward her nightstand. Bunny's phone rests atop a pile of books—*Notes of a Native Son, To Kill a Mockingbird, Song of Solomon*—her MacBook Air on the floor beside her bed, plugged into its charger. Bunny pulls her comforter to her chin. As Cate moves closer, Bunny pulls a hand out from under the covers and lifts her mask up over one eye. "What? What is it?"

"I just came in to check on you—your head any better?" Cate asks.

"If feeling like you're perpetually having an aneurysm is better, then, yeah, sure."

Cate laughs and sits at the foot of Bunny's bed. Bunny adjusts the mask back over her eyes, indicating a boundary she refuses to cross. She doesn't want to *look* at Cate.

"I heard about what happened," Cate says with trepidation, fully understanding that she's not part of the family, even though it hurts. The resentment creeps up again when she thinks about the time Bunny came to visit her in San Diego, before she moved to Washington. Chuck had taken Bunny on a trip to SeaWorld. At the time, Cate had received an internship at McDonald's. And when Bunny heard, she'd figured Cate was flipping burgers in the kitchen. It wasn't until Cate moved to Washington, and her internship came up in a conversation about her interview with a lobbyist friend of Chuck's, that Bunny had realized Cate had interned in their corporate office—not in the kitchen of the local Mickey D's. It gave a level of insight into Bunny's sheltered upbringing that Cate found both revealing and shameful.

"Honestly, she deserved it," Bunny says.

"I thought violence wasn't the answer, look at the shirt you're wearing."

"I threw a plate with fucking birds on it, hardly the same as an AK-forty-seven. The owners should thank me." Bunny leans her head into the pillow. Rubs her temples.

Cate can't help but laugh, thinking about smashed plates in some wealthy Georgetown home.

Bunny smiles when she hears her laughter. "See! You think they deserved it too! Greedy bastards."

"I'm not saying anyone deserved anything—we're living in complicated times. How's life at school?"

"It's fine."

"Heard you're hangin' with the boss's daughter?"

"Who? Oh, Mack—yeah, she's all right."

"Yeah?"

"Speaking of racist—I wasn't going to tell you, but your boss is one," Bunny says, adjusting her head into her pillow, satisfied with herself.

"What?" Cate asks, shock spiking through her at the quick change in tone. She shifts into work mode.

"Yep," Bunny says.

"What do you mean?"

"What do you mean, what do I mean—I heard him being one."

"When?" Cate asks, concerned, skeptical.

"The other day."

"How? Bunny, don't be preposterous."

"Where's my phone?" Bunny gropes aimlessly around her bedside table. Cate grabs the phone and puts it in her hand.

Bunny lifts her mask to scroll through her text messages. "Aha!" She presses Play on the recording and holds up the phone. Cate reaches for it.

"*Don't* touch my phone," Bunny says. "Just listen."

Mackenzie and her father's voices are heard as Bunny turns the volume up—: *"African American. . . . Running down the street like an idiot for all the neighbors to see . . . You had a young African American boy in our home who gave you drugs. Is that right? NO, he did not give me drugs! . . . Does this African American boy feel like home to you? Or does he feel different from home? . . . it feels complicated, Mackenzie. You wouldn't want to put yourself in any challenging position, would you?"*

Cate stays composed, taking this in. "Why do you have this? Who—who sent this to you? Did Mackenzie send this to you?"

Bunny smiles.

Cate reaches for the phone. "Let me see it, I need to verify this is even real."

"*Ah-ah-ah!*" Bunny yanks her hand away, still holding the phone. "My head hurts, and now yours must too."

Threatened, Cate feels her ambition catching fire, enough to make her want to grab Bunny by the neck, to push her out of the window.

Bunny pulls the mask back over her eyes. "You can get out now," she says. "Oh, and just because my mother told you to come up here doesn't mean you actually have to do it."

A punch to Cate's gut. She stands up, walks to the door, turns around and whispers, "Ungrateful bitch."

The Alibi Club

The oldest and most secret gentlemen's club in all of Washington, the club is located in an antebellum town house between two unsightly office buildings, just blocks away from the White House. Founded in 1884, it serves as a bipartisan gathering place for powerful politicians, lobbyists, judges, and businessmen where an alibi for their whereabouts will always be provided. For example, if a member's wife calls looking for her husband, someone will provide him an alibi. Only fifty men are members at any given time, and one must die in order for another to be admitted. No journalist has ever stepped foot inside. An air of mystery lingers outside as a government vacancy sign is often posted in the window—but this is just part of the game, to keep out those who are not welcome. Among the club's most notable members are and have been President George H. W. Bush, Henry Roosevelt, Thomas Gardiner Corcoran, Senator Mark Warner, Secretary of State John Foster Dulles, Speaker of the House Nicholas Longworth, and Senator Lamar Alexander—to name a few.*

---

* Sarah Booth Conroy, "A Peek at Privilege: Inside the Alibi Club," *The Washington Post*, June 22, 1992, https://www.washingtonpost.com/archive/lifestyle/1992/06/22/a-peek-at-privilege-inside-the-alibi-club/e18847d4-49d6-4f1c-81ec-23b9149acba2/.

The Laws of the Alibi

Now these are the laws of the Alibi,
Unwritten, unpublished, unsung,
And he who is wise will observe them,
Ere at noon from the yardarm he's hung.
Alibi-ites are a strange breed of cats
Whose origin is a marital mess,
So don't bring up your fancy begats,
We don't give a damn and care less . . .
Reserve the club for your private use.
Take care this privilege you not abuse,
And invite to your party whomever you wish,
Be it lady or woman or own private dish . . .
Don't let your party spill into the street
And create a noisome hubbub,
But maintain the aura of a gentlemen's retreat
Though we're licensed as a "bottle club."
Nothing will cause more trouble quicker
Than an angry woman loaded with likker
So remember that Shakespeare wisely warned
That "Hell hath no fury like a woman corned."
Once, a lady was rejected by her lover was ejected
From the center window second floor.
Despite her description the police blotter inscription
Read, "attempted suicide," but no more
But the facts of the case by the girl laid bare
That she was preceded by a bottle and followed by a chair.
So leave by the door no matter how tight.
Grasp firmly the handrails to left and right.

If the iron steps are out of place,
If the sidewalk comes up and slaps your face,
Don't fight the problem when the cops come by
To ring in "A drunk from the Alibi."
Go quietly with them to Number Three
Where Captain Pyle for a modest fee
Will provide you lodgings in good company.
Now these are the rules for the Alibi
Authentic, brief, and complete,
And he who is wise will observe them
Or land on his arse in the street.*

---

* If I tell you how I obtained this, I might have to kill you.

❖•CHAPTER THIRTY-NINE•❖

ate stands outside of a dilapidated antebellum town house: red brick, muddy green shutters, and an old streetlamp by the front door. A government VACANT sign sticks to the inside of a blurry glass window lined with velvet green curtains. The house is surrounded by modern glass high-rises.

Cate texts, I'm at the address you sent and all I see is a creepy government vacancy sign. Where r u? She spins around; the White House is just a few blocks away, secret service officers with their bulletproof vests and AK-47s, tourists taking selfies.

Come to the door, Doug replies.

Cate turns around like she knows she's being watched as the door of the town home creaks open. A strong whiff of mothballs fills the already polluted air—a sour, rusty smell like the breath of Thomas Jefferson risen from the dead.

As she walks in, a Black steward in a bow tie appears from behind the door like a ghost and closes it behind her. He says nothing, then lifts an old car horn to his lips and blows. Cate jumps from the penetrating noise—"Jesus!"—plugging her ears. The steward lowers the horn to his side and stares ahead as though Cate were invisible.

Cate pokes her head around the corner into the drawing room. A Victorian chaise and Welton dresser rest on a Persian rug fit for a king. *What is this place?* Leather-bound law books and old encyclopedia collections fill the built-in bookshelves. A crystal service bell waits on the antique burl-wood coffee table. Crossed swords hang on the opposite wall among other historical tchotchkes. It looks like an epic yard sale with American fairy tales hidden in every corner and crevice.

"Come upstairs," Doug says from the top of the single staircase, which hugs a wall soaked in damask wallpaper dating back to the Middle Ages.

Established as a secret institution in the aftermath of the Civil War, the club guards the ghosts of men from the grounds of Oak Hill and Rock Creek cemeteries, who are commemorated in the upper hallway in gold-framed photos of CIA directors, Supreme Court justices, secretaries of state, and presidents. The round table in the dining hall is set with pewter plates and goblets and Windsor chairs—like their very own American Knights of the Round Table. General Robert E. Lee's uniform hangs on a mannequin in the corner, still encrusted with his blood. The Alibi Club is the oldest, most secretive fraternity in all of America, where bipartisan power brokering is done and Saudi royals are entertained. Because the institutions of Washington live longer than the average male, the passing of the Alibi torch becomes the ultimate legacy.

Doug leads Cate into what is known as the poker room, filled with square tables, its walls covered in Japanese scrolls; legend has it that this is the room where General Eisenhower called for Operation Neptune—World War II's invasion of Normandy.

"Why did you have me come meet you at a museum?" Cate asks, annoyed.

"It's not a museum, it's an exclusive club, Cate," Doug says, defending himself and all of his choices in the history of his entire political career.

A workman enters carrying boxes of twinkle lights and several Christmas wreaths.

"Excuse me, we'd like to have some privacy," Doug says, shooing him out of the room, then turns back to Cate. "What's going on? Where's Walter?"

"He resigned, did you not check your e-mail?"

"He *RESIGNED*?"

It's no secret Cate's fighting for a rise in status, and Doug knows it. "Jesus Christ, what did you say to him?"

"In case you hadn't noticed since—since we haven't been seeing each other"—she pauses—"he has had an affinity for grazing my nipples and other inappropriate behavior. . . . The press was onto him, so I gave him a choice: resign with dignity or—"

"Is this the fucking emergency?!" Doug panics. Never mind that his press secretary was being sexually harassed and assaulted. He walks to the other end of the room by a green couch where a skinned boar's head heaves its snout. Cate looks away, tries not to gag.

"If you checked your e-mail, you would see that everything is *fine*. He's going quietly. He's 'retiring early' to spend more time with his family; he will not be moving forward on any future campaigns. That will be left to me. I'm being promoted in the meantime, which looks fucking *great* for you," she says, but Doug's not convinced.

"Christ, the press will catch on." Doug runs his hand over his shiny head.

"They've already talked to me. It's done. . . . But this *isn't* the emergency, Doug."

Doug flails his body, losing control over himself. "It *all* sounds like a fucking *emergency*—"

"The *emergency* is your *daughter*, and how she and Bunny both have a recording of you being blatantly racist—"

"That's impossible."

"—something about you needing your daughter to break up with her Black boyfriend because of the color of his skin." Cate lets this sink in. "Mackenzie's phone *has it*, she recorded it. Meaning: your voice is heard having a conversation with your daughter about how she had a person of color give her drugs, and something about if he doesn't feel like home then he's not love and basically that your parents would have been ashamed if she were ever to introduce him as part of the family. *Believe me*, I heard it."

Sweat drips from Doug's forehead, pit stains forming underneath his arms. He loosens his tie. "Well, I'm obviously not racist. . . ." Doug laughs manically, then pounds his fist into the air. "Betsy needs to get a grip on those girls. I knew it, I knew she shouldn't be hanging out with that Bartholomew girl either." Doug points his finger at Cate. "She's the one responsible for General Montgomery's son's overdose, you know."

"That's my cousin you're talking about."

"Oh, right—sorry, but—"

"But you're right, Bunny's become a liability."

Doug begins pacing across the room. "FUCK!"

"Look, we don't have a lot of time. I have evidence of two devices with the video, and who knows who else Mackenzie sent it to—and if either girl decides to post it, I mean, we're talkin' *viral*."

"Like Internet viral?" Doug asks.

The sound of creaking footsteps down the hallway prevents Cate from responding right away. Gordon Bay, the president's lawyer— eighties, disheveled hair, black bushy eyebrows, a hunched back— comes thumping down the hall with his cane. Framed by the poker room doorway, Mr. Bay stops to zip his fly, then looks over at Doug.

"Senator Wallace!" he says, delighted to see him utilizing the space as a new member of the club.

Doug switches gears as if he's fucking Jekyll and Hyde, a charming smile on command: "Sir." He goes to shake his hand. A young brunette bobbles behind Mr. Bay with a glass of bubbly. She wipes the corners of her mouth with her acrylic nails.

"Uhh, this is *Cat*," Doug says, looking at Cate. She looks back at him confused, irritated.

"*Well now*, don't you forget to tip." Mr. Bay winks. "You know the old blackmailing legend here, don't ya?" He tries to hit Doug in the arm but misses and almost falls over.

Doug guides him gently back out to the hallway. "I do, I do. I'll be sure to leave double the average, Counsel."

"Thatta boy."

"Make sure he doesn't fall down the stairs," Doug says to his mistress.

"I'm taking good care of him, Mr. Senator." She winks as they move away.

Cate stands, hand on hip, an incredulous look across her face. "Did you just imply that I was your prostitute? What is this? A flophouse for retired White House cabinet members?!"

"Relax, I told you, you're not supposed to be here."

"But I am if I'm your prostitute."

"Cate." Doug goes to her, cupping his hands around her flushed cheeks. "That was the president's lawyer, he *cannot know* about any of this. If it doesn't look good for me, it doesn't look good for you. Particularly in your new role as *communications director*," he says in a manipulative tone.

Cate places her hands over his and pushes them off her cheeks. "Fine."

"So I need to get Mackenzie's phone and you need to get Bunny's," Doug says, forming a game plan.

"And we need to not only confiscate the recording, but we need to scroll through their messages, their apps, anyplace where they could have potentially sent the video," Cate adds.

"Right."

"Doug, do you know how to go through the apps?" Cate gives him a patronizing look.

Doug looks flustered.

"Just get her phone and bring it to the office. I'll send for a fixer to clean it up," Cate says.

"Great—and you'll do the same for Bunny's phone."

"Yep. We don't have a lot of time. Where's Mackenzie now?" Cate asks.

"Christmas shopping with Betsy."

"Get hold of it, and I'll meet you at the office in the morning." Cate wraps herself in her trench coat, and heads for the stairwell.

"Oh, and Cate?" Doug turns to her. "I'm really not a racist, I swear."

Cate swings her purse over her shoulder. "You know, Doug, people who lie to others don't bother me—it's people who lie to themselves that end up getting completely fucked." A stare-down, neither one knowing if they can trust the other; then Cate turns away, leaving Doug speechless. As Cate descends the wooden staircase, the sound of a turbulent landing of God knows what—shattered porcelain and wood maybe—comes from the downstairs drawing room. Startled, she pauses on her way to the front door and peers into the room. Gordon Bay is sitting in a Chesterfield chair, staring at the floor. Split-pea soup oozes across the floorboards near the frayed fringes of a snapped rope—the dumbwaiter broke. He picks up the crystal service bell, panicked: *ding ding ding ding ding ding.*

❖ · CHAPTER FORTY · ❖

a black Suburban makes its way down a dirt driveway lined with anemic weeping willows and scattered haystacks. As the vehicle carrying Billy, General Montgomery, and his attorney approaches the old millhouse, an American flag whips around itself. There is only the sound of silence in the Blue Ridge Mountains as the middle of winter descends upon the grounds most notable for carrying the soldiers of the Civil War.

Having a farm in Upperville, Virginia, or nearby Middleburg, is a marker of wealth in Washington, a symbol that you are either a descendant of plantation owners or you are the first to begin building the desired legacy—*the American Dream.*

The general had bought the old property during the economic recession—a place for his in-laws to retire and a gathering spot for the family on weekends and holidays. Once a corn mill in the eighteenth and nineteenth centuries, it was the first plantation set on fire in the "burning raids" of the Confederacy as American troops marched up to the bloody battle of Gettysburg. When the general became chairman of the Joint Chiefs of Staff, when all the power and status he would claim in Washington culminated, this was the country home he'd chosen—his thumbprint pressed upon another part of history. The only spoiler was the perpetual smell of jet fuel and engine noise from the home just a mile down the road, where the scion of an American banking dynasty had added a goddamn airstrip for the private jet to fly his family to and from New York.

A roaring fire climbs up the stone chimney. Wooden beams cross fifteen-foot ceilings in the living room, where military sketches of various battles cover the walls between warped windowpanes. Carol sits in the corner of a beige sofa, her red reading glasses on top of her head. Crow's-feet stretch the length of her upper cheekbones; she's exhausted from the buried tears, her silent days escaping in books at the library. Her parents sit side by side opposite her, a simple couple just grateful to be there, as the general enters in his blue uniform. His lawyer and Billy follow in his shadow.

"Carol, Shirley, Bob, this is my attorney, Rod Bernstein. He's going to walk everyone through what we should expect in the next few weeks and how to handle it in public."

Rod Bernstein is one of the most prominent "fixers" in Washington; with a little too much Botox, he drives a Maserati and is currently having sex with a twenty-four-year old computer "engineer." He's the guy to call when a senator kills a prostitute, news of a president's shell company gets leaked, a congressman crashes his car after too many whiskeys—or when the nominee for secretary of defense is being investigated for war crimes.

Billy takes a seat next to his grandmother, who gives him a warm hug, smelling of lavender potpourri.

"Hello, everyone," says Bernstein. "So, we will start with you, Billy, because I know the general only needs you for part of this preparation for what we're about to be dealing with here."

Billy looks at his father, then to his mother at this discriminatory move—he's intentionally being left out of the "grown-up" conversation as punishment for his recent overdose; he's a liability to them now. The general stands next to Mr. Bernstein, arms folded, brow furrowed, zero shame regarding the hefty price he's paid to get him here.

Bernstein continues, "If the press follows you to school, to your basketball games, girlfriend's house, or whatnot, ignore them. *Do not talk to them*. If they heckle you, keep walking. Those tailing you are lowest on the totem pole, and despite it being illegal, no one with half a brain will care what you're up to *unless* the video gets released. The point is to keep your online presence clean, etcetera. But before I go to the video—"

Billy's grandmother interrupts: "What video? What video is he talking about?"

"Please, Shirley, do not interrupt him," the general says with the predictable irritation of a son-in-law, "he will get there."

"Okay, sorry."

"Before I go there, I want you, Billy, to keep your head and chin up when you walk, stand tall and proud. Appearances and first impressions are half of the battle. And if images end up online, you will at least look confident. Only celebrities look down. You are a product of a legacy that requires you to keep this confidence in the face of adversity."

"Yes, sir, okay," Billy says, his clammy palms folded in his lap.

"Now," Bernstein says, "if the video of you being waterboarded with champagne and using language that would be perceived as bigoted is released, we're dealing with something a little more serious."

"WILLIAM MONTGOMERY," his grandmother says, looking at him in disbelief and shame. He has betrayed her legacy, her daughter's legacy, his own good judgment, and their family's reputation. Carol can't bring herself to look at him.

"*IF* the video is released and catches fire with the media, it will call for a period of isolation. In which case, you will be driven to and from school by security. You cannot, at any time, be seen in public, as it will perpetuate the story in the gossip columns."

The general nods his head to concur with his attorney, despite being in uncharted waters.

"Presumably there will be threats, violent or otherwise—"

"Oh my God," Carol says, on the verge of tears.

"If so, we'll be monitoring, so there is no need to worry. I guarantee this, Carol. But, if it is released, at least it's now and not later, as the news cycle tends to slow down during the holidays. But it also makes the situation ripe for anything particularly salacious to go viral. So we'll need to keep watch. If it does, there is nothing we can do to stop it. You will need to ride it out as best you can, and complete the instructions given to you by my team regarding the isolation period."

There is a moment where Billy stays silent, prompting the general to say, "ARE WE CLEAR, WILLIAM?"

"Yes, sir," he says, a lump in his throat, his world closing in on him, the unknown, an unbearable feeling to hold inside.

"Great. So you understand?" says Bernstein.

"Yes, sir," Billy replies.

Bernstein looks to General Montgomery and says, "So I think we're done with him, yeah?"

The general turns to look at Billy. "William, you're excused now."

Billy struggles to ask his father if he can stay for the grown-up conversation, assuming Bernstein would serve as a great buffer, which might provide more wiggle room for a yes answer. He sits a beat longer on the couch, hoping someone other than himself will change their mind.

"I said, you're excused."

Carol pours herself a large glass of red wine. Billy stands and exits with his head down and takes a few steps up the old wooden staircase. Then, as quietly as he can, balancing on less-used steps, he tiptoes back downstairs and stands with his back against the wall, ear turned to the door—he's a soldier in his own home, a CIA agent, a private investigator; he wants to understand what exactly is happening to his father, the anxiety reaping each breath he takes.

Muffled sounds. Lowered voices. Scattered words. *"Naval base . . . Iraq . . . investigation has not yet been made public. Picking off a schoolboy . . . sniper . . . SEAL witnesses . . . blackmail. Over a dozen charges . . .*

premeditated murder and attempted murder charges are included in the indictment."

The sound of his mother's crying, his grandfather's belligerent rage, the general reassuring them, Bernstein: *". . . the president is on your side."*

Billy's heart pounds heavier with every word; he's consumed by shame and self-hatred for compromising the family reputation—the stakes have never felt so high. He feels violent inside, his hormones racing through his bloodstream, and suddenly all he can think about is calling Bunny.

❧· CHAPTER FORTY-ONE ·❧

*I*n the middle of the night, Doug creeps down the long hallway from his master suite and into Mackenzie's bedroom
while she is fast asleep. Holding his breath, he reaches for her cell
phone on the nightstand, unplugs it from its charger, then tiptoes
out of her room as fast as he can without getting caught. It's the next
morning when Teresa, the housekeeper, is in the kitchen packing
Haley's *Maleficent* lunchbox for the last day of school at St. Peter's
Academy before Christmas break that all hell breaks loose.

Mackenzie storms into the kitchen. "Where's my cell phone? Did
you take my cell phone? It's *gone*."

"*Niña*, check under the bed," Teresa tells her.

"I *did* check under the bed."

Betsy strolls into the kitchen wearing a pink floral kimono, her
hair pinned up in hot rollers, her foundation without the eyes and
lips done creating a kind of geisha look. "Good morning, sweet pea."
She pulls a coffee mug out of the cabinet. "Did you get your violin
practice in this morning?"

"Did you take my phone? *I can't find my phone.*"

Betsy pops an Illy coffee pod into the Keurig, slams it shut; above the sound of gurgling, she says, "Sweetie, why would I take your phone?"

"I don't know, but it's *missing*." Mackenzie begins throwing around pillows in the sun-room next to the kitchen, searching.

Betsy looks at Teresa. "Look at this, she's completely addicted, these kids have a serious problem." She sips her coffee without a solution.

Mackenzie knocks over a fake hydrangea arrangement.

"That's enough," Betsy says, storming over and grabbing Mackenzie by the arm. "You need to be out this door in thirty minutes."

"Stop!" Mackenzie swings her arm around, wrenching out of Betsy's hand, and begins to hyperventilate: "I have *notes* . . . for my . . . *test* . . . *ON MY PHONE!!!*" She stomps over to the kitchen island, frantically opening and slamming cabinet doors.

"All right, that's it, I'm calling your father."

"Good! Ask *him* where it is!"

Betsy holds her phone above her head; the sound of ringing over speakerphone. Teresa zips Haley's lunch bag, unfazed by the usual family chaos.

"Yes?" Doug says, picking up, a curious but playful tone.

Betsy locks eyes with Mackenzie, holding the phone midway between them. "Your daughter seems to have misplaced her cell phone and believes one of us took it."

"Oh no! Sugar pie"—Doug feigns surprise—"listen, I'll send one of my interns to do a sweep at the house today, we'll find it, don't you worry." Mackenzie stares at the phone. ". . . And look, babycakes, Christmas is around the corner—if you're good, Santa will bring you an upgrade, how about that?"

"I need *this one*, Dad, I have everything on my phone, I have my *life* on it."

"Okay, don't you worry, I'm stepping into the office now." Doug is actually stuck in traffic on Pennsylvania Avenue.

"Fine."

"Hey, Cate, will you send someone over to sweep the house for Mack's phone?" Doug says to his empty passenger seat.

"Thank you!" Betsy says.

"Thanks, Dad," Mackenzie says.

"Talk to you later." Betsy hangs up. "See? Now go get dressed, don't make your sister late for school. And *don't* forget your violin case like last time."

Mackenzie stands clad in her school uniform: green plaid skirt, black leggings, blue collared shirt, and gray V-neck sweater with *Fidelitas et Integritas*, the school crest, sewn on its pocket.

She scans her body in her bathroom mirror, reaches for her cell phone like a phantom limb, then remembers it's not there, just a bunch of loose music sheets in her bag and her violin in its case on the marble floor next to her. Mackenzie grunts into the mirror, "*Guuuuuaaaaaahhhhh!!!!*" As if it's Judgment Day, she flips her hair over to the left side of her head, carving out a part with her pointer fingers. Holding her breath, she lets her fingers crawl along the root of each piece of hair. She smudges her pointer finger against her scalp, scratching then collecting several hairs, releasing the ones she doesn't want; they fall like paper in the wind. For a moment, Mackenzie tries to stop herself, resist the pull, but it only makes her anxiety worse, like a truck driving into her lungs. She yanks without thinking, without any pause—like the tiniest stem in a dying garden, she yanks it hard and fast from the root, a crunching sound as it's torn from the skull. She exhales with pleasure, an easy look across her face once it's out of her head. She opens the palm of her hand; the tips of her fingers are covered in pink blood. She rinses them under the tap, and watches the pink water swirl down the drain.

"Mackenzie!" Betsy yells through the intercom. "We're going to be late!"

"I'll be right there!" She wipes her fingertips on an embroidered hand towel, then hops up onto the sink, scoots as close to the mirror as she can. Butterflies swirl in her stomach as she thinks about her upcoming exam, her father telling her Marty isn't good enough because he doesn't feel like home, her new violin piece. She parts her hair to the other side of her head, her fingers crawling along the roots. She rubs the root with her pointer again, her obsessive ritual, then curls the thin, tiny strand of hair around her finger and yanks hard, holding her breath. She exhales just as Betsy bursts through the bathroom door. Startled, Mackenzie turns her head and it hits the open medicine cabinet.

"*Ow!* Jesus, *Mom*, can you *knock?!*"

"What are you doing?" Betsy grabs Mackenzie's hand, sees the blood on her fingertips. "Wash this off right now."

"I am!"

"Let me see."

Mackenzie tries to swat her mother away. "Mom, stop!"

"Let me see right this goddamn minute." Betsy wrestles her, forcing her into a headlock, her diamond Cartier watch digging into Mackenzie's cheek.

"Ow!"

Betsy flips her hair over. "Oh my God, you're bleeding." Several new scabs have formed against the fresh patch of Mackenzie's bloody and picked roots.

"Mom, stop!" Mackenzie begins to sob, now limp in her arms. "Stop!"

"This isn't normal! This *isn't normal*, Mackenzie! *Why are you doing this?!*" she yells, letting her daughter fall from her arms as if she's dropped her over a cliff.

"I don't know!" Mackenzie sobs, up against the bathroom wall and sliding down to the floor.

"I'm calling the doctor right now."

Haley walks into Mackenzie's room with her backpack over her shoulders, ready for school. "Mom? What's going on? I'm going to be late!"

"It's your sister, we're dealing with an emergency. Teresa needs to take you. Go tell her I said she's taking you. . . . *Go!* The keys to the Jaguar are on the hook by the back door."

"Get out!" Mackenzie screams at her sister. Haley runs out of her room.

"Are you on drugs? Was it that boy, Billy Montgomery?"

"No!"

"You have to stop doing this, Mackenzie." Betsy squats down, puts her hands on Mackenzie's shoulders, and shakes her against the bathroom door. "Do you hear me? *You have to stop!*"

"Stop! I'm tired! I'm tired! I'm tired of performing; I don't want to perform anymore. I don't want to perform." Mackenzie curls over, buries her face in her hands as she sobs, rocking on her bath mat.

⁘ CHAPTER FORTY-TWO ⁘

*B*unny sits on the swan garden bench in Bishop's Garden smoking, her Doc Marten tapping its claw as she exhales. An arch of thorns over her head, and decomposing leaves stuck to the stone pathway beside her. She throws her cigarette into the fountain to her left, water spewing from the mouth of a stone gargoyle, gaping like a yawning cat. She crosses her arms and wraps them around her stomach, hunching over in her red peacoat, her freckles barely visible this time of year, faded against her translucent skin. She's wearing red Dior cat's-eye sunglasses to shield her eyes from the flat light now ripe for giving her headaches.

"What's with the sunglasses?" a voice asks from behind.

Bunny jumps and spins around. "Jesus, Billy. You scared me!" Bunny collects herself. Billy stands opposite her, black peacoat, tousled hair, hands in his pockets, dark circles under his eyes. Gaunt.

"The light, I got a headache," Bunny says. "Did you just climb through the bushes?"

"Yeah. Being followed." Billy ducks his head, peering out at the black Suburban parked across the street, tinted windows, government tags. "How come you're not responding to my texts?" he asks.

"I can't find my phone," Bunny says, the tension between them like sticky residue inside of an unfinished breakup.

"Can we talk for a second?" Billy takes a few steps closer to her and removes the sunglasses from her eyes.

Bunny winces, the light stinging. "*Ahh!* Can you *stop?*" she says, squinting up at him, a glassy veil over her clear blue eyes. "Give them back!"

Billy surrenders and hands them back. "Okay, diva."

"Fuck you. My eyes are sensitive to the light." Bunny puts them back on, takes a seat on the bench again.

"So did you give your money away?" Billy asks, sitting next to her.

Bunny sighs, annoyed. "Not yet." She feels the impulse to tell him about the Christmas homes tour but finds herself stuck in her own story, sinking in confusion, unsure of how to explain it anymore or what to say.

"Interesting." Billy nods his head.

"I don't want to talk about this, if that's why you came here."

Billy looks up to the sky, then puts his head back down as if looking up might reveal something he doesn't want to see. "My dad's being indicted for war crimes." The words slip out matter-of-factly, unusual for Billy when he's with Bunny, a more withholding and less sensitive tone.

"What?" Bunny says, confused. "That sounds like an oxymoron."

"Hah. I didn't think about that."

"What does that mean? *Indicted.*"

"Honestly, I don't really know, but I think it means prison. Unless the president pardons him, which, I don't know . . ."

Bunny looks down at her Doc Martens, kicks the claw of the bench with her heel. "Wow," she says.

"I know what you're thinking," Billy says.

"No you don't," Bunny says.

"Look, everything we have . . . *everything* my father built for my family was done on the backs of my dirt-poor ancestors—"

"Billy, everyone's families were built on the backs of their ancestors, this isn't *unique*. Why can't you just accept that the world we live in is morally bankrupt and *racist*? And that your dad probably *did* commit war crimes."

"Will you let me finish?!" Billy shouts.

"Finish!" Bunny shouts back, both of them angry about the same thing, but neither willing to hear it.

Billy stands, looking at her, fed up. "What I was going to say was that I fucking get it, *okay*? Is this what you finally want to hear—that it was all for nothing? That my father is going down in history as a murderer? *Your* family was responsible for the engine of our weapons of war, Bunny. I don't see anyone in your family behind bars." Billy throws his hands up in the air. "You honestly don't even know—"

"I do know, Billy!" Bunny leaps from the bench. "Why do you think I was trying to give my money *away*?" she yells, her temples pounding.

"Giving money away to a man accused of murdering your friend is not going to fix anything, Bunny!" Billy yells back.

Bunny stands in the cold, her lip quivering, on the verge of tears, when Marty comes sprinting down the stone steps, across the koi pond bridge, and through the garden to where they're standing. Out of breath, he throws his hands down on his knees. "You guys . . . oh my God," Marty gasps, pushes his glasses up his nose, "the video, the video of us, it's gone viral."

Bunny wipes a tear under her eye. "What? What video?"

Billy drops onto the bench and puts his head down between his knees. "*Fuck*," he whispers.

"The video!" Marty yells as if Bunny's an imbecile. "The video of us waterboarding Billy at Stan's party!"

"*Oh my God*—it was on Stan's cell phone, he had it," Bunny says, defensive.

"You're the one who filmed it, Bunny," Billy accuses her. "Give us your phone!"

"*I don't have it*, I don't have my fucking phone! *It wasn't me!*"

"No, wait, she's right, dude," Marty says, pulling up the video on his own phone, "this was Stan's phone. It was filmed on *his* phone—

and I can't find that little fucker anywhere." He begins to dial Stan's number.

"I tried him yesterday, he's MIA. And he didn't show up for our history final on Friday," Billy says, a rare mixture of panic and confusion building in his stomach.

"Fuck, man," Marty says in his upper register, "Harvard's gonna rescind my acceptance if they see this. My life is over, my parents *will* kill me." He sits down on the icy grass, flinging his North Face backpack to the side. "What the fuck do we do?"

Flooded with guilt for filming that night, Bunny's unsure of what to say. "I'm really sor—"

"*AGHHHHHH!*" Billy stands and throws a punch into the trunk of the three-hundred-year-old oak tree beside them, its trunk twice the size of the three of them combined. A loud crunch as his knuckles splinter the bark; blood oozes over his hand.

The hour strikes. The National Cathedral bells begin to ring—first the treble, then one after another in sequence, a crescendo of overlapping bells as the Washington Ringing Society commences its practice.

❧•CHAPTER FORTY-THREE•❧

*M*ackenzie steps out of Betsy's Jag wearing a brunette wig. After an emergency visit to her primary care doctor, Mackenzie has been diagnosed with trichotillomania (hair pulling classified as an obsessive-compulsive disorder) and immediately referred to a psychiatrist. Instead of calling the psychiatrist for an urgent appointment, Betsy took her to buy a wig and have her makeup done at the Tysons Corner Chanel makeup counter before taking her to school.

The waiting area of the school administration office has two plaid sofas facing each other and a large globe in the corner. Marty sits across from Chase with a stiff upper lip. Billy stands in the corner spinning the globe with his eyes closed, his pointer finger stopping on one of the seven continents. All three have been called into the principal's office after word about the video spread like wildfire. E-mails from the press are flooding the school's general mailbox. The school principal has seen the video; Marty's and Chase's parents have seen it; a message has been left for Billy's father—and everyone is on their way for a meeting with the headmaster.

*   *   *

Mackenzie follows her mother into the office, beset by the kind of high school dread due to a complete lack of confidence, brushing strands of the wig out of her eyes, and sees Marty waiting on the couch. He stands as she enters.

"Hey," he says, puzzled by her hair but too distressed to comment.

"Hey, what are you guys doing in here?" Mackenzie looks around the lobby area, pretending everything is normal, and sees Chase slouched over texting on his phone, Billy in the corner spinning the globe.

"Uh . . ." Marty puts his hands in his pockets, trying not to fidget. "It's, uhh, it's not good," he whispers.

"What happened?" Mackenzie asks.

"I'll, uhh, tell you later." Marty takes a few steps back as Betsy approaches.

"Hello," Betsy says, staring at Marty, who fidgets from nerves, pushes his glasses up his nose; the timing couldn't possibly be worse—meeting the mother of the girl whose virginity you've just taken.

"Mom, this is Marty," Mackenzie says.

Marty steps forward, sticks out his hand like a soldier with his chin out. "Nice to meet you, Mrs. Wallace."

Betsy smiles as if she's sucking on a sour candy, turns to Mackenzie. "Well, they've got my note, you can go to class. Teresa will pick you up after violin practice. I told her you could drive home."

"Thanks, Mom." Mackenzie's violin case dangles from her arm. "See you guys later," she says to them, relieved that Marty is amidst his own crisis, which allows her to escape a conversation about her hair.

As Mackenzie and Betsy part ways in the hall, Linda Williams comes barreling down the corridor in a pastel-blue cashmere sweater and Burberry quilted coat.

"Betsy!" Linda calls.

Betsy spins around. "Oh, Linda!"

Betsy stopped attending French classes after her interview at the Washington Club, and has stopped returning any of Linda's calls.

"Did you get my message the other day?" Linda asks.

"Gosh, I am so behind on my correspondence," Betsy says.

"Your daughter posted a meme of me and my daughter on a fake Instagram account, and it circulated through their class. Becca has cried every day after school."

"I'm sorry, Linda, I have no idea what you are talking about, and I have a meeting with my decorator in thirty minutes."

Linda does her best to remain civilized in a desperate attempt to regain her upper position in the friendship. "I'm just so confused, Betsy, as we're really not used to that behavior around here at St. Peter's Academy, and I would hate for the principal to find out— or for anyone to know—as it will reflect poorly on you and Doug. After all, I did just write a recommendation letter to the Washington Club on your behalf. . . ." Linda has no idea that rumors have leaked regarding her husband's sexual misconduct.

"I'm just curious, Linda, if you ever thought how knowing my family would benefit yourself? Particularly given Doug's rising public popularity. You know the ratings went up on Chris's show because Doug was on it. But a warning about certain allegations in the works would have been appreciated, given how sensitive the topic of sex has been, particularly given how delicate one's reputation can be. . . ."

Gaslit, Linda looks like she's seen a ghost. Stunned to silence.

"People talk, Linda. . . . *Oh*, what is that saying everyone in Washington uses? *We don't need a weatherman to know which way the wind blows*." Betsy walks up to the sliding doors, turns back. "Do send my love to Chris."

❦·CHAPTER FORTY-FOUR·❦

*B*unny shuffles up the cobblestone driveway, sunglasses on, lugging her heavy backpack as if she's just come home from war. Upon entering the front door, she throws her backpack down; it scratches the red toile wallpaper on its way to the floor, creating a rip in the façade of a family picnic. She strolls into the kitchen and sees Meredith standing at the stove, a beef stew boiling, a lit cigarette in her right hand as smoke and steam whirl up into the vent. Meredith is exhausted from the leaf blowers, the arborists grinding wood all day long, a perpetual engine spinning in her eardrums, sawing off limbs of her favorite tree. An antique trunk with golden latches is planted in the center of the kitchen, what's left of her mother's valuables she has yet to go through: black-and-white curled photographs of the farm in Middleburg, a debutante sash, stained white gloves. *Emily Post's Etiquette* rests on top of this treasure chest of an American Dream.

Ignoring it, Bunny finds her cell phone on the counter across from her mother. She runs to it.

"My phone! Oh, thank God." Bunny brings it to her chest, relieved.

"We need to talk." Meredith stabs her cigarette out.

"Can we talk later?" Bunny whines, kicking off her Doc Martens, her knee socks uneven, her plaid skirt and gray sweater begging to be thrown away after all these years.

Meredith sticks out her arm like a broomstick. "Stop right there. *Sit down.*"

Bunny rolls her eyes and slumps into the kitchen nook beside her.

"Have you been visiting the DC Jail?"

Bunny stares up at her, holding her tongue, a tactic she learned at a young age. Instead of filling the silence herself, she'll wait to find out how much her mother already knows, then gauge how to minimize the trouble, make it swing in her favor.

"Answer me." Meredith hovers over her, then whips her arm from behind her back and slams Bunny's Moleskine journal on the table in front of her. "Goddamn it, Bunny, we have all been through *enough.*"

Bunny's cheeks flush. "*Okay!* So I wanted more information about the case, what's the big deal?" Trying to minimize her connection with Anthony.

"You have been visiting a man who has committed *murder*. . . . This is—this is beyond inappropriate. . . ."

"*Inappropriate?*" Bunny mocks.

"Is this why you've been acting out? Because you've been having conversations with a man accused of murdering an *entire* fucking family!" Meredith is becoming unhinged.

"Well, maybe if someone would tell the truth, I wouldn't have had to do it!"

"*Christ,*" Meredith says, the back of her hand across her eyes and forehead. "How could you be so *stupid*, so *reckless* . . . to put our family in *DANGER* like this!"

Bunny scoffs. "*See*, you think we're in danger, don't you? We'd be in more danger if I *didn't* go, *didn't* see, *didn't* try to find out what's happening. I KNOW that the Banks family has killed innocent people, and we should make it right, we have a chance to make it right so it doesn't happen again. . . ." she warns.

"Elizabeth, goddamn it, I am at the end of my rope. You have stepped out of bounds—*OUT OF BOUNDS*, do you hear me? You have acted foolishly out of character. Not only have you tampered with their case, you have put yourself and our family at risk—"

"Then tell me the truth!" Bunny stands up.

"What more truth do you need, he was arrested, goddamn it! And I know what you're saying, I know how it looks, trust me I do, and I don't know what kind of game you think this is—some kind of *American trope fantasy* you're acting out because it was a Black man they arrested, but it's not going to fly with your father and me."

"*Trope?* Here's your fucking trope." Bunny walks over to *Emily Post's Etiquette* and slams her hand on it, its spine so old it pops off, pages slithering out like loose feathers. "You know what *etiquette* was founded on, Mother? *Racism, classism, CAPITALISM*—and by *etiquette* we mean *manners*, and by *manners* we mean *pedigree*, and by *pedigree* we mean *white*. Like those fucking ugly white gloves."

"Watch your mouth. If Mimi were alive, she would slap you."

"Well, that wouldn't be very *polite*, would it? Because being polite and having *manners* isn't the same as having *morals*, huh? *Nope, nope, nope.* It's about the way I hold my fork and wear my scarf and with-hold words and keep up the gatekeeping—like *you*. This—this—unspoken obstacle that controls access to money. Speaking of money, my money still hasn't arrived like you said it would. Just admit it—you're so scared of losing power not just for power's sake, but because of what might be done to you if you were no longer protected by it."

Meredith lifts her hand and smacks Bunny hard across the face. Bunny stumbles sideways, tripping over the vintage trunk; more loose pages of *Etiquette* go flying into the air, swaying between them, before reaching the kitchen floor.

"You do not have a monopoly on truth, you *ungrateful* child. Your place doesn't exist in this world without a social and economic hier-archy, your privileges, your education, the neighborhood and home in which you grew up—your grandparents would be *ashamed* of your uncalled-for juvenile behavior. Would you rather I cut you off? Dump you on a street corner downtown? Because I am goddamn close to doing it." Meredith's hands begin to shake as she reaches for her pack of cigarettes on the counter behind her.

Bunny holds her cheek and fumbles to put her shoes on with her other hand. "This is why they died, always some justification," she mumbles, on the verge of tears, "all those innocent people. And Anthony is next. . . ."

"That's it, I'm calling Georgetown Hospital's psychiatric department. This is *not normal*. You should have *never* been in contact with that psychopath; you could have been killed going down to that jail! When your father finds out, he's going to sue the whole *goddamn* city!" Meredith says, overcompensating for her own ugly truth—the lawsuits, the covering up, that Chuck in these very moments is meeting with attorneys in glass high-rises, blocking testimony by families riddled with cancer who can't pay their medical bills, whose minimum wage is so far behind inflation they can't eat three meals a day. That she is happy—relieved!—to be in negotiations to take over the Banks business assets, to stay forever planted as they were, as they are: *legacy pioneers* in the creation of social and economic hierarchy.

"Killed going down to that jail?" Bunny laughs. "Call the psychiatric hospital for yourself. I'm leaving." She runs down the hall and out the front door, slamming it behind her.

Mount Zion Cemetery

Clement Morgan was the first Black man to graduate from both Harvard College and Harvard Law School. He is buried "somewhere in the Mount Zion Graveyard" in Georgetown. "Somewhere," because the graves are cracked and crumbling in clustered piles; faded inscriptions and muddy land make reading any names nearly impossible. The cemetery, owned by Mount Zion Church, which was the first Black congregation of Georgetown, marks the burial ground of hundreds of the formerly enslaved and freemen. Unlike Oak Hill Cemetery, the "white graveyard" next door, there are no wrought iron gates protecting it from intruders, no immaculate cenotaphs and tombs, no gardeners watering its boxwoods every Saturday. Ravaged by neglect, it sits behind a run-down apartment building and beside an alley full of trash cans, dumpsters, and rats.

The eroding land remains a stark reminder of the racial and economic injustices as well as the gentrification that Georgetown has endured for over a century.* The graveyard may also have served as a hiding spot on the Underground Railroad. Those in the process of fleeing the terror of slavery were believed to have hidden in an eight-by-eight-foot windowless brick structure on the side of the hill that was used to store frozen corpses during winter.**

---

* "Death of a Cemetery: Mt. Zion's Disrepair," *The Georgetowner*, March 26, 2015, https://georgetowner.com/articles/2015/03/26/death-cemetery-mt-zions-disrepair/.

** "Mount Zion Cemetery's Underground Railroad Shelter," Atlas Obscura, https://www.atlasobscura.com/places/mount-zion-cemeterys-underground-railroad-shelter.

❖ CHAPTER FORTY-FIVE ❖

*B*unny sits on a bench in a deserted graveyard. She looks out at the opposite hill beyond the deep valley of Rock Creek Park, where she can see the lights of Billy's towering mansion through the cold and leafless woods. In the shadows, as the cloudy winter night hovers over crumbling graves, Bunny hears the sound of crunching snow. She turns her head to the right and sees two sinewy figures approaching her. Spooked, she pops up from the bench and ducks behind a tipping cenotaph; pulling down on her pink beanie, she squints to see who it is as one of the figures trips and slams into a headstone.

"Dude, are you okay?"

The sound of laughter.

"Fucking buzzzz killll," the other one says.

Bunny moves closer, shines her cell phone light straight into their eyes. "Marty?"

Marty, wearing a red beanie, puts his right hand up, squinting, holding a joint with his left. He jumps back.

"It's Bunny. It's Bunny!" she says. She moves her flashlight over. "Chase? What are you guys doing here?"

"What are *you* doing here?" Marty asks.

Chase swings a glass bottle of Russian vodka by his side. "Bunny Foo Foo hoppin' through the forest!" he laughs to himself.

"Don't fucking call me that," Bunny says, eerie echoes of Audrey teasing her in middle school. She looks at Marty. "I asked you first."

"We got kicked out of school," Chase blurts out, then takes another swig of vodka, sweat forming along his greasy hairline.

"What?"

"We didn't get kicked out of school," Marty corrects him, pushing his glasses up his nose as he moves closer to Bunny. "Harvard rescinded my acceptance letter."

"Oh, shit, no," Bunny says.

"Yep, me toooo." Chase chucks the bottle of vodka into a bush. He stumbles over toward Marty and wraps him in a drunken bear hug. "But we have each other."

"Shut up, Chase, you got into Rollins, not Harvard," Bunny quips.

"Harvard, *Schmarvard*!" Chase sings out, staggering. "It's all the fuckin' same if you're a rich man in *AMERRRIIICCAAAA!!!!*" He pounds his chest.

"Go home, dude," Marty says, "it's your bedtime."

"Nah, man," Chase says, "my dad is gonna hook me up to his lie detector again."

"So don't lie," Marty says.

"You're no fun, lame-ass." Chase pulls his cell phone from his parka pocket and calls an Uber. "I miss Stan-the-man!" He wobbles off toward the brick path, then shouts, "Texting Billy you two are alone in the graveyard!"

"Fuck you!" Marty yells back.

They watch Chase stagger off. Bunny greets Marty on the other side of a headstone. "Can I?"

Marty passes Bunny the joint.

"I'm sorry this is happening," she says, then inhales and passes the joint back.

"Well, it happened. The vodka and Purple Kush are numbing the pain though," Marty says, examining the joint.

Bunny puts her hands in her pockets; there's an ice storm coming. "Do you think it really matters where we go to school? Where we end up?"

Marty breathes in the cold air, looks up to the sky. "Did you know that the probability of any one of us going to St. Peter's Academy is less than getting struck by lightning?" He inhales the last of the joint, then kneels and rubs the roach into the dirty snow.

"Are you serious?" Bunny laughs.

"I did the research," Marty says. Standing up, he puts his hands in his pockets.

"I would have rather gotten struck by lightning," Bunny says.

Marty leans against the back of the bench, the marijuana pushing him into a deeper analysis of self. "It matters to me," he says, dropping into a more serious tone, "even though, if you look at it, at the probability—we've technically already won the lottery of life."

Bunny looks at Marty, and she feels a pang of guilt. "It's my fault," she says, "I should have never filmed you guys."

"Ah, don't worry about it, Bunny, we all took part."

"But I wasn't on camera, and it wasn't my phone."

Marty sniffles and straightens his back to sober up a bit. "Well, the truth is, my dad's position at Howard is probably enough to get me in there. And give or take a year, I'll just transfer somewhere else if I want. At the end of the day, I dunno, it matters and it doesn't— where we go to school. But I let my grandparents down, that's what's eating me." Marty shakes his head.

Bunny looks at him in wonder and in silence. She feels the opposite. She feels a kind of hereditary, genealogical disdain for her grandparents. And the shame feels invisible; she doesn't know how to respond.

"So I won't work for the CIA or the State Department, big deal. Sucks more for Billy, man," he says.

"What? No it doesn't. Why do you say that? Billy doesn't even want to go to the academy."

"Yeah, but his father's a public figure. Billy got trolled the hardest today, and it's only gonna get worse," Marty says.

"I haven't talked to him since earlier so I don't really know what's going on."

"He's been acting distant since even before the overdose—just super irritated a lot. What's going on with you guys anyway?"

"Nothing . . . it's . . . we broke up, I guess, but we're talking . . . more like fighting, still. It's the pressure from his dad, I know it. And then I did something that upset him, and it just brought up a lot of shit about our families and . . . expectations about who we're supposed to be, you know? But I think he might be starting to come around, given that his dad is *probably* going to prison."

"Yeah, General Montgomery's always been kind of a dick—but, fuck, you think he'll actually go to prison?"

"If the president doesn't pardon him."

Marty shakes his head. "First Audrey, now this, what's next?"

Bunny takes a pack of cigarettes out of her jacket pocket. Puts an unlit cigarette to her lips.

"Bunny and her cigarettes, so old school," Marty teases.

She stops herself. *So old school.* Bunny looks at the cigarette and snaps it in half, then takes the whole pack out of her pocket and stomps on it.

"Whoa, what'd I say?"

"Nothing. I'm done, *all right*? I'm done smoking cigarettes," Bunny says.

"*Okaaay.*" Marty looks at her with skepticism. An awkward moment passes. "What are you doing here anyway? Why are you all alone in an abandoned graveyard? It's a little creepy, Bunny. Are *you* okay?"

"Got into a fight with my mom . . . thinkin' about Audrey, wanted to hang among the ghosts of America's past, I guess."

"So you came to Mount Zion? This is my side of the tracks," Marty teases, "your people are buried over there." He nods toward the other side of a chain-link fence where Oak Hill Cemetery is—equipped with twenty-four-hour security cameras and where Bunny's ancestors are buried, still segregated from Mount Zion—a dark, visceral reminder of the priorities of preservation in American history.

"Yeah, well, I don't want to be on my side anymore," Bunny says. She looks over at Marty. She wants to tell him about Anthony; she wants to talk to him about what it's like being the only kid of color in her class; she wants to know what he thinks about the murders, about Anthony, whether or not he thinks he did it; she wants to know what he thought of Audrey's flaunted wealth; she wants to know whether he believes white people have an unconscious fear that if America were to obtain true equality, would the Black man do to the white man what the white man had done to the Black man? But in this moment, she is afraid to ask. She knows Marty is wealthy; his family lives in a cozy town house down the street crammed with overflowing bookshelves and the law degrees of his professor parents. Worried she might offend him, or say the wrong thing, Bunny finds herself resisting—it feels far too intimate—easier perhaps with Anthony, the two of them in different buildings, separated by a fake ID and a television monitor, where by circumstance she has more power, not just because of her family but because she is physically free. And she wonders if even thinking about all of these things makes her a terrible person.

"Do you miss Audrey?" Marty asks.

"Sometimes," Bunny says honestly, "but she could be a real bitch."

Marty laughs. "All right, you're being honest. We weren't that close . . . but it's still sad."

Bunny looks up, white flakes clustering in her strawberry eyelashes. "Do you think he's still out there?"

"Who?"

"The person who murdered her family."

"They arrested that guy though," Marty says.

"Yeah, but do you really think he did it?"

Marty exhales, exhausted, stoned, drunk. "I dunno, Bunny. . . . But, you know, my parents are skeptical. They told me not to tell anyone, though, out of respect for the family and all that. People just want to feel like justice has been served even if only on the surface. They got a face for the crime? Makes 'em feel safer even if it isn't true—but that's what my parents say, anyway."

Bunny looks at the snow collecting on the toes of her boots. "Yeah, that makes sense." She looks out into the woods toward Billy's house twinkling in the distance, too afraid to ask more.

Another awkward moment passes between them.

"Come on, let's get outta here," Marty says, "or we're going to get buried in the snow."

❖∙CHAPTER FORTY-SIX∙❖

Cate walks along the East Colonnade of the White House gazing out at the decorative Christmas trees, which have been spray-painted a menacing red, as if she's entering the gates of hell. The annual Christmas party is filled with members of Congress, foreign dignitaries, business leaders including Jeff Bezos, and country music stars just out of rehab. There are flying midgets (they prefer the term *midget* because the president said so) swinging from trapeze lines in the East Room delivering bags of sugar cookies embossed with the gold presidential seal to guests. The midgets were flown in from Las Vegas's MGM Grand Hotel.

Cate wanders along the red felt carpet in a black-and-white Rent the Runway gown and her late great-aunt's pearls, feeling antsy about Doug, when her work cell rings.

"Senator Wallace's office."

"Hi, Cate?"

"Speaking."

"This is Anne from the *Washington Post*. We spoke—"

"Yes, I remember," Cate says, turning her body away from clusters of cabinet members' wives and families, little boys in suspenders and girls with silk ribbons in their hair.

"Right, well, I'm just calling to let you know that our piece will be going live in a few days, and I wanted to give you one more opportunity to come forward with any sensitive information you might have about the senator's history of any sexual misconduct."

"Glad you got your corroborating evidence," Cate says, a smirk across her face as she gazes out the window at Doug on the White House's South Lawn walking an alpaca with bells around its neck. Haley and Mackenzie stroll next to him in their coordinating holiday dresses.

"I did," Anne replies. "It's not pretty, Cate."

"I'm sorry to hear that," Cate says. "He's clean, what can I tell you?"

Doug hands Mackenzie the alpaca leash, then pulls on his crotch. Cate squints her eyes.

"You have until ten o'clock tonight to call me back," Anne says.

"Merry Christmas, Anne." Cate hangs up, then calls Doug as she spies on him and his daughters behind one of the red Christmas trees. She sees him look at his phone and then press Ignore as she hears it go to his voice mail. Before Cate can call him back, she sees Betsy approach him on the lawn wearing one of her signature red capes. Holding a flute glass of champagne, she goes in to cheers him, puckering her lips as Doug leans in for a kiss. Cate drops her phone. A woman who seems about seven feet tall, in a sequined dress with feathers poking out of it à la vaudeville, reaches down and hands Cate her cell phone.

"Thank you," Cate says.

"Sure thing, honey."

The sound of a helicopter startles guests before they realize that Marine One, the president's helicopter, is descending from the sky preparing for a surprise landing.

"Haley, Mackenzie, look!" Doug shouts. The alpaca leaps from the deafening chopping sound, the rope yanked from Mackenzie's hand as the furry animal hops across the lawn in sheer panic. Two other alpacas run wild as well, having escaped the grips of bratty children.

"Come back!" Mackenzie screams above Marine One's engine, clutching her wig as she runs after it. Her heels catch in the wet grass.

Betsy sips her champagne, still as a posturing peacock. She points to a secret service agent and mouths, *Could you handle that? Thanks,* shooing him off to chase the alpaca.

"Haley, come on!" Doug motions for her to catch up to him as he jogs toward the helicopter like a kid at LEGOLAND, other scattered guests fleeing for a good view.

Haley slumps over in boredom, moans, "*Dad,* I *already* saw this. It landed on our soccer field last week, remember? *I told youuuu.*"

"Is that true?" Doug asks.

"We watched it land during PE." Haley rolls her eyes, cradling a special kind of apathy for an eleven-year-old.

From inside the Blue Room, Cate texts the senator: I saw you ignore my call, meet me in the Blue Room. She's standing in front of President Bill Clinton's portrait. The Marine Corps band plays swing-style Christmas music.

Doug enters, flustered, stressed. "Jesus, Cate, my family is here."

"That didn't stop you at a funeral. You assume I called you in here to fuck like Marilyn Monroe, but seeing as we're not fucking anymore, I thought I'd just relay the news that the allegations will be going live in the coming days."

"Okay, *whoa,* easy, easy," Doug whispers, looking around the room. "First, I thought we settled this—"

"Well, the reporter called me again, very, *very* sure this time that I had information about your office—your history of sexual misconduct. She was giving me a second chance to give her something."

Doug feels Cate's tone shifting from team player to threatening. His shame is so deep inside of him his cheeks don't even flush anymore. "Everything that's happened between the two of us has been consensual. I don't understand . . . what are you doing?"

A man dressed as a golden nutcracker walks by and offers them champagne. Doug waves him away.

"Oh, I know, Doug. But rumor is that you've been, and I quote, 'sticking your dick around town,' and not just in me—"

"Okay, Jesus, keep your voice down," he says, practically begging.

"You are my boss, and a friend of my uncle's, and, well, this isn't gonna look so good."

"I'm listening, I'm listening," he says. His eyes dart left, then right.

"I think everyone around here has always been a fan of the quid pro quo. So, for my silence, I'd like communications director when you run for president, maximum payout plus benefits."

Doug runs his hand over his bald head, *like the generals and the Corcorans!* "I'll have outside counsel send an ironclad. Okay? I have two daughters, Cate."

"Oh, I know you do . . . and one of 'em is still fucking her Black boyfriend." Cate smiles. "Merry Christmas, Doug."

CHAPTER FORTY-SEVEN

*a*nthony appears on-screen, his eyelid swollen shut; he has a gash on his right arm, stitches crisscrossing along what looks like a knife wound, a knot tied at the end holding his flesh together. Bunny picks up the blue telephone and presses it to her ear.

"Hey," she says.

"Hey." Anthony tugs on the edge of his stitches, an itch. Bunny winces and directs her eyes down, avoiding the wound. "Did you give them the money?" he asks, visibly anxious.

"I went to see your sister and . . . I'm sorry, she didn't want the money, Anthony," Bunny says, but with a cruel withholding—*Bunny doesn't even have the money.*

Anthony glares at her with contempt, a pervasive silence so strong she can feel it vibrating through the monitor.

"So what did my sister say to you?" he finally asks.

"She—she mentioned an agreement with the Banks company . . . I think. . . . Then she threatened to call the cops if I didn't get off her property."

Anthony fidgets in his chair, sniffs, rubs his right eye like he hasn't slept in days.

"Can you tell me about the agreement?" Bunny asks.

"It's the money they paid to keep us quiet," he says.

Frustrated, Bunny demands, "Why didn't you tell me this before I went over there?"

"Because you wouldn't have gone over there if you knew we'd been given money."

"Why would you assume something like that? Your sister was completely paranoid about me. And if you had warned her—she said you haven't spoken in months—why did you lie to me? You didn't have to lie to me. I would have still gone over there! I would have still tried to give her the money!" Bunny is working herself up, performing a kind of fake vulnerability, making her case for not being able to give him any money. A violent and manipulative navigation rooted in her shame and guilt for pretending to be someone else, for thinking she could help him. "I'm so sorry," she says, "there's . . . nothing else I can do."

As if coming down from a high, or from a false and angry hope, Anthony looks at her; it is the most vulnerable she has ever seen him. He knows what he's up against: *multiple counts of first-degree murder, armed robbery, extortion, theft, arson.* He'll get life in prison without the possibility of parole.

"I tried, Anthony," Bunny says, bowing her head.

"Then just help find me a lawyer! Find me a lawyer, I'm going to fucking die in here!"

"I'm—I'm a journalist, I—I can't. . . ." Trapped in her legacy of lies and warped fantasies of terror and victimhood and self-righteousness, Bunny is left with nothing but the reality that the system was designed for this.

Anthony nods, on the verge of tears, then reaches down off-screen where Bunny can't see. He comes back into the frame, composed, and holds up a copy of the *Washington Post* business section:

Bartholomew Industries to Acquire Banks Family Business
Assets in Monopoly over Chemicals Industry

"Do you know who this family is?" he asks her.

"I—I can't really see it, I'm having trouble reading—"

"Let me move it closer." Anthony thrusts the headline so it fills the entire frame of the monitor. Bunny reads it, her heart thumping; the words probe her deepest fears, her nascent narcissism and whiteness railing against the belief that he didn't do it, warping the truth, blind to the possibility: *Did my family kill them?*

Anthony laughs, a medicated laugh. "Sounds just like your family, Amazing Grace. Doesn't it?"

Bunny feels herself falling back into the shadows of her privileged conscience before the Bankses were murdered.

"Did you fuckin' lie to *ME*?"

"I—I—I don't know what you're talking about."

"YOU'RE THE FUCKIN' LIAR! I may die in here, Grace, but at least I'll die knowing the truth, while you may *never* accept yours."

Bunny's absorption of the Banks family legacy ignites a kind of new fragility within her she isn't sure she can withstand, it feels too big. *This door is closing on me.* She cannot escape her inner circle, the expectation that someone else will do it for her, will welcome her with open arms, without consequences—but there are always consequences.

She thinks of Billy and his father. She wants to run and hide with him. To think she could solve the problems of the world—how could she be so naïve? *Honey . . . you're not on this road.* She is *entrenched* in those problems, sinking in the quicksand of an antiquated life, romanticizing history, soaked in white paranoia within a hierarchy and nation stuck in its own imprisonment. *That will be her legacy.*

"I'm sorry," Bunny says to Anthony. "I'm so sorry." She hangs up the phone. Anthony looks at her through the screen as she gets up, rageful, scared; she is everything he thought she'd be. He wanted to tell her one last thing, but all he hears is silence.

Kicking Bear and the Ghost Dance

Matho Wanahtake, also known as Kicking Bear, was a chief of the Lakota Nation. He rose to prominence after the Battle of the Little Bighorn in 1876, in which American troops were resoundingly defeated. In 1889, he traveled to Nevada to learn what was known as the Ghost Dance from its leader, Wovoka, and bring it back to his people. The dance, which spread quickly through the western part of the country, was believed to help reunite Native Americans with their ancestors and protect against white colonialism, bringing back their land, their traditions, and their good fortune and causing the white man to "be swallowed up by the earth."*

Before the turn of the twentieth century, Kicking Bear traveled to Washington, DC, as a delegate for the Sioux Tribe fighting for more rights with the Bureau of Indian Affairs. During this time, he agreed to have a life mask made of himself. After his death, architect Glenn Brown, who designed the Dumbarton Bridge, lined the bottom of the bridge with fifty-six sculptures of Kicking Bear's face.**

---

*   Akta Lakota Museum and Cultural Center (website), http://aktalakota.stjo.org/site/News2?page=NewsArticle&id=8750.

**   John Kelly, "Those Carved Faces on the Q Street Bridge? Meet the Real Person They're Based On," *The Washington Post*, January 31, 2018, https://www.washingtonpost.com/local/those-carved-faces-on-the-q-street-bridge-meet-the-real-person-theyre-based-on/2018/01/31/61a66fca-05f6-11e8-94e8-e8b8600ade23_story.html.

CHAPTER FORTY-EIGHT

*B*illy is sweating, his shirt sticking to his back; it is days before Christmas and the weather channel signals a code orange. Billy feels the raw *whoosh* of cars passing by as he trails the edge of the sidewalk along Massachusetts Avenue—before the galas, the fundraisers and salons, the things *this town* tries so hard to cultivate, to make them feel important, to make them feel enough, to make them feel worth the weight of the world on someone else's shoulders.

Billy approaches the gates of the Russian ambassador's residence. He wobbles. He waits. He turns around to see if anyone—the *Washington Post*, the *Daily Mail*, that jealous no-name twentysomething who writes a Washington gossip blog—is following him. Instead of reaching for the bottle, the drug one last time, Billy makes a deal with himself: if his friend Stan answers, he won't do it. *He won't do it.* Stan would never betray him, *right*? He would never have released the video—on behalf of his father, on behalf of Russia.

Accustomed to lone helicopters flying overhead, Billy hears the sound of a government chopper churning in the polluted air, catching his attention for once. He looks up, then wraps both his hands around the Russian gates in front of him. *Where are the guards? Where is my buddy, Putin 2.0? Where is Stan?* Billy lifts his head: a lock and chain hold the metal gates together. He turns his back, holds his hand to his forehead like he's saluting the sun; he hears Bunny's voice like a whispering ghost, catching him in this righteous stillness: *Why are you so afraid of the dark, Billy?* He is not what she says he is: *She doesn't understand me, and she never will.*

An old white man approaches Billy with his chocolate Labrador puppy, all floppy paws and wobbly limbs. The white man: blue polo, yellow khakis, brown loafers, a walking Brooks Brothers mannequin. "We finally kicked those bastards out, eh? No one left to let you in, they've abandoned it—*heel, Bailey! Heel!*" The white man pulls the puppy away from Billy, who takes a few steps backward. Billy lowers his face to the ground, pulls his hoodie up over his head.

"Thank God, *send all the bastards home!*" The man cackles, an annoying laugh.

Billy doesn't understand what he means by this. *What the fuck is he talking about? Where did everyone go?*

Billy is unsteady, his mouth dry, his head light. He tries to speak but stutters, for Billy hasn't said a word to anyone in days. Waking up to the shame, the family name smeared, his legacy ripped from underneath him, and overwhelmed by the steps it would take to fix it, heal it, change it, *bury* it—to not become it. *It* is too much. Swallowing feels like a razor slicing through his guts, where the truth lives, day after day. He is a boy who cannot see the other side of disruption. He sees only his shadow, distorted from the bright sun and propelling clouds, shaking in the dead grass.

❖·CHAPTER FORTY-NINE·❖

*M*eredith sits before her computer screen fingering her cigarette, gazing every so often out the window—at the tulip poplar tree which is no longer there, only its phantom. She holds her phone to her ear listening to Chuck give her online banking directions for a separate account. Sunlight hits the side of her face, forcing her to hold up her hand like a shield. For all these years, the tulip poplar blocked the rays.

"Hold on," Meredith tells Chuck as she walks to her cherry-colored balloon curtain, kneeling on the floral love seat to tug at the cord, releasing the curtain's fold down the window. On the shelf next to her, her mother's white debutante gloves rest atop Sally Bedell Smith's biographies of Queen Elizabeth, Princess Diana, the Kennedys, William S. Paley.

"Okay, what's the log-in?" Meredith taps on the keyboard, throws on her tortoiseshell glasses to get a better look at the numbers. "Oh my God, Chuck." She can't believe the enormity of the number that she's looking at. "Will this get leaked to the press?" she asks, concerned.

"The transaction of assets will be estimated, but nothing personal," Chuck tells her.

"And the Bankses' will? Has it been settled?"

"Most of it was for Audrey—a couple hundred grand has been liquidated for a few cousins, but it's been dispersed, and contracts have been signed. It's done. None of the threatened lawsuits against the Bankses' side were credible."

"And what about us?" Meredith asks.

"Mer, the government—local and state—didn't have enough money and resources to prove it in court. The families don't have a leg to stand on—it's getting thrown out. I'm comin' home."

"Oh, thank God," Meredith says, exasperated.

"Just get Bunny under control, will you? I'm wiring the five hundred grand I told you about into her trust now—with a limit on what she can take out monthly. It's time for her to learn how to respect money," Chuck says.

"I made her psychiatrist appointment to get her on the medication we discussed. We can talk tonight. When does your flight get in?"

"Around nine."

"See you tonight, darling."

Meredith has known since childhood that a seed of sin plants itself long before its money grows. That once it's been planted, there is nothing you can do to determine where the roots will go, whether or not they will rot or flourish generation after generation. Most won't know until the tree has fully grown—and even if cut down, its roots stay gripping the soil underground. It is only in the erosion of itself that one can see its nasty tentacles—how many, how far, how wide they have spread.

Meredith lights another cigarette and crosses to the lead-lined Edwardian liquor cabinet, opening it to a display of inherited and magnificently mismatched decanters of single malt scotch, sherry, and gin. She takes a glass and pours herself a shot of gin. She shoots it, squinting her eyes, then slams the glass down next to an ancient bottle of Schnapps with a gold leaf floating in it. Curbing her impulse to call the psychic medium again, she takes a drag of her cigarette and flips on the nightly news.

". . . In breaking news, in the early hours of the morning the FBI arrested chairman of the Joint Chiefs of Staff, General Edward Montgomery, who had recently been nominated by the president to become the next secretary of defense. . . . It is believed that the president will not pardon him. General Montgomery's son William has also been under fire for a recent video, which went viral last week, showing him and several high school friends mocking US torture methods and using derogatory language on-camera. Some of those individuals were planning to attend elite universities in the fall next year, but it has been reported that those letters of acceptance have been rescinded. . . ."

Meredith stands riveted in front of the television screen, smoke climbing from the end of her cigarette like a slithering snake.

Bunny bursts through the front door, setting off the alarm; she grunts as she punches in 0007. Billy isn't answering his cell phone or responding to her texts.

"Bunny?" Meredith calls, not taking her eyes off the television screen—at a loss for words, her world imploding with scandal.

Bunny steps onto the Persian rug, preparing to confront her mother about the news Anthony showed her in the paper. She turns to the television screen, attention caught.

"Have you spoken to him?" Meredith asks.

"Oh my God." Bunny bolts for the front door. She races to her bike resting on the side of the garage. It'll be faster at this hour to ride her bike over the Q Street Bridge to get to Billy's house.

The temperature dropping, the icy wind burns Bunny's pale cheeks. She pedals faster and calls Marty from her cell, but he's not answering either. He had texted her while she was with Anthony, asking if she'd spoken to Billy; irritated, assuming it was about their breakup, she'd ignored it. Maybe it was, maybe it wasn't—maybe it was about everything.

Bunny's cycled this route a million times, but only now does its history seem to follow her: the muscular buffalo statues at the edge of the bridge, the Civil War hero atop his bucking horse, the stone faces of Kicking Bear, the Native American warrior who led the Ghost Dance ritual, lining the bridge.

Crippled expressions of looming gargoyles taunt her as Bunny reaches the grass of the Haitian Embassy where she hides her bike. She runs across the double yellow lines of Massachusetts Avenue and into the brick driveway of Billy's mansion. Out of breath, she lifts the front door knocker—a brass ring inside of a lion's mouth: *bam-bam-bam.* "*BILLY!*" she screams.

There is only silence.

She runs to the side of the house, where overgrown ivy has weaved itself through wrought iron gates. She stumbles upon a garter snake shedding its skin in the middle of the brick path; startled, she leaps, then trips and flies forward, skidding her soft palms into the ground. Bunny gathers herself and wipes her bloody palms at the chilling sight of the snake escaping its dead skin, *but it is still a snake,* and watches it slither back into the cold dirt. She looks up to her favorite gargoyle perched beside Billy's bedroom window—his mouth open wide, his sharp fangs hanging like knives—"*BILLY!*" she screams into the sky, then goes to unlatch the gate.

Upon entering the back garden she screams his name one last time as she approaches his hanging body. His swollen eyelids are red from broken capillaries and pregnant with trapped tears; his head hangs peacefully over the rope around his neck—his teenage angst, his fears, his rage, his shame, his love, all gone. He hangs from the back limestone balcony of his father's office below a stained glass window.

Bunny grabs his legs and swoops them into her arms, grunting with unleashed tears as she tries to lift them higher on her tippy-toes to make the rope loose around his neck, his knees pressed against her bulging cheek, but she's not tall enough. . . . *"SOMEONE HELP ME!!!"* His body sways around her. She lowers herself, trying to gather his feet in her arms, but her arms are too weak. *"SOMEONE HEELLLLPPPP!!!!"*

A security guard appears, panic-stricken as he runs to Bunny's aid and sees Billy's blue body dangling from the balcony. He calls 911, says something into his radio that Bunny can't understand, and bolts for the back garden of the embassy next door. He comes back dragging a patio chair and places it next to Billy's body, then climbs on top of it, lifting Billy's torso with his left hand, attempting to cut the rope with his right. Bunny looks up and sees Billy's recent tattoo in the light, the one he never showed her, below his quiet heart, an unfinished circle.

As the security guard briefs the 911 operator, Bunny collapses into a parallel universe, her heart slamming as she hunches over in prayer position, rocking back and forth, *". . . Please . . . please. . . .please . . ."* curling her back, she roars again and again and again *". . . Please . . . please . . . please . . ."* she gasps for air and Billy's body is taken away, red lights and blue uniforms surround her as she kicks her arms and legs, flailing, *"Get away from me."* Bunny falls to her side, bringing her knees to her chest, heaving and screaming in between blinding grunts.

❧ · CHAPTER FIFTY · ❧

Cate sits across from America's presumed future first family, Doug, Betsy, Mackenzie, and Haley, in a blacked-out limousine. She glances at Betsy's face, her tattooed eyeliner, her false lashes, her Botox and fillers, and hopes that one day she won't feel the same, remembering what Doug told her once: *My mother always told me to go for the pretty ones because they're the ones with the lowest self-esteem.* Thinking about what it must feel like to lose your beauty if that's all you ever had—clinging to a man whose inherent value somehow becomes your own. But Cate doesn't know how to climb out of the fishbowl she's thrown herself into; her desire for power always seems to give her whole self away. The thoughts, in these moments on the way to Billy's funeral, seem mostly abstract, but close enough for her to realize she doesn't want them.

Doug's cold withholding of affection, how quickly it left her, forces Cate to catch her breath. She swallows and lowers her sunglasses over her eyes and thinks about her father somewhere in a California prison, which is strange, because she never thinks about her father, not anymore. If she had been raised more like Bunny and less like herself, she wonders, would things have gone a different way for her? She thought she'd come to Washington to create herself, not find herself, and somehow she's been caught in between the two. The violence in her head castrates her circular emotions: *Aren't I worthy of love? Will my strategy work? Stop being dramatic.* Cate knows deep down that had she been given all of the harder things in life on a silver platter as Bunny was—the things she thought she needed to *win*—that her legacy alone would never be enough. People die, things change, it's simple. And even with all of the glory and status, no matter how she looks at it, something inside of her knows it wouldn't ever feel like enough.

Betsy looks at Doug, placing her hand over his. "Did I tell you we got accepted into the Washington Club?"

Doug, in a haze: "No, you didn't mention it."

"Well, we did." Betsy smiles wide before she remembers they're on their way to a dead boy's funeral. She picks up the newspaper displayed next to the empty flute glasses of champagne:

A RECKONING OF SEXUAL MISCONDUCT FOR POWER PLAYERS IN WASHINGTON

Cate studies Betsy again, watching her read the article. Betsy squirms in her seat, cracks her window. "Hot flash, phew!" she says, fake-smiling, when she reaches the end of the article—Doug's name absent among those of some of his oldest colleagues, whom Betsy knows quite well. Cate smiles in her direction for a moment as Betsy glances at her then quickly rolls up her window, a common unknowing of being inside a symptom of the patriarchy.

Doug turns back as motorcades blaze past them preparing to stop average pedestrians from *getting in the way* of government officials attending Billy's funeral. Doug remembers his brother, Ken, and he hates himself. He adjusts his tie and clears his sore throat, a cold coming on, tries to flip his thoughts to his pending bill again.

Someday I will be buried there, with the generals and the saints! Famous men. . . .

And just like that, Cate reaches into her pocket, scoops out her phone like one of her emotional rocks. She refuses to be painted as a victim under any man's power. But she *will* do something to thrust herself into the spotlight if it makes her look like a hero.

She texts Anne from the *Washington Post*: . . . but I do have this . . . She uploads the recording of Doug's racist monologue telling Mackenzie to break up with Marty. She hits Send.

By the end of the funeral, Cate's life will have changed. Photographers and reporters will swarm her; she'll be invited on every late-night political reporting news show and every panel. She'll be famous. She'll start her PR firm . . . she'll move to New York. She'll never look back.

Anne from the *Washington Post*: Holy. Shit.

Cate: You're welcome.

◦⃯◦

Bunny sits in the breakfast nook wearing black. Numb and heavy, she stares out of the aged-glass window forming a distorted reality as though she were hallucinating—a stray black cat tiptoes along the porch, its tail like the arm of a ballerina, twirling around a white column. With salad tongs, Meredith places a boiled hot dog on a china plate in front of Bunny. "You have to eat," she says. Away from the outside world, time stands still. Bunny has never felt more present inside of her own home before, inside of herself; she's so uncomfortable she wants to peel her skin off. Looking at her mother sitting across from her, the way her throat moves when she clears it and raises her eyelids, her pupils pinned to a random point on the wall between the floor and the windowsill, Bunny thinks, *Could I be brave like Billy suggested? Could I cut them off, could I run away? Could I survive?*

"My high school boyfriend killed himself," Meredith says.

The sentence lingers in the air between them for a long time. Bunny doesn't try to fill the silence. It belongs to her mother. She looks down at her soggy hot dog and swallows.

Meredith's eyes squint like she's trying to will the memory back to her. "I knew he was going to do it because he called me twice with instructions on what to tell his father." She picks up her fork and knife and begins to saw off a piece of her hot dog. "I remember my hair was wet."

Bunny picks up her fork. Her hand begins to shake like Meredith's.

Billy's funeral is in an hour.

"He hung himself with his father's favorite ties. He was a clever bastard."

Bunny bites off a piece of her hot dog, breathing out of her nose, and chews.

Meredith breaks her gaze from the wall and looks directly at Bunny. "Did you know that the idea of a utopia is inherently contradictory? No two people's ideals are the same, and can therefore never exist together. The human condition won't allow it. If the laws of the universe are correct, born out of utopia is dystopia, and that is a much more frightening place to live than somewhere in the middle. But no one really thinks that *deeply* about the world, Elizabeth." Meredith sighs and sticks her fork into her hot dog. "I am afraid history has done it again."

Bunny wants to know before it's too late: *How do you change the script of a storied institution?* Power can change in an instant, the *POW!* of a bullet, the ringing of a phone, the click of a bank deposit, the sentence of a crime—the touchdown of a tornado. It is not in the undoing, but afterward, in the sound of someone else's silence, when you know that it has left you.

Friends and family exit the glass doors of the Cathedral beneath the carved mural of a swirling God. The same photographers and bobbleheads as after the Bankses' funeral wait along Wisconsin

Avenue, arranging themselves in the order of their hierarchy—a cruel schadenfreude for the general and Carol's fall from grace, the two of them still sitting in the shadows of the great nave before tombs of famed generals. If shame could coil inside of grief, this kind will not find its way out.

Crows perch atop the angry gargoyles as pallbearers carry Billy's casket into the black hearse. A tiny American flag whips against its windshield as it drives away.

Bunny watches, a crinkled slit forming between her eyebrows where her mother likes to stick her finger ("Botox soon!" "Smile!" "Lucky girl!"). She staggers behind the crowd and backs into the nave, slipping into the Children's Chapel beside it. Cold as a ghost, Bunny tiptoes down the aisle between the little chairs where she learned to cross her ankles during nursery school prayers.

The altar before her is covered with candles below the mural of a baby Jesus—for the mother undergoing in vitro, the toddler with cancer, the stillborn, the secret abortion—but not one for the baby of the damned.

As Bunny reaches for a candle, she hears footsteps behind her. Spooked, she spins around.

It's Marty.

"Hey," he says.

"Hey," she says.

"What are you doing?"

"Just . . . lighting a candle."

Marty nods then turns around to leave.

"Marty?" Bunny calls out.

"Yeah." He turns back, pushing his glasses up his nose.

"Why do people come here?" she asks.

"To pray," he says.

"No, I mean to Washington. To *this* town?"

Marty puts his hands in his pockets, looks down at his shoes, rocks back on his heels. After a moment he looks back up at her.

Poised, he flashes a wry smile. "Isn't it obvious? *To change the world*, Bunny."

Bunny crinkles her forehead, pushing what's left of the irony inside of her out with a laugh. "Love you," she says.

"Love you too, Bunny."

Bunny turns to face the altar. Taking the unlit candle, she dips it onto a lit flame, lighting the wick like a sweet kiss. She places it back on the altar and kneels in prayer position. As her palms press against each other, sunlight ravages through the stained glass windows, forming warped shadows of angels on the wall behind her. And she remembers as a child all the times she sang "This Little Light of Mine"—when Billy pulled her hair and pinched her arm and she told on him for hurting her. The children's chairs still have their silk cushions embroidered with faded fairy tales: "Hansel and Gretel," "The Frog Prince," "The Pied Piper of Hamelin." And she misses him, she misses the way he'd play his ukulele for the gargoyles on his balcony, the way he teased her for her strawberry-colored hair but called her the most beautiful—otherworldly. She misses all those nights pressed close together in the rickety elevator climbing the inner walls of their history—all the times the ropes never snapped. She wishes she could tell him that she loves him.

As the light hits her, Bunny winces. She cups her hands over her eyes, falls into fetal position, and cries herself to sleep.

The year is 2020. As I write this, America has lost more than a hundred thousand lives to the coronavirus, our White House has gone dark, St. John's Church across the street is on fire, and protestors across the globe are marching and screaming and rioting in the wake of George Floyd's and Breonna Taylor's murders, among countless others. Meanwhile, our president is alternating between hiding in a bunker and calling on the military to shoot protesters with rubber bullets and tear gas.

I was born in our nation's capital, Washington, DC, in 1985, nurtured and educated inside of one of the most privileged communities in the world—the epicenter of institutional power—among the families of politicians, military officials, CIA agents, media moguls, ambassadors, lawyers, socialites, and philanthropists. Despite the District of Columbia being a primarily Black city during my childhood, I rarely socialized with people who weren't white, nor was I encouraged to do so. My parents readily ignored the city's massive economic disparity, inherently formed and generationally cycled as a result of our nation's history of white supremacy. And none of us were willing to examine our complicity in perpetuating it.

In 2004, while I was a college freshman in Los Angeles, my father, an associate of Jordan Belfort ("the Wolf of Wall Street"), was arrested for securities fraud, convicted, and sentenced to five years in a federal prison. He had stolen my social security number and left me nearly $100,000 in debt. Those dark years pushed me into a life of poverty, addiction, and loss, though my whiteness and the socioeconomic network I'd been handed in my absurdly privileged childhood protected me from any further institutional harm. I detail that experience in my memoir, *After Perfect*.

For many years I did not go back to the city of Washington, as it represented everything I thought I had lost and many things I was glad to leave behind. When I finally returned in 2015, it was for a reading of my memoir, and it was at this time that the idea for *The Cave Dwellers* began to emerge. During that visit, there was a story in the *Washington Post* about the murders of a wealthy Washington family whose mansion had been set ablaze. On the outside, the home and the family superficially reminded me of my own, and I was gripped by the media images of what are now known as the DC Mansion Murders. But any resemblance this story has to that tragedy ends there. This is a work of fiction. Any events and characters depicted were created from my imagination.

In the aftermath of my father's incarceration, I became deeply involved in criminal justice reform (although certainly not for his sake) and began to wake up to the inherent inequalities and injustices on which our society is built. If for this awakening alone, I'm grateful for my father's incarceration. I don't know that anything less could have opened my eyes.

But it wasn't until I returned to DC in 2017 to write this book that I fully internalized the extent to which white supremacy perpetuates itself, and how it unconsciously and consciously continues thriving in white communities through the abuse of political power, discriminatory clubs, galas, property, family inheritance, and greed, to name a few.

I went in search of information that would help me understand how and why the white, antiquated culture in Washington, in which

I'd grown up, was being preserved through the next generation. What I found was Robin DiAngelo's book *White Fragility*, which explained to me what I was experiencing. At a birthday party for a childhood friend I overheard one of the guests say, "Let's go downtown and hang out with the commoners." When I confronted him, bystanders laughed, and I was met with "I was joking!" and "He's a good friend," or "He didn't mean it like that." How did he mean it, then? And why were they defending him? DiAngelo's book describes this defense as a psychological phenomenon that happens to white people when confronted with white privilege: we become "fragile," expressing defensive emotions out of guilt, anger, fear, and centuries of silence.

Visiting my father in a minimum-security prison in El Paso, Texas, after spending my childhood flying in private planes paid for by the exploitation of others forged a sense of urgency within me to sound the alarm. But it was *White Fragility* that helped me begin to understand how to do it as a white woman. There were many other publications I read that inspired themes throughout the story. You will notice footnotes in the book where I provide historical context; a list of these publications is in the acknowledgments. But I am still continuing to learn and unlearn my own inherent biases.

I completed this book at the end of 2019. Given the current state of the world, I am encouraged that white Americans are being confronted with our whiteness and our personal responsibility to break subconscious and conscious cycles of classism and racism—that we are finally being challenged about what our whiteness means in our daily lives. However, I am also skeptical. So I ask: What does it look like and what will it take for us to break those cycles—institutionally, personally, and within our own families? Is it possible? These are the questions *The Cave Dwellers* sets out to explore.

❧• ACKNOWLEDGMENTS •❧

There are so many people for whom I owe an enormous amount of thanks. First and foremost, this book would have been impossible without my genius editor, Alison Callahan. Thank you for your unwavering belief in me. I am the luckiest to have you. Nancy Palmer and team: Molly, Carter, and Hope, for welcoming me back to Washington with love and open arms, and for giving me a room of my own. You are my family. Aaron Karo and Joshua Thurston, my first readers, my champions, thank you for taking my calls at ungodly hours. Thank you to my dearest friend and forever soul sister, Annie Hudson-Price, for your endless love and support, for your tireless legal work on behalf of those most vulnerable, and for our honest discussions on race and class. Thank you to Hannah Sward and Claire Titelman, for our weekly gatherings and critical feedback, and most important, your friendship and support. Alice Fox for countless hours listening to chapters and Valerie Johns for telling me I wasn't allowed to hand in anything until it was finished! To my agent extraordinaire, Peter McGuigan, and the entire team at Foundry Literary + Media, especially Kelly Karczewski for being one of the first to read. Thank you.

I'd like to thank the incredible team at Gallery Books/Scout Press for their hard work, Maggie Loughran for your fresh eyes, Brita Lundberg for your early support, Alexandre Su for bringing this to fruition, Joal Hetherington for your sharp eye, Lisa Litwack and Claire Sullivan for this clever and gorgeous cover, and Queen of the house, Jen Bergstrom. I'd also like to thank Aimèe Bell and Sally Marvin, as well as Bianca Salvant and Jessica Roth, for your early support.

I'd like to thank my friends on the frontlines of social justice in this country. Heather Warnken, thank you for your passion and dedication to restorative justice and all that I have learned from convening with you, you are forever my Swamp soul sister. Jim St. Germain, for your advocacy on behalf of the juvenile justice system and for picking up the phone when I called four years ago to tell you I wanted to write this story. Thank you for your encouragement and grace during our many discussions. Tony Lewis Jr. for your leadership in the District and your advocacy work on behalf of children with incarcerated parents. Sarah Comeau for your work at the School Justice Project and for sharing what you've witnessed. Carlton Miller for your work at Fwd.us and our discussions about families impacted by prison. I'd like to thank Amy Friedman and Dennis Danziger for your love and support and your tireless work on behalf of students impacted by prison and the founding of POPS The Club.

A lot of time and research went into forming the characters, historical inserts, and settings. I'd like to thank Richard Price, Lorraine Adams, Paul Hammond, James Frey, John Hudson, Luke Russert, Jeff Nussbaum, John Arundel, Tony Powell, Bob Weiner, Ben Lasky, Bob Costa, Bill Eggers, Will Rahn, Alexander George, Jill Schary Robinson, Valerie Woods, Alex Haight, Rob Bouknight, Ben Polk, Daniel J. Jones, and Caitlin Dietze for sharing your knowledge and expertise, and sometimes granting me access to certain figures and otherwise impossible locations. *You know who you are.*

I'd like to thank the Gritz family, Randi and Scott, and the McDowell family, Brianne and Alex, for your love. And the Seidlitz family, Ashley, Liz, Uncle Pete, especially my godmother, Anne Seidlitz, for your wisdom and love and our many dinners together.

Thank you to my best girls, Claire Woolner, Leanne Tomar, Christine Nolan, Catherine Trifiletti, Katie Shannon, Drea Renee, Jackie Aitken, Anusha Salimi, and Zoe Persina for being one of my first readers.

I'd like to thank Robin Muller for your tutorial on Plato's Allegory of the Cave all those years ago. Jacob Meszaros, Shirley Sacks, Albert Owens, and Roberta Villa for your early support and Elliott O'Donovan for photographing who I really am. I'd like to thank Luis and staff at Martin's Tavern and Roberto and staff at Compass Coffee and Jose and staff at the Tabard Inn. Thank you Judy Hudson for lending me your gorgeous home, and thank you Allan Loeb for answering all questions about writing and "the biz," and our decade-long friendship.

I'd like to thank my friends from MiQ: Melissa Kurstin, Chase Anderson, Emily Hohman, MacKenzie Kerrigan, Cedrick Yancey, Daniel Schwarz, and Will Harrington for your support.

I'd like to thank Melissa Randall for your faith in me, and my little bundle of joy, Ms. Zelda Fitzgerald, who always knows when I need a good walk. Lastly, I'd like to thank my parents, Gayle and Tom, for giving me a lifetime of stories to tell. . . .

The following authors have been some of my greatest teachers, and I'd like to thank them for their work: Robin DiAngelo: *White Fragility: Why It's So Hard for White People to Talk About Racism*, Ibram X. Kendi: *How to Be an Antiracist*, Kathleen Menzie Lesko, Valerie Babb, and Carrol R. Gibbs: *Black Georgetown Remembered: A History of Its Black Community from the Founding of "The Town of George" in 1751 to the Present Day*, Toni Morrison: *Playing in the Dark: Whiteness and the Literary Imagination*, James Baldwin: *Notes of a Native Son*, Ta-Nehisi Coates: *Between the World and Me*, Arthur Herman: *The Cave and the Light: Plato versus Aristotle and the Struggle for the Soul of Western Civilization*, Elijah Anderson: "The White Space," from *Sociology of Race and Ethnicity*, and Howard Zehr: *The Little Book of Restorative Justice*. Thank you.

The Cave Dwellers

CHRISTINA McDOWELL

This reading group guide for **THE CAVE DWELLERS** includes an introduction, discussion questions, and ideas for enhancing your book club. The suggested questions are intended to help your reading group find new and interesting angles and topics for your discussion. We hope that these ideas will enrich your conversation and increase your enjoyment of the book.

Introduction

cave dweller: a term, indigenous to Washington, DC, that defines a member of those families who have resided there for generations and whose bloodlines are woven into the warp and weft of the nation's capital

A compulsively readable novel in the vein of *The Bonfire of the Vanities*—by way of *The Nest*—about what Washington, DC's high society members do away from the Capitol building and behind the closed doors of their suburban mansions.

They are the families considered worthy of a listing in the exclusive Green Book—a discriminative diary created by the niece of Edith Roosevelt's social secretary. Their aristocratic bloodlines are woven into the very fabric of Washington—generation after generation. Their old money and manner lurk through the cobblestone streets of Georgetown, Kalorama, and Capitol Hill. They only socialize within their inner circle, turning a blind eye to those who come and go on the political merry-go-round. These parents and their children live lives free of consequences in gilded existences of power and privilege.

But what they have failed to understand is that the world is changing. And when the family of one of their own is held hostage and brutally murdered, everything about their legacy is called into question.

They're called The Cave Dwellers.

Topics & Questions for Discussion

1. Discuss Besty's continued obsession with affluent families and a life of luxury. Do you think she's satisfied when she's admitted to "The Washington Country Club" or will she always be a social climber? Why or why not?

2. Billy is the son of a general. They live in a home trimmed with Doric columns, and Billy speaks to his father with the respect one gives a

general. He lives a life of affluence with a guaranteed admittance to West Point. Why does Billy get upset when Marty teases him about his last name being the reason for the opportunities he has? Is there an underlying feeling of guilt—why or why not?

3. Bunny takes Mackenzie Wallace under her wing despite Bunny's mother, Meredith, insisting the Wallace family are "commoners." What do you think Bunny's intentions were in cultivating a friendship with Mackenzie?

4. Chapter 15 is a pivotal point for Bunny, Mackenzie, Billy, Marty, and Stan. How does their inherent privilege play into their grave mistake?

5. How does Cate assert her dominance over Senator Wallace in the crypt at the Banks family's funeral? How is this a pivotal moment for Cate's career?

6. Discuss Bunny's initial motives for visiting Anthony Tell in jail. How does Anthony's situation mirror the modern American justice system?

7. On the way to meet her mother for a Georgetown Christmas homes tour, Bunny finds out that her birthday check has bounced. As she tours the historic houses, Bunny's patience with high society dwindles. Discuss the causes that lead to Bunny's breakdown during the tour.

8. Are Senator Wallace's intentions pure when he reaches out to Lisa to apologize about his sexual misconduct? Why is his conscience constantly guilty when it comes to women and sex?

9. By the end of the book how have the teenagers changed? In your opinion, who has changed the most? Was it for better or worse?

10. Was it a shock when Senator Wallace's name didn't show up in the news story about sexual misconduct in politics? Why or why not?

11. What motives does Cate have to send the voice recording of Senator Wallace to the *Washington Post* reporter in the end? Why do you think she ultimately decided to hurt Senator Wallace?

12. We're never told who actually killed the Banks family. Who do you think committed the crime and why? Do you think the true killer will ever be uncovered?

Enhance Your Book Club

1. This book contains niche historical references between chapters, which explain pieces of history you may not have known. Have each member of your group pick their favorite historical reference and share why they feel it enhances the chapter.

2. Discuss different portrayals of Washington insiders and their children throughout other works of fiction or media. For example, *West Wing* or *House of Cards*. How does *The Cave Dwellers* (and its characters) fit in?

3. "Cave Dweller" is a term, indigenous to Washington, DC, that defines a member of those families who have resided there for generations and whose bloodlines are woven into the warp and weft of the nation's capital. Had you heard the term "cave dweller" before reading the book? Do you think this term accurately captures this group of people? And do you think there are families similar to the "cave dwellers" in Washington in other cities across America?